DOPAMINE SUPERSTAR

AMY SCARLETT

1

Everyone here thinks they're hot shit, but I don't recognise a single name or face. My feet balance on the edge of the diving board, soaking in the entrancing electronic music that drowns out the chatter of these party-goers. Neon purple washes over them as the garden lights replace the fading sun. From up here, the calming chlorine masks the stench of cigarette smoke and whatever fragrances are in this year. Time to liven things up. The Russian Courage I downed tonight should provide a decent shield. So I yell, "Hey, everyone. Look at me!"

In a second, I hit the empty water. I sink through the warm, dim depths, my clothes weighing me down faster, until my kickers touch the bottom. A low hum surrounds me. Lingering for several moments invites an oppressive loneliness.

I fight my way to the surface. With a gasp, I swallow the smoky air. Splutter and laugh. Can't believe I did that. The music gradually pushes through the residing water in my listeners. Now, do the special ones finally see me? Did I bring entertainment to their soulless conversations? Some shake their thinkers and turn away. Others glare and natter among themselves. Should be no surprise, but it still pisses me off. I'm no model, and my idea of fun doesn't involve standing around, gossiping, and looking pretty. Guess I'm just a crazy guy, but how can Kya call them friends?

A pair of familiar smart brown shoes stop in front of me at the pool's edge. My gaze trails up, over slender legs hidden in jeans, a long-sleeved shirt, and that grey waistcoat. Crossing his arms, my husband glares down at me. That expression spoils his soft face.

"What the hell are you doing?" he says.

"Having fun." I grin at him. "You should join me."

"Get out." He glances around. "It's embarrassing."

I scoff. "You care what they think?"

"Don't you?"

"No. I wanted to see how they'd react."

He rolls his eyes. "Out you come."

I reach for him.

"Use the ladder," he says.

I'm too weak for that.

"Please," I beg. "I might drown."

After a few moments of probably trying not to huff, he says, "I always have to drag you out of shit, don't I?"

He crouches and grabs my hands. As he pulls at me, I groan. He doesn't seem to care, and hooks his arms under mine to hoist my torso out of the water. My legs flail behind, as if detached. Between the two of us, we manage to get me completely out. Water streams from my heavy clothes onto the tile that runs around the pool. His front's covered in damp patches too. I'll be drenched for the rest of the night. Didn't really think this through.

"Kya won't be impressed." He stands and offers down his hand. "Let's get you dried off."

I smirk. "You gonna undress me?"

He raises an eyebrow. What's up with him? He was fine earlier.

"Come on, Madd," he says, and jabs his hand at me again.

So I let him yank me to my feet and guide me around the pool towards the small changing room building. I flash a smile to a staring model who's plastered in makeup and has her hair done up in a fancy bun. She sips from her cocktail glass and focuses on the tall, handsome guy in a suit next to her. He doesn't acknowledge me either. Can't these people lighten up? He's rambling on smugly about a Calvin Klein audition he's got. I cringe. Okay, he's not attractive anymore.

I traipse inside the changing room building. Connelly flicks on the light switch. I shield my eyes, then shut the door to kill the suddenly aggravating draught. Kya had to have an outdoor party in April, and I had to be dumb enough to jump in the pool. Think I'm sobering up a bit.

Connelly snatches a towel from the heated rack. "Take off your jacket."

"And what else?"

He half-smiles, but only for a moment. "You should probably take it all off. I'll get you some dry clothes from the house."

I struggle unsexily out of my leather jacket. Looks almost black now instead of dark-brown. I wring it out along with my shirt, then drop them on the wooden floor. He shoves the towel at me, which I fling around my shoulders. He really needs cheering up.

"I'll be waiting for you," I say, as smoothly as possible.

He looks me up and down, but not in the way I'd like, and folds his arms again. "How much have you had today?"

My gaze trails away. "Uh. Definitely at least half a bottle."

"Yeah. You're swaying."

Am I? I snicker.

4

He huffs. "Stop acting out. I know you don't like these people, but it's Kya's thirtieth. Don't ruin it for her."

How can he talk to me like that? Okay, I haven't been the most responsible twenty-eight-year-old tonight, but it's still a party.

"She's not as stuck-up as them," I say. "She'll probably laugh when she finds out."

"Oh, yeah. She'll find her brother-in-law embarrassing himself in front of her friends absolutely hilarious. You know, you're also potentially risking her reputation by pulling stunts like that. Did you ever think about that?"

I wouldn't have had to do it if they'd acknowledged who I am. Everyone here must know my and Kya's relationship to each other – it's no secret. You'd think it'd count for something.

"Conn, lighten up, man." I step closer and gently take his hand. "You're not one of them."

His jaw clenches. He retrieves his hand, and steps around me. "I'll be back in a couple minutes."

I watch him leave. The music slips in for a moment, but soon returns to a murmur. I've really pissed him off. I could've done worse. Could've pushed some of those people in the pool instead, like that guy who thinks he's the Joker with that ridiculous green hair – God forbid it get wet. I scrub my own hair with the towel and snigger. Imagine the others screaming that their pretentious designer outfits are done-for, that they'll lose their rental deposits. But I'd have to be way drunker to do any of that.

I yank off my sodden boots then squeeze into one of the changing cubicles. Balance against the wall while I battle out of my bottom half. The chlorine smell will disappear with a shower, but I can't be bothered, and I like it anyway. I dump my jeans, socks, and boxers on the narrow seat and dab my body with the towel. What's got into Connelly? I'm trying to remember when his attitude started. My mind's too blurry. It's not just the pool thing. I must've done or said something earlier this evening. I need us to be all right.

The main door opens again. Heels clop in. Tensing, I cling onto the wall. That's not Connelly.

"Maddix, you're a naughty one, aren't you?"

I really am, being naked while she's just on the other side of the door. I grin. Kya sounds playful. She's been on the wine – most likely too tipsy to care.

My thinker feels increasingly light. I rest my cheek against the cold wall. "Do you forgive me?"

"Don't be silly. You want a swim, go ahead. Just, uh, no skinny-dipping, all right?"

Connelly was over-worrying, as usual.

I laugh. "Oh, I wouldn't dream of it."

The door opens, and another draught creeps in. My skin starts to prickle. Hope that's Connelly with my fresh clothes.

"I'm sorry about this," he says.

"No need." Kya chuckles. "Make sure he puts these on. I don't trust him."

"Hey," I groan into the wall.

She clops out, and that bloody draught pricks me again.

The cubicle door opens. Crap. I didn't even lock it! Connelly stands there with a jumper and clean underwear looped over his arm.

"You didn't pack a change of trousers," he says bluntly. "You'll have to put those jeans back on."

I sigh. "Shit. Can't I wear yours? You're organised. You packed a spare pair, right?"

He hands me the clothes. "You think they'd fit you? I don't trust you in them anyway. Think before you leap next time."

I roll my eyes. "How long you gonna be mad at me? Didn't I say Kya would find it funny?"

"Mm."

I drop the clothes on the seat then turn to him and grip the cubicle frame above me with both hands. Being six feet, I don't even have to stretch. This'd make a decent photo. I've got an all right body for a naked shot – don't work out like those models, but still. If I was sober, though, I'd definitely need my clothes on.

"You can chill now," I say.

He raises an eyebrow. "Are you going to be good?"

"I can be." I give him a once-over. "Why don't you come in here and find out?"

I wink at him, and he cracks a smile.

"There we go," I say. "You love me really."

He stares at me. "Of course I do."

"So kiss me."

After a few moments, he leans up a little and presses his lips against mine. A hot flush runs down me. I was kidding about us doing that in here, but now I want to take him to the house and go upstairs.

Alas, I get dressed while he waits outside the cubicle. Alas? I must be wasted. I swear there's nothing more uncomfortable than putting on wet jeans. But the rest of me is dry, so I'll make do. When I stagger out at last, I glance about for my jacket. It hangs on the heated towel rack, along with my shirt and boots. I'll leave the shirt on there. They haven't had much time to dry at all, but it's better than nothing.

"Thanks, Conn."

He pushes himself up from the seat by the shower cubicle. "Let's get back to the party, shall we?"

I grab my damp jacket.

"Don't even think about it," he says. "Your jumper will be warm enough."

I tut. "I'm getting my phone."

I fish it out and hang the jacket up again. Don't even need to check whether he's giving me that unimpressed 'don't bullshit me' look. He's correct, though: I was very much going to put it back on.

After wrestling into my boots, I return outside with him. Thankfully, this jumper *is* enough to shield against the cold. Uplifting synth music swirls around us. Kya's lucky to have this luxurious Epsom house with no immediate neighbours. We'd never be able to afford somewhere like this.

The various groups of models seem to ignore us as we pass. Wonder if they all have big houses too. Plenty of flashy cars out front. And let's talk about these outfits: everyone's trying to squeeze into the hottest, shiniest dress or suit. Here I squelch in my boots, jeans, and jumper that barely cost over £100. Connelly's shirt, waistcoat, jeans, and shoes aren't the latest designer shit but he looks much classier than they do. I just want to tear it all off him, but settle with linking my arm with his.

The odd chink of glasses or eruption of what sounds like the fakest laughter I've ever heard distracts me from the conversation around us, but I do manage to catch the odd snippet:

"It's hard to find a good assistant. My last two turned out to be total creeps."

"I've always dreamed of working with L'Oréal."

"I know I shouldn't be eating these, but they're too delicious."

"Seriously, why did Kya invite him?"

That last one was aimed at me, wasn't it? I grimace, then stop myself.

Entering through the open patio doors, I stomp my feet on the mat.

Squint at the kitchen lights. A few people loiter here with their wine and cocktail glasses, eyeing us. I've had enough of their judging. I grin at them until they glance away. Kya stands between the kitchen counters and central worktop, illuminated like the star of the party she is in her white biker jacket. She sips from her glass then clinks it down and smiles at us.

"Hey, guys." She whips her pastel-pink ponytail over her shoulder. The colour of it matches her posh dress perfectly. "Maddix, thank you for putting some clothes on."

Laughing, I slip away from Connelly to lean my elbows on the shiny white marbled worktop. "You done with that wine?"

She snatches the glass away and mockingly glares. I sag.

"You need water." Connelly opens the tall fridge then dumps a bottle of the stuff in front of me.

"Where's my vodka?" I ask.

Kya raises an eyebrow and smirks. "You drank it all, wild guy."

"Oh, shit." I clumsily unscrew the water bottle.

Shaking his thinker, Connelly lifts himself onto one of the stools next to me. He still looks pensive, and he's jigging his leg, but not in time to the music. Is he honestly *that* pissed at me?

"You two okay?" Kya asks with a slight pout.

I gulp some water. Connelly nods with a half-smile, but he should know that won't fool her.

"Well, to be frank," I say, "your friends are bloody rude."

"Oh." Her dazed eyes glisten with confusion. "Are they?"

How can she be that blind?

Connelly sighs. "They're fine."

"No, they're not." I gesture the bottle in his direction. "You and I must be the only non-models here, and they let us know it." I tilt the bottle towards Kya, and struggle to contain a burning hiccup. "This one guy – green hair, my height, gorgeous pretty boy – when I told him I make conspiracy videos on YouTube, he scoffed and said, 'That's a job?'"

She cringes. "Sorry. He *can* be a bitch."

"Ignore him, Madd," Connelly says. "It's not worth it."

I roll my eyes. "It's all right for you, Mr. Social Media Executive."

Why'd I have to blurt that out? He hates me calling out his job title like that. I half-expect him to dive into another rant about how loosely 'executive' is used in his workplace and they should never have called him that because they don't treat him with the same respect as other 'executives'.

"I thought you didn't care what they think," he bites back.

"I don't." I hate lying, but it's better than the truth in this particular instance. "It's just hard to have fun when everyone's judging you."

"Well, congratulations, 'cause now everyone *is* judging you."

This jabs my already burning chest, but I can only scoff.

"Guys," Kya says, "please don't. I can't handle it when you fight."

I glare at the worktop.

"Sorry." Connelly swivels off the stool. "I'm going to the loo."

"You want another drink when you get back?" she asks.

"No, thanks."

He heads across the kitchen and around the corner to the hallway.

"Get him one anyway," I tell her. "He needs it."

"Mm. I think he's only had a glass of wine."

I smirk. "And how about you?"

She sips the last of her glass. "Lost count."

I snigger and gulp more water. If I keep this up, and don't sneak any extra courage from her liquor collection, I should avoid a hangover. She doesn't usually drink this much; she should hit the water soon too.

"You had a good birthday?" I ask.

Her eyes drift from side to side. "Yeah."

"What's it like being thirty, then? Scary as it sounds?"

She laughs nervously. "Ask me again in the morning."

Her smoky eyeshadow's so perfectly applied it appears airbrushed on – she must've got a professional to do it tonight. Her face is also plastered in a smooth, pale foundation. I have the advantage of knowing what she looks like without it and I can tell you she must be hiding invisible wrinkles and blemishes. Turning thirty must be terrifying for a model.

"Your birthday's coming up soon," she says.

"Yep." I sink to rest my cheek against the cold marble. My legs squash against my chest, but thankfully my knees don't push against anything under the counter. "Next month."

"You're both lucky you got another year yet. Then we'll all be in the thirty club together, won't we?"

"Yay," I groan. I really don't want to think about it. Instead, I focus on this new song's haunting tone, persistent bass, and seductively airy vocals. We've always been into the same type of music. I love that. I'm sinking into the worktop, becoming one with it and the song.

9

Something soft touches my hand. Fingers? I open my eyes. Kya's pink pointed nails.

"No passing out in the kitchen, please," she says.

I straighten up. Was I really dozing off?

"Sorry," I say, and swallow more water. Connelly will be back soon. I need to make him happy again.

"I should get back to mingling." With her empty glass between her fingers, she steps around the worktop then lightly squeezes my shoulder. "Will you be all right?"

That crazy, crinkled pattern running in a thin line down the front of her dress is right in front of my face. Looks almost flowery, with a gold zip hidden behind it. The black belt around her waist is so thin it's almost pointless. There's a small gold circular clasp, though. Squinting, I can just about make out an Aztec face.

"What's this?" I point at it.

She glances at it too. "Versace, dear. Now drink up, and I'll see you later."

Bloody hell. It suits her, but I hope she didn't spend her own money on that and they're sponsoring her to wear it instead. Anyway, I nod, down the rest of the water, and she clops away. Balancing in those heels while drunk is an art.

I bring out my phone from my back jeans pocket. It survived the dunk in the pool, but I'm still struggling to process the words on the screen. I fumble briefly, trying to bring up the YouTube app but pressing others instead. My video on replaced popstars I posted this morning has just under fifty thousand views. A little more than usual, but still underwhelming considering the five-hundred thousand subscribers I have. I sound ungrateful thinking this. But it's my job. As much as I love it, I still need to make money. And we need all we can get living in Tulse Hill. I try reading the comments – apparently there are two hundred-odd. The words still blur. I'd love to know what everyone thought, but I'll look at them tomorrow.

Where's Connelly? Can't still be in the loo. Unless there's a queue. But even then, he could use one of the three bathrooms upstairs. Three bathrooms sounds ridiculous, doesn't it?

With effort, I push myself off the worktop. Stash my phone away. Stagger across the floorboard of the kitchen, dining area, and main hallway that all flow as one. The ceiling lights bounce off the white walls. I squint again, and head to the little toilet by the front door. Call for Connelly. No answer. I slowly open the door enough to peer through the crack into the darkness. Definitely not here.

I turn and scuff to the stairs. A light's on up there. I gather the energy to pull myself up – that leap in the pool, on top of all this booze, has worn me out. The further up I get, the more the music muffles, until only the bassline vibrates through the floor.

At the top of the stairs, I almost stumble. Have to laugh at myself. Glance at the three bedroom doors on the left of the landing, the corridor on the right, then the bathroom door ahead. He's bound to be in there. I move forward, and the door opens. Connelly jerks slightly, and stays in the doorway. I grin at him, but his face falls blank.

"You following me?" he says.

"Might be." I look him up and down. "I want us to be all right." I take his soft, warm hands again. "Come dance or something."

"I don't want to," he says firmly.

I thought maybe he would've calmed down a bit by now. Maybe this'll work.

"I'm sorry for jumping in the pool. I can make it up to you."

He stares into my fuzzy eyes for several moments. I like that intensity.

"What exactly are you proposing?" he mutters.

I lean into him. Press my cheek against his. "Anything you want."

He could definitely use it.

"I don't want us to be gone from the party too long," he says.

"I'll be quick, then."

And I'll ignore that he'd rather go back to the party than spend the rest of the night in the bedroom. But at least he seems to be accepting my offer.

Keeping hold of his hands, I pace back and to the left, and lead him into our room.

My sense of time is shot. Feels like we've been at it for longer than twenty minutes. It's still too long according to him. He reckons it'll be obvious what we disappeared for. I try to tell him that he shouldn't care, and he gives me that condescending look I hate. I thought maybe he'd chill out, but he took longer to finish than usual. Was it me? Or was it this annoying apprehension he seems to have? I enjoyed it, but I'm not sure he did. Wish we could go further, wish I could do better, but maybe once everyone's left – at least he won't be timing it then.

Still sitting on the sofa in our room, he zips his jeans back up. I chuck the tissues in the tiny bin under the dressing table then check my hair in the mirror. It's mostly dry now, but humorously sticking up in odd places. I run my hand through to even it out. He grabs the comb from the table and thrusts it at me. Guess I'm combing it, then.

My woozy thinker allows me to smile as we leave the bedroom. He tells me to rinse my mouth out, so I slip into the bathroom to swish around some mouthwash. It's not the first time we've done that during a party. It sends such a thrill through me. Shame about him. He must've been remotely into it, though, or he would've pushed me off sooner. I just wish he'd fucking smile too.

We return to the downstairs hallway, and the hypnotic electronic music comes back into focus. Once level with the living room doorway, I tell Connelly I'm popping in to fix myself a drink. I know I don't need it, but I want to get plastered enough to not remember the awkwardness between us. He rolls his eyes and nods, then carries on through the doors into the garden. Why does he want to talk to them so much? Why can't I make him happy tonight?

I push open the double pine doors into the silent living room. The place dwells in darkness, save for the purple strip light that runs around the bar counter to the left. I step behind it and scan the row of bottles on the shelf below the big wall mirror. My gaze rejects the whiskey and rum, and settles on a large bottle of Black Cow vodka. Kya lets me have this occasionally. This is the best shit: better taste than Russian Standard. Wish I could afford it all the time. I should try other English vodkas, and Russian ones, to be fair. I'll pour a drink now and offer money for it later. Kind of desperate.

I place the bottle on the counter and retrieve a whiskey tumbler from underneath. As my slightly shaking hand unscrews the lid, a bright light hurts my eyes. The TV's on?

A rising and falling bassline kicks in through the speakers, with a moderate thumping beat. The white screen cuts to a close-up of a round stone-blue eye surrounded by black fur. It pans out gradually to show a rabbit sitting against a white background. Calming major-key synths ease in, along with twinkling chimes. What is this? Am I imagining it? I'm not that wasted yet. The synths rise slowly, then cut out. The beat and bassline remain, and a woman's voice joins them.

Her flawless pale face fills the screen, framed by golden hair. With an

unexpected smirk, those small shiny lips sing:
"What do you think you're doing here?
This has never been your scene,
and this is not your home.
You think you know everything."

She looks barely over twenty. Certainly sultry, and her large green eyes start to draw me in.

The synths return to mimic her tune as she sings:
"Pour yourself a drink.
Go on. Make it big.
You'll forget it all.
No-one will listen
and they never will.
Just forget it all."

It sounds almost cheery and uplifting, but those words ring depressingly true. I glance down at the open vodka bottle. How much should I give myself?

The camera focuses on the rabbit again. To the same synths and bassline as at the start, it stays still. We stare at each other. My mind feels cloudy again, worse than earlier.

As it cuts back to the young woman's face, she sings:
"Just hide away in the dark,
and stay there for forever more.
Just keep it all inside.
Forget what you think you know."
The twinkling chimes slip back in as she continues:
"Pour yourself a drink.
Go on. Make it big.
You'll forget it all.
No-one will listen
and they never will.
Just forget it all."

I grip the bottle tighter. Pour vodka in the glass all the way to the top. I was only planning on half of this, but fuck it.

The song's key changes up slightly. By this point, I don't think she's blinked once. She sings:
"And you'll never get near me.
Don't you even try it.

You can't hear what I'm saying
and you just can't handle it.
I'm gonna bash you down
before you even get close.
So go and lose yourself.
Forget it all and drown."

The same oddly juxtapositional footage of the rabbit plays again alongside the driving bassline and beat. I try to process. Was she seriously addressing me? The way she stared: it was like her gaze penetrated the screen and snatched me.

Her angelic face sings, with that hint of a smirk:
"Look into my eyes and go.
This world has never been for you.
Why are you even trying?
You know that you can never win."

And she proceeds to repeat the chorus, telling me to *"just forget it all."*

Then the music dies. The screen blacks out. It's only me in the darkness with my tumbler of vodka.

What just happened? How was it possible? I look down at my glass. Think I should pretend I didn't see or hear anything. Yep, that's easier. So I gulp down some English Denial. It burns, as usual, but I do like the sweetness of this one. Kya will definitely notice the missing chunk from the bottle. But she shouldn't get mad if I pay her back.

I take the glass with me out of the living room. Kya's music has been replaced by that familiar bassline and dancy beat. It's playing out here too? Loads of people are gathered in the kitchen. What are they doing? I stagger across the floorboard to them. Peer around the non-thinkers to see the TV on the wall that separates the hallway from the kitchen. Through hazy eyes, I watch with them.

The young woman on the screen smiles as she sings:
"The party's going on in here.
It's the greatest thing I've ever seen.
I never want to go home.
I want to see everything."

The same melody, but those weren't the lyrics, were they?

Some people bop along, while others gaze passionately. Kya and Connelly stand by the worktop, watching with the same sparkling, awe-struck eyes as everyone else.

With a beaming grin, the woman sings:
"Pour yourself a drink.
Gonna make it big.
You can have it all.
Everything glistens
and it always will.
You will have it all."

I may be rat-arsed, but those were not the fucking lyrics. What's happening? Frowning, I shake my thinker. Is this a dream? Did I pass out after all, or fall asleep upstairs after pleasuring Connelly? Did *that* even happen?

The woman sings:
'A light is shining in the dark,
and it will glow forever more.
We have it all inside.
It's something that you need to know."

I feel like I'm going insane. I gulp more English Apathy.

She sings the wrong chorus again. Everyone seems transfixed on the TV. They've packed themselves in here, with people even peeping in from the patio doors, just to hear and see this.

The woman's bright smile continues. She sings:
"Just sidle up near me.
I can help you see it.
Listen to what I'm saying.
You just need to embrace it.
Life will bash you down.
Don't let it get too close.
So believe in yourself
and don't let it drag you down."

What the actual hell? This is the complete opposite. I drink more. Maybe this'll go away. Maybe I'll wake up.

She sings sweetly:
"Look into my eyes and know
this world is but a stage for you.
You have to keep on trying
and believe that you can win."

The positivity is confusing, and sickening. But that last part's mainly the vodka.

After the final chorus, the song ends and cuts off as abruptly as before. Then a different music video comes on but Kya mutes it. I need to talk to her and Connelly. I push through the smoky, pungent bodies as carefully as possible. Avoid eye contact. They let me through, and among their murmuring, I catch:

"That was amazing."

"So inspiring."

"She was stunning."

"That bunny was so sweet!"

I force myself not to retort. Yeah, she was attractive, but the song was honestly meh – both versions! And the rabbit was random, plus a bit creepy.

Kya's face lights up. "Maddix, wasn't that great?"

How do I put my thoughts into words? "Uh..."

"It came up on the music channel," she says.

"Put it on again," someone calls, and others loudly agree.

Kya laughs and holds up the remote to rewind it again.

"What did you think of it?" Connelly asks.

Takes me several moments to realise he's talking to me.

"Uh, it was all right," I say. Will they believe me if I tell them what happened in the other room? This is probably still a dream anyway.

"You need more water," he says.

I lift the glass to my lips. "After I've finished this."

"I thought you'd drunk it all," Kya says.

I take a swig. "I'll pay you back."

She huffs but smiles. Presses the remote and the music starts again. Connelly's frown vanishes. He stares over at the TV, as does everyone else. The kitchen falls silent, save for the music. I'm not watching this for a third time.

So I scuff outside, and wander up the garden to the pool. How can everyone be so fixated on it? Who is this singer anyway? Never seen her before. Voice isn't familiar either. There's an airy cuteness to it. But what she sang in the living room was brash and demeaning. Maybe there *are* two versions, but the kitchen TV wasn't even on, right? Kya's been playing music through a docking station and speakers all night.

I sit cross-legged at the pool's edge. Gaze into the purple water. Can't stay out here long. Not drunk enough to ignore that chill, and my damp jeans only make it worse. The song's so loud that I can hear every detail,

16

like I can never escape it. I swig more English Oblivion and scrunch my eyes shut.

The world spins. This extra drink was a huge mistake. Well, I did want to forget everything. Let's see how much I remember in the morning.

If I concentrate hard enough, I can imagine Connelly's arm around me. His warmth. Want to lie in bed with him. Have him hold me until I drift asleep.

In my dizziness, I manage to muffle the song. Only half-aware of it ending. Chatter creeps into my listeners. People are coming outside again. At least they're not repeating the song a fourth time – not sure my thinker can take it. They all seem livelier than before, giggly and chirpy, like they've had a hit of something.

"Hey, Mad Max," a guy calls behind me. I recognise that annoyingly obnoxious tone. I crane my neck and there he is: green-haired Joker, a few feet away, grinning with a couple of his mates. Why the hell'd he call me that? I'm nearly throwing up in my mouth here. "Let us know if you're gonna jump in the pool again," he says. "That had us in stitches. I misjudged you, man."

It's one surreal thing after another, isn't it? Well, I'll take it, I guess.

"Uh, okay. Thanks."

"You want to get a drink with us?"

I certainly wouldn't go that far, though.

I hold up my glass. "I'm waiting for someone. Thanks, though."

He nods. "No worries. See you later, then. Have fun."

With that, he bounds off, and his mates give me a passing goodbye nod. How did I suddenly gain their respect?

A body slumps beside me. Please be Connelly. Oh, thank God. He smiles. "You all right?"

Sad to think this, but that smile looks weird on him tonight. He must've taken a hit too.

"What's going on?" I ask.

He gazes at the sky and sighs. "I don't know."

I frown. "Are you still pissed at me?"

"For what?"

This doesn't even make his face twitch. Did he seriously forget?

"Did you down a bunch of shots in there?" I ask.

He laughs. "No."

Could fool me.

17

He stares at me, and his expression falls. "Are you going to pass out?"

I *am* feeling lighter by the second, like I might detach at any moment.

"Maybe," I say.

"You want to lie down?"

I nod carefully. He springs up, helps me to my feet, and lets me grip his arm as he guides me through the crowd. Snippets of animated conversation: "I can't get enough," "It's just perfect," "It's got such an eighties vibe." The 80s always seems to be in. A lot of them type frantically on their phones. Surprised Kya hasn't continued her playlist to fill the void. I see her through the patio doors in the kitchen, jabbing the remote at the TV. Is it broken?

As we pass her, she says, "It's gone. I don't understand."

Images of another video flash in reverse on the screen. She stares with dazed frustration.

"What?" is all I can say.

Connelly leads me down the hallway. "That song just disappeared. It's bizarre."

"What?" None of this makes sense. Why's my hand empty? I stop. "Shit. My drink... I left it, by the pool."

"I'll get it later. For now, you've had enough, okay?"

I groan. But that stuff's good. Some random person will probably help themselves to it.

I either didn't say that or he's ignoring me, as he aids me up the stairs and says, "I'll take care of you."

This soothes me. When my heavy legs reach the top of the stairs, I pull on his arm to make him stop. He's blurry around the edges.

"I love you," I say.

He smiles. "Love you too."

This is the guy I married. Who was that imposter earlier?

He leads me to the bedroom. I stagger through the dark and flop onto the bed. Soft cushiony heaven. Through narrowed eyes, I see his silhouette approaching. The landing light seeps in behind him through the open doorway. He undoes my jeans.

"If we're gonna do this," I say with a smirk, "you'd best shut the door."

"Relax, big guy," he murmurs. "I assume you don't want to sleep in wet jeans."

"No," I mumble.

He yanks them down and I twist my body so that he can tug each leg off. With a bit of effort, my skin's left bare. I hear my jeans crumple on the floor. Can't help swelling with anticipation.

"Sure you don't want to join me?" I say. Not sure how much *I'm* capable of, but I could certainly take it.

"You need to rest, love." He leans over and kisses my forehead. Makes me sink into the bed. I feel something soft drape over my legs – a blanket, maybe. Ask him to lie with me, but don't think the words leave my mouth.

*

White pillow. Can't lift my aching thinker. Must've slept through the whole night. With a grunt, I roll over. Connelly's not here. Did he even come to bed? I manage to pull myself up to sit. Expectedly, there's the heaviness and grogginess. The blanket still covers my legs. How I didn't kick it off I don't know. I try to ignore the wave of sickness in my chest as I yank off the blanket and swivel my legs off the bed. Don't remember how much I drank last night, but it must've been more than usual because of all this pressure on my skull. Connelly brought me to bed, didn't he? My jeans are draped on the radiator. I certainly didn't do that. Bless him.

Carefully, I push myself up, stretch out my back, and move to the radiator. Slip into my lovely, dry, warm jeans. Much better. Shame they smell a bit. I'll shower before we go, but for now I'm starving. Barely ate anything yesterday.

After popping to the loo, I sluggishly make my way downstairs. Light floods the hallway from the glass ceiling above the dining table and patio doors. Squinting, I continue on past it to the kitchen area. Connelly sits at the worktop, flicking through his phone. A steaming cup rests on the marble.

"Any hot water left?" I ask.

He glances at me. "Oh, morning. Yep. Plenty."

I scuff to the cupboards in front of him. Take out a random mug.

"How do you feel?" he asks.

"Pretty shit." I pour water from the kettle into the mug. "Thanks for helping me to bed."

"You were completely out of it." He doesn't carry any venom with this – just seems to be stating a fact.

I dump two tablespoons of coffee in the water and mix it a few times. "Did I miss anything?"

"Not much. Everyone left by eleven."

Definitely not party animals.

I clutch the hot cup to my chest with both hands and slide around to face him. "I did tell you I'm sorry for jumping in the pool, right?"

"Yep." He sips his own coffee and smiles. "Several people joked about it, actually."

"Oh, really?" I do vaguely remember Joker coming over and laughing about it. "So you're definitely not still pissed at me?"

He frowns. "I never was."

I stare at him for several moments. Don't blink. Is he serious?

"You were well moody at me," I say. "Said I was embarrassing."

"I don't remember that. I did laugh, though."

"What? How much did *you* drink?"

"Only a few glasses of wine."

I glare into my dark coffee. This makes no sense.

"Look," he says, "I'm not mad at you, okay? Don't worry."

He sounds sincere, and he wouldn't mess me about. But maybe I remember it wrong.

I sip gently at my coffee then place it on the worktop. Pull out my phone to check the time: 10:05. My replaced popstars video's bound to have way more views and comments by now. As I bring it up to look, light footsteps descend the stairs and cross the hallway to join us in the kitchen. Wonder if Kya's thinker's as bad as mine. Bare-footed, she comes over in a white sleeveless top and tracksuit bottoms. Her pink hair's tied in a loose bun instead of scraped into a high ponytail like last night.

"Maddix." Smiling, she moves behind her brother to go to the fridge. "Nice of you to rise with the rest of us. And Happy Easter, by the way."

I snigger. "Yes, Happy Easter. Did the wine treat you well?"

She grabs a bottle of water from the fridge. "I'm on a detox today – let's just put it that way."

"Ah." I should probably do the same, but won't. "What about chocolate?"

"I may sneak a few truffles."

I smile at this, and then at my video statistics: just over seventy thousand views, around three hundred comments, one thousand likes, and an inevitable one hundred dislikes. As long as the likes far outweigh the dislikes, all's good. It's doing well, but I guess it could be better. Maybe if people hadn't been watching that *other* video last night. I hate relying on as many people as possible to watch the ads. Earning revenue from the 15% of viewers that actually do this leaves me with about 50p per thousand views. Times that by seventy and... I can't do that in my foggy thinker right now. I bring up the calculator and groan: £35. Nearly as much as Black Cow. Yeah, it's not great. Thank God for my patrons. It's a business world, with too many people trying to earn money. But I still get much more than when I started a few years ago.

"You guys want breakfast?" Kya asks. "I can do the usual fry-up for you."

"Yes, please," I answer immediately. My stomach grumbles even more imagining it.

Connelly smiles at me, which warms me more than the coffee. "That's a yes from me too, please."

So she takes out some massive packets of scrumptious bacon from the fridge and piles them by the stove. I step aside to give her space, then she brings out frying pans, oil, and a carton of eggs.

I flick through a few comments on the video:

'Great vid as always man, keep it up.'

'Britney DID NOT die in an effin crash.'

'I can't believe these clone theories are still a thing, people still believe this shit?'

'Ur so hot omg.'

'I love Avril – don't understand why these people can't accept she's changed. People change. Music evolves. Get over it!'

Smirking, I roll my eyes at the predictable 'hot' comment – at least a few on every video these days. As I don't personally believe any of the cloning theories myself, and made that perfectly clear, I can't take offence at the 'get over it' and 'this is ridiculous' comments. Well, except Taylor Swift *does* scarily look too similar to Satanist Zeena LaVey for me to ignore that one. I'll get the usual barrage of for and against arguments, and I'll lie in bed at home and entertain myself with them later.

Thinking about popstars is jogging my memory about that song from last night, and I was even complaining about it earlier when I was going over my statistics, but I get easily distracted sometimes. I can't remember exactly how it went, but I can see that woman's face clearly.

"Did you ever find that video again?" I ask them.

Kya cracks an egg and drops the yolk in the pan. "I tried for ages to get it back. Conn and I have been searching online for it this morning too."

I frown at the TV. "That can't be possible. Is there anything in the news about it?"

"It's *all over* the news," Connelly says.

He stretches his arm over the worktop to pass me his phone. The headline jumps out in big letters at the top of the article: 'Mystery Pop Artist Unveils Captivating Video Then Deletes All Traces'. How did she manage that? There's no footage whatsoever? She couldn't just delete stuff from everyone's phones and computers, but loads of people have stated that anything they captured is gone. The article writer seems more in awe at this than concerned!

What the hell? They've used a stock image of a rabbit, but it's white... The article even mentions a *white* bunny. I know the lyrics were originally different for me, but the rabbit was black both times. Think I'll need to move on for now before it swamps me.

Reading on, they say the song, entitled 'Something That You Need to Know', globally aired at 9:33 pm UK time on TV music channels, radio stations, and YouTube, only to disappear ten minutes later. Thousands of online sources agree that, from memory, the YouTube video was three minutes and thirty-three seconds and the account's name was blank. How can the account be blank? But more strangely, how did I see a different version?

Kya cracks another egg. "It's like the singer decided she didn't want the video published after all. But I have no idea how it vanished from the rewind on TV. That's impressive."

"Apparently, *any* footage of it is gone." I hand Connelly back his phone. "You can delete a YouTube video or get it taken down easily. But she would've had to hack into people's devices to 'delete all traces'."

Connelly frowns at his phone and starts scrolling.

"It really sucks," Kya says. "That song was great."

I almost gawp. "Does the clear breach of privacy not disturb you?"

Her expression seems to turn vacant. "I'm not sure."

What's wrong with her?

"Have the music channels not released any statements about where they got the video from to air it in the first place?" Connelly asks.

"Every one so far claims they don't possess it. They say their systems glitched, like they were hacked."

That should've been the focus of the article headlines!

"See: another breach of privacy," I say. "That's probably why she somehow deleted all traces of it, then, and took it off YouTube to avoid legal repercussions."

The hob clicks on, and the bacon starts to sizzle.

Kya shrugs. "I just wish I could hear it again."

I nearly slam my mug down. Why is she not reacting to the obvious issue here?

"Me too," Connelly says. "It seriously might be the best song I've ever heard."

Not him as well! Everything's backwards. Am I still asleep?

"Music doesn't normally impress you," I say, playing along.

"I know, but something about it made me feel...exhilarated."

"Yeah," Kya says, "it was like a burst of new life and inspiration."

I shake my thinker. "You wouldn't say that if you heard my version."

They stare at me. I kind of blurted that.

"I saw a different video," I say. "Well, it was the same one, but different. I can't remember how it went, but she was cocky and horrible: not inspiring at all. Plus, what colour was the rabbit for you guys?"

"Uh, white," Connelly says.

I stand dumbfounded.

"Why?" Kya asks me.

Doubt they'll believe this, but: "It was black for me."

A few moments of silence. They glance at each other as if I'm talking shit. I should've recorded the bloody thing – not that it would've done any good!

"You did have a whole bottle of vodka," Connelly says.

Is he serious?

"And some of my good stuff," Kya says, "which we managed to salvage and put in the fridge for you, by the way."

"Oh, thanks," I say, then glare at the floor. At least she still doesn't sound annoyed about that, but they're both dismissing me. Hang on. I've just remembered: "Kya, was the TV even on?"

Her eyes narrow. "It was on when that music started."

"But you didn't turn it on yourself?"

"...No. Huh. I guess I didn't question it."

Another oddity she conveniently didn't consider.

"The TV in the other room turned on by itself too," I say. "I never touched it."

"Maybe the people who were in the kitchen before us did it," Connelly suggests. "In any case, it's not worth getting worked up about."

23

I hold out my arms. "What about mine?"

He smirks. "You remember that time we were at the uni campus bar and you were bragging about all the pool matches you'd won against me, but we'd never once played pool?"

I huff. "That was ten fucking years ago, man."

He raises his hands. "Okay, sorry. Just saying that you don't always think straight when you've been drinking."

That's not the point!

"There's been no mention of another version online," Kya adds.

Scrunching up my face, I bring up an Internet tab on my phone. "*Someone* has to back me up on this."

I scour countless articles and comments, even as we tuck into our delicious fry-up around the dining table. I could eat three plates of this. Kya's chewing carefully through her fruit salad – must feel sick. I still do, but the food's helping.

"That was a good turnout last night," Connelly says to her.

"Yeah," she says a little glumly. "To be honest, I didn't know a quarter of them. Well, I know who they are, but I don't *know* them."

Figures. A bunch of people there were honestly not her type at all. Connelly's undoubtedly tilting his thinker and frowning. I glance up from my phone. Yep.

"I asked the models I'm friendlier with to invite them," she explains. "Before six years ago, none of them probably would've turned up." She shrugs. "Thought it'd be cool to have some new famous young faces at my party, then they'd post about it online."

"I guess that makes sense," Connelly muses.

It does, but shame they weren't actual friends.

"Problem is: so far, they *have* posted pictures, but only of themselves. No mention of me."

Not really a shocker.

"That sucks," Connelly says.

"Yep. And the real kick in the teeth: there was even an agent who turned up, trying to scrounge some work."

"Oh. I missed that."

I did too.

"You guys had disappeared."

Connelly stops eating and stares at me. If he could blush, he'd definitely be doing it right now. He's adorable. I smile at him. Kya's too busy focusing on her salad to pay attention to us, which I'm sure he's glad about.

"Still not found anything?" she says to me.

Nope, and can't concentrate anyway. "Nothing. It's unbelievable."

"How did it go? Like, what was the chorus?"

I stay silent as I try to retrieve the lost words. Why am I drawing blanks? I'm hardly helping myself here. This is both frustrating and terrifying.

"I don't know," I say.

She stares at me as if perplexed.

"Madd, maybe you should look into it later," Connelly says. "Try to enjoy your breakfast."

I try not to sag. He knows what I'm like when I go into investigation mode; surely he understands it's not that easy? Besides, this time, it's more important.

As I chew on a piece of egg and bacon, I scan the deep recesses of my muddled mind for the answers. But yet again, blanks. I *will* figure this out, one way or another. Even if everyone claims I'm a deluded drunk. Because either way, out of nowhere, a mysterious new pop artist has unconventionally thrust herself into our lives and triggered the conspiracist in me to find out how and why.

2

You know, I love a good mystery. This one certainly provides fuel for an interesting video, maybe even a series. I just know my judgement will be questioned, though. Will anyone believe me?

As Connelly drives us back to Tulse Hill, I continue searching online until my phone's battery falls to 10%. I was already half-cut before we left the house yesterday and forgot to pack my damn charger. Connelly didn't bring his either. And everyone on the road's ridiculously slow!

"Will you stop jigging your leg, for God's sake?" he says. "You're distracting me."

I growl under my breath and try to keep my leg still. "Not much else I can do. Would you please put some music on at least?"

"No distractions!"

Why does he always have to snap at me? And why's *he* in such a bad mood? He's not the one in a hurry to get back.

We get stuck at a set of traffic lights. I have to make progress on this whole thing, even if only in my head. I haven't found anything new. Most of the articles are clones of each other. Everyone seems confused, fascinated, and desperate to hear more. The song wasn't that great – hardly original. How has it captivated all these people? How did it manage to hack into the music stations and all those devices? Why and how was the footage deleted? Was it a publicity stunt, to promote intrigue? Will the artist publish anything else, and when? Surely she can't reveal herself now? Last I checked, hacking's illegal. Several of these stations, both on TV and the radio, are demanding she come forward, but not to reprimand her. They want to carry on airing the song. Are they seriously saying she'll avoid any legal ramifications because it was that good? This is insane.

After what feels like an eternity of wanting to tear my hair out, we pull up outside our small flat block.

I slide straight out of the car. "Finally!"

I grab my rucksack from the back.

Connelly huffs and says, "I went as fast as I could."

I've no time to explain who I was really frustrated with. I dart inside the building. Sickness pokes my chest again – staring at the phone screen for ages hasn't helped – but I push past it. Connelly isn't far behind me. He's muttering. I don't want to know.

Once I've unlocked our front door by the main staircase, I hurry inside our narrow flat. Drop the rucksack on the floorboard by our bedroom door then turn into the studio room. Barely hear Connelly say, "Bye, then." I know he gets annoyed at how I shut myself away, but the quicker I get this out, the more info I can share with everyone. Let's face it: after a glass or two, I'll probably forget what little I can recall of the version I saw. Plus, after I've done this, I can change out of these chlorine-infested jeans. I may have showered at Kya's, but putting these back on was bloody horrific.

I push the door shut, plummeting the place into dimness, then squeeze between the camera tripod and sofa and slip behind the black curtain. Leaning over the desk, I pull open the blinds to let in the daylight – not too bright, so should be fine for the video. I slump in the computer chair, rest my aching back against it, and bring out my phone. Wish I could've recorded a video in the car, but the battery wouldn't have survived it. I retrieve the charger lead from the desk drawer, connect it from the phone to the computer tower, and jab the power button. This'll be strange; I haven't shot an unscripted video for a long time. If I end up rambling, I can always edit it down. Quality won't be as good, either, but I need to get this out. I take a silent, readying breath, hold the phone in front of me, and tap record.

"What's up, everyone?" That was lame. Everyone says that. Oh well. Roll with it. I try to smile but just look tired and nervous. "My name's Maddix A. If you're new here, I normally talk for twenty to thirty minutes, analysing different conspiracy theories, but I needed to get something out quickly today because, man, I've got to talk with you guys about this."

And hopefully won't get too much backlash for it. I straighten up. Put on a genuinely serious face.

"I'm sure you've all seen or heard of the song that aired last night: 'Something That You Need to Know'. Everyone's going crazy over it already, especially since no-one knows who the artist is and now it's been completely deleted. Every screenshot or video of it has been erased." I hold up my finger. "Which means someone, maybe the singer herself, must've hacked into people's devices. And no-one seems disturbed by this! Seriously, does *anyone* care? What about you guys?"

I pray at least one person sees sense or has the courage to admit it. Now for the tough part, though:

"What's even stranger is: I heard a different version, guys. I was alone when I saw the video for the first time. The tune was the same, the beat, the cuts, all of it, except the rabbit was black not white, and the lyrics...

they were demeaning, like, God, I can't remember what she was singing, but it wasn't uplifting and inspirational like in the version everyone's talking about." I stare into space. My stomach aches. I probably sound crazy, but someone has to believe me. A bunch of my subscribers have been with me since the beginning. They have to trust me. I look into the camera again: "Please, if anyone knows anything, let me know in the comments. I've been searching online, high and low, and there seems to be no mention of it. If I remember more, I'll do another video. Definitely expect to see more on this because, wherever this song came from, it's certainly caught everyone's attention. So, until next time, I'll see you then."

I stop the recording. That felt way too short. Wish I could remember more. My credibility doesn't sound great, but it'll be even worse if I mention how much booze I had, or that the TV switched on by itself. These bags under my eyes don't help either. Weird uploading a two-minute video. It'll probably get more clicks for being shorter, though. If my subscribers are as obsessed with this thing as everyone else seems to be, they'll click for sure. I keep the title blunt: 'I've Heard a Darker Version of that New Mystery Song – Have You?' Now I have to wait for the comments. One way or another, I'll make a proper video on this – I just need more information.

I spend a while on the computer, refreshing multiple news sites every five minutes and compiling as much as I can in a folder called 'Mystery Song'. It sucks, but it'll do for now. I've found a few more interesting accounts of what happened. Apparently, the song made it to prisons and hospitals, playing for prisoners and patients, and even for doctors performing surgery. Surely that had to cause major issues? Unless they were able to continue working while listening? If anyone *did* die from a distracted doctor, I doubt the media would admit that. Of course, there are also countless cases of people who were driving at the time and missed the video part. Hearing it seemed to be enough to spark their intrigue, but they've all expressed huge disappointment over not seeing it like most others. Even a large potion of homeless got to experience it, either through outdoor speaker systems and screens, or through monitors displayed in shop windows. But what about anyone who was unconscious for whatever reason, or those without access to *any* media devices? There must be a tiny pocket of people who didn't experience it at all – they're just not speaking up.

Hoping to find a semblance of sense, I flick to the comments on my video. Most of them tell me they have no idea what I mean while also gushing over how inspirational the singer is and cooing over the bunny. Looks like they've fallen for it too. Everyone's being dismissive, some even going as far as to claim I'm making this up for attention, to get those clicks. Stomach pain's back. I don't recognise a lot of these users – they're probably not subscribers, just any one of the swarm that's inevitably searching for anything on this song. I've never seen so many people losing their minds in the comments.

How could my self-professed number one fan Tinfoil-Canis not have spoken up yet?

As I finish typing the first paragraph of my video script, Connelly knocks on the door. I call him in but stay staring at the screen. The words start to blur. Think I need a break.

Connelly slips behind the curtain with me, and sets down a red Lindor Easter egg box on the desk.

I grin, and my gut would start pining for it if it wasn't full from breakfast. "Aww. Thanks, love."

"You're welcome," he says tiredly.

I'm especially grateful after how I've been ignoring him since we got back.

My chest tightens. "You did say you didn't want anything this year, right?"

"...No."

Oh, shit. Is he messing with me? His eyes are dead serious. I can't even pretend I'm hiding something – I'd need to sneak out and buy it right now and it'd be totally obvious.

"Crap." My stomach twinges. "Sorry, man. I'll go get you an egg."

"You don't have to." His jaw's clenched; he's miffed. Don't know why I thought he didn't want one. They'd better not have sold out everywhere. He rests an elbow on the back of my chair and leans forward to read the screen. "You're really going to tell everyone about the weird version you saw?"

"I already have. Posted a short video about it earlier." Can't help sounding miffed myself. "No-one else has come forward yet."

Should I have waited and scripted the video after all? I'm happy my voice is out there, but I hate rushing things. If I'd thought about my phrasing, I could've more likely persuaded others not to throw all that negativity at me.

"Well, hopefully someone will," he says. "If not, lay off the vodka for a bit."

Rubbing my eyes, I sigh and lean back. "You still don't believe me, do you?"

He straightens up. "I believe you saw something. I just don't understand."

"You would've seen it too if you'd come with me, instead of buggering off to mingle."

"What?"

"All you cared about last night was those bloody models and what they thought of you. What could you possibly have to talk about?"

He clenches his jaw again. "I told you weeks ago that I want to branch out and get more involved with Kya's life."

"You're gonna manage all her friends' social media too?"

"No. Only hers, for now."

How many people is he thinking about 'branching out' to? Would he consider helping me if I was on social media?

"If you get loads of rich clients and I get famous on YouTube," I say, "maybe we can finally move out of this place. You could have your own proper study, and I could have a bigger studio."

"That's the dream." Sighing, he gazes out of the window. His green eyes always look warm and calming in the daylight, but today they waver with trouble. It's not just about the egg, is it?

"What's up?" I ask. "Where's that excitement from last night?"

"I don't know. I'm kind of crashing."

I want that happy Connelly back. Stretching my arms above me, I say, "I need a break. Why don't we do something?"

"I think I'm gonna lie down, actually."

Maybe those few glasses of wine hit him harder than he admits.

Hiding my disappointment, I say, "Okay," and he leaves. Well, talking of drinking, I could use one, so I push myself up and leave too.

I head down the short hallway and turn right into the kitchen. Get myself a quick glass of cold tap water and find myself staring at the fridge. Connelly brought home that leftover Black Cow for me. Tempting to have a slither. But we all know I can never stop at that, and I need to have a clear thinker for this.

While snacking on my deliciously smooth Lindor egg pieces, I slog away at the script until I've done a substantial amount. Maybe writing a video with a hangover isn't a brilliant idea, but I have to get this out. Knowing my luck, by the time I upload it, it'll all be old news or there'll at least be a new development. By the end of it, I've got a tired buzz: that worthwhile satisfaction of decent chocolate and completing a script. I'm ready to do this.

I flick on the painfully bright box lights and camera that point at the sofa. Transfer the script file from computer to laptop then set up the document on the laptop screen in line with the camera. Press record, sink into the sofa's soft fabric, and close my eyes. Nearly drift off. I jerk awake, shake out my shoulders, and tap my cheek a few times. I shouldn't do this when I'm hungover, but needs must.

"Right." I clear my throat, stare at the camera, and take a long breath. I count down from three, and widen my eyes to look more alert. "Hi, there. My name's Maddix A., and today we are talking about *that* song. You know the one: the mystery pop song 'Something That You Need to Know', which hacked music stations and devices around the world last night – all at the same time, I found out. No delay to allow for time zones, or rates at which certain devices can receive signal." I hold out my hands. "That's impossible, right? But no-one seems to be questioning that, or how it even made it into secure places like prisons and hospitals. From what I can find online, everyone, all from different countries and cultures, seems enamoured: obsessed, even. Where did this thing come from, and who made it?

"Quick side note: I posted a video this morning where I asked you guys if anyone had seen or heard the same version as me, with darker lyrics and a black rabbit instead of white. No-one seems to know what I'm talking about, so please, if anyone watching this experienced the same thing, let me know. I am going nuts researching into this and not finding anything. Honestly, Gene Ray's time cube theory makes more sense than this."

I laugh nervously. I uploaded my video on that a few months ago – hopefully, most of my viewers will get the reference, at least.

"Let's continue on for now." I lean forward. "Currently, no-one recognises the singer. No information is known about her, or whether she was the one who leaked the song. No-one can even work out what country it originated from.

"Apparently, according to thousands of sources, every trace of footage that anyone managed to capture of it was automatically deleted. That sounds absolutely mental, and I've not personally seen any concrete evidence of this. It could just be a rumour going around to conjure more mystery, but surely if this song is as well-loved as it appears to be, everyone would be desperate to share any footage they have?" I try not to get wound up at this next bit. "What about you? Did this happen to you? If this *is* true, it means some person out there, or organisation, has access to all of our devices. But no-one seems outraged by this."

These lights are making my headache worse. Thankfully, this won't be as long as usual since there's limited information available.

"Does anyone who's heard this song actually hate it, or not think much of it? There are bound to be those of you who haven't even heard it. But so far, all I can find is everyone saying it's 'inspirational' and 'life-changing', including loads of big-name stars." Insert celebrity Twitter screenshots here. "And the people I was at a party with last night listened to the thing three times then came away acting seriously high on life. It was surreal."

I've left out that they're normally snobby, miserable bastards – don't want to get in trouble.

"A few sites have posted some lyrics from memory, trying to decipher the song's meaning. Interesting how those haven't been deleted! Anyway, I'll link those in the description." I clear my throat – a tiny thing to edit out. "They differ from person to person, but one phrase remains unchanged: 'You can have it all.' Now, the overarching theme seems to be: don't give up on your dreams, don't let life drag you down, anything is possible. We've heard this many times in music, going back generations. So what makes this one different? What has drawn so many people to it? Is it because now of all times, when the world seems to be getting madder by the minute, we need this message?"

I straighten up. "Please, let me know in the comments what you love about this song. It's certainly caused a stir. People are desperate for more, and I am too, to be honest. I want to find out where it came from and why it's already captivated the world." I clear my throat again – remember to edit that out as well. "By the time I post this, there's bound to be further developments to this investigation. I know my video today has been way shorter, but hopefully in my next one I can go into a deeper analysis, depending on how much more this all develops." I smile – haven't done that enough. "Thank you for watching, and I'll see you soon. Bye!"

I sigh. Push myself up from the sofa and switch off the camera. My intros and outros are still seriously lacking. Thought I'd keep it simple with the 'Hi, there', but that doesn't make me stand out, does it? I'm certainly not going back to saying that cringey 'Hello, fellow conspiracists,' and I'm not doing any silly hand actions. It was bad enough when Connelly walked in while I was practising one.

Anyway, wish I had more to talk about. Maybe I could've mentioned the legal ramifications the publisher will or won't face after hacking all those music stations. I'll go into that another time. My thinker hurts too much and I need to edit the video together yet. I'll have to delay the release of my follow-up on the continuing mystery of who assassinated Princess Preciosa – maybe by a week or two. Who knows how many videos I'll make on this mystery song, and I should release them consecutively for consistency. For now, I put that to the back of my mind and prepare myself for editing.

Several subscribers have sent through permission to show screenshots of their comments about the song. I gratefully thank them then slip them into the video. Always more credible to provide backup, and I'd never repost without their consent. I spend a couple hours editing – would be less if I didn't have to refresh the news sites and YouTube every five minutes to check for updates.

I nearly fall off my chair when I see that my little video from this morning has over two-hundred-and-fifty thousand views – usually takes several days for my recent stuff to hit that count. I can't keep up with the thousands of comments, but I'm trying hard to. Any one of them could provide new information or a fresh perspective. Why do people post comments that are basically a copy and paste of others'? But in this case, it shows me how many people believe or have experienced the same thing. And the more I read, the crazier I feel. How can *no-one* have seen or heard what I did? There's no mention of any devices suddenly turning on, either. Was it really the booze's fault? Could I have reached for the remote without realising?

Within the first twenty minutes of being live, my new video gets over ten thousand views. So I delay no further and crack out the Black Cow to celebrate. Success never tasted this sweet. Increasingly more people are posting videos about the song, but still no-one has a clip or anything different. I notice a new trend among the comments section, though: people are complaining about feeling drained, like a comedown, and now they're even more desperate to hear it again so they can experience that rush from yesterday. Connelly suddenly felt wiped out this afternoon. A song can't cause that. They must be winding down from their excitement and can't think how else to describe it. I collect screenshots of their comments anyway, in case I decide to discuss it later. It feels kind of cheap to be putting out the same type of content as many others – this topic's top of the trending list right now across all media platforms. But I have to remind myself: I have something to offer that no-one else does.

Eventually, I refresh YouTube for what must be the thousandth time, and a private message notification appears. Finally. How did it take this long? I bring it up, and lift my glass to my lips. Freeze. Tinfoil-Canis has responded at last: a brief private message that leaves me stunned. It says, 'Hey, man. I've just seen your two latest videos and I need to tell you that I know exactly what you're talking about. I heard it too. I'd love to discuss it with you. TC.'

I read this several times before I remotely process it. I've had several conversations with this guy over the last few years. We always tend to agree. He's been the most generous contributor to my Patreon fund, consistently donating £50 a month. Connelly's called him a 'suck-up groupie', and I guess he's right in a way, but I'm still indebted to him. The guy obviously had something going on this morning that stopped him from instantly leaving a comment on my latest videos, but I did break my 6 pm upload schedule. I don't know him well enough to truly tell if he's lying, but I'm pretty sure he wouldn't do that. Suppose the only way to know is to test how much he can tell me. In any case, I have to follow this up.

After a long sip, I type back: 'Hi there, Tinfoil! Thanks for your message. I'm intrigued. Do you remember the lyrics? Were they different from what everyone else says they are? Let me know. MA.' I'll leave it at that for now. Hopefully, if he's telling the truth, and does remember the lyrics, even if only some, it may jog my memory too.

I sip my English Apprehension and refresh the page. Loads more generic, unhelpful comments flood in. I may have now found someone who saw what I did, but I have to keep an eye out for others.

It takes me a few moments to register I have a new private message. Maybe I should slow down on the vodka. Tinfoil says, 'Maddix, as always I appreciate your quick reply! This was the chorus: *Pour yourself a drink. Go on. Make it big. You'll forget it all. No-one will listen, and they never will.*

Just forget it all.' My thinker feels lighter by the second. Those words. That *is* what she sang. He continues, 'I have the rest of the lyrics but would love to discuss them with you in person. What do you say? Would you mind at all if we were to meet? TC.'

I frown at this for a while. How can he know the whole song? He must've listened to it with pen and paper in hand and jotted like crazy. And why would he want to do that? More importantly, he wants to meet face-to-face? Is that an ultimatum? Will he stop giving me money if I say no? I mean, considering how dedicated he's been to my channel, and for such a long time too, surely he deserves a meeting with me? It'll be great to shake the hand of the guy who's genuinely supported my career more than my parents ever have. If he really does have the other lyrics, this'll be beneficial for the channel too, not to mention emotionally rewarding to discover I wasn't imagining the whole thing in a drunken stupor.

Anyway, where will we meet? Where does he even live? I should bring Connelly with me.

I reply, 'Tinfoil, it'll be brill to meet you. Especially after all the support you've given me. Those lyrics definitely ring a bell. I'd love to hear the rest of what you've got. Do you have an idea where you'd like to meet? MA.'

He knows I'm from London, but I've no clue about him. His YouTube profile's practically blank. He's never uploaded anything, either. He could be anyone. Is this a good idea?

He quickly comes back with: 'I live in Lambeth. You're from Central London too, right? Pick a place and time. I'm flexible :) TC.'

My eyebrows dart up. I never realised we lived so close. It's about a thirty-minute car ride to Lambeth. I snicker into my glass. This is nuts. Hard to believe, but not impossible. Also, it's quite cute how he still mimics my sign-off style.

This narrows meeting places down by a great deal. Obviously, we should meet in public, but somewhere loud enough to drown out our conversation – don't want people overhearing. And it should be as soon as possible. Would he be free today?

I reply: 'How about Costa in Brixton? Nice halfway point. As for time, are you free later this afternoon, or is that too short notice? MA.'

I finish the dregs of my glass and stare at the screen, at our surreal exchange. I've never met a fan. No-one's outright asked before. But the chances of him being so nearby: they're unreal. Granted, most of my fanbase is from the UK, but a great deal is from America too. Good job this guy's on my doorstep.

He replies, 'Maddix, not short notice at all. I'm always ready to go! How about 5, then? TC.'

Smiling, I type, 'OK cool. Who should I look out for? MA.'

Now I should find out who I'm dealing with exactly.

He says, 'I'm a fairly small guy. I'll be wearing a black beanie and a massive grin :D TC.'

I snigger. He could've given me more to go on, but let's face it: he'll recognise me immediately.

'By the way,' he adds. 'I just paid you an extra £50 for your trouble. Hope that's OK. TC.'

I almost fall off the chair again. Fucking hell. This guy's mental. His words blur together. I don't know how to respond. Everything I can think of doesn't sound good enough.

Eventually, I settle with: 'Thank you so much, man... You didn't have to do that. I really appreciate it. I'll see you later! MA.'

I should've added more, about how I don't know what I'd do without his support, or ask him why he feels like I'm worth this much. But that'd make things awkward, and I've just been given more money. I've got vodka to get!

I rush out of the flat block and follow the path up to the main road. The brightness stings my eyes. As I head to the zebra crossing, I check for new comments on my phone. More people claiming I'm lying or mistaken. A whole bunch of confused reactions. I roll my eyes, but there's that stabbing pain in my gut. I don't get this. There still aren't any videos similar to mine. At least I stand out in the crowd in that respect, but it's frustrating because no-one seems to be taking me seriously. My community knows what I'm like: I always focus on facts, and I'm no liar. How can they suddenly doubt me? I don't need this negativity! I need more vodka. Fuck it. I'll get two bottles.

Crossing over the triangular island at the centre of the intersection, I shove my phone in my jacket pocket. Need to stop staring at screens for a bit, and once I've got some Russian Apathy in me, I should calm down. So I follow the road for a couple minutes past the terraced houses, trying not to think about this whole situation. The trees dotted along here bring me shade from the sun until the last little stretch where I have to shield my eyes. At least the sun offers some warmth against the bitter breeze.

The Co-Op sits on the corner of the T-junction, opposite The White Hart. I miss hanging out there with Connelly; we'd have a meal and drinks at that pub every two weeks, but it got expensive. Now I take the cheaper, quicker option of getting drunk off booze from the Co-Op. But nothing quite beats that cosy feeling of eating a tasty meal and sipping a well-mixed beverage with my husband in a place where other people are enjoying the same. Just don't go there on a noisy Saturday or when the bloody football's on.

I slip through the supermarket's automatic double doors and almost head straight to the till. Connelly's egg! I divert to the confectionary section. Plenty of chocolate. No eggs. Fuck. Why did it slip my mind this year? His absolute favourite's Hotel Chocolat, but the nearest is in Battersea about twenty minutes away, and I really don't fancy a trip back to my hometown. I'll order it online – hopefully, I can get next day delivery. For now, to make sure he has a treat to snack on today, I pick up a large Dairy Milk Turkish Delight bar.

I take this to the till, which somehow has no queue. Behind the lovely shop assistant lies a rainbow of bottles. All that to choose from, but I'm only interested in one thing.

"Same as usual?" she says with a tired smile.

"Two, please."

"Oh." With raised eyebrows, she turns to retrieve two bottles of Russian Standard, scans them, then puts them on the counter. They sit there enticingly. Today is a very special day. Thank you, Tinfoil.

"How's it going?" I ask.

"It's been a little dead in here."

I glance around. It *is* suspicious for a Sunday lunch time.

I press my card to the reader, it beeps, and she thanks me.

"What are you up to today?" she asks.

"I made a video on that song from last night."

"Oh. The one that's been in the news?"

"Yeah. Did you hear it?"

"Yes. It woke me up, actually." She lowers her tone. "You'll never believe it, but it just started playing from my phone."

My eyes widen. Kya's kitchen TV must've turned on alone after all. This is the confirmation I needed!

"Same thing happened to me," I say, trying to contain my excitement. "The TV switched on to play it... I *knew* there must've been others who experienced this. No-one seems to have been brave enough to admit it – online, anyway." Or maybe their comments were instantly deleted. "I know this is out of the blue and probably weird, but could I possibly record you saying that? Even if it's just a voice clip."

She appears to tense up. Glances away for a few moments then shakes her head. "I'm not sure I should. I'm sorry."

Is she just too self-conscious? Or is she worried about getting in trouble?

"Is there anything I can say or do to persuade you?" I ask.

Her focus hits the counter. "I'd rather not."

As frustrating as that is, I don't want to make her uneasy. Guess even if I *did* get a clip, people would say I paid her.

"That's fine," I try to say as nicely as possible.

"It's all so weird," she continues. "But I *am* glad I heard it because it was brilliant."

I shrug. "I've heard better."

She gasps quietly, and starts bagging my items up. "What sort of music *do* you like?"

"All sorts. Normally chill-out stuff. But not pop."

She nods. "Me neither, but this one was special."

My thinker tilts. "Why do you think?"

"I..." Her mouth stays open as her eyes search for the words. "I'm not sure."

How interesting.

"Well, I'm looking into it." Smiling, I collect my bags and edge back towards the doors. "I've got to dash. I'll see you later, yeah? Take it easy."

"You too." She gives me a tiny wave, and I leave the shop.

Maybe the place is dead because everyone's off trying to find that song. I shake my thinker. Unlikely. It's honestly not worth that much attention anyway. I realise that's ironic.

Once home, I pour myself a small glass of Russian Calm and start swigging. Nothing like more alcohol to beat a hangover. Our bedroom door remains shut, so I slot Connelly's chocolate in the fridge. How will I get to Brixton? Can't be arsed to take public transport, and Connelly's coming with me anyway. We should drive. Wait, though. I need to convince him to come in the first place. He'll be his suspicious, protective self, which isn't always a bad thing, but I need him to go along with me on this one.

I down the rest of the glass and clink it down on the kitchen side. My thinker whirls. I smile. At least the vodka will steady my nerves. I stagger down the hallway to our bedroom. He can't still be asleep. I creep in, just in case. The room's nice and dark. He lies on top of the quilt on his side. I whisper his name. No answer. I move closer. Carefully perch beside him. His eyes are closed, and his breathing's slow. He looks gorgeous, but I have to wake him.

Saying his name again, I gently place a hand on his arm. He slowly comes to, and all the while I'm desperate to get out my news.

"What is it?" he croaks.

"Something crazy's happened."

He sighs and rubs his eyes. "Why do most of our conversations start like this?"

"I'm serious. You know Tinfoil-Canis?"

He glares at me. "How could I forget your biggest fanboy?"

"Sorry." I try not to laugh. "But he saw and heard the same thing as me. He sent some lyrics, and honestly, they look right."

"Okay," he says with a frown.

"He wants to see me, in person, to discuss it." I grin. "It'll be cool to finally meet him."

His frown deepens. "Where are you meeting?"

"Costa, in Brixton. He actually lives in Lambeth. Can you believe it?"

He pauses, as if processing. "He happens to live close to you? Have you even seen what he looks like?"

"No, but he did describe himself. Why does it matter?"

"You could be meeting *anyone.*"

I slide my fingers down his arm. "That's why you're coming with me."

"Too right I am." He kind of snaps this, taking me by surprise. He *is* cute when he's protective, though. He hoists himself onto one elbow. "When's this happening?"

"Five o'clock today."

His eyebrow shoots up. "Seriously? I bet you want me to drive too, don't you?"

I smile as sweetly as I can. "Please."

"So you *have* been drinking again."

"...Yes."

He rolls his eyes. "You sure you want to be drunk when your 'biggest fan' meets you for the first time?"

"Hey, I am *not* drunk compared to last night. I feel fine right now."

"Have you had lunch?"

"No. That breakfast was massive. Oh, I did eat the egg you gave me." That reminds me: I'll need to order that Hotel Chocolat egg for him. "I left you a little gift in the fridge for now. But you *will* be getting an egg."

He laughs under his breath. "Okay. Thank you, then."

I'm glad he's not refusing it.

"You went out?" he says.

"Yeah. Tinfoil gave me another fifty pounds so I treated myself to two bottles of vodka and got you a temporary chocolate gift."

Uh-oh. There's his judging face.

"What?" I say.

"I suppose you've forgotten about paying Kya back for the Black Cow."

All I can do is look away and grimace. I feel terrible that I didn't even once think about it.

"And I suppose you drank it today too," he says.

I smile. "I didn't even know I was going to get that money. We just won't tell her, and it'll be like before."

Frowning, he glances down at me. "Have you even changed?"

What's he talking about? I follow his line of sight to my jeans. Oh, crap.

I snicker. "You know what? I got so wrapped up in the video I forgot." I must've got used to the chlorine smell too. "I'll change before we leave."

"You will change *now*. In fact, get off the bed." Wish I could tell him to stop being bossy, but I'll never hear the end of it. "Get out of that jacket too. I'll stick them both in the wash."

Groaning, I push myself up. He does too. Guess it would be good to have a clean jacket for meeting Tinfoil. I stay rooted for several seconds, staring at the bed. Could do with a nap myself. Need a break from that screen. But yeah, I shouldn't get into bed with dirty clothes.

I start struggling out of them as Connelly brushes his hair back over to the side with a smooth hand movement. He looks sexiest after a nap, although he doesn't agree: knackered eyes, messy hair. There *is* another instance where he looks exactly like that, minus the clothes.

"Has anything else about that song shown up?" he asks.

Wish he'd focus on my bare legs and exposed boxers instead.

I drag myself out of my daydream. "No. It's still a total mystery."

He sighs, and genuinely seems disappointed. "I dreamt about it last night, and again just now."

I frown at him. "Seriously?"

"Yeah. Both times, I was back in Kya's kitchen, listening to it with everyone again. I felt amazing."

Wow. It made more of an impression on him than I thought. But that's not the first time I've heard that.

"A few comments were like that," I say. "Well, they said they'd listen to it in their dreams if they can't in real life, but I thought that was wishful thinking."

His eyes widen slightly, as if in awe at the memory. "It was so vivid. I mean, you know I normally get vivid dreams, but I could hear it, note for note, word for word, everything about it."

"Do you remember the lyrics, then?"

"Not really." He winces. "It keeps going. It's fucking frustrating."

I huff. Tell me about it. "Well, Tinfoil seems to have some answers, about the different version, anyway."

"Any news will do." He shakes his thinker. "I don't know why, but it's constantly on my mind, ever since last night. I thought taking a nap would help."

I stare at him again. Music's never really been his thing. I'm not sure he's ever even had a favourite song. How can this one have infected him and everyone else so much? I'm going to get to the bottom of this. It's just another of life's many mysteries I love to explore. But this time, without sounding too cliché, it's personal, and I need help. First, though, let's sleep off some of this drunkenness.

"Talking of which," I say, "I'm taking a nap too."

"Good. You *are* going to remove those boxers, right?"

I glance down at them then smirk. "Why? Do you want me to?"

His eyebrow arches. "Yes. They'll stink of chlorine now."

I sag slightly. Didn't think about that.

I slip my thumbs under the hem. "As you command."

He watches blankly as I slip out of them. He's like that a lot recently. What have I got to do to make him loosen up?

"Before you fall asleep, I'm getting you a pint of water." He starts making his way out. "You're going to drink the whole thing."

I salute him, but he doesn't see as he's already out the door. It probably would've irked him anyway.

Don't want to kill this buzz, but I do need to be much more sober to meet my biggest fan. My gut should be flipping about it. Once most of the booze wears off, though, I can assure it will be.

3

Well, I can walk without staggering, and my thinker's not as light as earlier. I run gel through my fringe so it sticks up respectably instead of jutting out at all angles. At Connelly's request, I brush my teeth and swish some mouthwash around. He even makes me down more water. I get it: he doesn't want me turning up even remotely drunk. It wouldn't be professional, and I owe it to Tinfoil. I must admit, though: a tiny buzz wouldn't hurt, and would certainly help with these nerves.

To go along with my fresh boxers and jeans, I switch into a different jumper then grab my jacket from the tumble-drier. Connelly wants me to shave, but I bat him away. I like my fine stubble. I'm good to go.

In the car on the way to Brixton, I play out different scenarios. Will Tinfoil be overexcitable, withdrawn from nervousness, or casual and treat me like any other person? I'm clearly more than that to him. Not sure how I'd prefer him to behave.

Connelly parks in the usual car park on Ferndale Road, by the rail bridge. It shuts at 6; Tinfoil and I have an hour to talk things over. Connelly says if I want to stay out longer, I can get the bus back. Depends how well this conversation goes, I guess. But I understand why he doesn't want to stay out, as he has the joy of getting up at 6 tomorrow morning for work. I wonder if Tinfoil has a job.

I ask Connelly to lend me some cash for me to buy us a round of drinks. I can see he nearly says no, so I lean in and kiss his neck, then he rolls his eyes and reaches in his pocket.

We cross the road and pass the rail bridge's peeling white brick wall. The fresh air sobers me up a little more. As we walk by the independent cafés that sit below a row of small flats, I draw in a silent, deep breath. The sun warms my back. I focus on this for as long as I can to keep my nerves at bay. Connelly has to remind me, though:

"I hope this guy's telling the truth."

I frown. "Why wouldn't he be?"

"He could be stringing you along just so he can meet you."

We fall silent. I hope it's not true, but I get why he said that. I'm sure Tinfoil's had plenty of opportunities to suggest meeting – why wait until now?

"What do you actually know about him?" Connelly says.

I suppose I was waiting for this.

"Well, he says he's twenty-six, and he was born in England but his parents are from Japan. And now I know he lives in Lambeth. Other than that, I can only give you a list of conspiracies he does or doesn't believe in."

He doesn't respond for a few seconds, but when I check on him he's clearly trying to hide a clenched jaw and says, "Right. Okay."

"...Please don't grill him."

"Don't worry. I'm staying out of it."

I try not to sigh with relief.

At the end of the road, we turn onto the main one. The roaring of cars and buses aggravates my thinker. A coffee should help. We pass TK Maxx, Foot Locker, New Look, and under the bridge that demands in big green letters, 'COME IN LOVE'. This city needs to pay more attention to it.

Opposite the underground station, and beneath the second bridge, we spot our meeting place. Among the spattering of passing people, a grinning guy stands out. Looks about our age. Under that black studded beanie hat, his dark hair spikes out. He's pale, and judging by his slender face and neck, I think he's slim under that hoodie. I push my stomach pain down and try to walk straighter.

As we get closer, his brown eyes practically twinkle in the light. He's about a thinker shorter than me, but I'm a tall guy. I straighten up and give him a smile.

"Maddix." He holds out a hand. "Hi. My name is Akihiro Tamotsu."

"Hello." I shake his warm hand for a few moments. "Tinfoil-Canis, I presume?"

"Yes. Call me Aki, though." He chuckles. "Thank you so much for this."

"You're welcome."

I'm not sure who I imagined when I thought about him before, but it's surreal to hear his proper name and see the guy in the flesh. He must feel the same.

He looks at Connelly, who says, "Hi."

Is that all he has to offer? His smile seems friendly enough, but his eyes are guarded.

"This is my husband Connelly Durand," I say.

"You're married? Wow. Nice to meet you." Aki shakes his hand too. "*Both* Durands."

"Actually, that's not *my* name," I point out.

"Oh. Different surname?"

"Never you mind," Connelly says, in that awful, blunt way that makes me want to hide in shame.

Laughing, I gently elbow his arm. "A story for another time, yeah? Let's get inside. I'm dying for a coffee."

Thankfully, Aki doesn't appear to flinch at his rudeness. He beams at us. "Let me get you both one."

"No," I say. "Drinks are on me. It's the least I can do."

Because of all he's given me, I can't pass up an opportunity to give back in some way other than sending him a link to my videos a week early as well as cutting room floor material.

"Really?" he says.

"I insist."

Hope he doesn't ask for anything expensive.

Costa's pretty busy, as usual. Hopefully, we can find a corner somewhere. We join the queue at the serving counter, and Connelly goes off through the stone archway into the back area to scout out a table.

I can't help noticing Aki staring at me in the corner of my eye.

"Are you okay?" I ask.

Sheepishly, he glances down. "Yeah. Sorry. I just can't believe I'm standing next to you."

I'm like a celebrity. I feel my face grow hot. Oh God. I'd better not be blushing.

"Well, believe it," I say.

He chuckles to himself again. Surprised he hasn't asked for a selfie yet.

Connelly hasn't returned, so I assume he found us a table.

"I'm sorry about my husband." I try not to burn up even more. "He's very private."

Aki bats his hand dismissively. "No offence taken."

Oh, thank God for that.

Fortunately, we don't queue too long, and Aki only wants a small espresso. Added to Connelly's regular cappuccino and my regular latte, the cash barely covers it, though. And now this tip box taunts me. Is Aki expecting me to tip? All I can contribute is the pittance of change they gave me. Well, other people are waiting to be served, and it's better than nothing, so I slot it in. Don't think Aki even notices – he's too busy inhaling the steam from his cup. Might as well have kept the coins!

Through the stone archway beside the counter, Aki and I step into the wide, bright seating area. At the back, Connelly's scrolling on his phone at

45

a table on the end of the long red padded pew. I go and sit beside him and Aki takes the chair opposite, with the small table between us. No-one's directly next to us, and hopefully it'll stay that way. I dread Connelly's reaction to what we're about to discuss. Wish I could ask him to give us five minutes alone, but I know he'll insist on staying. Guess I can understand his suspicion, but he should relax a little, especially now that Aki seems cool with us being married. I've hinted that I'm gay on a few videos before – it should come as no shock to my 'biggest fan'.

"You get any change?" Connelly mutters to me.

I didn't even think he'd want it back, let alone immediately.

Grimacing, I whisper, "I tipped it. Sorry."

He visibly suppresses a sigh over the rim of his cappuccino. Great. Another thing for him to be annoyed at me about. I don't need or want this tension right now.

Aki slips off his shoulder bag, takes out a black notebook, and dumps his bag under the table. Will all the answers lie in that tattered book, or did he make it up so he could meet me? The chatter around us and whirring of the drinks machines in the other room will mask our conversation, at least.

"I believe I have it all in here," he says.

I sip my Steaming Sobriety, and it slides smoothly down my throat. "Show me what you've got."

Grinning, he flicks open the book to just over halfway and turns it for me to see. Among the black squiggles and crossings-out lie those familiar lyrics:

What do you think you're doing here?
This has never been your scene,
and this is not your home.
You think you know everything.

My eyebrows dart up. "Oh my God. This is it."

I sing along mentally to the jaunty, taunting melody:

Pour yourself a drink.
Go on. Make it big.
You'll forget it all.
No-one will listen
and they never will.
Just forget it all.

It's spot on so far. Almost too good to be true. As much as I was desperate to find another person with the same experience, to prove I haven't gone insane, I'm actually a little disappointed. Wasn't expecting that.

Connelly leans in to read it too. As I'm about to ask Aki how he got it all down, Connelly snaps: "That's not right."

He takes us both aback.

"Conn?" I say.

"Those aren't the lyrics." He glares at Aki. His face flushes. "I can't remember exactly what they were, but it wasn't this shit."

So much for staying out of it. What's with the aggression? He's out of line, and I want to tell him, but I daren't make this more awkward. Aki stares back at him, but I can't work out if he's flustered, offended, or both.

"Of course it's different from what you heard, Conn." I try to keep my voice level. "The whole point is that we didn't hear what you did."

"But it's ridiculous." That jabs at me, but I endeavour to ignore it. "And it doesn't make any sense. You were drinking at the time, right? So if you really did hear those words, and they were targeted at *you*, at least they related to you in some way." Where is he going with this? Wish he'd change his tone. "What about you, Aki? Were you drinking too?"

He never did mention that. We both wait with bated breath for his response.

"Uh, yeah, I had a vodka and coke."

He drinks vodka too? Another thing we could potentially bond over, I suppose. But I guess that really does mean the lyrics weren't tailored specifically to me. That uneasy mixture of relief and disappointment washes over me again.

Connelly doesn't add anything else, but still looks tense as hell. I'd squeeze his knee if I didn't feel like he'd bite my hand off.

"What exactly happened, then?" I ask Aki.

"Well, I was in my room making notes at my desk about Grand Unified Theory – your video last week got me really interested in it."

I smile at his flattery.

His eyes widen as he continues, "Then my laptop brought up a new tab by itself: the video was playing on YouTube. I noticed there was no uploader name, no options to like or dislike or do anything with it. But I could replay it. So I jotted down the lyrics out of interest, and I'm glad I did because it disappeared soon after."

As gratefully as I can, I say, "I'm glad you did, too."

47

Nodding, he impressively necks his espresso.

Connelly's still silent. I take this opportunity to continue reading:

Just hide away in the dark

and stay there for forever more.

Just keep it all inside.

Forget what you think you know.

"It's coming back to me," I say. "How ironic that it's talking about forgetting something."

He lifts a finger. "That's the idea, though. It told you to forget, and you did."

I frown. "I forgot because I was wasted."

Shit. I blurted that. Didn't want anyone to know. Will he keep that secret?

"No," he murmurs, and leans forward. "It's possible you would've forgotten anyway, wasted or not. I'd only had one drink, but when I woke up this morning, it was a blur, even the tune. When I read my notes, though, it rushed back to me. And that's happened to you too now, right?"

I stare at the words again. "Yeah. But what are you saying?"

"So far, we seem to be the only two people in the world to have seen and heard the official version."

Connelly chips back in: "What makes you think *yours* is official? Maddix heard ours too, when he joined us all."

"Yeah. That *is* odd. I never got a chance to see the other video. But I know about it through what people are saying online, and it just sounds dodgy to me: the way everyone was left feeling high."

"We enjoyed the song. That doesn't make it dodgy, or unofficial."

I can see both sides, but we can't discern the truth yet.

"We can't be the *only* two people who heard and saw what we did," I interject.

"Why not?" he says. "We're both clued in on all the weird shit that goes on. This is just another one of those things. It could be another form of brainwashing. She made sure to reach as many people as possible, through seemingly impossible means. And anyone who didn't experience it is nowhere to be heard, like their voices are being silenced."

I've researched some crazy stuff over the years, and even believed it, but a brainwashing music video that *only* two conspiracy theorists saw the official version of?

"Stop already," Connelly says harshly. "No-one is brainwashed."

I want to believe that too, but can't help suspecting Aki might be right.

"What would be the purpose?" I say.

Aki taps the page. "Keep reading."

I take another sip of Soothing Sobriety then focus on the lyrics again. Skip over the repeated chorus and read:

And you'll never get near me.
Don't you even try it.
You can't hear what I'm saying
and you just can't handle it.
I'm gonna bash you down
before you even get close.
So go and lose yourself.
Forget it all and drown.

Those were the demeaning and aggressive words I couldn't remember. That awful feeling I had while hearing it returns.

"She's threatening us," Aki says, "like we're onto her. But she won't let us ruin her plan."

"What?" I screw up my face. "What plan? I don't even know who she is."

"It doesn't matter. It's like she's saying even if we do find out who she is, we won't be able to do anything about it."

"What are you talking about?"

He leans even closer and whispers, "I'm saying this chick is gonna be the next big thing. This hack and deletion stunt was to get everyone's attention. But she targeted us personally with the real video to warn us off because she knows we have a shot at exposing her."

Is there acid in this coffee? Because this is beyond far-fetched. But maybe I should humour him, to see how far his theory goes.

Connelly scoffs. "Or maybe she's goading you because you actually mean nothing to her."

I frown at him. He must be playing along, but he's still being overly standoffish. I just want to shake him.

"We must mean *something*," Aki says, "or she wouldn't have bothered singling us out."

I'd rather not mean anything to her if it puts us in danger.

"How did she hack into your specific laptop, then?" I say. "And how did she very specifically turn on my sister-in-law's TV that was in the room I happened to be in at the time?"

He stares unblinkingly at me. Must've thrown him. "That's what I can't figure out," he says at last. "Apparently, no-one can suss out how she did it. People on the other side of the world were asleep, not to mention others who were locked up. The only way she could get them to listen at the same time was to hack into any device she could... Makes me wonder."

"Wonder what?"

His eyes narrow. "Who, or what, she really is."

I brace myself. He's never expressed spiritual beliefs in previous YouTube debates. Will he now?

"You're about to make another ridiculous claim, aren't you?" Connelly says.

My jaw clenches as I repress the urge to tell him to shut up.

"She obviously has immense technological power," Aki explains. "Or friends in high places."

I sigh internally. Good. We're still within the realm of reality.

"How does she know *we'll* expose her?" I ask. "And expose what exactly?"

"There must be more to her than what meets the eye. Not sure how she could know about us, but you're certainly a well-known conspiracy theorist."

"Seriously? I have five-hundred thousand subscribers. A fair amount, sure, but there are actual famous conspiracy theorists out there."

"I don't have the answers yet, man. We're gonna have to find out."

Indeed.

I read the final verse:

Look into my eyes and go.
This world has never been for you.
Why are you even trying?
You know that you can never win.

She does seem to be taunting us. Is it egotistical to think she could've crafted a different version for me and Aki alone? That's what a deranged, obsessive fan would believe, surely?

Well, this has been a lot to think about. I lean back and take a longer swig of Steadying Sanity. We *will* just have to wait for what happens next.

His eyebrows push together. "Do you think I'm crazy?"

"Yes," Connelly says curtly.

I squeeze my mug until my hands twinge. Aki seems nonplussed by his answer, and seems to be anxiously awaiting mine. At this stage, I'm genuinely unsure, but I can't think straight with all this tension.

I force a smile. "I fancy a lemon muffin. Conn, would you get me one, *please?*"

It means more money, but it's the best idea I have.

His stare drifts between us. Please don't explode. I asked nicely!

Finally, he sighs, pushes himself up, and leaves. A weight lifts from me.

"I am really sorry about him," I mutter to Aki. "He's not normally this bad."

His eyes narrow. "He *was* suspiciously distressed by those lyrics."

If everyone *is* brainwashed, will they have the same reaction? Pains me to imagine, but we have to share this.

"So, he thinks I'm nuts," Aki says. "Do you?"

Persistent, isn't he?

"No," I decide. "I've heard worse. But this does all seem like a bizarre dream, so maybe *I'm* crazy."

He grins strangely. "Come on, Maddix. Thought you didn't believe life was a dream?"

I stare at the froth on the surface of my Swirling Sobriety. "Can you convince me I'm awake?"

Am I still asleep at home? Passed out at Kya's? It'd certainly make more sense.

"You're scary when you talk like that." He laughs, almost nervously. "Don't let it get to your head already. We've barely begun."

I focus on the page again, at all the words. "I do want to see this through. It's not every day I'm personally involved in a conspiracy, and people should hear the full story."

"Exactly." He slaps his hands down on the table, either side of the notebook, making me flinch. "It's exciting, isn't it? I honestly can't believe it, but we're in this together."

His chuffed expression is sweet, but his wide eyes are off-putting. It's still odd for a stranger to be elated simply from being in my company, but he feels less of a stranger after his several years of support. Plus, I have a face to a name now. If I'm to solve this worldwide mystery, he certainly has the zeal to help me. His theory about us being targeted seems unlikely, but should we be worried at all, or should we feel special and privileged to have this separate experience from everyone else? There must be others. They just haven't come forward yet. We'll find them.

"Would you like to make a video with me?" I ask.

His grin drops into what looks like another gawp, bigger this time.

"Really?"

"Yeah. You can help me explain to everyone what we heard. We don't technically have concrete proof, but when did that ever stop a debate?"

Is he seriously tearing up? If so, I'm both flattered and slightly embarrassed.

"I would be bloody honoured," he says.

"Brilliant. So, when are you free?"

"Well, any time of the day, any day of the week. I'm between jobs at the moment."

I hope that's not for long, considering his continuing sizeable Patreon donations.

"How about tonight, then?" I say.

"Are you sure? Such short notice."

"The sooner the better. Could be a new event tonight for all we know."

His gaze drifts down to the notebook, then back to me. "What about your husband?"

Fuck. I should've asked him first. Why do I let myself get carried away? Now I need to convince him to let Aki come to ours. That'll be fun.

"I'll go run it past him." I rub the back of my neck. "If you'll excuse me, then, I'll be back in a minute."

Aki nods and I use the table to pull myself up. My gut churns. I move through into the other side. Connelly's several places from the front of the queue. He gives me that intense stare, and not the good one. Great start.

I sidle up to him and murmur close to his ear: "I'd still like that muffin, but I was wondering if we could get it to go and also take Aki home with us?"

After a pause, he leans away and blankly says, "What?"

"I want to make a video with him."

"Oh, really?" he mutters. "And, what, you've just invited him over? You barely know him, he's clearly off his rocker, and I haven't even tidied the flat."

"The flat's fine. We'll be spending most of the time inside the studio anyway."

He rolls his eyes. Wish he wouldn't.

"I've been chatting to him on and off for five years," I add, "and he *is* the guy who's been donating the most to me. This would mean a lot to him." His expression doesn't change. My gut canes to the point where I struggle not to grasp it. "Do you seriously think we're 'off our rocker'?"

"I said *he* is. I'm worried he's dragging you into his insanity."

We move a couple of steps along the queue.

"But we both experienced it," I insist. "It's worth investigating."

"I don't like the idea of you being alone with him in our house."

As much as I adore his protectiveness, he needn't worry so much. I smirk. "I'm big and strong. I can handle it."

"That's irrelevant. He's still a stranger, with questionable motives."

Understandable, but he just doesn't give me that vibe.

"Well, I won't be alone with him if you're in the other room." I carefully grip his hand. "If I need help, I'll yell, okay?"

He sighs quietly. I need him to trust my judgement.

"Can he come over tonight, then?" I say.

He appears to gaze up at the bright menu boards. Hate when he drags things out like this.

"Did you already tell him he could?" he asks.

I contain a grimace. "I suggested it. Said I'd run it past you."

He tuts. "Now I'll be the dick if I say no."

I shouldn't have put him on the spot. I enjoy my impulsiveness, but sometimes I swear I wilfully forget he doesn't appreciate it.

Still not looking at me, he says, "If he tries anything, or seems remotely out of order, he's gone."

"...Is that a yes?"

"Mm-hmm."

I throw my arms around him. He seizes up. I know he doesn't like public affection, but it's not like we're kissing, as much as I want that. I pull away before he gets any more pissed then return to Aki. He eagerly straightens up.

"It's a go," I say.

He covers his mouth. His eyes bulge up at me for several moments before he lowers his hands and says, "Thank you so much." He grabs the book, and with one hand snaps it shut. "This is gonna be awesome."

If Connelly's uncharacteristically aggressive reaction's anything to go by, we're going to get a lot of backlash for this. Some may take our word for it, but loads of people, especially my crowd of 'haters', will call bullshit. We have no evidence, and this'll be the first time I'm presenting an opinion without it. The video will certainly rake in the views, being controversial and featuring my first ever collaboration, but pre-empting all the negativity makes me crave more alcohol.

53

Connelly drives us home. The whole twenty-odd minutes he spends in silence while Aki and I plan our video. I reckon he's given up trying to dissuade us. As I eat my delicious lemon muffin from its takeaway bag, I try to shove away his sceptic, moody glances and focus on Aki's animated face in the mirror.

From the back seat, he gestures excitedly and asks me, "Will it be scripted like most of your other videos? Can I sit beside you on that sofa? Maybe we could take turns reading out the lyrics – what do you think?"

I answer yes to them all. That's how I pictured it, anyway. We shouldn't need to jazz it up, as the content alone should grab people's attention.

By the time we get through the front door of our flat, I've visualised the script layout. Need to type it up before it starts to degrade. I barely give Aki a chance to look at the place; I head straight for the studio and flick on the light. Don't know where he imagined me living, but I'm sure it wasn't in a tiny flat in Tulse Hill. Well, I try not to care what people think about it. Not like it's our forever home. Connelly's undoubtedly still stressing that he hasn't vacuumed and cleaned for our visitor, but it's still pretty spotless from the deep clean he did the other night. The studio's as tidy as it'll ever be, although this could be a hovel and Aki would likely gawp at it like he is now.

He glances around as he steps in behind me. "Wow."

It's only a small converted bedroom. Obviously doesn't take much to impress him. Connelly's probably right, though: it's bound to be stuffy in here – I just never notice. So I leave the door open to let the air circulate. Hope it doesn't smell musty, or God forbid, stink of booze.

I step over the box light cables. "Mind these."

Aki gives a quick nod, follows me, then grins and jabs his thumb sideways. "That's epic. I remember when you got it."

I smile at him. He's talking about the big silver plastic play button from YouTube, displayed in its glass frame above the sofa. One-hundred thousand subscribers was an amazing milestone, but it's grown five times bigger in the last two years. Shame it has to double on top of that to reach gold. Can't imagine reaching a million, though. I still view that silver play button with pride, but after seeing it every day, the novelty's kind of worn off.

I yank open the curtain to reveal the desk. Will he be amazed by this too? I prod the power switch on the computer tower then turn to him. Of course, he's ogling over what's just a desk stacked with books, post-it notes, a monitor, and a computer. My empty glass is still here from earlier – I pray he can't smell the vodka.

"You all right?" I ask.

He shakes his thinker a little, as if returning to reality. "Yep."

"You want a drink? I'm going to the kitchen."

"You have any coffee?"

I nearly laugh. "You want another one already?"

He cringes. "Oh, I'm kind of addicted."

I know that feeling well, but not with coffee.

"How do you take it?" I ask.

"Black. Strong. No sugar."

I reserve that blend for hangovers – couldn't do it all the time.

I grab the empty glass and move to the door. "Make yourself comfortable on the sofa. You did help pay for it."

His wide eyes dart to it. "Really?"

I give a short nod. He approaches hesitantly and lowers himself onto it like it's precious. The thing only cost about £100 in a sale, but a quarter of that was his unknowing contribution.

"You gonna pay me back at some point?" he says.

I tense up. I used to worry about that when he first started giving me money. Has it all come back to bite me in the arse?

He beams at me. "Kidding, of course."

Struggling to hide my relief, I snigger and leave.

Connelly's in the kitchen, wiping down the small U of counter-tops. I stifle a sigh. I told him the place looks fine, but he never listens. We can never both function in here, either; I'll have to wait 'til he's done. For now, I discard my glass on the side.

"I told you we'll be spending most of our time in the studio," I murmur.

He opens the bottom cupboard, pulls out the bin, and tosses in a clump of wipes.

"Suppose you've left *that* a mess," he says.

I burn up. "It's not that bad."

He thrusts the cupboard shut and turns to me with that sour face.

I know Aki's waiting for me, but I need to clear this up: "What was with you at Costa? You were pretty rude."

It honestly doesn't feel natural for *me* to berate *him*.

Frowning, he mutters, "I'm sorry. Seeing those words made me furious.

It shouldn't have, but it did."

At least he's apologised, but his whole behaviour still unnerves me.

"We're going to find out what's happening," I say. "For now, just try to relax, yeah?"

His gaze trails away. "There's washing-up to do."

I roll my eyes. "If that helps. Can you boil the kettle while you're there, then?"

As he fills the kettle, I grab a fresh glass and mug from the overhead cupboard, and deliberate over pouring myself some Russian Comfort. I need to survive until later; need a clear thinker for the typing, recording, and editing. Should take a couple hours, then annoyingly, another half an hour to upload.

From the big bottle in the fridge, I pour water in my glass instead. The low hiss of the kettle fills the cramped space, soon joined by gushing water from the taps. All of that's more pleasant on the listeners than him huffing at my drinking, and at least he won't do it this time. As I return the water bottle, I spot his chocolate bar still in the fridge. Must be saving it for tonight in front of the TV.

The kettle boils quickly. After spooning two heaps of coffee into the mug, I add the water. Hope that's strong enough!

With the glass and mug, I hover in the doorway. "See you later."

He keeps his back to me as he carries on washing up. "Yep."

I'll cheer him up later. I have to. I'll be better than last night 'cause I won't be blotto this time.

I return to the studio. Try to shake away all lustful thoughts, but don't succeed. Would Aki still look pleased as punch to sit on that sofa if he knew the things Connelly and I have done on it? Well, he gets to keep that grin because I won't tell him.

He thanks me for the mug and cups it contentedly with both hands.

I sip my water. "Right. Let's get to action."

"Yes." He reaches across to put his glass on the round black side-table then slings off his bag and dumps it on his lap. As I move to the desk, he fishes out his notebook and stretches it out to me. "It starts on page thirty-three."

"Thanks." I take it, slump in the desk chair, and swivel it to face him. After another swig, I reach back to put down the glass and flick to page thirty-three. Not that I'd pry anyway, but I'm mindful to avoid reading anything else in this potentially personal notebook. "Like I said earlier, I'll draft out something as quickly as possible then you can have a look and decide which parts you want to speak. You can also tell me if I've forgotten anything."

"Sounds great." Smiling with that twinkle in his eyes again, he pulls out his phone. "And I'll search for news and updates."

I give him a thumps-up. Hopefully, we can keep on top of all the latest gossip and/or reports, but depending on how things progress, I might be wishing for a bigger team and budget to put this all together.

After about half an hour, we're ready to go. It's been unusual but refreshing to have a collaborator. I've still done the bulk of the writing, but credit for the script also belongs to Aki now. I tell him I'll acknowledge this in the video description, and ask if he wants me to include a link to his channel. He says, "No, thanks. I don't post anything, and I don't particularly want to be inundated with messages." Fair enough.

He's ecstatic to start recording. His leg won't stop jigging as he sits beside me on the sofa with the microphone between us. His eyes don't even squint from the box lights shining on us. If he can't keep his composure while recording, he might come across a bit mad, but at least he'll maintain my work's established enthusiastic tone.

"Right," I say. "I'll move each page of script along with this." I hold up the mouse to show him then place it next to me on the arm of the sofa. "It's silent."

He nods. "Clever."

"If either of us messes up a line, don't worry. Just say it again and I'll cut it out."

He nods again and straightens up. "I'm ready when you are."

I push myself up, press record on the camera, and return to the sofa. "I'll count us in." Once he acknowledges this, I force down my fear and clear my throat. "Three, two, one." I check he's looking in the laptop and camera's direction before saying, "Welcome, everyone, to another exciting conspiracy video. My name's Maddix A., except this time I have with me a long-time fellow conspiracy theorist: Tinfoil-Canis." I gesture to him.

He gives a little frantic wave. "Hello."

I smile. "Tinfoil reached out to me today and told me that he shared the same experience I did regarding a different version of the mystery song that hacked the Internet and music stations worldwide: 'Something That You Need to Know'."

"Yes," he says. "I too heard and saw the same video that Maddix did last night. Like everyone else, I was able to watch it three times–" He holds up his fingers. "–before it was taken down. I did, however, manage to jot down the lyrics." He picks up the notebook from beside him, but fumbles while flicking to the appropriate page. I'll cut that down so it runs smoother. He lifts the book and points at the page. "Of course, I understand that a lot of viewers out there won't believe this, as I could've written anything down. But we feel like we need to get this out there anyway, so we will now share what we heard with you."

He lowers the book, and I nod slowly. I'll splice the lyrics over the top as text for people to read as they listen. Reading from the laptop screen, we take turns reciting each verse and chorus. Aki stutters in a couple places – I'll quickly cut that out. Presumably, he's not used to this, so no big deal.

"Obviously," I say, "this version is not about enjoying life and being the best you can be. The singer taunts us, tells us to give up. It's almost like she's threatened by us. She's trying to tear us down, destroy our confidence."

"It's definitely strange," Aki says animatedly. "Why is she targeting us in particular? Has anyone else experienced this version?"

I put my hands together. "Please, if anyone else knows what we're talking about, let us know in the comments. We're desperate to find out what's going on. This singer has continued to elude the police, as well as everyone else who's investigating the hack, the video's origin, and even her identity. She managed to somehow turn people's devices on to get this song to play, and yet this detail never made it to the news. Three people have confirmed this to me in person now, and it happened to me." I dare there to be opposition on this one – everyone would've experienced it, whether they admit it or not. Some may not realise it, though, if they walked into the room and it was already playing. "We *will*, of course, put out any evidence we have if and when we can find it, or if anything else happens. For now, though, all we have is our word, and it'll be interesting to see how many of you out there believe us."

And I honestly don't think many will regarding most of it. I want to make my peace with that, but the likely impending repercussions make it impossible.

"Again, my name's Tinfoil-Canis." Aki places a hand on his chest. "It's been a pleasure to be featured in one of your videos, Maddix. Thank you for giving me the opportunity."

"Thank *you*." I smile and lift my eyebrows at the camera. "So, watch this space for any progression with this surreal case, and until next time, I'll see you then."

I think my intro was better, but that outro isn't working no matter how I say it.

Aki gives one final grin and wave, and I can't help snickering at the cuteness and how much he seems to have enjoyed this. I stand up, move a few steps forward, and end the recording. My legs are unsteady, even before the booze.

"Right." I sigh. "All done."

He clasps his hands together. "Oh my God. That was fun. Thank you so much." His smile drops. "Sorry if I'm being too much of a fanboy here."

I laugh. "You're fine."

He sags a little. "What next, then?"

"Well, my normal process would be to wait a day before editing, but that was a short one and it needs to go out ASAP, so straight to editing I go."

"Can I help with anything else?"

I wish I could say yes, but I'll get this done faster myself.

"I just need to get my head down now," I say.

"Okay." He springs up from the sofa. "Well, I suppose I should go now, then. Leave you to it."

"You know where you're going?"

"Yep. There's a bus stop nearby. I got the route figured out."

"Brill."

He slides the notebook back in his bag, slips it on, and collects his empty mug. "Oh, one thing I've always been dying to know. You don't have to tell me if you don't want, but... what does the A stand for, in your name?"

Suppose there's no harm in him finding out. "This is between you and me, okay? But it's my surname: Aitken."

That probably answers a question he may have had following our conversation outside of Costa: the one Connelly cut short.

He smiles. "Awesome."

Talking of personal things, I add, "Before you go, do you want to exchange numbers? It'll be quicker to get hold of each other if something urgent pops up."

He almost gawps. "Really? That'd be great."

I still can't get over how he treats me like a celebrity, but I find it more flattering than disturbing.

After swapping numbers, I escort him to the front door, and lean briefly around the kitchen door frame to pop his mug on the side. As he loiters in the front doorway, Connelly appears from the living room beside us.

"How did it go?" he asks.

"Successfully," I say.

"It was great," Aki says. "We're gonna attract a lot of attention with this one."

Connelly folds his arms. "Bad attention."

Realistically, he's right about that, and I'm unsure how to deal with it.

"It's okay, though." Aki forms a fist. "People need to hear the truth."

They may need it, but most of them won't want it. We're technically discrediting the song that's captured the general public's hearts and obsession... I need a drink.

Connelly raises an eyebrow. "Uh-huh."

He apologised to me earlier, but not to Aki. Looks like he won't. What will it take to make him trust him?

"Anyway," Aki says, "thank you for inviting me into your home, both of you, and for letting me be a part of this. It's been an honour."

I nearly scoff with a smile and say, 'Yeah, I got that,' but give him a short nod and say, "You're welcome. Safe journey back. I'll contact you later once I've posted the video."

"Great." He bows. "See you later."

We say goodbye and he practically bounces down the hallway and out of the building's main door.

I close up and sigh with a chuckle.

"Bet he was interesting to work with," Connelly says.

"Certainly was." I twist towards him. "Now what's up? You're still pissed, aren't you?"

He glances down, and his eye twitches once. "That song. I seriously can't stop thinking about it. I've tried distracting myself with the TV, a bit of reading... nothing works."

His deep frown shows pure frustration. This only further proves that this song is more than what it seems.

"I need to edit and upload the video." I step closer and stroke my fingers down his arm. "But after that, I can help take your mind off it."

He sighs. "I wouldn't say no."

It was a long shot, so I'm shocked but pleased.

I grin slowly. "It's a date. See you soon."

I kiss his cheek and he nods with a tired half-smile. Pulling away from him, I nearly turn into the kitchen for some vodka. No. Need to stay as sharp as possible to put this together, and it'll take me about an hour as it is. I'll have a drink while it's rendering, and by the time it's done that, as well as uploaded and processed to YouTube, I should've had a decent chance to psych myself up for Connelly's distraction.

4

The video's up. My stomach wrenches. Thinker's worn out. It's definitely weird that I've uploaded three videos in two days. Normally, I'd say that'd hurt my view count, but they've been topically spot-on with what's trending. That does leave a sour taste, one that should be fixed by this glass of Russian Contentment. But I'm dreading the reaction. Did I rush through the editing too much? Will everyone loathe it? At least Aki should be happy with it.

He's already commented: 'Such an honour to work with you! I look forward to where this investigation leads :)'

I smile, but stop as I keep scrolling. Here they are, the negative comments that hurt in more ways than one:

'What the hell you guys going on about?'

'Who's the random guy?'

'You two must be high. WTF?'

'Maddix a week ago: doesn't believe in conspiracy theories without solid proof. Maddix now: starts his own conspiracy without evidence.'

'This guy's clearly a maniac, Maddix. Don't let him drag you into this craziness!' Connelly practically said these exact words at Costa.

'Haha, real funny. You're both idiots.'

'Get a life. Seriously.' Oh, never heard that one before!

'Interesting theory but come on, guys.'

'Stop spreading hate. It's an amazing song. Don't twist it into something it's not just to get attention. You're better than this.'

Some of these are from randoms, but a lot are from long-time subscribers who've always been supportive until now. It's not like I haven't faced criticism before, and not all of them have turned out as aggressive as I feared, but it still makes me swig the rest of my vodka. How will Aki take it? I'll hide the ones that include him in a bad light. If he asks to read them, if he hasn't already, I guess I shouldn't stop him, but for now I can save him the potential confidence knock. Besides, there *are* nicer ones:

'New guy's cute. Where'd you find him?'

'You two make an interesting pair. Maybe more collabs in future?'

These are, of course, prefaced with the song being the best thing they've heard and they don't know why we'd dare say these things. They do wish they could hear our version, so they know what we're 'going on about', even though it sounds awful in comparison. At least *some* of these people want to indulge us. They *have* to trust me. I've never pulled anything like this before.

The like to dislike ratio's about 20-80. I'm grateful for the small handful of likes, and surprised considering our slant. Are those people perhaps *not* brainwashed? But seriously, five-hundred dislikes in ten minutes? Fucking hell. That doesn't sit right in my stomach. View count's through the roof, though: five thousand and counting. Goes up more every time I refresh the page. Everyone's tuned in, I guess, desperate to find out anything they can on this bloody song. Baffles me to comprehend just how much this has affected everyone. I'm both dreading and looking forward to seeing how much the statistics have exploded once I'm done with Connelly. I've found it useful to watch other people's videos in the meantime. They're all acting like raving teenagers. It's quite terrifying, although slightly amusing too.

I really do need a break. I lick the dregs in my glass then push myself up and stagger out of the studio. After quickly using the loo and freshening up, I follow the chattering from the TV. I lean in the living room doorway. Connelly sits, arms crossed, on the black L-shaped sofa, watching a show I don't recognise. He doesn't even snigger along with the canned laughter. Looks like he's put on any old crap just to take his mind off that song. When he notices me, he uses the remote to switch it off. A soft orange glow surrounds him from the standing corner lamp next to the window. I've always found it romantic. But that intense stare isn't filled with romance. It's more carnal and desperate. That's okay too.

*

My hazy eyes open to the dim living room. I'm still lying face-down on the sofa next to Connelly. His arm wraps around my bare hip and his warm crotch presses into my leg. This and the fact I left my T-shirt and socks on stops me from getting cold. I do want to cuddle in bed instead, as we barely fit on here together, but I'm too knackered to move. My body's sticky and aches – it's never comfortable doing this on the sofa, no matter how drunk I am.

I'm overjoyed that he decided to go all out with me – must've been a couple months since the last time. Hopefully, I managed to distract him for a while. I certainly wasn't thinking about any of that while he was letting loose on me. I think a fair amount of time has passed. I dozed off. By Connelly's slow, deep breathing, I'd say he's asleep. It's probably late enough for bed anyway; maybe I should encourage him to relocate with me to the other room.

White light shoots out of the TV screen. I jerk and scrunch my stinging eyes.

"What the fuck?" I whisper.

Are we lying on the remote?

"What is it?" Connelly murmurs into my back.

"The TV." I slide away from him and scramble to a sitting position. He does the same, but slower. I stare at the blank white screen, waiting for something else to happen.

He groans. "Maddix, what's going on?"

"I don't know," I croak. Man, I need a drink. I glance around and see the remote on the carpet in front of us, next to my boxers. "It just turned on, by itself."

"...What?"

He probably doesn't believe me. Well, if any other weird shit's about to happen, I'm capturing it. So I lean forward, grab my jacket off the floor, and yank out my phone. I bring up the camera, aim it at the TV, and press record. Quality won't be great. I'd go and turn on the main light, but don't want to miss anything.

The TV screen shows a white floor at camera level stretching out into a bright distance. A tiny black dot appears. What is that? Gradually, it approaches us, hopping in a straight line towards the camera. A rabbit? Yes, definitely. But not just any one.

"It's the rabbit from the music video," I murmur.

"Really?" Connelly leans around my shoulder to watch.

It gets closer then stops and stares down into the camera. Its nose twitches as if inspecting it. Is this a new music video? Where's the singer? Everything's still silent. Uneasiness builds in my gut. The rabbit's blue eyes lock with mine. Then it lunges at the camera. All we see is black. And something flies out of the screen, into the room, and thuds onto the carpet.

I draw up my bare legs with a scream. Connelly cries out too. It's here with us! Am I dreaming?

"What the fuck?" Connelly almost shrieks. "Kick it!"

I frown hard at the creature that sits in front of us, nearly like an ornament save for the twitching nose.

"Oh," Connelly says. "Is that actually a rabbit?"

Did I get that on camera? I stop the recording and quickly jump to the point where it leaps out of the screen. It did happen, and I have proof. Bit grainy and the light from the TV's overexposed, but it still shows enough detail. This is definitely going online later!

As I press record again, it continues to stare at us.

"How did this happen?" Connelly leans around me to peer down. "It's really there, right?"

I slide slowly off the sofa to kneel in front of it. Wish I'd put my boxers back on now. Why isn't it running off? Doesn't even look scared. Can I touch it? I carefully hold out my hand, palm turned upwards.

"Don't," Connelly whispers.

I keep my hand just under its sniffer. Maybe I should've washed it first. In any case, it doesn't bite me, so we seem to be on good terms. Its whiskers tickle my skin. I can definitely feel that. It has to be real – I just don't understand how.

"We have to get that out of here." Connelly edges off the sofa, gently gathers his clothes up from the floor into a pile, and steps back into his boxers.

"Where would we take it?" I mutter.

He slips into his shirt. "The nearest vet that's open?"

"And tell them what? It's not a wild one. You don't get black rabbits in the wild, right?"

"...What do you mean black?"

I frown up at him. "Well, that's what it is."

He frowns back. "Are you pulling my leg?"

"No." What's he playing at?

His eyes widen, and his lips stay parted as if in shock. "Maddix, it's white."

I stare at the creature until it blurs. This doesn't make sense. One of us must be colour-blind. Or this is another case of me seeing this damn bunny differently to everyone else.

I stop recording and play the first again. Hold it up for him to see. "How about on here?"

He squints, and after a short pause, says, "White. Now stop messing about. I'm going to find something to put it in. Keep an eye on it."

He leaves before I manage to respond. I'm totally thrown. I hear him rustling and banging about in our room next door. Why hasn't this thing even flinched? They always try to flee. Then again, this special little bunny spawned from my fucking TV. I wave my hand in front of its face. No reaction. Click my fingers. Nothing. Just more nose twitching.

Connelly returns with an empty Amazon delivery box. He's stabbed several holes in the top. "This'll do. Now we just need to lure it inside."

"I don't think it'll need much luring."

He creeps closer, crouches beside us, and keeps the empty box open in his lap. "What's with this thing? It won't move?"

"It doesn't seem to be in shock. Its ears are lying flat. Think that means it's quite happy sitting there." After several moments of us just watching it, dumbfounded, I say, "I'll try picking it up."

"I'm not sure that's a good idea."

"Well, there's no point luring it into a trap or whatever. It's not trying to avoid us, and it's not frozen from terror."

Connelly studies it, and cringes when I carefully scoop my hands under it. I lift it with one hand under the chest and the other supporting the back legs. It's super soft and fairly light. I lower it into the box, and Connelly folds the flaps back down.

He sighs. "Well done."

I grab my boxers, push myself up, and wriggle into them. "Are you *sure* we should take it to a vet?"

"What else can we do?" He manages to stand, still firmly holding the box. "It doesn't belong to us."

"I disagree." He's frowning at me, of course, so I continue, "It certainly doesn't belong to anyone around here. Unless one of our neighbours' pets found a way to teleport through the TV!"

His frown stays. I don't know what I want to do: keep the rabbit to study, and see what else happens, or get it the hell away from us.

As I try to process this freaky shit, I struggle into my jeans. It *would* be beneficial to get the thing looked at, but I'm still unsteady, my heart won't calm down, and I just want to sleep.

"Can we wait 'til morning?" I ask. "I'm sure it'll be fine in the box."

Connelly places it on the floor. "We go *now*."

I groan. I really need to freshen up, then.

He grabs his own jeans and sits on the sofa to pull them on. "This is fucking insane. I'm not dreaming, am I?"

I rub my forehead. "I thought the same thing."

66

He buttons himself up, shakes his thinker, and stands. "We *have* to take this to someone who knows what to do, okay? It'll be in better hands with a professional."

I focus on the box. "True. And we'll certainly be popular showing them *the* rabbit, from *the* music video."

"You don't know that's what it is. How is that even possible?"

I throw out my arms. "I don't know. But it's a spitting image, right? And the TV turned on by itself, just like it did the other night for me *and* you guys."

He raises an eyebrow, and doesn't blink.

"That's what happened," I go on. "Surely you have to believe it after what you just saw?"

His gaze falls to the box. After a few painful moments, he says, "However this rabbit got to us, it doesn't belong here. We need to hand it in to the right authorities."

I clench my jaw. He's in denial. I am too, I guess. After all the crazy stuff I've researched into and not believed despite 'sufficient evidence', this has happened in front of me, and I'm not as drunk as last night. I do want to keep an eye on this thing and understand what it's doing here. But it does scare me, and needs to be assessed sooner rather than later. Connelly's on the most sensible track, as usual.

Between us, we search for nearby vets or clinics that are open this late at night then head out to Streatham. Can we even afford this? Connelly hasn't mentioned anything about the impending cost, but I'm sure he's fretting about it too.

I sit in the passenger seat with the bunny on my lap. The journey will only take five minutes, apparently, so it won't have to endure being in the box much longer. Not that it's even tried to escape. It's barely made a noise. I press my ear to the box. Its whiskers or something brush against the cardboard, and I can just about hear snuffling over the deep hum of the car. Still doesn't quite feel real.

Connelly drives us through several streets lined with smart terraced houses. They're nowhere near as impressive as Kya's, but this size would probably be more ideal for us. Connelly hasn't said a word – just silently follows his phone's sat nav. Doesn't look perturbed anymore – only focused. We should still be dozing naked together. He finally seemed relaxed, and this fucking rabbit screwed everything up.

We reach the long high street, and even though it's only been a few minutes thanks to lack of traffic, I can't bear the silence anymore.

"Are you okay?" I ask.

After several more moments, he mutters, "I don't know. What about you?"

I sigh. "Me neither."

"...Maybe this isn't a dream. Maybe your friend slipped hallucinogens in our Costas."

I scoff. He's suspicious enough to believe that, but it's not at all possible.

"Well, they took four hours to kick in, then we shared the same hallucination." I shake my thinker and stare out at the passing shops and town house blocks. "Aki wouldn't do that anyway."

"You don't know that. And technically, we do see something different."

I frown then glance at the box. "Oh, 'cause you reckon this thing's white?"

"It *is* white."

I roll my eyes and tense my jaw again. It's not like we're arguing between tan and brown. These are literal opposites. Well, we'll see what the people at the clinic think.

We pull up outside the emergency veterinary centre and park in the dotted bay along the pavement. We can only stay for thirty minutes, but hopefully we won't need longer than that. The clinic's nestled between a fitness centre and dry cleaners. Various businesses stretch both ways down the high street, lit up with street lamps. We've driven through here before but never had a reason to stop.

The big window to the side of the clinic's front door is frosted over so we can't see in. The door's glass panel lets out a bright glow, though, stinging my eyes. After requesting to be let in at the buzzer, Connelly holds it open for me. I carry the box to the reception desk but keep it pressed to my chest.

"Hi," I say to the woman lounging in the chair behind the desk.

She glances up from her mobile phone. Dark bags hang under her bloodshot eyes. Has she been staring at a screen all day like I have?

"You found a rabbit?" she annoyingly repeats Connelly's words from the buzzer.

"Yep. We don't know who it belongs to."

She nods. "Someone will be out to see you in a minute. But just so you're aware, our out of hours consultation fee is two-hundred pounds."

I grimace. Is she joking? I thought it would be more like a hundred, and that's savage enough!

"Okay," Connelly says stiffly. "Thanks."

I don't want to look at him right now. I feel sick.

She quickly types on her computer then scrolls on her phone again. I'd think she's being rude, but I can see from here she's looking through YouTube. I know she could be searching for anything, but I can't help wondering if it's what I think.

After sitting in the waiting area for hardly any time at all, another woman comes out to greet us. Seems a little livelier than the receptionist. She takes us to a small private room, which is, again, too bright. My headache's rapidly worsening. I place the box on the table in the middle of the room. The vet stands on the other side and grins at us.

"You two have had an interesting Easter gift," she says. "Funny, since you can't even buy them this time of year."

Connelly and I glance at each other. Odd thing to say, but at least she's making light of it. I try to smile.

"We found it outside our flat building," Connelly explains.

Her thinker tilts slightly. "Have you asked around to see if he belongs to anyone in the area?"

Would she honestly expect us to buzz each flat and knock at every house, especially this late? Either way, we both know this rabbit doesn't belong to anyone.

"Yes, as many houses as we could," I tell her, because it's easier.

"Okay, well," she says, "let's have a look at him, then."

As she slips on her thin gloves, I open the box. The bunny just sits there, twitching its nose like before.

"It seems completely tame," I say.

The vet leans over to peer in, and carefully scoops it out of the box. Holding it to her chest, she observes it for ages. A pain grows in my stomach. Can she tell this isn't a normal rabbit? She's not even doing any checks.

Connelly crosses his arms. "Is everything okay?"

I agree with his impatience; I just want to go to bed, and this vet's taking her time, seemingly gazing into the creature's soul.

69

Her intense eyes drift to us at last, but focus directly on me. "He came for you."

She seems dead serious.

"What?" is all I can say.

More gut-churning silence then she says, "He belongs to you."

I just lock stares with her, unblinking. What does she mean? This doesn't make sense.

"He is *not* ours," Connelly says firmly.

"He is Mr. Aitken's," she says.

My frown deepens. Thinker feels crushed in a vice. "How do you know my name?"

She doesn't answer. Does she know me from YouTube? I've never revealed my surname.

I glance at Connelly. "Did you tell anyone here our names?"

"No," he says, and shoots wide eyes at her. "What's going on?"

She lowers the bunny back into the box. "We cannot take him. He must go home with you."

Connelly laughs. "What?"

I glance down at the rabbit. This is a sign. It must be. It's unbelievable, but if this isn't a dream, and he really leapt out of *my* TV... I have this indescribable feeling in my gut.

"We *have* to take him," I say.

Connelly glares at me as if I'm insane. "We can't look after him."

"I'm at home all day. You won't have to worry."

His thinker tilts. "You're serious, aren't you?"

I take a deep breath and sigh quietly. "I guess I am, yeah."

His jaw tightens. Eyes bulge. Fuck. He's going to shout. He asks the vet, "Can we have a few moments alone, please?"

She nods and leaves, almost robotically. What's with her?

As soon as the door shuts, Connelly jabs his finger at the box. "What the hell is this? We are leaving this thing here. God knows what it really is. Don't let her pressure you into keeping it."

I lean a hand on the table to stretch out my aching side. How can I convince him?

"Are you listening to me?" he mutters.

I straighten up. "Yes. Look, I don't know how to explain it, but I need to keep him. I need to find out how and why he came to us, and how that song's related to all this."

He chucks his hands in the air. "That fucking song. I swear!"

"Don't you want to find out more? We have *the* rabbit, from *the* music video, like I said."

"This is crazy. Listen to yourself, to both of you." He shakes his thinker then scratches the back of it frantically. "Is this a set-up? An Easter prank?"

"Conn, this is real. No joke."

Hands on hips now, he says, "Okay, then, how can we afford this? The appointment alone is two-hundred quid."

There's only one way for now: "You pay for him and I'll pay you back."

His eyes narrow. "That's your fucking answer to *everything*. You keep making promises. And recently, you keep breaking them." He's right, but I've had different reasons for that, some better than others. I may be taller than him, but the way he's sneering at me so condescendingly makes me feel small – I bloody hate it. "This is going to cost *a lot*."

"I did say let's wait 'til morning."

"That's not the point. You just expect me to cover everything. Do you know how expensive it is to keep our flat up and running? No. You don't, because I pay the bills."

I start overheating. First, he's wrong, and does he have to do this here? He's obviously kept most of this to himself for a while; he could've waited a bit longer until we got home.

"I help with rent," I say, "and food."

"Yes, you do, but what about gas, electric, water?" He's making me feel tinier by the second. "Consider all of that next time you expect me to dish out money for the upkeep of a rabbit or a new camera or a round of drinks for you and your biggest fanboy!"

I check the window on the door to see if the woman's peering in and listening. Thankfully, she isn't.

"I finished paying you back for that camera two months ago," I say.

"You said you'd finish paying me back *four* months ago." Good point. He huffs. "Don't do that to me again. I can't keep going into our savings."

I glance down. I do still feel awful that he has to do that, but it annoys me how he has to mention it so often.

"I'll find a way," I insist. "Even if I have to beg for more patrons."

Doubt I could bring myself to, actually. Why did I say that?

He crosses his arms. "If we take this rabbit, we're only keeping it for as long as we figure out what to do with it, and you're paying me back

71

immediately, okay?"

I smile internally. Knew I could get him to come around. Shame we had to fight, though.

"Yes," I say.

He shakes his thinker then peers down into the box. "We don't even have any supplies for it. And nowhere will be open now."

At least we won't have an issue with our landlord – she actually allows pets.

"We can ask the vet if she'll give us a case to keep him in for the night," I say, "then I can go out and get stuff tomorrow morning."

He sighs. I know this is a big responsibility to take on, but he won't need to fret about it at all.

"I'll set something up in the studio for him," I continue. "I'll do the cleaning out and stuff too."

"Do you even know the first thing about looking after a rabbit?"

I pat the bulge of my jacket pocket where my phone is. "I'll Google it."

A knock at the door, and it opens. The vet steps in and says, "Everything all right in here?"

Connelly sighs again. "We'll take him."

Before we leave, the vet does a health check, but only because we insist. She's acting bizarrely, as if possessed, and hasn't grinned at us again since she first greeted us. The bunny's in top condition, at least. He manages to appear pretty normal considering he spawned from a TV. The vet can't exactly determine his age, but assures us he's not fully grown yet. The most pressing issue, though: his colour. She says he's white. And there it is: more proof that something's either wrong with me, or the rest of the world.

Apparently, we don't need to return this carry case. Wonder if it'll come out of her pay packet. She even donated an old clean blanket for him to sit and sleep on. He has a temporary water bottle set up too. I'll slice up a carrot for him later. It'll do until I can head out in the morning.

On our way out, we return to reception. I prepare for Connelly's mood to hit an all-time low at the invoice. But the receptionist's still transfixed on her phone, even after he tries getting her attention. I hear my voice. It's my latest video. She's just caught up? She frowns harder by the second. Uh-oh. Better get out of here.

Connelly catches my arm and mutters, "We still haven't paid yet."

She hasn't even glanced over at us.

I just coax him towards the door. "Let's go. She won't even notice."

That was mad. Out of everything that happened, Connelly's more worried about us avoiding the payment. I tell him, "If they want to get hold of us, they have our number. But they were off anyway, and for now we get to keep our two-hundred pounds." He bites back, "*My* two-hundred pounds!" All I can do is recede into my seat.

At home, I beg him to let us have the carrier in the bedroom, so I can keep an eye on our new house guest for the first night. He insists he's not sleeping with 'that bloody thing' in the same room then banishes us to the living room. Won't even let me hug him. I'm totally discarded. Passing the kitchen, I resist the urge for another drink – feel sick enough already. I get his fear and frustration, but now I have to sleep on the sofa and wait until tomorrow to make things better between us. Stings even more considering we were dozing so peacefully together in here earlier.

For ages, I'm on edge that the TV will turn on again. The rabbit watches me from the carrier on the floor in front of it, almost taunting me. I keep staring back at him in the half-light, feeling like I'll go insane. Sometimes I drift off, then jerk awake as if I shouldn't have because he could've killed me in my sleep. Ridiculous. I want to check my videos, or do anything to take my mind off it, but struggle to tear my eyes away. I shouldn't believe he's more than he is, but he jumped out of our fucking TV. We both saw it.

One particular thought persistently plagues me: why the hell is he not white to me?

Let's run with the crazy theory that he changes colour depending on whether the person looking at him is brainwashed or not. Is the black-or-whiteness rooted in his follicles, or based on an otherworldly external source? Aki would have a field day with this. I can't wait to show him. But for now, I might be able to answer the question myself.

I manage to pull myself up, throw off my blanket, and turn on the lamp. Stand and jab my finger down towards the creature.

"Behave while I'm gone."

It's risky, but I'm not carrying him with me.

I leave to cross into the kitchen. Fumble in the drawer. Grab the scissors.

A few hours have passed. I can't take it anymore. Connelly will be getting up for work soon anyway.

I stagger into the bedroom. The dim early daylight filters through the blinds. Connelly's on his side, all wrapped up in the quilt like he usually is when I'm not there. No time to admire, though. I kneel beside the bed. Gently shake him.

"Conn. Wake up."

His face scrunches with a groan.

"I have to show you something."

He sighs. "Why?"

"It's important."

My stomach's either about to stop aching only a fraction, or get much worse.

As soon as his dazed eyes open, I hold up the tiny clump of hair. "What colour is this?"

That frown I loathe returns with a vengeance. "Are you fucking kidding me?"

I know I'll have a *lot* of making up to do for this, on top of everything else, but I've been losing my mind all night.

"Just tell me," I say. "Is it black or white?"

"It's still white," he says through gritted teeth. "What the fuck is wrong with you?"

Those words always stab me, especially coming from him.

My gaze drifts to the fine hair between my thumb and fingers. "After being cut, it doesn't change for either of us."

"Wow. That's so fucking weird, Maddix."

Wish he'd stop swearing at me.

My eyes bulge at him. "What *is* weird is that it grew back. Took about half an hour, but it did." He frowns harder, so I add, "He didn't leave any droppings or anything either.... He's not natural."

He's silent for several moments. He doesn't believe me, does he?

Seeming to study me, he says, "You didn't sleep at all, did you?"

I grimace a little. "I may have got an hour."

Huffing, he rolls onto his back and chucks off the quilt. He'd better not be insinuating I made this up.

"Go check the thing yourself," I say. "I left the smallest bald patch on his tail, but it's gone. And his case is clean. The only normal thing he did last night was eat his carrot."

He sits up and grips his thinker. "Maddix, it's too early for this shit. I

74

barely slept either, but I certainly got more than an hour."

Tensing my jaw, I glance away. He'll continue doubting me until he sees for himself. If he's anything like me, he was probably expecting to wake up this morning and find it was all a dream. I don't know if I'm glad it wasn't.

He swipes his phone off the bedside table. "I have to get ready for work."

I manage to drag him into the living room while he's darting about, eating an apple on the go. He resists at first, but I demand that he looks at the rabbit. I scoop him out of the case, which I point out is spotless, then twist my body while awkwardly holding him and get Connelly to inspect for bald patches. He finds none, of course, and says, "Yes. That's bizarre, all right? But I can't deal with it right now. Put him back in the case."

He whisks off, nearly leaving me dizzy. Why must he put work above *everything*? As I slot the amazingly well-behaved bunny inside his tiny prison, I have to tell myself: you can hardly talk.

Before Connelly heads out the front door, he pops in and interrupts me as I'm scrolling through the overwhelming onslaught of confusion and negativity in my YouTube comments section.

"Are you sure it's wise to publicise you have the rabbit?" he says.

"People have to know, and it'll definitely direct more traffic to my channel."

His eyebrow shoots up. "Even if it's negative?"

I glare at my phone. Too tired and out of it to put on my mask. This latest video: I've never had so many people collectively disagree with me. One-hundred thousand thumbs down. What the fuck? I've never seen anything like it. Do they hate me that much, or does barely anyone want to entertain the idea that another version of the song exists? Being called a liar honestly stings. And now I'm going to make things much, much worse.

"That video you recorded last night," he says, "you're absolutely sure there's not one sign of–?"

"–No-one will see our lovely bodies."

Even if the TV had caught our reflections, the quality wasn't good enough to make out any details.

"Okay." He comes over to the sofa. "Anyway, here's my card." He holds it out, and my fingertips grip its edge. He sternly says, "You are *not* to use this for anything other than the bare essentials. No booze."

As if I would. I repress my frustration. "Yep."

"Call me if anything happens."

He releases the card into my possession then leaves without our usual kiss goodbye. I really will have to wait until later to destroy the residual badness between us. At least I have plenty to distract me in the meantime.

I need to make a new video ASAP. Might have to push back a few of the already scheduled ones depending on how many of these I make. Need to get the bunny sorted first, though.

As I shower and get dressed, all that negativity makes me dizzier and sicker. Keep forcing myself to focus on the positive: my latest video has just over seven-hundred thousand views already! And it does have a small bunch of likes. My other recent videos are getting more views now too. Feel like pouring a pint of Russian Celebration – perhaps Commiseration, too. But I need to drive. Well, first I need a coffee to wake up properly. Don't trust my eyes to stay open.

After a strong one, I squeeze into my car and set my phone to take me to Pets at Home in Sydenham. It's slightly closer than Battersea, and I still have no intention of returning there – Mum and Dad moved away years ago, but I bloody hate the place. Think I've made the right decision to leave the rabbit indoors, as another car journey may upset him. At the moment, he seems like the most zen creature in the world, but you never know. Actually, maybe I *should* go grab the little bugger that kept me up all night... No. He'll only slow me down.

I huff and start driving. Now's as good a time as any to call Aki. Want him to find out first-hand rather than through the video I post later. So I turn on my handsfree and dial his number.

He answers after a few rings, sounding elated: "Maddix. Hi."

"Hi, Aki. Hope I didn't wake you?"

"Not at all. I'm always an early riser, whether I have a job or not."

"Good. Something bat-shit insane happened last night after you left."

He gasps. "What?"

"I need to show you. Are you free to come to mine today?"

"Again?" He chuckles. "I'd love to. What time? It'll take me about forty minutes."

"Okay. If you aim to get to me in an hour and a half, then, by ten?"

That'll give me time to drive to Sydenham and back and set up the hutch or cage or whatever I end up buying for this thing.

"Awesome," he says. "I must admit: I'm very intrigued. Give me a hint?"

The traffic lights ahead of me turn amber. I speed up to avoid having to stop. "Let's just say: I had an unexpected visitor."

I try not to spend too long at Pets at Home. Ask a shop assistant to help me pick out the essentials, coming away with a bag of grass, hay, and straw, as well as a sturdy grey hutch and metal mesh play pen. Connelly shouldn't flip when he finds out how much this all cost as he *was* expecting it, right? The damn hutch was £45 alone. I could've got a smaller cage, I guess, but apparently rabbits need an area to hide and I also don't like the idea of it not being able to hop around a bit. Don't want to torture it. I don't know if this thing truly is a rabbit, but for now I'll treat him as such. The hutch just about fits on my back seat – the legs can be assembled at home – and it should fit in the studio, if I create some space. It won't be ideal, but our flat isn't suited for bunnies, and he decided to impose himself on us anyway, so he'll get what he's given.

Back at home, I set up the hutch just inside the studio in the corner. The rabbit's still contentedly twitching his nose in the carrier. Good; no destruction. Well, as happy as he looks, I'm sure he'll feel even better in his new hay and straw filled hutch. I carefully transfer him inside, and the first thing he does is hop into the private compartment. Weird to see him moving again at last. Exhaustedly, I lean forward to peer through the wire mesh into the dark area, where he's observing the grass I put in the food bowl. Well, that's him sorted for now. I leave the carrier on the floor beside the hutch. Don't even need to clean it out. Something must be wrong with him – that's not even factoring in the regrowing hair. The vet didn't notice anything, although she wouldn't if he has a digestion issue or secret ability to regrow stuff... What if I cut off his ear?

Lack of sleep is fucking me up. I need to just accept that he likely functions differently, considering his origin, and I might never understand. But I need to!

A buzz at the front door makes me jerk. Is it 10 already? I check my phone. Yep, on the dot. I push myself up and head out to let Aki into the flat building. His grin's wider than ever, and he's not wearing his hat today, meaning his short, fluffy black hair gets to shine and flick out fully at the bottom.

"Thank you for inviting me back here," he says, "and so soon."

I'm sure Connelly won't appreciate it, but Aki needs to see this.

I let him into our flat and guide him straight to the studio door at the end of the hallway.

"You ready?" I say.

He clasps his hands together. "What is it?"

I step in, he follows, then I gesture to the hutch.

His eyes contract. "No way. You got a bunny?"

Thankfully, the rabbit's returned to the main area so that Aki can see him.

"Yep," I say, "but not just any one."

Let's see how quickly he connects the dots.

He crouches in front of the hutch and peers in. "Hang on. A black bunny, with blue eyes?"

I laugh with relief. "You think it's black too?"

His thinker whips around to gaze up at me. "Yeah, like the one in the video."

"Connelly reckons it's white, as does the vet we took it to." I pull out my phone from my jacket. "It appeared in our living room last night. I don't understand how, but watch this."

I bring up the video, forward it to just before the rabbit jumps through the screen, and hand him my phone. Frowning, he watches, jerks a little, then frowns again.

"What?" is all he says.

"It's fucking crazy, but both Connelly and I saw it happen."

His eyebrow rises. "You didn't edit this?"

"No." I sigh. "You believe me, right? This vet checked him over and he seems normal, but she was acting so weird. She knew my surname somehow, and said he belongs to me."

"Okay... Odd."

"Yeah. Now I have to look after it. I need to know how and why this happened."

His focus drifts back down to my phone. He taps the screen, seemingly watching it again. His eyebrows dart up and he shakes his thinker. "I don't know, man. I really want to believe you, but this doesn't make sense."

He has the evidence right in front of him!

"All I can think is that he's been sent to me," I say. "I'm just glad you still see him as black too."

He stares at the rabbit for several moments. "You think it's the actual one from the video?"

78

"It has to be. Plus, the TV turned on by itself."

His thinker tilts. "People won't believe this."

"They won't believe he doesn't seem to crap or piss, either."

"Really?"

"His carrier and hutch have been constantly clean."

He studies the inside of the hutch as if puzzled.

"But he eats," I continue. "So looks like he'll eventually blow up like a balloon and explode."

"Aww, no. I hope not."

I smirk. "Maybe I should cover the room in plastic, just in case."

"Maddix!"

"What? I don't want him ruining my equipment."

He chuckles, but nervously, I think.

"Anyway," I say, "it gets even more mental." I pause for dramatic effect. He seems to wait anxiously. "His hair grows back."

"...What?"

"I cut a piece off last night, and within half an hour, it was back." Unsurprisingly, this doesn't alleviate his frown. "I'll prove it!"

I hop over a cable and thrust aside the black curtain. Prise the scissors from my messy desk drawer. Return to the hutch.

"You are officially scaring me now," Aki says seriously.

"No. It's okay. I won't hurt him, and the hair *will* come back."

I open the hutch door and try to take hold of him. He darts to the furthest corner again. Wow. Is he scared, or just avoidant? In any case, he's emoting.

"He wasn't like this last night," I say.

"I'm surprised he *let* you anywhere near him with those." Aki snickers. "He clearly doesn't trust you to get scissor-happy again."

I huff and close the door. "We'll get him later. For now, I need to make a video about him." It'll get way more views than yesterday's. I'll just have to drink my way through the inevitable fallout. "No matter how many dislikes it gets."

"Oh, that *was* devastating. Made me feel like it was my fault."

"Not at all." I run my fingertips over the smooth scissor blades. "Everyone's messed up over that song."

"Yeah, but even if they're brainwashed, screw 'em. You *have* to make a video about this rabbit. They have to see it, whether they believe it or not. Maybe it'll snap them out of it."

"I'm *going* to do this." I smack the scissors down on top of the hutch. "Do you want to be in it too?"

He smiles. "I'm honoured you would ask me again, but I think it should just be you. It's your experience, and your fans might more likely believe you."

I glare at the floorboard. "I don't know. A lot of them seem to be turning their backs on me already."

A fact that could ultimately affect my livelihood, in more than one way.

I only get to briefly reflect on this because Aki interrupts my thoughts with: "*I'll* never abandon you."

He grins at me, I assume sincerely. I return it and say, "Thank you."

It *is* satisfying to hear, but with him being my 'number one fan', it's hardly a surprise.

He goes back to studying the rabbit. "Have you given him a name yet?"

I twist my mouth in thought. "I actually haven't... How about Sleep-Thief?"

He laughs. "What?"

"I got barely an hour last night thanks to him." I sigh. "Otherwise, I have no clue what to call him."

"Hmm."

"You can name him, if you want."

His grin returns, and he places a hand on his chest. "Really?"

"Sure. I don't mind."

He'll probably come up with something better than me anyway.

"Oh my God. Okay." His dark eyes light up and glance at the bunny again. "How about... Shinpi? It's Japanese for mystery."

My eyebrows lift. "Huh. Interesting, and apt. I like it."

He clasps his hands together again. "Brilliant."

Shinpi doesn't even flinch. He's truly the bravest bunny I've ever seen, except for his sudden fear of me with the scissors.

"You want a drink?" I ask.

"Oh. Yes, please. You got any coffee left?"

"I do."

So I head to the kitchen and start boiling the kettle. Lean against the counter and stare at the overhead cupboard where my Russian Solace dwells. All those nasty comments rush through my thinker in jagged circles again. I would've thought a large handful of my subscribers would be on my side. Thought they respected me. It's like all the praise they've ever given has melted away from the acid they've poured over my channel. I'm a liar now. Well, quite frankly, as Aki says, 'screw them.' I scoff at myself. As if it's that easy. I have to keep showing them this stuff, because it's *my* truth, and if they're being brainwashed, they have to know.

Aki appears in the doorway, with his hands in his hoodie pockets. "Don't let it get to you, man."

I snigger. "Can you read my mind?"

"I can just tell."

I half-smile, grab a mug out of the cupboard, and place it next to the kettle. After grabbing a teaspoon from the drawer, I ask, "Black, strong, no sugar, right?"

"Yes, please."

I scoop a couple spoonfuls of coffee into the mug, pour in boiling water, and hand it to him.

He breaks the silence with: "Thanks muchly."

"Mm-hmm." My gaze trails to the cupboard again. One drink to start off the day can't hurt. I might sneak it into a coffee of my own once I'm alone.

"Have you written a script for the next video," he says, "or are you gonna freestyle it?"

"Well, I want to get this up as soon as possible, so I won't have time to do a script." I retrieve my mug from the draining board and dump one spoonful of coffee in it. Might as well make it black if I plan to add booze. "Also, it might be a bit awkward trying to hold the rabbit and read from my laptop at the same time."

"I can help by bringing him to you so you don't have to leave the sofa. I've handled a rabbit before."

"Oh, cool. Thanks." I fill the mug with leftover hot water. "You go wait in the studio. I'll be right in."

He nods then zooms off down the hallway. Without further hesitation, I open my cupboard, snatch the vodka, and add a splash to my coffee. I don't know what Aki would think about me drinking on the job, let alone this early in the day. But I need this, to lift my spirits – no pun intended – and thrust me away from the gnashing jaws of criticism.

The box lights illuminate me and the sofa, but only my top half will be in frame to start with. Shinpi sits completely still on my lap. I'm more than grateful for the animal's oddly tame nature. I straighten up and clear my throat. Aki stands beside the camera, counts down from three with his fingers, and presses record. The clip I recorded on my phone last night will play before this.

"Hello, everyone," I say, almost flatly compared to usual. "What you just saw is unedited footage I, Maddix A., captured last night of what has left me honestly questioning everything I know. A lot of you are going to call me a liar, again, and I don't blame you." Tried to say that without too much animosity. "But everything I've said is the truth. Please, if you've made it this far, give me a chance to explain." I sigh and glance away as I try to remember the wording I came up with five minutes ago. I'll edit that out and cut straight to: "I've never experienced anything like this before. But a rabbit appeared on my TV and literally leapt out of it. I know most, if not all, of you will say I faked the footage, but I honestly don't know how else I can prove it, except... the bunny's still with me."

I raise my eyebrows at Aki. He presses a button on the camera to hopefully zoom it out so that more of my body's in frame. Then he twists, opens the hutch, and scoops out the rabbit. He passes him over to me like a pro. I clutch him to my chest, and check with Aki before continuing. Again, I'll edit out that little exchange and fade into:

"So, yeah. Here he is." I clear my throat quietly. "Um, now, a question for you all: what colour is he? I'm very keen to find out what you guys say, because I genuinely believe this is the bunny from the 'Something That You Need to Know' music video. He even has the same blue eyes."

Shinpi continues to comfortably lie in my arms with his nose twitching against my chest. At least he trusts me, but I do intend to grab those scissors again soon.

"He's ridiculously chill, you guys. I honestly don't understand it." I shake my thinker. "I don't understand a lot about the last couple days... But I've decided to keep this little guy. I have to find out, somehow, why he came to me, and how. I know it's impossible. I thought many things weren't possible. But now I don't know." I laugh. "So, come on. Tell me what you think. Am I still making this up?"

I feel a rant bubbling under my tongue. But I shouldn't give in. I ask Aki to stop the recording and he does. Feels empty not doing my cheery outro of 'see you next time' and whatnot, and that intro sucked, as always. But I can't bring myself to be fakely happy; those comments have pissed me off, and I'm feeling angrier the more I think about them.

"You didn't mention the hair thing," he says, "about cutting it off and whatnot."

Nor his lack of defecating.

"I figured I have no proof yet, so there's no point telling them." I scoff. "In fact, they'll probably think my recording of him jumping out of the TV's been manipulated, so maybe there's no point at all."

He wags a finger at me. "You can show *me*, though. I'm dying to see this magical hair."

Guess we could try again. I almost ask him to get the scissors and make sure Shinpi can't see them, but part of me reckons it'll give the creature a heads-up, as if he can understand English. Stupid, but who knows at this point?

Aki seems to read my mind, or already be thinking the same. He sneakily swipes the scissors and approaches us with them behind his back. I make sure to keep a remotely firm grip on Shinpi, in case he tries to bolt again. Aki crouches before us, strokes the rabbit's head, then in an impossible flash snips at his tail. Shinpi flinches, but thankfully doesn't leap away. Aki holds up the tuft of hair with a grin.

"How the fuck did you do that so fast?" I say.

He winks. "I'm skilled."

I chuckle nervously.

"Now I suppose we wait," he says.

5

Within an hour, I quickly edit the video, render it, and now it's uploading to YouTube. It *is* a nice change of pace compared to my usual lengthy editing time. Depressing to know, though, that these videos will get way more views, just because of the subject matter. I've made sure to set the thumbnail to me holding the rabbit. If that doesn't get more clicks, I don't know what will. People love bunnies, and it *is* Easter.

Oh, crap. I haven't ordered Connelly's egg yet. Why do I let myself get distracted like that? This second, even stronger Russian coffee doesn't help. Maybe the egg will put me in his good books again, even if slightly. I bring up a new tab for the Hotel Chocolat site. Not much left in stock, unsurprisingly, but they have one here he'll love: large, extra thick smooth milk chocolate. Just about affordable, too, even with the few quid for next day delivery. I suppose I do still have his bank card... No. I wouldn't, and that'd be ludicrous. How could I consider that? Now I fear I really am skint, though. At least I already have plenty of booze.

Aki's still on the sofa here, checking his phone for any comments on my latest videos that stand out from the new norm of 'you're lying' or 'WTF?' I'm grateful for his help, as I can't bear to read one more comment that says I'm just an attention seeker or that my opinion means nothing. I realise I'm only opening myself up for even more shit with this next video, but they have to see it.

I hit publish.

"There, it's live," I announce, and spin in my chair to face Aki. "If they don't like it, fuck 'em."

I finish off my mug and revel in the comfortable numbness.

He glances up from his phone and stares at me. "Is there booze in that?"

Shit. Am I slurring?

"What if there is?" I say.

Shouldn't have phrased it like that. He'll think I'm rude. Oh, bollocks.

"I was just wondering." He smiles. "It's no big deal."

He's not judging me?

"We haven't checked Shinpi," he adds. "It's been way over half an hour."

My eyes bulge. "God, you're right."

I shoot out of the chair. Nearly stumble over a cable. Curse under my breath. Aki doesn't react verbally, but I don't want to check to see if he's mimicking Connelly's unimpressed eyebrow.

As I reach the hutch, I turn to him anyway. "You're better at handling him. You get him out."

He gives a short nod then joins me. Opens the hutch and coaxes Shinpi into his arms.

"Not going to hurt you," he murmurs. "Just taking a look. I promise."

He stands with the bunny, and tilts his thinker to check out the tail. I peer closely at it too, and nothing seems out of place.

"You see?" I say.

He laughs, as if in a pleasant shock. "How about that? It's good as new."

I study the creature all over. "Maybe we could shave off everything. See how quickly *that* grows back."

His brow arches up. Eyes contract wider than I've seen them. "Please tell me you're joking."

I straighten. "Pfft. Of course I am... mostly."

It'd be cruel, sure, but an interesting experiment and an easier way to prove it.

Frowning, he snickers anxiously. "I'm gonna put him away for now, okay?" He slots Shinpi back inside the hutch. "Anyway, I could do with some snacks. How about you?"

I *am* hungry. I often neglect food. Probably don't even have enough left in the bank for biscuits.

"There's a Co-Op down the road." I lean on the hutch for balance. "*You* can get stuff. Think I blew the last of my money today."

Why did I admit that? Gut's burning with more than just the vodka now.

"I'll get you something," he says.

The burning worsens. I don't want to owe anything else.

"You don't have to do that," I tell him.

"I don't mind. After everything you've gone through over the last few days, you deserve it. And don't worry about paying me back."

He knows how to win me over.

I slowly smile. "Okay. Thank you very much, then."

"Just so I know, though, what time do you need me gone by?"

I shrug. "Maybe six? Connelly gets home after that."

"Cool... Does he even know I'm here?"

I never did tell him. Mixture of being too nervous and forgetting. Surely he won't be too mad?

"No. But it's fine." Another lie I have to force myself to be content with. "Let us depart."

As we walk briskly up the cold street, I resist checking my phone for comments. Need to wait until I've got a nice glass of Russian Indifference to hand. We pass over the zebra crossing and alongside the smart terraced houses. What kind of place does Aki live in? I *should* get to know him better, really.

"Do you live alone, or...?"

He glances around and mutters, "Well, don't tell anyone, but I still live with my parents. Frustrating when you're nearly thirty."

Another reminder that I am too.

"Hey, it's okay," I say. "Moving out's expensive."

"Mm. Especially when you have no-one to move out with."

That *is* a shame. I just smile sadly.

"You and Connelly," he says, "you don't share the same last name. What *is* that about?"

Looks like neither of us are worried about personal questions. At least Connelly's not here to shoot him down this time.

"We didn't fancy taking the other's name," I say, "and didn't like how they sounded together, so..."

Connelly preferred us not taking each other's names. I kind of went along with him. Wouldn't have minded joining them together if they flowed better.

"Aww, okay. How long have you been together, then?"

"Uh, since uni. We met at Lambeth College in our Media undergraduate class, so we've been together about ten years. Married for three, though."

"Wow." He grins. "Must be true love."

I grin too. "Well, we drive each other crazy, so it must be."

It's refreshing to chat with him about anything other than conspiracy theories, as much as I enjoy that.

We reach the Co-Op in no time. Connelly and I will need another bag of carrots now that we're sharing with Shinpi, but I'd have to ask Aki to get it for us. I'll stick to this packet of Oreos. We can go without carrots for now, I'm sure... Why am I being so accommodating to this creature, whatever he is?

I've been standing still, stuck in my thinker for what feels like ages. Quicker we get home, quicker I can continue drowning my thoughts.

As Aki's browsing the sweets, I lean in closer to ask, "You drink much?"

He straightens up and mutters, "I prefer things that give me more pep, like caffeine, but I drink too from time to time."

I nod slowly, and find myself watching him for several moments as he scans the shelves. Thankfully, he doesn't spot me. I sigh. "I wish there was a way I could give back to you, as a thank-you."

He places a hand on his chest. "Aww. You don't have to do that."

"I know." I smirk. "But I want to."

His eyes wander in the direction of the checkout. "Well, what was the booze you were drinking at home?"

My own eyes widen a little. Don't ask me to buy you any. You already know I have nothing.

"Vodka," I say. "Russian Standard."

"Hmm. Okay. How about I pick up a pack of Monster energy drinks and I share some of your vodka?"

I snicker, and try not to show my relief. "If that'll make you happy, it's a deal."

So we return to the studio with our beverages and snacks, ready to face the music. Shinpi watches us through the wire mesh. I try to ignore him. Slump on the desk chair, gulp down vodka, and bring up the comments on my phone. Aki swigs from his drink and does the same. He's pretty brave mixing Monster and vodka together. If *I* made a habit of that, I'd probably get a heart attack.

"Bloody hell," he says. "We'll never get through all of these."

Over a thousand comments already. Insane.

"You read the ones at the top," I say, "and I'll scroll down a bit and start from there."

He clears his throat. "Right. Well, top comment: 'Maddix, I've watched your videos for the last year and a half and I genuinely thought you were a smart, down-to-earth guy. Now I'm thinking you need to get help.'" He cringes at me, but I tell him to keep going. "'Sorry but I don't know how you expect people to believe this. Cute bunny, man, but I'm afraid you can't fool me.'"

I sigh. Great start, although it's not like I wasn't expecting it. I don't even want to know who wrote that.

I read some from my screen: "'I don't believe this for a second.' Short and sweet. 'I want whatever this guy's smoking.'" I scoff. "'How the fuck could this be real? You blatantly went out and bought the thing. Enough of this attention seeking. It's getting old already.' These people really can't write to save their lives."

Aki rolls his eyes then gazes at his phone again. "'You're absolutely crazy. And you're obsessed with that song. I am too, but hey!'" He scrolls a little. "'Convincing footage. Almost had me there.'" His eyebrows dart up. "Ooh: 'More videos of the rabbit, please. I don't care if it *is* the one from the video, although it'd be awesome if it is. Just show us more bunny. He's too cute. I adore his eyes.' Well, at least that person wasn't being nasty. Oh, and they said the rabbit's white."

I glare into my glass. "I saw loads of people saying he's white too. What a shocker."

He knocks back several gulps. I do the same and grimace slightly from my burning chest.

"'Why are you doing this?'" he continues. "'Actually think you might be schizo. Get yourself checked.'"

I laugh. "Believe it or not, that's not the first time someone's said that to me. Just because I genuinely believe the original moon landing was fake."

"It *was*." He scowls at the phone. "They shouldn't be saying these things, though. It makes me mad."

I'm flattered that he'd get upset for me. I remember him and several others standing up for me once in an extremely toxic comment section.

"Well," I say, "I'm going to take your advice and try not to let them get to me." I lift my glass to my lips again. "Easier done with Russian Comfort."

"I'll drink to that." He swigs from his glass and carries on scrolling. "'I can't take it anymore. I need to hear that song again, even if it's a few seconds.'"

Frowning, I shake my thinker. "I honestly don't get it, man."

"Neither do I. I mean, I assume the other version has the same sound, just different lyrics?"

"Yeah."

"It's really nothing special."

"I know, right?"

So great that he agrees with me. We seem to be in tune with everything surrounding this song.

"The rabbit," I say. "We still seem to be the only ones who think he's black."

His gaze drifts over to the hutch, and his eyes widen. "You don't think we're cursed, do you?"

I pause sipping, and some of the vodka trails back into the glass. I can only stare at him. Did he say cursed?

"We only see the darker versions," he goes on. "That can't be a good thing."

I don't even believe in curses.

"Well, I've always seen Shinpi as black. But when I joined everyone else in the other room at that party, I did hear the 'normal' lyrics."

"Why would she let you hear both?"

I shrug. "Maybe she was toying with me, trying to make me think I was remotely like everyone else for a moment? Or just wanted to drive me nuts." I keep drinking. "In any case, I'd say us seeing the black bunny's more like a gift."

He screws up his face. "How, when you're being ostracised by your own community?"

I stare into the glass, at the pitiful amount left. "We have a unique perspective. They just don't understand, or don't want to." I sigh. "I really want to stay excited about this whole thing, but it's hard when no-one believes you."

"Mm. And I suppose at least you're pulling in a bigger audience to your channel. Negative attention's better than no attention, in a way."

Wish I could accept that.

I let my arm hang loosely over the chair, keeping a light grip on the rim of my glass. My thinker rolls to the side with another sigh. "This isn't how I imagined it all going. I mean, yeah, having a channel about conspiracies is controversial anyway. But now I've started my own conspiracy, and I just wish my subscribers wouldn't so quickly dismiss me. It fucking happened, and I've shown as much proof as I can." I raise my voice: "Good job I haven't told them about the regrowing hair and constantly clean cage!"

Nothing is as it should be. Even Black Cow isn't black!

He narrows his eyes as if in thought, swigs his drink, and says, "We need to make them believe you."

"How?" I groan.

He raises a finger. "Everyone says you faked the footage, right? That's easy to do with digital. Maybe you could get a disposable film camera, and keep it handy for if something else happens."

That might actually be worth trying. Didn't think of it before.

"That's an idea... For now, though, I need another drink."

"Already?" He glances at his. "I haven't even reached halfway yet."

"Drink up, then."

Smirking, I push myself up and scuff to the kitchen. Legs feel light, almost disconnected. Another one then my thinker should feel the same.

I pour my next lot of Russian Numbness. Should I ask Aki to keep scrolling through the comments but only tell me if anyone says something substantially different? Can't handle more bad stuff. After a while, it's just mindless repetition, and it hurts more than it should.

His footsteps approach, and his glass plonks down next to mine, empty. I laugh. "Wow."

"Yep. I drank up." He smirks, as if proud of himself. I tip more vodka in his glass then he grabs his energy drink from the fridge. As he tops up his concoction, he says, "All this is making me wonder what else out there is real, you know?"

I lean back against the counter, clutching my glass to my chest. "For once, I'm trying not to think about it in too much detail."

His eyes widen. "But we have to find out."

"How?"

He takes a long swig then stares at me. "Has something like this seriously never happened to you?"

My gaze wanders. "I don't know. This is definitely the strangest."

"What about aliens? I know you said in your Most Credible UFO Sightings Around the World video last year that you've never spotted any yourself, but you also said you thought it's ignorant to think we're the only lifeforms in the universe."

"And I still hold true to that. But..." I lift a finger then knock back more vodka. "There's always the possibility that certain things or events are the work of aliens, but we have no concrete proof. I've always been open to the idea of their existence. I've just never seen anything that's obviously linked to them."

He raises an eyebrow. "Until now."

"What?" I frown for several moments. "Are you saying the bunny's an alien?"

"Who knows? Plus, that singer, or whoever made the video, hacked the Internet and broadcasting stations without a trace."

I scoff. "I'm sure you don't have to be an alien to be an expert hacker."

"Okay. But focus on the rabbit: how it travelled through your TV. Surely some paranormal/extraterrestrial shit was going on there? Plus, its hair growing back."

I've obviously considered it, but can't quite bring myself to admit it.

He spins and leaves. Guess we're returning to the studio. I pull myself away from the counter to follow him. Stagger into the studio and lean back on the door frame. He kneels in front of the hutch, peering in at the potential alien.

"How about we take a proper look at him?" he says.

"You mean, like, get him out?"

"Yeah."

"Uh, okay." I swig again, put my glass on the small table next to the sofa, and grab the wire play pen from beside the hutch. "In case he decides to actually hop away. Might not trust us after snipping at him twice."

I set it up on the floor to create an open pentagonal area. Aki opens the hutch and carefully retrieves Shinpi. After placing him on the floor inside the pen, we kneel either side and watch him as he sits there twitching his nose like always.

"Maybe I should put a towel or some paper down," I say.

"No point if he doesn't 'piss' or 'crap', as you so eloquently put it."

I laugh again. This whole situation's hilarious, really. The vodka helps me see it like that, anyway.

"Tell us what you are, Shinpi," I say.

He stares up at me. Nose stops twitching. Body seems to freeze, as if not even breathing. My smile falls. A haze clouds my eyes.

*

Softness beneath me. Dim ceiling above. Thinker's light. Am I lying on the studio sofa? My heart pounds. I clutch my chest. Gasp.

Aki leans over me. "Maddix, are you okay?"

"What's happening?" I croak. "How did I get here?"

"You passed out a few minutes ago." He chuckles. "I thought you were done for."

Why is that funny?

"How much have I drunk?" I ask.

"Much more than me. What's the last thing you remember?"

I try to lift my arms but can't. "Uh, we got the bunny out."

Frowning with an amused smile, Aki says, "That was, like, two hours ago. We've been drinking and chatting in here since then, and you ate all the Oreos."

Another reason I feel sick, then. Am I really so wasted I've lost two hours? This doesn't usually happen.

"Aki, I can't move." I sound scared, and pathetic. "Vodka doesn't do this to me."

I barely feel his hand on my shoulder. He says, "It's okay. You're okay."

"No." My thinker rolls from side to side. "Let me up... Help me up. Please."

He hooks an arm under my back and holds the other in front of me. I grip it and pull myself up. Dizziness crashes over me. But Aki keeps me in place. He must be strong if he can support me, especially dead-weight like this. He's not even muscly.

I glance over at the hutch. Shinpi sits inside. Did I put him away? Did Aki?

"What time is it?" I ask.

"I dunno. Just past three?"

I take a steadying breath. "Good. I have three hours to sober up before Connelly gets back."

"How you gonna do that?" He grins. "You wanna jump in the tub and I'll hose you down with cold water?"

I swallow, and stare at him. He seems serious, but he can't be, right? I just laugh, nervously, I think.

"Too weird?" He snickers. "Okay, how about we go for a walk? Get some fresh air. You can show me around."

"Uh, I dunno if I should go out like this."

"Come on. It'll be fun."

He manages to move my legs so they hang over the side of the sofa, then he hoists me to my feet with his arms tucked under mine.

"Fucking hell," I murmur. "You're strong."

Not sure if that's insulting. But I do know the room's swaying.

He laughs. "I know."

He keeps one arm linked with mine as he guides me out. My legs are beyond jelly.

"What about Shinpi?"

He presses forward, forcing me down the hallway. "He'll be fine. Seriously, stop worrying."

Before we leave the flat, I just about remember to swipe the key from the dish by the door.

We stagger out into an overcast mid-afternoon. What day is it? I'm ridiculously fucked up. Only several hours of sleep will cure this. And water. I should've drunk some. I try to turn back. My legs push forward. I seriously don't feel in control. This is terrifying. Can't even feel the cold.

Aki clutches my arm. I barely feel it. We take a right at the top of the road. Those towering terraced houses unnerve me. I try not to look at them.

"Where are we going?" I drone.

"I dunno. I'm following your lead, man."

I open my mouth to question this. Nothing comes out.

We head left. Begin the long stretch of Norwood Road. Connelly drove us up here last night. Nothing but houses. The expensive ones.

"This place is pretty nice," Aki says.

"We want to live in one of these," I blurt. "We'll never afford it."

"But your channel grows bigger every year. More and more people support you."

The sickness in my gut crawls to my chest. "How much longer if they think I'm a nutcase?"

"You'll prove them wrong. Then everyone will listen to you and practically throw money your way. They want the truth. Only you can show them."

All of that was slurred, but fills me with a warm feeling of, what, hope? I *want* to be positive about my future. But these people, these bloody usernames, want lies.

"Mm," is all I can utter.

"I believe in you. And so does Connelly."

Regret crashes through me. He'll hate that I'm wasted again. But this is worse than at Kya's party. And I've drunk nowhere near as much. This doesn't make any bloody sense.

We carry on and on. Pass the houses lucky enough to have front lawns. Aki's talking. What the hell is he saying? The sky's turning a darker grey. Or is it my eyes?

I hear him at last. He whispers, "You wanna tell me where we're going?"

Terror grasps my throat. My voice cracks, "No idea."

We're finally approaching the end of the road. We cross the T-junction. Cars have whooshed by now and then. I've nearly called for help, but feel like I can't.

Past a row of independent cafés and restaurants, we stagger over another T-junction. Brockwell Park stands before us, surrounded by wooden fencing and trees just starting to bud. I'm fighting hard to resist this compulsion. My legs command me to go in. I know something terrible waits in there. Legs yank me through the tall metal gate anyway. Take us up the wide concrete footpath.

Our feet touch a vast stretch of grass. I glance ahead and can't understand what I'm looking at. A large black rectangle, on its side. A billboard? No. A massive TV, standing in the park. It looms over us. I need to leave. I try, but my body freezes. The air falls silent, and heavy. A worse terror jabs my gut. I try to open my mouth, to beg Aki to drag me away. It clamps shut. No sound even forms in my throat. He's not saying anything either. Is he suffering the same fate? That thing doesn't belong here. Neither do I.

White flickering from the screen attacks my eyes. I can't close them. I'm a fucking statue. What's happening around me? Anything? Has time frozen? Why am I thinking this? I need to shield my eyes. They're on fire! My arms won't lift. Stop doing this to me! Whatever I did, I'm sorry. Whatever you want, take it. The pain is blinding. I can't bear this!

Something pricks the back of my thinker. It gets lighter. A hole seems to open up.

*

The darkness clears. Feeling returns to my heavy limbs. I can barely move them. Am I lying on the grass? I'm still in the park. Passed out again? Pain grips my thinker. The field's empty. I manage to push myself up so that my elbows support me, and glance around.

"Aki?" my voice croaks.

Where did he go? Did he seriously run off? Maybe he's getting help. No-one else is around. I just want to scream, 'What the fuck is happening?' But can't muster the energy. How long was I out for? Why did I even come here?

I fumble in my jacket pocket then pull out my phone. Call Aki. It rings and rings. My stomach twists increasingly tighter. Nothing.

Hang on. There's a missed call from Connelly and... Mum. What the hell? She only calls at Christmas. What could she possibly want in April?

Well, I can't deal with her right now. I need Connelly.

After several agonising moments, he picks up: "Hi. I assume I caught you recording or editing?"

"I'm in Brockwell Park," I say shakily. My throat's so dry. "I fainted, or blacked out, I think."

"What? Are you hurt?"

"Just a headache."

"Okay." Doesn't sound angry – not right now, anyway – just concerned. "What exactly happened?"

My eyes sting. Where *is* everyone? Can't even hear or see any cars in the distance.

"Maddix?" he almost snaps.

I try to mentally shake myself. A dark fog wraps around my brain. I can't focus on the memories leading from setting out with Aki to waking up just now. "I went for a walk with Aki," I explain, "but then I passed out, and now he's gone. So's everyone else."

"Have you been drinking?"

Was it too much vodka and not enough water? No. I saw something in this park. I swear I knew what it was when I initially woke up, but now a blank space exists. A sickening fright gnaws at my chest.

"Something was in this park," I mutter.

"What?"

My wide eyes dart around at the grey silence. "Oh God. Why can't I remember?"

I clutch my stabbing heart. Hate everything about this. Need to run home.

"How much have you drunk today?" he persists.

"It's not the alcohol's fault, but I don't know what it was."

Every time I nearly break through, the fog grows stronger, as does the pain.

He sighs. "Maddix, find somewhere safe to sit. One of the benches near the entrance, if you can. I'll come pick you up in ten minutes."

I bring the phone away from my ear briefly. 4 pm? "But you're at work."

"I'll tell them it's a family emergency," he murmurs.

I don't want to be responsible for getting him in trouble. But I need him. And his excuse *should* be acceptable.

"Okay," I say.

"Be careful," he says firmly.

Tears form. "I love you."

"Love you too. See you soon."

It warms me to hear that when I know he's mad at me.

We hang up. When he gets here, maybe he can help me understand this mess.

I throw as much strength as possible into pushing myself up. Glad no-one can see me struggling like this, but I do wish I could spot just one sign of human life. My brain finally registers the distant tweeting of birds in the trees. What's up with my senses? I still can't even feel the cold.

Staggering across the grass, I try to call Aki again. It goes to voicemail. Might as well leave one:

"Aki, it's Maddix. Where are you? Not gonna lie: I'm pretty scared, man. I passed out again. Not the booze this time, I swear, and I woke up and now you're gone. Last thing I know for sure is that we were walking out of my flat and up the street... Just tell me you're all right, okay?"

I hang up. He'd better get back to me soon. I make it to the park entrance gates, and still can't see any people or cars in the street up ahead. Where have they vanished to? We should've never left the flat. Now I'm in this crazy situation, though, I have to find out what's going on.

I leave the park and cross the road. For my body's sake, I should probably stay sitting like Connelly said. But I just want to check the immediate vicinity. From the pavement, I can't see through any of these houses' windows – I'd have to walk up the stone paths leading to their front doors, and I'd rather avoid getting arrested for trespassing. So I wander over again, and enter the little Maxy Supermarket.

Just to the left inside, the young shop assistant leans forward on the counter, with his phone close to his face. I stagger over. You'd think I'd be used to feeling light-headed with all the vodka I drink these days, but this is awful.

"Hi," I say to him. "What's happened to everyone?"

He just continues to gaze at his phone intensely, as if transfixed.

I step closer. "Hey. Mate, can you hear me?"

Still no answer. Either he's bloody rude, or that screen's absolutely fascinating.

I edge nearer, rest my hand on the counter for support, and peer down at his phone. He jerks back before I can see. His eyes bulge at me, and he takes out a white wireless earbud from his ear. He's got another one in, though.

"Sorry." He still looks alarmed. "Didn't know you were here."

Well, you shouldn't be on your phone.

"What are you watching?" I ask.

He seems to laugh nervously. "Why?"

Guy can't be older than eighteen. But he's not too young to intimidate if I have to. If he knows anything, I have to get it out of him.

"Are you okay?" he says. "You look like you can barely stand."

I'm not about to tell him I drank too much and fainted in the park, but I *will* repeat my original question: "Where is everyone?"

His face scrunches. "What do you mean?"

"People." I'm feeling sicker by the second. Need to lie down. "No-one on the roads. No-one walking about."

His gaze drifts past me. "Maybe they went inside to watch it."

I hold back a huff. "Watch what?"

He grimaces, like he's said too much.

"Tell me what it is," I say firmly.

"You'll only twist it," he snaps.

I raise an eyebrow. "Excuse me?"

He clasps his phone to his chest with both hands and pleads, "Please, don't ruin this for us. I've seen your videos. All you've done is bad-mouth her."

Wow. My videos are reaching further than I thought.

I frown hard. "Is this about the mystery singer?"

"Yes." He sighs, but at himself, I think. "About half an hour ago, a new video went live: an interview, with her."

Something in my gut lurches: maybe excitement, or fear, or the God knows what amount of vodka. I *have* to see this. He seems guarded about his phone, so I pull out mine. Bring up YouTube. Shit-loads of messages. I spot one that starts with: 'Omg, you're so lucky.' What are they talking about exactly? Anyway, surprise, surprise: this interview's top of the trending list. Over a billion views? What the fuck? How's that even possible in half an hour? Especially for a BBC News video. The thumbnail shows a blonde woman with a flower crown, smiling past the camera. That's her, all right. I tap the video, flip my phone so it fills the screen, and turn up the volume.

A man with slick, greying hair and a smart suit talks to the camera in front of a large window that overlooks the tall, shiny buildings of central London: "Good afternoon. Breaking news." His face lights up, and he sounds ecstatic. "The mystery singer who became an overnight sensation with her music video 'Something That You Need to Know' has joined us here in the studio for her first public appearance." He turns sideways to address her off-camera. "Hello, and welcome to the BBC."

It cuts to her sitting in an armchair in front of the same window, smiling as graciously as she was in the thumbnail. Her stunning dress appears to be made entirely out of the same rainbow of flowers from her crown. I can't believe she's even there. Is this real?

"Hello," she says softly.

"So, please, tell us about yourself," the presenter says impatiently off-camera.

With a cheeky smirk, she holds her thinker high. "What exactly would you like to know?"

She sounds British, but like upper-class.

"Well, how about you introduce yourself? There are millions, if not more, people out there dying to know your name, where you come from–"

"–What my favourite colour is?" She chuckles, then he does too. Even the shop assistant in front of me stifles a laugh. He must've seen this several times by now and still thinks it's funny? Doesn't get so much as a lip twitch from me. She runs her short blue-painted nails through her wavy hair. "Okay. Well, my name is K-Rin. And where I come from..." She presses a finger to her glossy lips. "It's a secret."

Interesting, and frustrating, response. Also, weird name, but what was I expecting? Must be fake.

"Okay." The presenter laughs again. "Well, K-Rin, what *is* your favourite colour?"

"I like all colours. The whole spectrum."

"I can tell by your beautiful dress."

She glances down at herself then grins. "Thank you."

"Anyway." The presenter leans forward. "The song. Please tell us how it came about. What inspired you?"

As interested as I am in that too, shouldn't he focus on how she hacked the music and radio stations? Where are the police?

"I believe the world right now could benefit from more positivity." Her smile remains, but she carries a slightly sad tone. "People need to believe in themselves, in the potential they can bring. Everyone has been dragged down and made to feel like they can only be this or that. And if they can find that courage to live their dreams and not let anyone stop them, they can find true happiness."

I shake my thinker slowly. Great sentiment, but it's not that simple. It's hardly an original message, though nothing's original these days.

"Happiness is very important," the presenter says.

"Yes. And obviously, everyone finds it in different ways. With my music, I hope to inspire those who want to make a positive impact on the world, and even those who don't, to take that first step."

"Why through music?"

Her eyes shift around, as if in wonder. "Music transports people into a dreamworld, where their imagination roams free. Anything is possible there."

She's quite on the money about that. Music has probably been one of the most influential mediums. It's also been amazingly successful at brainwashing.

"You're certainly right," the presenter says, "and what an astounding song you have created. Are other people behind it too?"

"All me," she says proudly.

"Wow. And will you release the song officially?"

"Yes, and it will be free."

His jaw seems to drop. "Free? Why not monetise it?"

"It is not about money. This needs to be accessible to all. Everyone deserves to be happy."

I can't tell if she's genuine or just arrogant.

The presenter flashes a grin at the camera then stares at her in awe. "What a refreshing attitude. More people in this world need to be like you."

Is this for real? It's a joke, right? Everyone's in it for money, whether they admit it or not. Why the fuck hasn't he mentioned her illegal hacking? Unless that's legal now?

She glances down with what looks like a flattered smile. Trying to be modest now?

"The cute little bunny in your video," the guy says, "can you tell us about him or her? Does he or she belong to you?"

"He *was* mine," she says, with a sad pout, "but I gave him away."

I tense up. Squeeze the phone with both hands.

"Why did you do that?" the presenter asks.

Her thinker tilts a little. "Someone else needed him more than me."

His eyes widen. "Who is this lucky person?"

I stop blinking. Chest tightens.

"I *would* respect his privacy," she says, "but he has already shown the world on YouTube."

I wipe my forehead. No way is this real.

"I don't use YouTube personally," he says. "Who is he?"

"A YouTuber by the name of Maddix A."

My gut lurches. What the fuck? Millions of people have watched this. Now they all know! I'm grateful for the exposure, but this isn't how I wanted it.

I glance at the shop assistant, who watches me intensely. Well, I guess this explains his attitude towards me.

K-Rin calmly addresses the camera: "I request that everyone respects Maddix. Try not to send him horrible messages. Yes, he has posted a few slightly disparaging videos about me, but he is simply mistaken. Running a conspiracy theory channel, it's in his nature to question."

I scowl at the screen. She's acting like she knows me. At least she's telling people to go easy on me, though, and not exactly handing out my *full* name and address. In any case, can't believe I'm being talked about on TV. It's frightening, and seems wrong without my permission. On the flipside, my channel's traffic should skyrocket. Must check my statistics.

"I hope my presence here helps to convince him of my existence," she continues.

The presenter screws up his face. "He doesn't believe you're real?"

"I think he was on the fence. Hopefully, it is clearer now."

I laugh under my breath. Yep, you certainly seem real enough. But I won't stop questioning your intention and how you've managed to make everyone obsessed with you in two days.

"I'm sure it is," the presenter says, "especially now you have graciously given him your rabbit."

"Yes. I'm hoping he will look after him. After all, I'm sure he wouldn't hurt a single hair on his body."

She smiles, but with obvious cockiness. How does she know I cut Shinpi's hair? That was clearly a dig at that, right? Is she warning me not to attempt it again?

"I'm sure he'll be kept safe," the presenter says. "Regarding your song, 'Something That You Need to Know', are you able to give us a release date?"

She lifts her thinker again. "This Sunday, sixteenth of April."

His eyes light up. "Ooh, that's close."

"There will be a new video to accompany it."

"Oh, really?"

"The one that streamed Saturday night was a prototype, simply to showcase the song. The official video will be available on the sixteenth."

His mouth drops. "I can't wait."

What the hell has she conjured together as the 'official' version? And how will I hear and view it compared to everyone else? She has six days for the hype to build. People will go crazy waiting for it.

"K-Rin, it's been a pleasure and honour to talk with you this afternoon." The presenter holds out his hand, which she shakes softly.

"Thank you for having me."

The video fades to black.

I lower the phone slowly. I did just watch that, right? She mentioned me by name, didn't she?

"What are you gonna do?" the shop assistant asks. He looks wary, like I might explode.

"Not sure," is all my weak voice can muster.

"Please don't post any more bad stuff about her. She isn't a conspiracy."

He sounds so desperate, as if it'll hurt him personally if I tarnish her image any further. I just stare at him, expressionless, unable to accept that this random guy is telling me what to do. I don't interfere with *his* job. He's just like many of the usernames who disagree with me, and the millions if not billions she's infatuated.

I leave the shop. The crisp air hits me. Thankfully, he doesn't shout after me or anything.

I return to the edge of the park and wait for Connelly. Surely he must've seen or at least heard about this interview? He never mentioned it. How will it affect him? Hopefully, he won't feel like our privacy has been compromised – our address wasn't revealed. People who know us will undoubtedly speak up. Is that why Mum called? Bloody hell. Must be. But what about our neighbours? They haven't come knocking so far after uploading those videos about K-Rin – they might not have seen them anyway – but now she's announced to the world that I've got her rabbit, they're bound to show up. If they're infatuated with K-Rin, they *should* listen to her request and respect me. That really does shock me, though. She could've destroyed me. What's her play?

Need to check my channel statistics. I bring up YouTube on my phone again. Have to grip the iron bar of the gate to stop myself falling. Over two-hundred thousand more subscribers, in half an hour? That's nearly half of what took me seven years to accumulate. And my K-Rin videos have reached several million views each! Absolutely astonishing. My chest leaps with flattery and pride, but also panic. Don't think I want to read the comments. There are thousands. I need Aki to go through them for me. Where the fuck is he? Is he aware about any of this?

Connelly's car pulls up. A few others have finally started driving by too. I jump into the front passenger seat and shut the door quickly.

"Are you okay?" he asks.

"Complicated question. Did you see that interview?"

"Yeah. Everyone at work's been watching it. It's bloody insane."

"You never said when we were on the phone before."

"It's why I tried calling you in the first place. But then I was more worried about you fainting in the park."

Fair enough.

"Get your seatbelt on," he says, so I do.

He starts the journey home, and around the first street corner, some cars drive by us. There are still fewer than usual for this time of day. Are the others seriously inside, continuing to watch that video?

"Your mum's been trying to get hold of me," he adds. "I messaged her saying I couldn't answer. She wanted you. I assumed you didn't pick up because of your normal aversion to talking to her, but guess you were unconscious."

I roll my stinging eyes. "It'll only be about that interview."

Connelly gives what looks like an apprehensive smile, "Congratulations on your first TV appearance, kind of."

I scoff. "Can you believe the cheek of her, though? K-Rin was acting like I'm mental."

"At least she was nice about it."

My eyebrow arches. "Are you defending her?"

"I'm just saying she could've been worse."

"Mm. Well, she got me two-hundred thousand more subscribers, so..."

"Bloody hell." He laughs a little, as if in disbelief. "Fantastic."

I smile out at the houses, which we pass quicker than normal, then shake my thinker. "This guy in the shop just now begged me to stop posting bad stuff about her. But K-Rin told everyone to respect me, so even if I upload more of these videos, people are less likely to be hateful towards me. And as long as YouTube continues to let me monetise these videos, that ad revenue will be rolling in."

"People will have to watch at least thirty seconds of the ads for it to count, though, right? Don't you think they'll skip them to get straight to your theories about K-Rin?"

I frown at him. He has a point.

He turns a corner rather fast. I grip the door handle. Keen to get home? Or making the most of the fairly empty roads?

"It's weird," he says. "A part of *me* doesn't want you to say anything negative about her. It doesn't make sense. But as long as you can handle the backlash, whatever the intensity, you should keep going."

His encouragement pleases me to no end.

"It's promising to hear that from you after how you've been recently," I say. "Is the song still plaguing your mind?"

He focuses on the road. "Honestly, not as much. I've barely been able to concentrate today, though. Hardly anyone got any work done. As soon as that interview was posted, they all got so hyped – even the boss did."

"But you didn't?"

"I was excited, sure, but not as much as them."

Is the brainwashing wearing off for him already? I frown harder, but it hurts too much.

"Anyway," he says, "how are you feeling?"

"I'm fine, but still light-headed. Don't remember what happened, at all."

He glares at the road. "You never did tell me how much you drank today."

"Honestly, I don't know."

"You said you were with Aki?"

"Yeah. But he vanished, and won't answer his phone."

"And you don't have any other symptoms besides a light head?"

"Well, I feel a bit sick. Why?"

That clenched jaw returns. "Did he come into the flat? Do you still have my bank card?"

Does he seriously think Aki would've stolen it?

I fish inside my pocket and pull it out. "It's safe. He only came 'round so I could show him Shinpi."

"Shinpi?"

"That's what he named the rabbit."

"Fucking hell." He huffs. "If he tells anyone where we live, they'll come knocking for that rabbit. That thing's just as big a celebrity as its owner."

"K-Rin told everyone to respect me, that he belongs to me."

"Yeah, so if they don't knock, they'll be hanging around outside like paparazzi."

I nearly laugh. "You know how nuts that sounds?"

"This whole situation is nuts," he raises his voice. "A mysterious, unknown singer teleported a rabbit to you through our TV, apparently!"

"I still can't explain that," I admit.

"Look, either way, I'm not comfortable with you bringing that guy into our home and getting drunk."

I fold my arms. "Why? What exactly's going to happen?"

"Anything." His eyes bulge at the road. "You don't know him, not properly. I can't believe I have to tell you this."

I just fall silent. He doesn't need to talk to me like that. I wouldn't have invited Aki back if I thought he was dangerous in any way.

Thankfully, we soon make it home. Well, there's no paparazzi. Connelly scouts out every room with that persistently tensed jaw. He's still pissed at me, but surely he'll calm down when he realises nothing's been stolen or anything? Would've thought he'd relax at least a little now he has his card back. He *has* been quiet, though, ever since I mentioned how much I spent on Shinpi with it.

Lying on the sofa, I rest my thinker on the arm. Tempted to go to bed, but my mind's too active. What's the latest news? What are people saying about me? Have my patrons left me? Staying subscribed to my channel to see what I say next about K-Rin I can understand, but they wouldn't continue to actively give me money if I'm trying to denounce her. My gut churns as my finger hovers over the YouTube app icon on my phone. The Patreon app beside it taunts me too. I just need to suck it up and check. So I open YouTube and brace myself for the inevitable shitstorm.

I bring up the Notifications menu. I told it a while ago to stop alerting me about people's comments, and I'm relieved I did now that my videos are getting thousands of them. But apparently I have over a thousand private messages. My eyes strain at the screen. How can I read them with this dizziness? Are they seriously all about K-Rin? Are they attacks on me? I can't deal with them all right now, but I can look at a few. So I tap the one at the top of the list:

'Dear Maddix, I've been watching you for a year and always been a fan. I've never made a request before but could you please do more videos about K-Rin's rabbit? I just signed up to your Patreon and I'd love to see more K-Rin content. You must be honoured. I have to admit I'm a little jealous lol! Anyway, I won't take up any more of your time. Thank you for all you do!'

That's from wishfulthinker99. I've seen their comments on many previous videos – I'm grateful they've stayed polite and respectful as usual. Looks like I have a new patron, which is great, but it does surprise me.

The next is sPIkyCAke: 'Maddix my man, totally sorry I called u a liar in ur last vid. Pls forgive me. Can't believe K-Rin sent u her bunny. Still not sure about the jumpin thru the TV thing mate but u clearly have somethin special. Gotta admit ur theories are wild but keep goin, it's intriguing.'

Ah, yes, I remember this guy saying something like: 'WTF. Such a liar. Disappointed.' At least he's changed his tune. Just a shame it took a stranger on TV to convince him.

My eyes close. Can't take staring at a screen any longer. If I have this many messages now, how many will I have when I wake up?

Connelly's footsteps approach. He sighs. "Well, the flat and rabbit are both fine."

Crap. I've been reading about that damn rabbit but didn't think to check on him. Not used to having anything *to* check on, and I just focused on lying down.

"Thanks," I say.

Knock at the main door. If I wasn't out of it, that might've made me jump. Frowning, Connelly steps back out into the hallway to answer it.

"Hiya." An excitable, husky female voice. Is that the lady from upstairs? Oh God, no. "Sorry to bother you, but I just saw the news today. You and your husband have K-Rin's bunny, don't you? I went on YouTube and saw Maddix's videos. I didn't know he was a YouTube star."

Well, I'm not a star, but that does sound good. Guess she wants to see the rabbit. If I had the energy, I'd pull myself up and go whisper in Connelly's ear not to invite her in, but he's naturally way ahead of me.

"I'm afraid if you want to see the rabbit," he says, "we're not letting people in. I hope you understand."

"Oh, of course." She laughs coarsely. Woman needs to stop smoking, but at forty-odd, I suppose the damage is done. "I just wanted to congratulate you both. You will pass on my congratulations to Maddix, won't you?"

"Thank you. And yes."

"Okay, then." She laughs again. "Take care, both of you."

"Thanks. Bye-bye." And the door shuts. I don't know how he always manages to put on that polite tone when he absolutely hates people knocking. He returns to me and sighs. "I suppose you heard all of that."

"Yeah. Apparently, I'm a star." The word feels golden on my tongue, although tarnished by the fact that she came here for Shinpi, not me.

"Mm. I'm just glad she didn't try to force her way in."

That *is* fortunate. I don't know the woman well enough to notice if she's being uncharacteristically respectful in that way.

I gaze back at my phone. "Don't suppose you'd be willing to help me with my abundance of private messages?"

"What would you want me to do exactly?"

"Just filter through them to see if there's anything other than gushing over K-Rin or asking me to do more bunny videos."

"Uh, okay."

"Brill. Thanks." Closing my eyes, I reach the phone up to him. He takes it and slumps on the end of the sofa by my feet. Must barely be enough room for him.

I start to doze, but can't switch off completely. Static buzzes in my thinker. This doesn't happen from too much booze. Maybe tomorrow, with a clearer mind, I might remember what happened in the park.

"Everyone's certainly going on about the rabbit," Connelly says at last. "And God, some of them can't write at all."

I roll my eyes inside my skull. I know. I said that earlier. But that doesn't matter right now.

"Um," he says in that elongated way that worries me.

"What?"

"There are several people saying they see the black bunny too."

My frown rips through my forehead. I fight past it. "That can't be true. Only Aki and I can!"

"'Maddix,'" he reads out, "'I've always seen the black rabbit, like you, but was too afraid to come forward about it.'"

My whole body tenses. "Bullshit."

"I thought you were desperate to find others who experienced what you did?"

"I was. But they're sending this straight after K-Rin's interview? Suspicious as hell." I glare at the floor. "If they'd come forward when I was practically begging them to, I would've more likely believed them. Now they're lying to me... do they call that respect?"

He briefly lets me stew, then says, "Let's look at this tomorrow."

"No. What else is there?" I'm feeling increasingly sicker, but need to know. By his taut expression, I'm assuming I said that rudely. "Please. Just a bit more."

Sighing, he carries on skimming. "A bunch of people say they've donated to your Patreon. You should check that out."

My eyebrows painfully dart up. Grimacing, I say, "Come out of YouTube and open the Patreon app. It'll log in automatically."

"Okay." He taps the screen a few times.

My stomach still churns, expecting the worst. Maybe *these* people have donated, but have I lost most if not all of my other patrons?

His thinker tilts. "How many patrons *did* you have?"

I grip my gut. "Eight-hundred-and-fifty."

He looks perplexed, and shocked. It's bad, isn't it?

"What's the damage?" I ask.

"...It says you have one-thousand-three-hundred."

My jaw drops. "What?"

Has it really jumped up by four-hundred-and-fifty in a day? It took me seven years to get to eight-hundred-and-fifty.

He shakes his thinker with a smile. "At one pound a patron, that's bloody brilliant. You should definitely set up higher tiers. I've been telling you to for years."

I have to see this. I reach sideways towards him and he returns the phone. Gaze at the screen for a while until the figure blurs. Hope it's not a glitch because £450 extra a month, before tax? I won't say no! Maybe higher tiers *would* be good, but right now I've nothing extra to offer any £2 donators compared to the £1s. How many more people will have subscribed and pledged by tomorrow? I'm glad I'm already lying down. I'll have to post a thank-you message to everyone, but I need to recover first.

My phone vibrates. Mum's calling, again. I never phoned her back.

"You not answering?" Connelly says.

"It's my mum. I'll ring her tomorrow."

The vibrating's so aggravating I hang it up before it reaches voicemail.

"Mmm," he says. "You'd better message her at least, or she'll keep bothering me... Anyway, you still want me to go through your messages?"

"No, thanks. I need to rest. And you probably have Kya's stuff to work on."

"I do indeed." He pushes himself up and brings out his phone. "Oh, I have a message from her, actually." He taps the screen and starts reading. His expression turns intense. What is it now? I go to ask but he says, "She's doing a photoshoot tomorrow."

"Well, that *is* her job."

"It's a personal shoot. And this is the inspiration for it."

He holds up his phone. It's a screenshot of none other than the world's newest pop sensation in that dress and crown made of flowers. No bloody way.

"She also says she wants to talk to you," Connelly says. "She has a 'favour to ask'."

I frown at the floor for several moments. What could she want from me? Then my eyes drift to the open living room doorway. Of course. There could only be one thing.

6

New day, another groggy thinker. This is the worst I've had in a while. God, on top of my other bender, I drunk so much yesterday I'm surprised I made it to bed. Wait, what happened yesterday?

I fight the urge to close my eyes again, then apprehensively roll over in bed to check my phone. Why am I awake this early? I bring up YouTube. Tap on my channel. My jaw drops.

"What the fuck?" I shoot up in bed. Push past the pain in my skull. Connelly groans next to me. My chest tightens, as if trying to contain my erratic heart. "Two million!"

"What?" he croaks.

I can't tear my eyes from the impossible figure on the screen. "I have just over two million subscribers."

He shifts onto his side to face me. "Are you serious?"

"Yes!" I laugh from excitement. "That gold YouTube play button's mine now!"

He pulls himself up to peer at my phone. "You've got enough for two." Shock replaces his tired tone. I know I woke him up, but his alarm would've gone off soon. Anyway, just imagine two gold play buttons!

Must check Patreon. I open the app, and my hand smacks against my mouth. This is too surreal.

"What is it?" Connelly asks. He leans in closer again, and raises his voice: "Four-thousand-two-hundred-twenty-five patrons?"

I shake my thinker slowly in disbelief.

"How many did you have last night," he says, "just over a thousand?"

"Yeah," I manage to utter. After tax, I should earn about £3500, more than I've ever made in a month! And that's not even including the YouTube revenue. Now I really should add a higher donation tier than £1, but still need to think about what I could offer in return that doesn't overshadow Aki's benefits. Normally, I'd question how this happened. K-Rin may be the primary reason, but I'm too ecstatic to be annoyed about that at the moment.

"Congratulations," Connelly says at last, and rubs his eyes. "We should go out and celebrate."

I grin. "Awesome idea. Maybe tonight?"

"Sure." He reaches over to the bedside table for his phone then starts tapping and scrolling. "Where do you want to go?"

Need to go through all my messages. I bring up the private message menu on YouTube. Where should we eat? My eyebrows dart up. Nearly five-thousand messages. I can't cope. Do I fancy Japanese, Indian, Spanish, Mexican? Too many options, but for some reason I have the compulsion for food that'll blow my brains out. Really need someone to go through these damn messages. Won't have time today. Maybe we should just go out for drinks. No. I want food *and* drinks. Hopefully, my headache will disappear before then.

"Gold Lotus," I say.

He nods slowly. "Why am I not surprised?"

"You love it there too."

"Yeah." Think he'd look more thrilled about everything if he didn't seem like he's struggling to keep his eyes open. "I'll book a table when I get to work."

"Thanks."

I'd better get a move on if I'm to make it on time. I push myself out of bed and put my phone back on charge with the lead on the bedside table. Need as much juice as possible while I'm out, and I'll even bring my power bank this time.

Connelly climbs out of bed too, runs a hand through his short, messy hair, and scuffs to the wardrobe to take out his smart shirt. He looks shattered with those sunken eyes. Can't imagine what mine are like.

"How are you feeling after yesterday?" he asks.

I hold my thinker. "I know I drank a lot – that's for sure."

He pauses, and raises that judgemental eyebrow at me. Oh, no. Here we go.

"You do remember passing out in the park, right?" he says.

I stare at him for a few blank moments, then sickness and fear ripple through me. Flashes of wandering absolutely blotto with Aki to Brockwell Park. The searing pain in my eyes. Then nothing but darkness. How could I forget? Where did Aki go? Has he left me a message? Tried to call? I check my phone again. Well, it's a no for those last two. Did he really do a runner, or worse?

"Maddix?" Connelly says firmly. He's got that impatient frown now, still standing there awkwardly holding his shirt.

"Yeah, I remember."

No drinking today, until maybe later, of course. We still need to celebrate. Meanwhile, I have a big drive ahead of me, and a creature to

110

look after.

"Go careful today," Connelly says, and finally lays his shirt on the bed.

"Don't worry. I will."

He raises an eyebrow. "You sure you're up for it?"

I should be annoyed that he's doubting me, but I understand.

"Yep," I say.

He hesitates then says, "Call me if you need me."

I nod carefully.

"Also, I've been thinking," he adds. "I really think you should continue using Maddix A. in public where possible."

"Oh, I'm planning to."

"Good. The amount of attention you and that rabbit are getting..." He lays his shirt on the bed. "Has *anyone* been aggressive?"

"Not so far. Why?"

His face scrunches. "Huh. I imagine loads of them must be jealous, and when people get jealous, they can act out. You wouldn't believe the nasty shit I've had to remove from Kya's account."

That *is* saddening to hear, but he's right. I haven't considered the potential ramifications of their envy.

"Anyone who *has* expressed feeling like that has been fairly good-natured about it," I say. "From what I've seen, anyway."

"Hope it stays that way."

His anxiety is infectious. I'll have to keep an eye on the public's reactions, especially after today.

After jam on toast, painkillers, and a quick but careful hot shower, I struggle into my jumper, jeans, boots, and jacket then load Shinpi into his carrier case. He's compliant as always. Hasn't eaten much of his food, so I slip a carrot and some hay in next to him. I fill up the case's water bottle with fresh tap water, and now we're both set to go. Probably won't have to worry about him having any accidents since I still can't find evidence of droppings or bodily fluids, but I put a blanket in there with him anyway. Does this rabbit even have blood? Stupid thing to wonder, but he's not exactly natural, is he? Is he really an alien like Aki suggested? Freaks me out too much to entertain.

I've had to Google some things, but I'm pretty confident about this forty-five minute journey with my new pet. I place him on the front passenger seat with the case door facing me to keep an eye on him. He'll have the pleasure of watching me drive, too. The seat belt wraps firmly around the carrier. I've also set the aircon to cool – it's not hot in here, but apparently he might still overheat, so it's not worth risking. What if I crash and something bad happens to him? Will K-Rin hunt me down and slaughter me? I'll try not to think about it; just drive as safely as possible, and hope for the best.

All the way up the A23 through Brixton, a mixture of thoughts keep circling my mind. I'm still overjoyed but thrown and terrified by my subscriber and patron increase. What will this mean going forward? What if this K-Rin fascination dies fast, and people drop away from my channel and pull out of Patreon because they no longer want my content? I was getting by with my original support; guess I won't lose *everything*. You know what, though? I need to test this: maybe bring my originally scheduled part two video on Princess Preciosa's assassination forward again. See what their reaction is. I've always had more to say, and always will. I'm more than my discussions on K-Rin and her silly bunny-thing!

Seriously, though, why did she give *me* her rabbit? Why would she give it to anyone? She thought that would change my opinion of her? I know what I saw that night at Kya's party. Aki saw it too. Why's he now missing? Did she 'take care' of him? Is it my fault? How will the public react to me? Despite being branded a liar, many people still want to watch my videos – although only the K-Rin ones, I fear. I'm grateful for any kind of interest, but I need them to believe me. Need to look into Aki's disposable camera suggestion. Problem is: even if I can find a remotely cheap one, it'll still be too expensive. Can't ask Connelly for more money, and I won't. Need my payments to come through *now*! Could ask for help from my subscribers, I guess, but it'd be too embarrassing to admit I can't even afford a crappy, little disposable camera. I'll have to suspend the idea for now.

As I follow the traffic slowly over Waterloo Bridge, the low golden sun looks beautiful over the water. Calms me briefly. Wish I could down a few shots to kill my nerves. Screw my banging headache and sickness. Shame I pretty much only have buildings and cars to focus on for the rest of this drive in bloody stop-start traffic. You never do quite get used to it.

My phone vibrates in its stand on the windscreen. Mum again. She's never been so insistent to get hold of me. I did message her that I'd phone her later, but she obviously can't wait. Might as well get the conversation over with.

I answer with hands-free: "Hi, Mum."

That sounded robotic, but it's hard pretending to be happy to talk to her.

"Maddix! Me and your dad can't believe it. We saw on YouTube: you were on the BBC News!"

She seems delighted. I knew that's why she's been calling. Is she just congratulating me, though, or does she want something?

"Yes," I say, "and let me guess: you're so proud that you *had* to call now, despite it being, what, about five-thirty in the morning for you?"

"I couldn't sleep. It's all too exciting. You have so many subscribers now, though I honestly don't get how." There's that confidence in me I sorely missed. I had loads of them *before*! "Be careful with what you're saying about K-Rin."

I squeeze the steering wheel. That bitch got through to Mum too.

"At least you're watching my videos," I mutter.

"We're glad you're doing well. We really are. But you shouldn't lie to people. It's not right, or fair."

I roll my eyes. She'd likely be saying this whether brainwashed or not. "I'm not fucking lying. I never do–"

"–We both feel like you would benefit from counselling."

She's seriously cutting in with that? I get that my videos are hard to believe, but there's nothing wrong with me.

"You never believe anything I say." I brake for the hundredth time, and stop a little too close to the car in front. Huffing, I yank on the handbrake. "Did you really just call to berate me? 'Cause you're killing my mood."

"I did say we're happy for your success. But we're also worried."

I snarl out at the traffic ahead. "Since when did you start worrying about me?"

"Don't say that."

"Why not? As soon as I moved out for uni, you and Dad fucked off to Barbados and never came back."

We've already had this argument. It never gets resolved. Don't think it can.

"Please, stop thinking about it like that," she says curtly. Why isn't she reprimanding me? Is it the brainwashing?

"Just admit you couldn't wait to get away from me."

"I told you before: we were getting away from everything else there, and you had just started your own life."

You know, their reasons don't matter anymore. They hardly call. Never visit. Didn't come to the wedding. Didn't even post a card.

"I'm on my way to a photoshoot," I say. "My headache's getting worse. If you have nothing else to add, I need to go."

After an annoying pause, she says, "There's one thing."

"What?" I almost snap.

"If you get to meet K-Rin, let us know what she's like. And send pictures."

I squeeze the wheel tighter. Want to scream. She's unbelievable.

"Okay. Bye, Mum!" I jab the hang up button on the screen and huff again. "For fuck's sake."

That went about as well as I expected. Now I really could do with some shots.

Once I make it through King's Cross, the pace picks up. I turn into the final long road, and pass a range of old industrial buildings with discoloured bricks and shabby windows. Is this really the right place, or is the sat nav confused again? Parking bays line both sides of the road but the signs tell me they're for permit holders only. I keep going until I come level with a three-floored black-bricked building that looks in much better shape than the others: High Sky Studios. At least I made it here, even if a little late. I reverse-park into one of the couple spaces left in the parking bay just in front. The sign here says I need to call a number to pay. Sucks that it's not free, but it's not extortionate. I stick two hours on it, as I doubt I'll stay longer than that, and get out of the car.

I unload Shinpi from the passenger's side. He's still contentedly twitching his nose in his case. Hasn't even touched the carrot, or made any messes. Well, I'm relieved about that last part.

"Fucking weirdo," I mutter to him, then kick the car door shut and lock it with the remote.

We stand outside the big double frosted glass doors. I press the buzzer, and a man's voice speaks clearly through the circle of tiny dots on the intercom: "High Sky Studios."

"Hi. I'm here to join Kya. My name's Maddix A."

"Oh, yes. Please come in!"

That was incredibly enthusiastic.

The door unclicks. I push it open and squeeze in with the carrier. The young guy waves at me from behind a pale wood and marble counter. His eyes are brighter than the cream walls. I approach him with an uncomfortable feeling in my gut. Does he know who I am? Will he tell people I'm here? He grins down at the carrier in what looks like awe.

"Kya told me you were coming." He glances at me then back at the rabbit. "It's an honour to have you here."

I'll pretend he's solely aiming that at me.

"Thanks," I say. "Where can I find her?"

"She's on the first floor. Studio room three." He gestures in front of himself to the open A4 book on the counter. "Please sign in first, and I'll give you a lanyard."

I nod, and rest the case on the shiny floor while I fill in the diary with my name and car registration.

The guy leans forward and murmurs, "What's it like to be chosen by K-Rin?"

I feel like a celebrity myself now. So daunting. I just drop the pen back on the counter and sigh. "To be honest, it's still all very surreal."

He chuckles. "I bet. Well, if you need anything, let me know." He hands over the lanyard, I slip it around my neck, and he gestures again to his right. "You'll find the lift just over there."

"Thanks." I retrieve the case from the floor, make my way over to the lift, and press the button. Can almost see a clear reflection in its door. This place is pretty fancy for the road it's in. I've never been to a photography studio. Don't know how this one ranks with others in London, but it must be good if Kya uses it for her professional shoots.

During the ten-second ride up, several thoughts flash through my thinker: I still can't believe I have over two million subscribers and four thousand patrons; need to make a thank-you video; there are way too many comments and messages to sort through; need to contact Aki; can I record any footage of this photoshoot for my channel, and would Kya appreciate the extra publicity? I need another painkiller.

I emerge in a long bright corridor. As I move across the wooden flooring, I check behind to see if I'm tracking mud – thankfully, no. The walls are lined with abstract, colourful canvas works that blend portraits of beautiful models with neon light patterns. None of them have been untouched by a digital brush. They do look cool, though.

I pass studios 1 and 2, and find 3 at the end of the corridor. The heavy door opens to a large white room flooded with light from the floor to ceiling windows on the other side. Once I'm done gawping at the impressive overhead lighting rigs and big standing box lights I wish I could take home with me, I notice Kya getting her makeup done on the far right. I make my way over. Her gaze meets mine in the lit-up mirror attached to the counter she's sitting at. I have to double-take her: she's wearing a realistic long wavy golden wig that makes her look scarily identical to K-Rin, but she's still in her loose clothes.

Framed with blue eyeshadow and mascara, her eyes bulge at me. "Maddix. I'm glad you made it!"

I stop nearby and say hi to her and the makeup lady, who nods to me but doesn't so much as half-smile. Guess she's not one of my new fans. She plucks a little pallet of powder and a brush from the organised makeup mountain on the counter.

Kya swivels on the stool to grin down at Shinpi in his carrier. "He is mega cute. Thank you for bringing him."

"Mm-hmm."

The woman beside her raises an eyebrow. "I thought they don't allow pets in here."

Wow. Someone who's not jumping for joy at you, Shinpi – unless she's simply skilled at keeping her composure.

Kya straightens up. "They made a special exception considering he's a famous bunny."

I try not to roll my eyes at the ridiculous notion. "He won't make a mess, either."

"Really?" Kya turns her body towards the mirror again.

"Yep." They won't believe me if I tell them the real reason, so I say, "He's very well trained."

"Oh. Excellent."

"Hmm." The makeup lady leans in to dab Kya's cheeks with a pale shimmering powder. She's treating both Shinpi *and* me like we're normal. Is she one of the lucky unbrainwashed people?

"Excuse me," I say to her. "What colour do you think he is?"

She pauses. Stares at me as if unimpressed, almost the way Connelly does. "Is that a serious question?"

Why the surprise? Has she not seen my videos?

"Yes," I say bluntly.

She carries on prodding Kya with the brush. "White, of course."

Bugger.

I contain a sigh. "I would've thought you'd be happier to see him, then."

"I *am* happy, just busy." She sweeps the brush across Kya's cheeks. If

116

she *is* being genuine, it's refreshing and intriguing to see that not every brainwashed person turns incessantly hyper. Connelly was only like that for a short time then he was crashing hard. Affects everyone differently, I guess.

I place the carrier gently on the floor then look at Kya in the mirror. "What's *with* the K-Rin cosplay anyway? You don't normally dress up like other people."

"I know," she says. "But she's such an inspiration, and so beautiful."

She sounds besotted. Does she not care that I believe K-Rin may be forcing her to feel like that?

"Do you have a dress like what she was in yesterday?" I ask.

"I have something similar but I reckon it looks good enough considering the extremely short notice I gave my stylists."

"Okay."

Her smile fades. "Are you all right, Madd? You're not your usual self."

Can she tell how hungover I am? Do I still stink of it? I tried so hard to cover it up.

I shrug. "It's been a crazy few days."

The makeup lady fishes through a tiny black bag on the counter.

"Oh, yes." Kya's grin returns. "Massive congrats on the two million subscribers, and your mention on the news."

Smiling, I rub the back of my neck. "Thanks."

The lady holds up a small tube of lipstick and says to Kya, "Ready? We're almost done."

She nods, faces forward properly, and keeps still. Then once the woman's applied the subtle pink to Kya's lips, she stands back and seems to admire her work. She's definitely done a great job. I actually feel the hate bubbling inside me.

I wait on a fancy leather sofa in front of the windows while Kya gets into costume in another room and the photographer sets up his camera and tripod in here. Tempting to nap for a bit, but not in public, and I've been reading these private messages on my phone instead – have to sift through all this eventually. Several praise me on my recent success, but most not because of my new subscriber count. No, people are delighted, and still only modestly jealous, that K-Rin chose me as her pet's new guardian. I mean, really? Grateful as I am, this is still odd: no-one's being aggressive, like Connelly and I have been fearing. No doubt thanks to her request. All this gushing's down to her, though, and nothing I've personally accomplished. That tastes more bitter than this coffee.

One kind username has sent me links to several 'breaking news' articles, all discussing me! Breaking news? I'm heating up already. Titles screaming variations of 'Who is Maddix A.?' I'm a mystery now too. Never thought I'd see that. Seriously, *I'm* more important than this other story that's been pushed to the side about loads of criminals in prisons admitting to their crimes? What a shambles.

Reading on, seems some of the 'celebrities' who were at the party have come forward claiming they recognise me. Wonder if they think any higher of me? Of course, there's a strong rumour circulating these pages that I'm the same Maddix who's related to Kya. Didn't take them long. Kya's obviously doing that thing where she cuts herself off from the world while she works or she would've mentioned this earlier. Well, I'll certainly confirm the rumours with the video I'm planning today. I honestly don't know how to feel about all of the speculation and attention: excited, flattered, disturbed, or terrified. Either way, it's too much.

Looks like this guy's lapping it up, though. An article about the BBC presenter who met K-Rin pops up under the related news section. The picture shows his beaming face with the caption 'First person to publicly meet K-Rin after her worldwide debut expresses ecstatic new enthusiasm for life'. In my grogginess, I didn't even consider him. According to the article, he's been inundated with requests for information on K-Rin. Sounds familiar. But weirdly, he states the whole encounter's a blur for him now. All he knows is he's been left with a constant feeling of joy and appreciation for life that's inspired him to help others, saying everyone should do the same if they can. Good as that is, seems like he's experiencing the high that everyone got after hearing the song, except he now apparently feels nothing *but* joy. It's like any negative emotions bounce right off him. Ideally, that *would* be great, except it's not natural. He seems absolutely brainfucked.

That interview from yesterday apparently already has the second highest view count on YouTube. Fucking hell. That's ludicrous, and bizarre, especially as the rest of the top ten are music videos. She'll probably hit number one tomorrow. With that in mind, how do I not have even more subscribers?

I return to my messages and come across one I wish I'd seen yesterday. Sent around the time I passed out in that park, this is apparently from a

BBC journalist, asking for an interview. Is this real? They want to hear my reaction to being gifted Shinpi, how I know K-Rin, and how I feel generally about the whole situation. Guess it makes sense for them to reach out to me next, and isn't too shocking considering all those articles on me. But would it do me any good? Should I ignore it? I can't deal with this!

The door up ahead opens. I straighten up, discard the coffee mug on the unit beside the sofa, and slide my phone away. Kya strides out in her colourful flower dress. Her bare feet tap quietly across the floor. We never did see K-Rin's feet in the interview; who knows what her shoes looked like, if she even wore any? Kya's golden wig glows in the sunlight. I genuinely think she's prettier than K-Rin, even with those fake wavy locks. The blasphemy levels would be unreal if my viewers heard me admit that.

Kya flashes a passing smile at me. I can only stare. Now she's closer, they really have nailed the look. The dress is maybe slightly longer, and the flowers don't quite cover the whole thing. The thin patches of black netting give the dress a more varied texture, and again, I think I prefer it to K-Rin's. She walks to the area between the large white backdrop and the photographer's setup.

"Let's do some solo shots," he says, fiddling with the lens on his big camera, "then we'll bring the rabbit over."

Kya grins over at me. "You got that, Maddix?"

I nod.

Another lady comes out of the back room. Think she's Kya's assistant or stylist – I've seen her before, and definitely spotted her at the party. In flared pin-striped trousers, she clip-clops over to them. Doesn't even glance my way. I'd just smile awkwardly anyway. The photographer points over at the main door. The assistant nods and shakes her hips from side to side over there. If she's playing to the two guys in here, it won't work on me. She flicks a switch, and the blinds behind me start quietly rolling down. The room descends into darkness, save for the box lights pointed at Kya.

Leaning on the arm of the sofa, I watch her standing silently for several moments. The photographer's poised in position, but doesn't say anything either. Don't they normally point and order models around? Kya gazes out, unblinking, glowing in the darkness. Holds her non-thinker high. Her eyebrows relax. A content expression washes over her.

The camera flashes, and again. She stares straight at it. Her smile seems different: genuinely happy. The longer I watch, the camera flashes slow down, like in slow-motion. The room fills with light, peaceful air. It seeps into me, and I soak it up. Thoughts disappear.

Kya outstretches her arm to me. Takes me a few moments to register what she wants. I push myself off the sofa. Carefully pick up the case. Take it over to her. Thinker still feels light. I gently lower myself, place it on the floor, and pull open the grated flap. Grinning, she crouches and holds out upturned hands. Shinpi hops out. She scoops him into her arms and slowly stands. He's just as well behaved with her. I close the case, move backwards with it out of the light, and leave it on the floor by my feet. I stay standing, behind the camera and just off to the side. Watch the flashes capture the peaceful, proud K-Rin holding her beloved rabbit. She makes sure his head faces toward the camera. He twitches his nose, as always, and isn't fazed by any of it.

Something burns in me. The longer I look at them, the worse it gets. Darkness fogs my mind. I've never felt like this. It terrifies me, but also feels so natural. Takes several more camera flashes of those glorious smirks before I realise what I'm feeling:

Deep, endless spite, so dark I see nothing else.

My fingers itch to prise the bunny away from Kya. Can't explain why. As soon as I do, I practically shove him back inside the carrier, and all I can think is: why were you so well behaved? Thankfully, Kya doesn't seem to pick up on my weirdness and pushes on as normal. She asks if I can send Connelly the 'sneak preview' images to post on her Instagram tonight. The photographer says he'll get the edited photos to her by tomorrow. Now that's dedication. He must've taken hundreds with the amount that flash went off.

Anyway, I need to get out of here before my bad mood makes me say or do something I'll regret. I grab Shinpi, say goodbye, and Kya thanks me with great enthusiasm. It's hard to even look at her on the way out. What's wrong with me?

Once I emerge outside in the fresh air, the dark fog slowly but surely starts to clear. I take a long, steadying breath.

As I drive down the boring stretch of Caledonian Road, I call Connelly on the hands-free.

"Hey," he says, and sighs. "How'd the photoshoot go?"

I pass under the rail bridge. The brief shade comforts my aching thinker. When I get home, I'll definitely have a nap.

"Kya's stylists did a brilliant job," I say.

"As always. Did the rabbit behave?"

I glance at him in his case on the passenger seat. Why was I so angry about that? "Yep. Even more proof that this thing isn't real."

Connelly laughs so quietly I barely hear it. Guess he still can't get his thinker around this.

"I'll send you some pics when I get back," I say. "Kya wants them up tonight."

"Oh. Okay."

Everyone's reactions will be interesting.

"By the way," he continues, "don't suppose you've had a chance to see, but there are articles about you."

"I did see. And I'm a bit overwhelmed, to be honest. It's only a matter of time before they figure out who I am. They're already onto a winner."

"Mm." He sounds guarded as ever. While I understand that, I would've thought he'd congratulate my growing popularity like he did yesterday.

I glance either side of the road at the endless restaurants, pubs, shops, and miscellaneous businesses built into town houses. Nice to see the council's continued attempt at making this place greener by dotting trees along the pavements.

"How's work going?" I ask. "You're not rushing me off the phone. I assume things are relatively calm?"

"No. I need a break. Hardly anyone else is doing any fucking work. Just sitting there talking about you know who."

I frown hard at the road. "Seriously?"

"Yeah." He sighs again. "I'm trying my best not to engage in it. We've got to get this new marketing campaign live across all platforms by the end of the week. And I'd love to chat all day too, but *someone's* got to work on this or we'll all be in deep shit."

"Can you not report this to your manager?"

"I would, but he's slacking off too!"

"Then you can't get in trouble, right?"

"I dunno, man. But I'd better get back to it. I'll see you later, yeah? I booked us a table at The Gold Lotus for seven o'clock."

I can't help grinning at that last part. "Okay. Thanks. See you later."

I'll tell him about the interview request from BBC when he gets home. I still haven't even decided.

"Bye," he says, and hangs up.

I hate hearing him stressed. How can he be expected to do all the work? Makes me want to march to that office and slap sense into everyone. Well, hopefully he can unwind tonight.

Shinpi goes straight back in the hutch when we get home. The carrier's spotless. How is there not even one speck of hay or carrot left? I wasn't joking when I said to Aki I reckon the thing will explode from all this eating and no shitting. In fact, I've never actually seen him eating, or drinking, or sleeping... This needs to be rectified, and I have a sneaky idea how.

I slot a new fully-charged battery in my camera, and place the other on charge. Set the tripod in front of the hutch and lower it so the camera has a perfect view of Shinpi. I'm going to catch you tonight, you little bugger. I'll leave the studio light on as even if the camera had night vision, the image would be grainy as hell. I just won't mention it to Connelly or he'll bite my head off about wasting electricity.

Wish I could implement the same technique with capturing Shinpi's hair growing back, but I'd have to keep him completely still for at least half an hour and make sure the camera's zoomed in close enough to see. Don't think it'd be wise to touch him again, though, if K-Rin really was warning me, and unsure how far he'll trust me anyway after the stunt Aki and I pulled. What the hell happened to the guy, for Christ's sake? Most of his visit yesterday's a blur. I was blackout drunk, but shouldn't have been. How did it all go so wrong?

In the kitchen, I peek inside the recycling bag we keep on the floor by the doorway. His energy cans are here. I could do with another caffeine hit, actually. God, that coffee at the photography studio was vile. Anyway, yesterday's vodka bottle is here too, empty. Now I *know* I shared this with Aki. He only had a little booze, I think, which means I must've had most of the bottle. He said we were chatting for two hours after we got out Shinpi, but I don't remember a single detail. I must've carried on drinking, but I've never been too drunk to remember what I've done. First time for everything, I guess.

I bring out my phone. Still no return messages or voicemails from him. Maybe he decided to ditch me. He got what he wanted: a peek into my life, and his five minutes of fame on a collaboration video. But he seemed too enthralled by this K-Rin mystery to run away already. Did he black out in the park too? No. He had nowhere near enough booze. Talking of which, a few shots would definitely calm me, and I have another bottle in the cupboard. I sigh and shake my thinker. Have to leave the stuff alone, at least until later. For now, I need to nap so I can have a clear thinker for scanning through more messages.

*

Buzzing down the hallway wakes me. It's not that lady from upstairs again, is it? No, she would've knocked. This person's buzzing us from outside the flat building. Whoever it is has disturbed the wonderful nap I was having. As I pull myself out of bed, I check my phone. It's been about three hours. I do feel much better than earlier, at least.

I leave the flat and notice a delivery guy through the glass of the main door. Connelly's egg has arrived. Perfect. I take it into the flat and leave it on the kitchen side.

Staring at a screen for a while might only bring back my grogginess, but needs must. I return to the studio with a pint of water. Load up YouTube on the computer and nearly spray my water across the keyboard. Just over a thousand more subscribers since this morning! And the view counts of my K-Rin videos have skyrocketed. I sit in awe for a brief time, unsure how to process it, or the influx of messages.

Need to send out a thank-you to everyone. Just a short handheld video will suffice. I pull out my phone, bring up the camera, and hold it in front of my face. Use the camera as a mirror to flatten some hair that still sticks up from my nap. I do look a lot more fresh-faced after my nap, so let's do this.

Raising my eyebrows, I sigh with a grin and tap record. "What's up, everyone?" Why did I say that again? Oh, what the hell? Roll with it. "Well, I just want to say thank you to everyone who's subscribed to my channel and/or my Patreon, as well as, of course, those who have continued to support me. Bloody hell, guys! I did not expect this." I run a hand through my hair and glance away briefly. "You have no idea what this means. I honestly thought I was going to...aggravate a lot of people. And, well, I have, but most of you seem really intrigued by what I have to say on this whole K-Rin situation."

I clear my dry throat. "Some of you have been asking why did she give her bunny to me, do I secretly know her, and stuff. The answer is: I have no effing clue why she wants me to look after her rabbit. I had no say in that. I've never met her. I wish I had a way to contact her. I have *so* many questions. But, honestly, I *am* grateful for all this because it's drawn so much attention to this channel that it's almost unreal." I hold up two fingers. "Two million subscribers. Seriously, I am bloody stoked."

I chuckle to myself, then feel dirty. As much as I *am* stoked, I *hate* the method in which I gained the popularity. Shouldn't admit that, though.

"Let me know if you want to see anything in particular – eg. more of the the bunny, other conspiracies you want me to cover, or whatever. I'll keep you all up to date with anything else that happens." I straighten up. "On that note, thank you again, everyone. Until next time."

I stop recording. That won't take long to upload. I transfer it to the computer, and while it's processing on YouTube, I open a separate tab. Just remembered my plan of bringing my second Princess Preciosa video forward. I schedule it for tomorrow evening. Now we'll have to wait and see whether it gets more views and likes than usual, or less.

Unfortunately, my ever-growing list of private messages still awaits me, so I check them out. Most people ask the same things:

'How did you really get K-Rin's rabbit?'

'Why you?'

'What's it like being chosen?'

'Did you really see a different version of the video?'

'Will you tell us if you hear something different when the song officially releases?'

'Can you show us more of the bunny? Does he have a name?'

'How long have you known K-Rin? What's she like?'

It's quite overwhelming. Hopefully, my latest video will answer most of that. But I feel like I'll need to put together a Q and A, or I'll just be endlessly copying and pasting the same responses to everyone. That reminds me: a bunch of people *have* been asking me to follow that trend of answering the top 5 Google questions about myself. I haven't even looked – been quite anxious about it. Suppose I could at least check them out; if all the recent positive comments are anything to go by, Google shouldn't throw up anything too nasty.

I bring up a new tab for the search engine. Type in the phrase 'is Maddix A' and a list of auto-completed search options appear underneath:

'Is Maddix A telling the truth about K-Rin?'

There it is. But the fact that they *have* to ask that question is a promising sign.

'Is Maddix A going to do a video with K-Rin?'

If only. Maybe then I could shake her and force her to admit *her* lies.

'Is Maddix A going to make another video with K-Rin's rabbit?'

Well, they won't have to wait long for that answer.

'Is Maddix A in London?'

Of course people are looking for me, and all for one reason, I imagine.

'Is Maddix A insane?'

That question was bad enough on my old conspiracy videos, let alone being asked enough times in Google to make the top 5!

All of these pretty much relate to K-Rin in some way. Makes me want to scream.

Fuck this. Today should be about celebrating. I just wish Aki could join me. Will he see this new video? Will he reply to any of my calls or messages? Should I be more worried about him?

I pull out my phone, and stare at his name on my call list. Is it worth trying to ring him again? Guess there's no harm. So I do, and nearly jump out of my seat. Vibrations, behind the curtain. I spin in the chair and yank the curtain aside. Where the hell's it coming from? Did he seriously leave his phone here? My listeners lead me to the sofa. I kneel and shove my arm under the cushions. My hand finds it down the edge. Shit. No wonder he didn't answer.

After patting the cushions back in place, I plonk my butt on the sofa and hang up the futile call. I turn his phone over and study it. Didn't notice yesterday, but it's literally the same make and model as mine – I know it's a popular brand, but still. If this has been here all along, it only reinforces the burning question: where the fuck is he? Wouldn't he have come back for it?

I tap the power button on the side of the phone. Strangely, he has a plain black lock screen wallpaper. Battery's nearly dead. I return behind the curtain, sit at the desk, and plug my charger lead into it. No lock on the phone, so I load up the home screen. I know I shouldn't pry, but the guy's missing and something on here has to help.

I frown at the screen. The only apps he has are: Calendar, Camera, Clock, Mail, Maps, Messages, Phone, Photos, Safari, Settings, and YouTube. He's deleted everything else? No games, even? I bring up Photos: nothing in it. Messages: one chat log, between me and him. Really? Phone: only calls are to and from me, and I'm his singular contact. What the fuck? What about his parents? Did he get this just for me? Is it a burner phone?

Expensive one, if so. This tells me absolutely nothing about him. My stomach twists uncomfortably. This is getting scarier, and now I don't know what to think.

Out of interest, I bring up the YouTube app and it automatically signs in as him. I might be able to get some personal details from here. I open his account settings. Here's his e-mail address. Maybe I could check his e-mails, then. Can't believe I'm even considering that, but I've come this far. I can't find his home address on this list, of course, as it only shows the country under Location. I know he's from Lambeth, but I'm not exactly going to scour the place up and down for him. So it's time to try his e-mails.

The Mail app logs straight in. I nearly sigh with relief, but I'll wait until it's proven useful. My eyebrows shoot up. Inbox is empty. Junk and Deleted Items are too. Did the guy clear it all out, or is he that good at staying on top of it? Surely he'd keep something? Nothing in Sent, either. No subfolders. Bloody bizarre. There's only one more thing to try, and I can't do it from the app. Need to log into his account through the website, and that won't let me in automatically. I'd have to hack my way in, just to find an address that he may or may not have listed in his account settings.

I shouldn't be doing this. Aki knows where I live. If he wants the phone back, he can come and get it. But if something's happened to him, well, what should I do? With no-one on his contact list, how am I supposed to tell anyone? Maybe I should wait a day or two, then hand the phone to the police and they can take it from there.

For now, actually, there's one more thing to search for: any social media accounts. He may not have the apps, but he could have an account. So on the computer, I bring up Facebook, Instagram, and Twitter. Searching his name on all three brings up results, but none of the profile pictures or locations match. This particular Akihiro Tamotsu doesn't have a social media presence. No e-mails, photos, or contacts. No messages, either, other than those between us. It feels like he did exist, but now doesn't. Am I going nuts? Or is he, or someone else, trying to make him disappear?

7

My thinker needs to slow down. Can't help fretting over Aki or any of this K-Rin insanity. I want to be psyched about tonight, but now I'm going nuts over how me posting this new video is breaking news! Every site I check, I'm the top story: the fact that I uploaded something. 'Maddix A. Thanks Fans for 2 Million Subscribers' and all variations of. Wish I could feel excited about that, but it's mostly terrifying and ridiculous; they're only that hyped about it because I might mention new information about their beloved princess or her bunny!

Might indulge in those shots now, to take the edge off. I've nearly finished getting ready to go out. Got on my best black jeans and red button-up check shirt. Just need to gel my hair. Connelly will be back soon, but I've time to grab a beverage.

I head to the kitchen, take out my bottle of vodka, and plonk it on the side. Stare at it for a while. At first, I'm not sure why. The longer I look at it, the less I want it. What's up with me? Too worried to drink? The idea of it turns me right off. Okay, well, I still need *something*.

Connelly has no wine left in the fridge – not that I'd dare touch it. It *would* be better if I turn up to the restaurant sober anyway. Oh, there's still a can of Monster here. If Aki drops by again, I could buy him another one. I've never been big into these, but it'll certainly be refreshing and energising. So I pull out the can, pierce it open, and push the fridge shut. The whoosh of fizz from the can resonates in me. It's a strange feeling of familiarity. As it slides down my throat, the fruity bubbles kick straight into my system. Bloody hell. It's better than I thought. In fact, it's fantastic, which makes it the first fizzy drink I've loved.

Gulping from the can, I make my way into the bathroom next door. I sigh with satisfaction then rest the can on the edge of the bathtub. Using the mirror in front of the window, I dip my fingers into the gel pot and run them through my hair. I've already shaved the stubble from my face and dabbed on some aftershave, so I'm about ready to hit The Gold Lotus with Connelly and celebrate.

I step back to study my reflection. Tilt my thinker and frown. Thought maybe I'd look at myself with pride from my recent success. I do feel it, of course, but what's stronger is a sense that I'm missing something, that things still need doing, that this is only the beginning.

As Connelly drives us down the straight lamp-lit road through Tulse Hill, I sort through my private YouTube messages on my phone. More and more congratulations, and people honestly can't get enough of that damn rabbit. Well, I remembered to press record before we left and I'll leave it running all night. I'll catch him in the act, doing whatever it is he does to make that food and water disappear. It has to be an act, and everyone else will see. But as with the hair thing, do I really want to show the public? If they believe it, they might see him for the freak of nature he is and have less interest in my channel. Or maybe they'll have more.

"You *are* feeling up to this, right?" Connelly asks.

"Yeah. Why? Do I not look like I am?" I thought I'd scrubbed up well enough.

"Actually, I can't believe how quickly you've bounced back from what happened in the park."

"Mm. It's weird. I had a massive headache this morning and felt a bit sick, but after a nap, I'm fine now."

And very grateful for it.

"Huh," Connelly says. "What did your mum want, by the way?"

I nearly sag. I'd managed to block her from my mind until now.

"She was like, 'Well done for getting on the news but stop lying to people.'"

"Oh. Right. At least she called, I guess."

I'm just surprised she didn't insist that she and Dad look after Shinpi instead. That would've been the perfect ending to a shitty conversation.

I scoff. "I don't want to think about her right now."

Hopefully, he'll take the hint and drop it. I already feel the anger sizzling in my chest.

"How's it going on the channel?" he says.

"Pretty crazy. I'm *breaking news* again. Just because I posted a thank-you video. Can you believe that?"

He nods slowly. "With how mental everything is at the moment, yeah."

"A BBC journalist asked me to do an interview earlier as well. Don't know if I should, though."

"Oh." He actually sounds impressed by this. "Well, they must want to hear your side of things. It'd probably be a good opportunity to reach more people, too."

"Yeah. But either way, I'm getting more subscribers by the minute. I'll probably reach two-and-a-*half* million by the end of the night."

He sniggers. "Dinner's on you."

"Hey, I won't get paid until about another two weeks. For now, my wallet's just as light as usual."

Especially after the amount of vodka I've bought this month already.

He huffs. "It shouldn't be this early in the month."

There he goes again. Thing is: I know he's right, but hate that he is.

"Hang on a second," he says. "Are you expecting me to pay for this?"

I stare at the blurry text on my phone, not even reading it. All I want to do is shrink into myself. "No."

After several horrible moments, he bites out, "You are such a liar."

That word makes me burn all over and want a strong drink. Too many usernames have thrown it at me. The issue here is: I did lie this time.

"I'm sorry, okay?" I try to say as genuinely as possible. Still can't look at him, though.

He scoffs, which also triggers me because it tells me my apology means nothing to him. "Surely you can contribute a tenner? A fiver? Otherwise, dinner's definitely on you *next* time we go out, all right?"

"Yeah," I mutter. I do agree it's only fair, but I can't offer anything otherwise I can't get more petrol this week. Even then, I won't be able to put much in, but hopefully enough to get me around quickly to any necessary places. Anything could happen surrounding this K-Rin situation. Food *will* be on me, though, at some point.

"I might not have space left later for that egg," he says, with residual spite.

I scroll through my messages again. "That's okay. No rush, obviously."

But you'd better still eat it.

"It does look lush," he says.

I manage a smile. "I knew you'd like it."

Watching the line of trees and flat blocks pass by is a welcome break from the phone screen, and our conversation. But I promptly get back to sifting through the messages as the drive will be over soon and I don't want to do this in the restaurant.

"You had any weirdos contact you yet?" he asks.

"I've had multiple requests to meet up, but I haven't replied."

"Mm. I suppose you haven't heard from Aki?"

"Nope." Oh, I haven't told him yet. I pull Aki's phone out of my jacket. "He left his phone at ours."

Connelly glances at it with a frown. "You'd think he would've come back for it."

I won't mention that the only stuff on it seems to relate to me – don't want to freak him out.

"We'll see," I say.

"Anyway, did you have to bring that? Leave it in the car."

I almost scoff but hold it in. Like hell I will. I just tell him, "Okay," and slip it in the side of the door for now.

We reach Brixton Car Park within ten minutes. I love how close this place is; we only have to walk five minutes down the high street. I appreciate Connelly letting me link arms with him as we stroll through the dim sunset past several multi-storey office buildings. Not the poshest area, but not the worst in Brixton, that's for sure. If my channel continues to grow at this rate, we might be able to afford a bigger flat. We both want one, so I know he wouldn't refute it.

Ignoring the spattering of lingering car fumes, the cool, refreshing air clears my thinker. I love nights like this. When we're out and about on the city streets, it feels like anything's possible.

We pass under a bridge, cross the T-junction, and hit the first set of high street shops. Most of them are shut, of course, but it means we get to appreciate the detailed, colourful graffiti artwork sprawled across the roller shutters: abstract shapes, people's faces, dogs with top hats. The street doesn't seem as busy as usual, though; plenty of restaurants are still open, and glancing inside, not many people are dining out tonight. It *is* a Tuesday, and we normally go out on Fridays, to be fair. The roads are emptier too. It's a little odd, but makes our walk more pleasant, at least.

The Gold Lotus sits under a long row of flats. In a way, I wish we lived in one of them – all we'd have to do is go downstairs for instant great food and drinks. Especially now I've had this pay-rise. Wouldn't be as special after a while, though.

We unlink arms to step into the big open-planned restaurant. Haven't been here for a couple of months, but the place hasn't changed: still bathed in a warm orange glow, tables lined up perfectly with bigger ones in the middle and smaller ones against the floor to ceiling windows, extensive bar along the back wall, and that lush, spicy aroma. Only a few couples are in here, so it's quiet, save for the calming flute music in the background.

One of the regular chirpy waiters comes over to greet us, but if it's possible, his smile's wider than ever. "Maddix, Connelly, we have been anxiously awaiting your arrival. Welcome!"

Both our eyebrows dart up. Not surprised that he recognises us by now, but the eagerness? Can only guess it has something to do with me being *breaking news*. Even the other waiters stop to grin over at us. Should we be scared or flattered? Connelly and I just smile and say, "Hello."

The waiter picks out two menu cards from the wall then takes us across the shiny dark floorboard to our two-seater table in the centre of the line of windows. The other patrons watch us too. Do they know who I am? I try to ignore them and drape my jacket over my chair. Connelly does the same, revealing the grey waistcoat he wore to Kya's party, but with a white shirt underneath instead of blue. He always looks smarter than me, but I never really try. We sit and pull ourselves in against the table. The waiter places down the menus then straightens up with his hands clasped to his chest. I can't help smiling.

"Just to let you know," he says, "everything is on us tonight."

I stare at him for several moments. Did he really say that?

"Are you sure?" Connelly asks, just as baffled as me.

"Oh, yes. You have been here many times. We want to show our gratitude. Besides, any friend of K-Rin's is a friend of ours."

I force myself not to frown. Do they seriously believe I'm her friend? Well, guess I should play along.

"Thank you very much, then," I say.

"Yes," Connelly says. "Thank you."

The guy goes on, "Maddix, we have all subscribed to your channel."

I exchange a shocked look with Connelly then glance at the other waiters, who still watch me with big smiles. Everyone else ogles us too, with intrigue, I think. It's quiet enough in here for them to hear our conversation. I'd normally be slightly bothered by this, but right now I feel an overwhelming pride and appreciation.

"Thank you," I say to them all.

The guy nods to a colleague, who briskly heads to the bar. "To celebrate your two million subscribers, please accept something from us, on the house."

The other waiter comes over and places a bottle of Moët and Chandon on the table. This takes us both aback. On the house? The stuff's worth about £50. We thank them again. Not exactly going to turn down a free bottle of decent champagne!

"You want to crack this open now," Connelly asks me, "or wait 'til we get home?"

"Oh, I'm very much up for opening it now."

So they kindly pour us a glass each, slot the bottle in an ice bucket, and leave us to read through the menus. All the waiters have resumed working, and the other tables are chatting and eating again. The fruity champagne slides beautifully down my throat, leaving that pleasantly slight afterburn. Smiling, I sigh.

Connelly leans forward and mutters, "You're like a celebrity now. It's crazy."

"I know, right?" Grinning, I sip more champagne, and he does too. I honestly never thought this day would come, especially from having a channel about conspiracies. Suppose it's mainly thanks to K-Rin. When she's not a hot topic anymore, will people still want my videos? I shake myself. Can't keep worrying about that. I'll deal with it when it comes. For now, I need to make the most of this.

"Excuse me." A tall guy in a white buttoned-up shirt and smart trousers appears beside our table with his hands clasped in front of him. "Hello. I am the manager here."

We say hello. He's not about to tell us the staff made a mistake and we'll have to pay for the champagne, right? Judging by his lit-up eyes, I doubt it.

"As the others have already probably told you," he says, "we very much appreciate your continued patronage. And we were wondering if you would be okay with us taking a picture of you together at the table tonight?" I nearly ask him to repeat, and feel Connelly's wary expression without even looking at him. The manager explains, "This would be to display on our wall. You're the first celebrity to dine with us."

He actually said it, and directly to me. Surely Connelly will end up being famous by association? Anyway, he and I exchange glances as if trying to communicate with each other. I don't have too much of an issue with it – guess I'm shocked and flattered more than anything else. It'll help boost their business, I'm sure. Connelly seems reluctant then smiles nervously.

"Sure," I say to the manager as pleasantly as possible. "It's the least we can do."

Especially since they're gifting us a free meal tonight.

His face bursts with excitement. "Thank you very much. One second, then, please."

He disappears off. I brace myself for whatever Connelly's been dying to say.

"We're going on the wall," he murmurs. "Is this really happening?"

"To be honest," I say, "I'm struggling to wrap my thinker around *any* of this."

He nods intensely and sips his champagne.

The manager soon returns with a digital camera – nothing as fancy as mine but decent nonetheless. He directs us to stay with our bodies facing towards the table and thinkers towards the camera, and asks us to pose as if clinking our glasses together. I grin as big as I can without being scary, and hope Connelly's at least put on his friendly face. Once a few shots have been taken, the manager thanks us profusely then leaves again. I couldn't even get a word in to thank him for their offer of paying for our meal. I'll mention it on the way out.

People are watching, of course. Wonder if they're jealous or simply in awe? If Connelly's noticed them, he's clearly ignoring them.

"Okay, now that insanity is over." He peruses the menu then snaps it shut. "No point looking, really. Already know what I want."

I'd agree, but I'm viewing my favourites without any keenness. Not sure why. I really do fancy something different, and more thrilling.

When the waiter returns, Connelly orders his standard vegetable gyoza, yaki udon, and soda water. But I go for the fiery lamb skewers, Korean Wings of Fire, and a can of Red Bull. Connelly frowns at each request, and waits for the guy to leave before questioning me:

"You know you ordered the spiciest stuff on the menu, right?"

Smiling, I lean back, sip more champagne, and say, "Yep."

"I thought you hated lamb, too."

"I haven't had it in years, and I just really fancy trying it again."

It *is* £3 dearer than the chicken and peanut satay, but hey, tonight it's free.

"And since when do you drink Red Bull?" he asks.

I smirk at him over the rim of my glass. "There a problem with that?"

His eyebrows relax but he continues to stare at me. "No."

I can't explain it, but that can of Monster I had at home's given me a craving for it. Mixing energy drinks and booze will be interesting.

Connelly nurses his champagne then pulls out his phone. After tapping the screen a couple times, his eyes widen, and he says, "Kya's photoshoot teaser's doing well on Instagram. Over two-hundred thousand likes already. I posted it not even an hour ago."

I gaze at all the tiny bubbles in my glass, how they rise to the top and burst one by one. "What's she hoping to get out of this?"

"Same thing as you, I guess. More followers, support, and exposure."

Huh. Seems like we're both using K-Rin for our own gain.

"Well," I say, and raise my glass, "this one's on K-Rin. Thank you *very* much, wherever you are."

He chuckles a little and raises his glass too. I do feel a tad sick thanking her, but try not to dwell on it.

Oh, man, Connelly having his phone out's reminded me I haven't checked Aki's. There's no subtle way to do this, so I lean around the chair to rummage in my jacket pocket. I pull it out and try to check it as quickly as possible, but of course, Connelly's on me like a shot.

"You brought that fucking thing in here?" he mutters. "I told you to leave it in the car."

No messages. No calls. I sigh and clumsily stuff it away.

"Sorry," I say. "But he could contact at any moment for all we know."

That disappointed glare. Fuck. I ruined things again, but I needed to, for my peace of mind, although now he's pissed at me again and it's not like I can drag him to the men's for a quickie. God, I need to stop thinking like that.

"What is wrong with you?" he whispers. "We finally get to spend some time together and you're more concerned about that fucking phone. You're always buried in technology. Hiding out in that bloody studio. You don't even eat with me anymore."

I grow hot. More shit he's been harbouring. Keep telling him he needs to mention this stuff sooner to avoid this happening.

"I've been busy with the channel," I say. "And it's easier to eat at my desk."

He shakes his thinker. Need to break the tension, especially now we have an audience. Be romantic. Win him over. Just do it quickly. I hate that I suck at this.

"I'm sorry, Conn. I'll make more of an effort. Maybe we can even cook together again, like we used to." The words trail out of my mouth. He stares intensely at me. I'm not sure how, but the words just keep coming: "After ten years, I should treat you better. Should treat *myself* better." I reach out and hold his hand gently on the table. "Just know that I *am* going to make things right."

134

He blinks, frowns, then raises his eyebrows. "Where did that come from?"

Honestly, I have no sodding clue, but I'll take it. I just squeeze his hand and smile.

When the starters arrive, Connelly carefully chews his vegetable gyoza parcels. I power through the lamb skewers. Despite their spiciness, they taste amazing – in fact, it's *because* of it. I've always hated too much spice. Don't know how my palette's suddenly changed. In any case, I'm loving the food so far, and that's all that matters.

We're getting through the champagne pretty quickly. Well, I am. Connelly's limiting himself to a single glass, as he's driving. A few of these get me sloshed, even with food to soak it up. Connelly's glass makes him grin adorably. Doubt they'd give us a second bottle for free, so I might move on to a cocktail next.

In the corner of my hazy vision, I swear I spot people holding up their cameras to us at various points. I utter this to Connelly and he says it's possible but just ignore it and don't draw attention. How is he not more annoyed? Maybe the champagne's made him more tolerating. Or perhaps he thinks I'm making it up and he's playing along. People are definitely still watching us. It does unnerve me but at the same time continues to fill me with flattery, especially since some nearby tables have ordered the exact starters as me. Can't be a coincidence. I just smirk into my glass.

My main dish is certainly far from healthy, coated in this sticky sweet and spicy sauce. But my God, these are the best chicken wings I've ever had. They make the duck I normally order plain and dull. I have to keep rinsing my mouth with the champagne and Red Bull to manage the burning, but man, it's worth it.

As Connelly sucks up his noodles, he regards me with a frown. "You're bloody insane."

I snigger and lick the sauce off my fingers. "You sure you don't want to try any?"

"They're all yours."

I don't get how this isn't unbearable. It's possibly the best meal I've ever had.

Once our plates are cleared, I read through the cocktail menu with dazed eyes.

"You not going for The Old Fashioned?" Connelly says.

"Mm. Nah. After all that spice, I need something sweet."

So I call over the waiter and request the sweetest drink on the menu: The Amazing 'O'.

The waiter nods with a knowing smile.

"Oh, man," Connelly says amusedly, "what's in that?"

I snap the menu shut. "Vodka, Kahlúa, Baileys, Amaretto, and whipped cream."

He raises his eyebrows, and when the waiter leaves, he says, "Very fancy."

"What can I say?" I neck back the last of my champagne. "I'm a fancy bitch."

He laughs, and the way his nose crinkles turns me on a little. "What's got into you tonight?"

I rest back. "I'm just really happy."

Or drunk. I can't always tell the difference.

I swear they put extra booze in that cocktail because I can barely feel my legs. I'm not as drunk as yesterday, but I'm getting there. Have to keep hold of Connelly's arm on the walk back to the car. He tried leaving a tip as we left, but they refused it. They've been so generous. I want to stay out all night. Don't know where exactly we'd go next, but maybe we don't need to go anywhere. I'd love to just sit and bask in the cool, fresh night air. Connelly probably wants to go straight home. It *is* a work night.

"Wanna try popping in somewhere else?" I say. "Who knows? We might get more freebies."

"I think we should head home, to be honest," he says, predictably. "Don't take this the wrong way, but I'm surprised you're being treated this nicely considering your stance on K-Rin. And it definitely got busier in there than usual."

I scoff. "Well, the lovely lady did tell everyone not to disrespect me."

"Hmm. I mean, The Gold Lotus might've been a lucky exception. You should try a random place."

"Yeah."

I spot a bar on the other side of the high street. Barely remember to look both ways before pulling Connelly over there.

"I didn't mean now," I hear him say, but plough on. Don't even notice what the place is called. Go in anyway.

Dim purple and yellow lighting. Slow, steady dance beat with synth arpeggios alternating between minor and major. Decent vibe, and at a moderate volume for once. Place has that musty, sharp booze smell. Makes me crave shots. Fair amount of people in here, and some are staring at us already. Normally, I'd feel slightly intimidated, but being recognised has had its perks so far tonight.

I manage to nab a spot at the bar. Connelly squeezes on the end next to me. My hazy, hungry eyes scan the rainbow smudge of bottles. Need something exciting. I can do vodka shots at home.

"Excuse me," the guy beside me calls above the music.

My gaze trails to him: some young 20s lad, shorter than me, of course, with a pretty glint from the reflected light in his eyes. He grips the shiny bar with both hands.

"You're Maddix A., right?" he asks. "The YouTuber."

He doesn't seem aggressive, more fascinated.

I lean my elbow on the bar and grin down at him. "I am."

"Oh, wow." He beams back. "I literally just subscribed to you. You make some interesting stuff."

"Thanks."

Being approached in public like this is still too much like a dream.

"Let me buy you a drink, man," he says. "What you having?"

And it keeps getting better. Can hardly believe it.

I scan the colourful bottles again. "Well, I haven't decided yet. Definitely a shot or three."

"What about your mate? Who's staring at me, by the way."

I check on Connelly. He is indeed observing the guy with his typical suspicion of strangers.

"Want anything?" I ask him.

He shakes his thinker.

"No thanks, then," I tell the guy.

He nods curtly. "You after a good kick?"

"Yeah, but with some sweetness."

He lifts an eyebrow. "How about sambuca?"

"Hmm. Maybe. It's been a while."

"Don't you hate sambuca?" Connelly asks near my ear.

I frown briefly. Last time I tried it, I nearly threw up. Now I really crave it, like I know it'll be better this time.

I slap my hand against the bar and say to the guy, "Go for it. Make it raspberry."

"Okay."

He laughs then manages to catch the bartender's attention. The guy hasn't noticed my presence yet – seems too busy.

Connelly clutches my arm and speaks into my ear: "You're mixing a lot."

A hot rush through my body nearly makes me grab him and press him against the bar. I barely manage to resist.

I wrap my arm around his waist from behind. "I'll be fine."

"You passed out yesterday from just vodka."

"There was other stuff going on. You know I can handle my booze."

Surely he believes me? I don't want to check his expression, though. Talking of which, I really do need to find out what happened.

Before I know it, the pink shot sits in front of me. The guy gulps his Coke and whatever while watching me.

I pick up the shot glass between finger and thumb, thank him, and down it in one. The raspberry's sweet sharpness lasts two seconds. Now my throat and chest burn. I give a short cough then relish the rush to my thinker. Not as bad as I remember.

He laughs again. "How is it?"

"Pretty good, actually."

He sips his drink. "Hey, would you mind if I got a selfie with you?"

Really? Wonders never cease!

"Okay." I try not to sound too astonished.

Grinning, he pulls out his phone, touches his shoulder against my arm, and raises the phone in front of us. He aligns our image on the screen and we both smile at the camera. Once the flash goes off, he checks out the photo. Hope I look presentable.

"Thanks a lot," he says.

"And thank *you* again, for the shot."

"No problem." He continues to stare at me, and finally I start to feel uneasy. "This might be a crazy question, but do you want to swap numbers? Maybe we could hang out?"

Is he coming on to me, or only trying to get closer to a celebrity? Let's face it: it'll be because of the same reason as everyone else who's been messaging me online recently.

"Sorry," I say as nicely as possible. "I'm not giving my number out to anyone at the moment."

He holds up his hand. "That's cool. I get it. Thanks for talking with me, though. Have a good night. I look forward to your next video."

138

He seems genuine enough. Didn't even have any questions about K-Rin. I give him a small wave as he wanders off with his drink into the crowd.

Connelly has an almost thunderous face.

"What's up?" I ask.

"We are not hanging out in bars if guys, or girls, are going to try giving you their numbers."

Didn't even think about him just then. Got caught up in the moment.

"I'll politely decline, like I just did, and it'll be fine," I say.

He rolls his eyes. "Well, I think you've had enough fun for one night. It's Tuesday, don't forget. Got work in the morning."

Knew he'd mention that at some point. But he's right.

I groan. "Okay. But I'm coming back."

Clutching my arm, he guides me out. Has to steer me away from more awe-struck voices.

On the dark drive home, I nearly slip into a dizzy but peaceful unconsciousness. One thought keeps me awake: I need to find K-Rin.

"How would you even do that?" Connelly asks.

Did I mumble that last part aloud? Oh well.

"She clearly watches my videos." I pull my thinker away from the window. "I could ask her to contact me. Plus, that'll prove to everyone I'm not as pally-pally with her as they think."

He frowns at the road. "She must be still in the UK, at least, considering she was broadcasting live from Marylebone yesterday."

"She's got to be in London, yeah."

"Well, if she doesn't reach out to you, someone at the Broadcasting House should know something."

"If they're not sworn to secrecy."

My gaze latches onto the blurs of light from the passing street lamps. Part of me still wants to thank her for this sudden career boost, but I hate myself for it. Was that even her intention anyway? She wouldn't care about the success of a little YouTuber, especially one who's trying to defame her.

I struggle to straighten up. "Oh my God. I've been so blind."

"What?"

"Diversion tactics," is all I can get out.

He sighs. "Full sentences, Madd."

Through the crazy fog in my thinker, I try to pick out a coherent sentence: "She's trying to soften me up, make me like her, stop me from investigating."

"Really?"

"She's distracting me with success. Even taken away the person who was helping me spread 'false' theories about her."

"You really think she took Aki away?"

"It makes the most sense."

He shakes his thinker. "That's insane, even for you."

I clench my fist in my lap. Hardly feel it. I know I'm right about this.

"Check through his phone," Connelly says. "Contact someone he knows."

"I can't."

"Why?"

Oh. I never told him. Guess he'll have to find out now.

"There's no-one in his contact list," I explain, "except me."

His wide eyes glance at me. "You serious?"

"Yeah. I think it's a burner phone."

"Okay... Is there nothing else on it, like an address, so we can find out where he lives?"

"Not that I can see. I looked into his social media accounts. Turns out he has none, actually."

He goes silent, and continues to frown hard at the road. Does he believe me? Is he struggling to grasp it all? With him on that.

"When I meet K-Rin," I say, "I'll demand she tell me where Aki is."

His jaw tenses. "Please don't get in trouble."

"I won't."

He sighs again. "Look, if you do meet her, I'll make sure I'm there with you, okay?"

Is he being supportive or controlling?

I slowly smirk at him. "To make sure I behave, or maybe get a selfie?"

He rolls his eyes. Obviously not in the mood for jokes, and intriguingly not jumping at my suggestion.

"All right," I say. "You come with me. But it'll be in a public place, in case she tries any brainwashing shit."

He doesn't reply. Maybe when he meets her, he'll understand what I'm talking about, or he'll just warm to her even more. Is it such a good idea to bring him along? I don't fucking know right now.

"Maybe we can convince her to take her rabbit back," he says.

"As much as he freaks me out, he's doing wonders for the channel. Let's keep him a little longer." I put on an angelic tone: "Please."

That jaw won't relax. His focus remains on the road.

"He'll stay in the studio, out the way," I continue. "Plus, I would've thought you'd be honoured to look after him. Everyone else would be."

"Yeah, well, I'm not everyone else," he snaps. "I like her, yeah, but I didn't sign up to look after her bloody pet!"

I frown hazily at him. So he's not brainwashed the same way. Still semi-brainwashed, right?

"Do you still have her song stuck in your head?" I ask.

"Not really. It comes and goes. But it's not driving me nuts anymore. How much everyone at work goes on about it does, though."

How interesting. Well, I'm bloody relieved, but this does now complicate things a bit.

I stagger into the flat after Connelly. Lean back on the door to shut it. He turns to use the key but I'm blocking him. I stare at him, and he stares back. He's tense again. I just want him to chill, to be as happy as he was at the restaurant. I clutch his shirt and pull him into me. Plant a kiss on his warm lips. We kiss deeply for several moments. Hope all that alcohol washed away most of the spiciness. My thinker grows lighter. Body gets hotter. I'm riled up. I need him, and I think he needs me. We both need to lose ourselves again.

He pulls away slightly. Gazes at me with a small frown.

"What?" I say. "Was that not good?"

After a few beats, he says, "It *was*, just...different."

I don't know what he means. But if he enjoyed it, that's all I care about.

Keeping his face close to mine, he reaches around me to lock the door. I stay still, but my knees want to buckle. I'd drop down right here if he wasn't funny about doing it in the hallway. He hangs the key on the peg by the door. Locks eyes with me again. I'm going to make sure we both enjoy the rest of the night.

*

Connelly's sadistically cheery vibrating alarm wakes me up. Weird. I normally sleep through it. My aching thinker forces my eyes closed, until the alarm goes off again. He never lets it go off twice. I haven't even felt him stir. So I reach behind to gently shake him.

"Conn, you getting up?" My throat's drier than usual. Mouth feels disgusting.

No response. I shake him again. He groans and finally slaps his phone to turn off the alarm. I gather the energy to roll over. He lies on his back with scrunched eyes.

"What's wrong?" I murmur.

"I can barely lift my limbs," he rasps.

"That my fault?"

His lips twitch. "Probably. I'm exhausted."

I smirk. "I'll take that as a compliment."

It *was* one of our best nights in a long time, and I'm shocked he went all out with me again so soon after the other day. How did I even keep it up with that much booze in me? Talking of which, I don't feel as sick as I should after all that mixing. Didn't even get up at 3 am to chuck up. The oddest thing about yesterday, though, was how I seemed to lap up the public attention. I reckon the drinking's to blame for that one.

His eyes open at last to gaze at me. He's adorable when he's knackered. But there's a warmth in that expression I haven't seen for a while.

"I want to stay with you today," he says. I almost ask him to repeat it.

"What about work?"

"I'll see if I can work from home. Normally, they hate last minute things like that, but they've been ridiculously lax with everything this week – I doubt they'll care."

As much as I love him wanting to spend time with me, I can't help saying, "Not like you to work from home voluntarily, though."

He rolls his eyes. "I'm already sick of them all going on about you know who. If I stay here, I'll get stuff done and I can spend time with you, too."

It'll be great to have someone to talk to during my downtime, but it'll be a problem if he knocks while I'm in the flow of writing or editing – he does that sometimes at weekends. At least he knows not to come in while I'm recording.

I smile. "Come in to me when you get bored. Just knock first."

He nods slowly then stares at me for ages. I relish in his fierce gaze that, although exhausted, appears like he's ready to go another round or two. There's a new light in his eyes. I thought I'd witnessed every possible expression from him, but what is this? Reminds me of the adoration I saw in Aki when we met in person. Makes me feel like sparkling gold. And the other thing that does that is how loudly I made him scream last night. I didn't know I still had it in me. The flat above must've heard, but I don't care. I haven't felt this good about myself for years.

"You're making that video for K-Rin today, right?" he says.

My stomach twinges. "Yep."

"Let me know how it goes, then."

"Mm-hmm." I'll worry about it in about an hour. My thinker could do with more rest. So I close my eyes again. "Need my lie-in first."

"Okay. Well, I'm going to phone my boss."

"Mm."

He shifts in bed and I hear him slide his phone off the bedside cabinet again. It'll be strange having him around during the day, but definitely a nice change.

*

I've barely dozed for any time at all and Connelly's kneeling beside the bed, trying to wake me.

I groan into my hands. "No."

Don't make me regret you being at home already.

He murmurs, "Sorry, but you need to see this."

Has there been a development?

He raises his phone. "This went up last night while we were..." He clears his throat. "Try not to freak out."

He said that so gravely, how can I not?

Takes me several moments to focus on the screen, but once I've stopped squinting, he presses play on a video.

A suited guy sits in front of a colourful backdrop. "This evening, we have a surprise guest, a lovely lady who has promised to enlighten us on one of the world's biggest burning questions at the moment: 'Who is Maddix A.?'"

My eyes bulge at Connelly. He stares intensely back.

"Please welcome the mother of the YouTuber himself: Laurel Aitken."

Applause erupts in the studio audience. Jaunty music plays. A dark-haired woman joins the guy on stage and grins at the camera. That can't be her. She never wears dresses, or that much makeup. But the longer I study her round face and big green eyes, the more the screen blurs. It *is* her, and I suddenly wish I didn't exist.

I can't process it properly to start with. Among the pleasantries, her bullshit comments of "I always knew he'd be successful" and "He had a great childhood" stick out. When they show a picture of a sullen teenage me with her and Dad at Legoland, though, I snap out of my haze.

"He used to love Lego," she chuckles. "But he still enjoys trying to figure out how things fit together. I admire that about him."

No, she doesn't. She used to reprimand me for my constant 'unnecessary' questions – one of the main reasons she's never supported my channel. Now the whole world has seen this stupid photo that I've always hated. Bet she won't tell them that she spent most of that day having a go at me for not being happy enough. How could I when she and Dad were bickering over everything?

Connelly places his hand on my thigh. Must be making it obvious I'm close to flipping out. I *am* burning up.

"Out of everyone," the presenter says, "K-Rin chose your son to look after her rabbit. Why do you think that is?"

She fiddles with the pearl on her necklace, probably showing it off. "Well, in her BBC interview, K-Rin made it seem like it was a kind gesture, to try to win his trust. I think he does secretly adore her as much as everyone else, but he's in denial." I dig my nails into the bed sheet. Can't stand hearing her say that too. "Hopefully, he'll come around soon enough."

"Why do you think he's in denial?"

Because people are allowed different opinions! Because I'm not brainwashed!

"Maddix has always strived for greatness," she says. That *is* true. "Honestly, he's probably jealous of K-Rin's fast rise to fame." And the bullshit continues. Like an idiot, the guy nods. She looks sad, but I can guarantee it's put on. "As he was growing up, whenever he pursued a project or took part in competitions, he'd almost sabotage himself. He'd spend too long in bed, or procrastinating, and sometimes give up entirely."

I shake my thinker. Can't believe her audacity. She shouldn't be talking about this, and I'm not as bad as that anymore. Everyone will say I'm lazy!

"He's certainly been tenacious when it comes to his interest in K-Rin," the guy adds. I appreciate the defence, but I was tenacious before she came along!

"Yes. And as much as I do apologise for the claims he's made against her, I'm honoured that she chose our family."

144

"She didn't choose our family," I snap at the screen. "She chose *me!*"

Connelly squeezes my thigh.

"Turn it off," I say, and he does.

I cover my face again. Wish I'd stayed like this and not let him show me that.

"I'm sorry, Madd," he says, as if reading my mind.

My hands slip, and I push myself up to sit on the bed. "How could she do that? Doesn't *anyone* need my permission to talk about me on TV? Please tell me my dad had the sense not to appear."

He joins me on the bed. "He wasn't there."

One point to Dad, then.

"She's always wanted to go on TV, and as soon as she gets the chance, she swoops in." Can't help sounding spiteful. "Now everyone knows my name... Did she blurt out our address too?"

"No," he says tensely, "but she revealed you have a husband, and gave out my name. They even showed a picture of us. And now everyone who's been gossiping about us knows for sure that we're married to each other."

I'm both glad and annoyed that I stopped watching.

I frown so hard it spikes my headache. "Gossiping?"

He sighs. "Our outing last night made it to social media–"

"–What?"

He taps the screen a few times as I wait with torturous anticipation. "They *were* taking pictures of us at the restaurant. Raving over our meal choices, especially yours. Gushing over how cute we look together."

My face grows hotter. "Really? Show me."

He tilts the phone to reveal an example sneaky snapshot on Twitter of me holding his hand. The comment underneath says: 'couldn't hear exactly but they made up <3'

Oh God, I get why he's pissed. I'm not thrilled either, but at least they reckon we're cute. And they're praising my meal choices? I wouldn't even normally eat that stuff.

"Others were speculating what we were arguing about," he bites. "They're saying I clearly had an issue with you bringing out that phone, and because you use it to talk to K-Rin, I *may* have a problem with *her.*"

I rub my forehead. These stupid, nosy usernames.

"Our conversations should remain private, like they always have," he says. "They have no right to talk about us like this." I get his anger. They've tainted what was a spectacular night, too. "Don't get me wrong: I'm happy for your channel's success and everything, but I am *not* comfortable with this. I'm getting messages through Facebook and Instagram now asking about my relationship with you, K-Rin, and that stupid rabbit!"

Huffing, he thuds his phone down beside him.

"I'm sorry this happened," I say.

"It's not your fault. Guess I should've expected it with how popular you are."

I admit the word 'popular' fills me with an embarrassing pride and happiness, but I don't want us to be spied on, nor for the public to know every detail. It's not like I can convince them to stop; they'll do what they want regardless. I suppose they *are* at least respecting us enough not to *physically* bombard us.

I'd rather focus on these gossipers, but Mum keeps searing her way back in. I know they would've recognised us anyway, but she's opened us up for even more speculation, and potential ridicule. The whole world now knows our names, that I'm gay for sure, and will believe I have a loving, supportive mother!

I grab my phone off the bedside unit.

"What are you doing?" Connelly says warily.

"I'm calling her. Don't care that it's three in the morning or whatever for her."

He touches my arm. "Wait until you've calmed down."

That insistent stare eventually convinces me. I know she likely won't take it in, but she needs to know what she's done. She deserves to have her non-thinker bitten off... I don't want her blabbing to the world about that, though.

I squeeze my phone until it hurts. I'll calm down, but it doesn't change the fact that even from eight-and-a-half hours away, she still manages to crush my spirit.

"We'll get through this, okay?"

I love when Connelly uses that soft tone. I pull him into a hug and he strokes the back of my neck. Can I stay like this for the rest of the day, or maybe forever?

8

As crazy as this morning was, I need to throw myself into my work. Won't be able to record the video if I've just come off the phone from Mum, so I'll postpone calling her a bit longer. These messages flooding through from an abundance of usernames are getting on my last nerve already, though. Nothing but compliments towards her. I knew they'd fall for her act. I'm relieved and shocked that no-one's jeering at my publicised homosexuality – bearing in mind, it's been spread *all* over the world – but her lack of boundaries and falseness was unbearable. The latter was blatantly obvious, or at least to me. Apparently, towards the end of that interview, she told the presenter that she and Dad catch up with me a couple times a month. Makes me want to scream into a glass of Russian... God, I'm too riled up to think of a name for it.

To make things worse, the comments are in for my part two Princess Preciosa video that went up last night. Could've checked them while I was out or when I got back, but wanted to enjoy myself. If I'd have looked, I would've needed more booze. Every *single* comment mentions K-Rin or the bunny, begging for more content about them! I was afraid of this, so I shouldn't be shocked, but this fad has already killed what my channel used to be. Does no-one care about Preciosa's assassination anymore? She wasn't just strangled by thin air! Someone slipped in, without leaving a trace. All the palace security footage was wiped, and yet not by any of the staff. Extra kick in the balls: it has about half the views my normal conspiracy videos tend to get by the next morning. Hardly any likes, either. I imagine, then, that whoever did watch was scouring it for any tiny piece of information about their newest star.

I need a shower to calm down. Need to check on Shinpi first, though. I enter the studio. Why did I leave the light on in here? Oh, shit. The footage! I retrieve the camera from the tripod. The battery's minutes away from dying. It did well. Now let's see if it got anything.

Hang on. He hasn't touched his food, or drink. I peer in at him suspiciously as he lurks in the corner, giving me that creepy side-eye.

"Did you do this on purpose?" I mutter.

He doesn't answer.

I slowly switch my focus back to the camera. With what's left of the battery, I start reviewing the footage from the beginning. Fast forward through different points to see if anything changes at all. But Shinpi defiantly chills in that corner the whole night.

When I glance up at him in real time, it takes me a few moments to realise: his carrots, hay, and water have vanished. Oh, you little fucker!

I spend the next half an hour trying not to lose my composure. So tempting to go screaming to Connelly, and the world, about what I just witnessed, but Shinpi won't let me get proof. The creature has it out for me, I swear!

Feel too sick for breakfast. Stomach's playing up, thanks to all that spicy food. Why did I do this to myself? The stress of this morning isn't helping, either. Anyway, once I've showered, finally brushed my teeth, and dressed in my jumper and jeans combo, I manage to put on my game face and record my video. Keep my phone off, even while editing. Need to watch it through one last time now. I lean back in the chair and click play:

Sitting on the studio sofa with Shinpi in my lap and the box lights illuminating us, I beamed at the camera. "Hi, guys. My name's Maddix A., and this is just another quickish one to say thank you again to everyone who's subscribed recently, and to those, obviously, who are still subscribed. Nearly two-and-a-half million now. Unbelievable!"

I laughed, a little weirdly. Could edit it out but I'll keep it in to show a bit of modest shock.

"A *lot* of you have been requesting more bunny screen time, so here he is." I glanced down at him. He sat completely still, twitching his nose, like the bugger did all night. At least he cooperated with me for *this*. "He doesn't really do much, but there you go." I raised an eyebrow then smirked at the camera. "He actually had a busy day yesterday, though. Got to take part in a photoshoot with the beautiful and talented London model Kya Durand, who most of you likely know is my sister-in-law." My smirk died. "Thanks to my mother's surprise interview, a fair bit about me has been leaked. If you haven't seen it already, please don't watch it. Quite a lot about what she said was embellished."

Shall I edit that last part out? I genuinely don't want the public seeing it, but is it better for them to think those 'great' things about me and my childhood? Yes and no. I'll leave it in; can't bear lying.

The preview image from Kya's Instagram of her smiling over her shoulder at the camera fades in beside me and Shinpi. "Kya has a whole K-Rin themed photoshoot coming shortly to her Instagram, featuring the real bunny himself, so make sure to head over there and keep an eye out."

The Instagram logo pops up under the image with a line of text reading her user tag: '@kyaDurand'. That needs to be slightly bigger. I pause the video, amend the text, save it, and press play again. The image and text stay for another five seconds. "I'm looking forward to seeing how it's all turned out. Should be really good. Kya did a spot-on job." And she's bound to get loads more followers now.

Should I move me addressing K-Rin to the start of the video? I'm going to call it 'Bunny Photoshoot + Message to K-Rin' or something similar, though, and I'm sure she watches all my stuff anyway. I still don't understand why I was spiteful towards Kya during the shoot. I've never harboured any bad feelings for her. She deserves the publicity. It's just a shame she has to do it by looking like K-Rin. These pictures make my skin itch, which is awful because I genuinely believe she's gorgeous. I seriously need to keep my thoughts and feelings under control when I see her next.

On the video, I straightened up and said, "Anyway, the last thing I want to mention is to K-Rin herself." My tone turned serious. "K-Rin, since you kindly gifted me your pet rabbit and put out a good word for me, I'd love to thank you in person. If you're still in central London, and it's convenient for you, we could meet somewhere – public, of course, but not swarming with people." If we can even manage that in central London. "Let me know if this'll be possible. It'd truly be an honour."

I reckon I looked and sounded sincere enough in that last bit. Felt sick saying it, but at least it should get her attention.

The video wraps up, short and sweet as my current ones are. Certainly less stressful to edit. Should I have gone into more detail about Mum? How would I break it to everyone? I'm already holding back details about Shinpi. It's torture, but much simpler this way. Don't want the backlash.

It doesn't take too long to upload. I'll leave it ten minutes then check for comments or messages.

I could do with a coffee refill. So I push my aching body up and head out to the kitchen. Hear a cupboard shut and almost jump. Not used to company during the day. Connelly fills the kettle up at the sink.

I place my mug next to his on the counter. "Add enough for me too, please."

He glances over his shoulder at me, says, "Sure," and carries on filling. Odd to see him in a baggy shirt and bottoms on a Wednesday morning. Actually wish he was in those tight office trousers that shape his arse so perfectly. I step back and lean on the fridge to admire him anyway.

He sets the kettle boiling then, folding his arms, rests sideways on the counter. "You'll have to pop out soon and get more at this rate. How many cups have you had?"

"This'll be my third."

He raises an eyebrow. "Haven't been making them Russian, have you?"

I hold my thinker high. "Nope."

"Oh." He smiles. "You do surprise me."

Smirking, I cross my arms too. "Like I surprised you last night."

He looks like he could blush. Wish he would.

"I can't remember the last time you got on top like that," he says. Neither can I. It was a compulsion I had. He must get bored of me lying on my front and letting him do most of it. As good as it feels for me, I can't blame him. He glances down. "I know I haven't been especially 'into' it recently."

He doesn't usually talk this openly about it. Guess I might as well take the opportunity to do the same.

"You had me wondering if I was doing it wrong," I say.

He straightens up. "No. Work's been stressing me out. I feel like I can't relax and let myself enjoy anything." He sighs and smiles. "It was good to go out last night. What happened afterwards was just the perfect end."

My body comes over with a hot flush. "Perfect?"

"Yeah."

He stares at me with that adoration from earlier. Normally, I'd feel flattered, and as I'm sober, probably blush. But right now, what overwhelms me is pride. It burns.

He seems to shake himself back to reality. "Anyway, how did the video go?"

"Good, thanks. Just need to wait and see now."

"I'll watch it when I go back to the bedroom."

I nod. "How's working from home?"

"Peaceful. I don't have to stay on my feet for hours printing and assembling marketing shit for my boss. And he's not pestering me every ten minutes... He was uncharacteristically chill about me staying home. I didn't even have to explain why." He scoffs. "Of course, I heard some of the guys in the background mocking me."

"What? Why?"

"They were like: 'Oh, I bet he wants to stay home after last night!' Guess they saw the photos of us at the restaurant."

I sigh. For a second, I thought they somehow found out what we did when we got home.

"Ignore them." And that's *me* saying that.

"Yeah. All of them in that office have been acting high this week."

"I'm telling you: it's brainwashing."

He frowns at the floor. "It's something. My boss hates pop and dance. He's a full-on metal head. But this song's captivated him. He went on for twenty minutes in our Monday meeting about how it's given him a new zest for life."

I shrug. "Same as everyone else."

"Yes. But he shouldn't be sharing that with the whole marketing department on a busy Monday morning." He rubs his forehead. The kettle clicks. He spins on his bare heel to start filling our mugs with water. "If it *is* brainwashing, why is it not working on us?"

"We do seem to be an exception. Aki as well. But you *were* hooked with the others to start with."

He mixes in the coffee, clinking the spoon against the mugs. "Well, when I heard it that night at Kya's, I *was* as besotted as everyone else. But that's definitely gone now."

I smirk again. "I'm obviously a good influence on you."

Half-smiling, he chucks the spoon in the sink and hands me my third Caffeine Focus. How am I not bouncing off the walls already?

"Tell me as soon as you hear anything from K-Rin," he says, "if you do."

"Will do, love."

I lean in to kiss his forehead. The bright affection in his eyes looks alien, and I don't know what exactly I've done to deserve it, but I'll take it.

"You haven't phoned your mum yet, have you?" he says.

Why'd he have to spoil the moment?

I sigh. "No. But I think I'm calm enough to do it now. It'll still be quite early for her, but I don't care if I wake her."

"Okay. If I hear shouting, though, I'm coming in."

I should be fine, but can't promise I won't.

If I could, I'd take this outside, but don't want anyone overhearing me berating my own mother. Studio will feel too claustrophobic. So I choose the living room, leaving the door open a crack. As I wait for her to answer, I pace around the small space. Ignore my cramping stomach as best I can.

"Maddix!" She's way too lively for what should be early morning for her. "I'm glad you called."

She won't be saying that in a second.

"You can drop the act, okay?" I say. "Unless you're still on the air."

I hope the bitterness oozes from my tone.

She doesn't acknowledge it: "I take it you saw my interview. Wasn't it amazing? I reached out and they invited me in immediately."

Out of desperation. Because they are just as hypnotised by K-Rin as you.

"Yes. It's bloody marvellous how you got to finally live your dream of embarrassing me and leaking private information about me and my husband on national television."

She tuts. "The clip got more views online than any other interview for that show. This'll get you more exposure than what you'd ever get with your other videos, even that Princess Preciosa one."

My eyes bulge. Kick me while I'm down! Is she seriously insinuating this was in *my* best interest? Also, hearing her gush over views is almost too cringey to bear.

"You mean it will for *you*," I say. "I don't need any more exposure, and Connelly certainly doesn't want any!"

"Maddix, I don't understand. You're practically a celebrity now. You should own it. I would've thought you'd be ecstatic."

"I am, but it's overwhelming sometimes, okay? It happened ridiculously fast, and *I* wanted to be in control of how much the public knows about me." I grip my thinker and take a breath. "You didn't even ask our permission. You just waltzed on there and did what you always do: completely disregard my feelings."

I hate how she gets me worked up like this. It doesn't suit me.

"Maddix..." She actually sounds taken aback.

"Listening to you going on about our happy family life was a kick in the teeth. Wonder how everyone would react if they found out you forced me into most of those competitions and told me countless times that 'failure isn't acceptable'."

"...You know your dad and I have only wanted the best for you."

I scoff. "Dad never pushed me. And at least he didn't go on TV discussing our personal lives... In fact, why haven't I heard from him yet? You speaking on his behalf again?"

"Your dad's very proud of you. He's just been busy."

I growl under my breath. Why can't the man ever grow a backbone?

Anyway, this is pointless. I'm not getting anything out of her, don't want to be wound up any more, and I've got stuff to do.

"I need to go."

As I'm about to give her one last reprimand, she cuts in with: "Before you do, I need to tell you that we're actually planning to visit the UK."

My eyebrow shoots up. "Why?"

"We were hoping to see the bunny, and meet K-Rin. I'm sure you could put in a good word for us. Maybe get us a discount at a decent hotel. Failing that, we could stay at yours for a few nights. It'd be no trouble, right?"

There is so much wrong with what's coming out of her mouth. I can't deal with her anymore.

"Are you fucking kidding me? I can't get you a discount, and you *cannot* stay here. The place is small; we only have one bedroom. And I have no idea how to get in touch with K-Rin anyway. Stop leeching off my success!"

"But–"

"–No. From now on, do as K-Rin says and respect my wishes: do *not* talk about my life with anyone else." Can't believe I have to say that. "And please, do *not* come to the UK if all you're interested in is K-Rin. Got it?"

"...Okay, we won't." She sounds disappointed, but I give no shits. Then somehow, her unbearable cheeriness returns: "Take care, dear."

My thumb slams the hang up icon. Chest stings even more now. She's clearly under K-Rin's influence, but the sad thing is: brainwashed or not, I still reckon she would've done this.

I briefly report to Connelly, who gives me another hug. He's glad I convinced Mum not to turn up here. I'm starting to chill, but there's still work to do. I return to my desk and place my mug beside the mouse to cool. Tempted to slip a generous amount of vodka in it, but I need to stay sharp. After a deep breath, I'm ready to refresh YouTube. I doubt K-Rin's responded, but I'm still apprehensive for it. Many new private messages, but none, unsurprisingly, from her – just the same standard stuff. The comments on this video, though... I gawp at the several thousand of them, all variants of:

'Yes, more bunny!'

'K-Rin needs to see this!'

'Surely you've already met?'

'Can you do a video with me?'

'I can't wait for a collaboration between you two!'
'Meet K-Rin and you'll love her as much as we do!'
'That photoshoot sounds amazing!'
'That model looks just like her!'
'Tell us everything if you talk to K-Rin!'
'These are exciting times!'
'What did your mum embellish exactly? Tell us!'

Guess I should've expected to be questioned on that last one, but I'm not elaborating. I've never seen such an explosion of comments within ten minutes, and those views – Christ, there's a few-hundred thousand. Can't see a single negative one so far, either. This hot rush makes my heart stutter. It's scary, but feels right. Belongs. I feel so arrogant thinking – no, knowing – that I deserve all this positive attention. And I'm not even drunk.

A text pings on my phone. Mum? My mood dies. Stomach twists. What could she possibly want after that call? Is she telling me she's squealing to the world that I had a go at her? No, I'm sure she'd want to keep that secret.

The text reads: 'I meant to say while we were chatting that as a celebrity you really must dress smarter for your videos.'

My fist slams down on the desk. I won't even dignify that with a response.

Lying on the studio sofa, I hold my phone above my face and scroll through the endless comments. Not one from K-Rin. She must've seen the video by now. Is she ignoring me? Stringing me out? She knows I'll be refreshing constantly, waiting for a reply. Am I only promoting her further with these types of videos? I mean, I publicly *thanked* her. Said it'd be an *honour* to meet her. And why am I not more overwhelmed by these comments? They may be positive, but this many would've floored me before. What's up with me? I sigh.

Oh, fuck. I've done it again. I should be trying to find out what happened to me and Aki in the park the other day, and what am I doing instead? Lying around, waiting to be contacted by the person who likely made Aki disappear in the first place! I need to get back on track. Think I just needed my exhilaration from earlier to ease up.

My thumb refreshes the inbox a few more times, probably from force of habit. A new private message appears, titled 'Interview Request'. Another one from BBC? Shit. I didn't even decide on the first. Don't want them to twist my words or make me out in a terrible light. But maybe I should put my fear and paranoia aside and use this to my advantage. As Connelly said yesterday, a BBC interview will get my side of things out to even more people. It *won't* be to lie and show off like Mum did. And working for the broadcasting channel that interviewed K-Rin, this journalist might have info on her whereabouts. Then who knows, I might be able to find out what happened to Aki too?

I push myself up, stride out two steps across the corridor to our bedroom door, and knock.

"Yeah?" Connelly calls. I pull open the door and rest on the frame. He spins in the chair, away from his cluttered laptop screen, and raises an eyebrow at me. "What are you smirking about?"

I place a hand on my chest. "I have an interview with a BBC journalist this afternoon."

His eyes widen. "That's very short notice, but okay, wow. You decided to go for it."

"Yeah. I'm hoping it'll give me a better chance to meet K-Rin."

"So you're going on TV?"

"No. It's a back and forth over audio chat which will be uploaded to YouTube and transcribed into an online article. But why *didn't* they invite me on TV?"

I should be relieved, but I'm oddly disappointed.

"They might've thought it'd be quicker to get you over the phone rather than arranging a physical appearance. Or they're building suspense for the public."

I shrug. "It's a start."

Why did I say that?

"That's still cool," he says. "I hope it goes well."

"Thanks."

For some reason, any nerves I had from yesterday about the idea of being interviewed have nearly all disappeared, even in spite of my private life being recently exposed. How am I this chill?

"Oh, by the way," Connelly says, "Kya's invited us over again. Tomorrow night, for dinner. Kind of a belated birthday celebration for Mum and Dad to join in."

And now the nerves are back.

"Your parents will be there?"

"Yeah, as they couldn't make it to the party. And tomorrow's the only night they're free this week."

I run a hand through my hair. Glance at the dark carpet. Is there a way I can get out of this?

"Come on, Madd. We haven't seen them for months."

"That won't change how they feel about me. Maybe you should keep it a family thing."

He sighs, and lifts his left hand to show off his gold wedding band. "You *are* family. I'm sure you'll all get on civilly. You've done it before. Just don't drink too much."

After how much I've downed lately, I don't fancy the idea of drinking a great deal again any time soon. It never goes over well with the Durands anyway. Wish I could get on with them – not like I haven't tried – but after ten years, what are the chances? I'll go to this dinner, though. Of course I will. I'll put myself through it for him, and Kya.

As this interview will be audio only, no point reapplying any hair gel or sprucing myself up again. Before I slump on the studio sofa, ready to take the call, I check on Shinpi. He's resting in the dark corner of his hutch, his spooky blue eyes reflecting in the light. The longer I stare at him, the more familiar he feels to me. It's peculiar.

I sip my Caffeine Enthusiasm. I've honestly lost count how many I've had. Should be getting shaky right about now, but they've kicked me more into productive mode. Don't even feel like any shots to calm my nerves about the interview, because the anxiety about it is non-existent. Where did I get this confidence from?

The phone vibrates in my hand. Unknown number. A thrill rushes through me. I straighten, and answer the call.

"Hello," a woman says. "Is this Maddix Aitken?"

"It is."

"Hello, Maddix. This is Salma Merlo from the BBC." Her voice is fairly deep and smooth. "Thank you so much for accepting my call. Are you still available for the interview?"

"I am."

"Excellent. As I said in my message to you earlier, I will record this conversation and it will be uploaded tonight. I will do a countdown from five when I'm about to record. Are you happy with this?"

She's so formal, but still comes across friendly enough.

"Yeah," I say, and sip my Caffeine Confidence.

"Okay. I will begin in five, four, three, two, one." She clears her throat. "And we're recording. This is Wednesday twelfth of April 2023. Salma Merlo interviewing Maddix Aitken. Hello, Maddix."

"Hello."

"So, you're a YouTuber who creates content on conspiracy theories."

"Yes. Been doing it for five years now."

"And your channel has gained immense popularity this week after you uploaded various videos centring on a theory concerning a different version of K-Rin's song 'Something That You Need to Know'. You have certainly had a unique take on it. Most perplexing is the video you posted of K-Rin's rabbit jumping out of your TV screen. Can you explain how you made that video?"

I take another sip. "Well, not many people believe me, but that video's absolutely genuine. I don't understand it myself, but somehow K-Rin sent that rabbit to me."

"K-Rin announced to the public on the BBC News on Monday that she gave you the rabbit to look after. In one of your latest videos, you explain that you had no idea that she would do this."

"That's right. I'm actually trying to get hold of her to ask her why."

"Do you think perhaps she sent you him as a way to communicate to you?"

I frown over at the hutch. "What, to prove she's real?"

"It's quite a show of trust to bestow her beloved pet to someone else, especially someone who has been heavily critiquing her work. Maybe she wants to extend an olive branch to you. I believe your mother Laurel Aitken said a similar thing yesterday on Evening Barbados."

I try not to sigh and nearly say, 'Leave my mum out of this.'

I force a laugh. "An olive branch would be a message or a phone call."

"Has anyone else so far contacted you regarding sharing the same experience of the song?"

"Other than a guy I did a collaboration with on Monday, no."

"Only you and this other guy have heard and seen a different version?"

"That I know of."

I won't mention that he's now gone missing. Dread to think how they'll spin that. Have they even tried contacting *him* for an interview?

"Most people on YouTube and social media don't seem to believe this other version exists," Salma continues. I tense up. I know what's coming.

She says, "Some are claiming that you are simply trying to gain attention, that this is another conspiracy theory opportunity for you."

I wonder what *she* believes.

I try not to sigh. "I've seen these comments. I can't blame them for being sceptical. *I* would be. But loads of people, like you said, are just interested in seeing any K-Rin-related material, no matter what the angle. I mean, I'm just trying to understand what's going on. She became an overnight sensation. I want to know how she did it, and why practically no-one else in the world saw what I did."

"So, this other person you mentioned, who *did* see what you did: have you had previous connections with him?"

"Well, he's been a subscriber of mine for five years, and an avid supporter."

"So, you could say that maybe he played along with you?"

Is she seriously insinuating that he lied to me, to meet me and do that collaboration video? That *was* Connelly's suspicion. Is that why Aki's now gone?

"Maddix?"

I mentally shake myself. "No. He showed me all the lyrics he'd written in his notebook the night the song aired. They were exactly what I'd heard, and I hadn't told anyone what they were."

"Okay," she says bluntly. Again, don't know if she believes me, but I don't care, just as long as she doesn't convince everyone that Aki and I are lying. "What do you think about K-Rin? Do you believe she has negative intentions as suggested in your videos?"

Now that's a loaded question.

I choose my words carefully: "I can only go by what I know. She's clearly very talented at what she does. She's perfected the art of winning the attention and adoration of the public. I don't know what she's planning, but I want to find out."

I could say much more, but I really shouldn't.

"You've been trying to reach out to her, in a video you uploaded this morning. What would you like to say to her?"

If she watched it, she'd know. But I guess this is for the benefit of anyone who hasn't.

"I want to thank her, for the opportunity she's given me to increase my audience." That does sound slightly self-centred and still sickens me to say, but I need K-Rin to think I'll be approaching her in peace. "I'd also like

158

to find out who she is, how she pulled off her multimedia hack, and why she chose me exactly. She's a complete mystery, and I love mysteries."

That second half is true, but I hate my overly friendly tone.

"Well, Maddix, I hope she contacts you soon. A *lot* of people will want to hear what she has to say, especially as her song 'Something That You Need to Know' is being officially released in four days on Sunday sixteenth of April. Everyone is looking forward to it." She clears her throat quietly. "Thank you for speaking with the BBC today, and we wish you all the success with your channel."

Oh, it's over already?

"Uh, thank you," I say.

"Okay, and end recording." She sighs. "Thank you for your time, Maddix. We will be uploading this at six tonight."

"Cool. Thanks." I lean forward. "Before you go, though, I have to ask, *off* the record: will anyone at the BBC Broadcasting House have any info on where to find K-Rin? I mean, when she left, surely someone followed her, or tried to?"

She pauses for several moments. "To be honest, I wouldn't know; I work in an external office. You'd be best contacting the Broadcasting House directly. I'm sure they'd be happy to help if you tell them who you are."

I huff under my breath, and stare at the carpet. Directly it is, then. If anyone knows where she is, or if she's even been sighted, surely it would be all over the Internet by now? Maybe no-one knows, but it's still worth checking out, especially as I've yet to hear from her.

"Okay," I say. "Thanks, then."

"I'll send you a link to the article and video when they go live."

"Thank you."

And we hang up. Well, that could've gone worse, but it could've gone better. I don't want this to sway anyone against me. I know not many believe me anyway, and I can't seem to do anything else to prove it, but I don't want to be shunned outright as an attention-seeking conspiracy theorist liar. I shouldn't care about it, but I *do* want to prove myself right. If I can get K-Rin to admit there are two versions, everyone will have no choice but to believe me. As one of the only people to have heard the other version, everyone will want to talk to me. That kind of popularity should scare me, but right now, I'm glowing inside thinking about it.

A quick Google search gives me the number for the BBC switchboard. From the computer desk, I call it on my phone. After going through the options, it finally lets me talk to a human.

"Hi," I say. "My name's Maddix Aitken. Your studio interviewed K-Rin on Monday. I just wanted to ask if she left any contact details. I've been trying to get hold of her."

The guy on the other end groans. "You're not the only one."

"Oh." Guess I really shouldn't be shocked.

"We are not giving away any details regarding K-Rin."

I frown at the desk. They either have nothing, or they're protecting her.

"I'm sure you can tell *me*," I say. "I'm *Maddix Aitken*, the YouTuber K-Rin was talking about in the interview. She gave me her rabbit."

He sighs again. "And you're about the fiftieth person to say that over the last two days. I will have to politely request that you do not call this number unless there is anything else I can help you with."

Seriously? People are pretending to be me? I'm freaked out and flattered, but now this random switchboard handler doesn't even believe who I am? Can he not recognise my voice? I'll have to go there myself. Show them my face. I'd like to see them deny me then.

After checking for an address, I push myself up. Go to leave the studio, but Connelly's on the other side of the door. That should've made me jump, but I tilt my thinker instead. Unlike him to be idly standing around.

He cringes slightly. "Sorry. I just wanted to hear how it went. I could practically hear your side of it from the bedroom anyway."

"Well, it went all right. But no-one will tell me anything about K-Rin, so I'm paying them a visit."

"What difference will that make?"

"Switchboard guy didn't believe who I was. Turns out I have a pack of impersonators."

His face screws up. "Oh. How far exactly is the Broadcasting House, then?"

"Half an hour. But probably more, thanks to traffic."

"That's a long way to go if they turn you away."

I hold my thinker high. "Don't worry, love. I'm certain they'll tell me something."

"Okay." He stretches up to kiss my cheek. I nearly melt. "Good luck."

Would've expected him to warn me against it, or force me to stay home, but suppose I'm actually sober today.

160

The traffic through Westminster is aggravatingly heavy. Maybe it would've been quicker to take the train, but who knows how much the ticket would've been? I've still got a bit of petrol, and a spare fiver I can top it up with if necessary.

To keep me calm, I listen to my downtempo ambient mix. Felt pretty confident when I left the house, but the longer I stay in the car, the more time I have to doubt myself. Can I pull this off? What if I come away with absolutely nothing? Will K-Rin reveal more about herself to the public once her song goes live? Or does she want to keep the mystery going? She can only hide for so long. If she has people protecting her, someone's bound to sell her out eventually. Even if I get nothing from the BBC today, I have to find her.

The final stretch of Regent Street's a bitch. The traffic's worse than snail-pace. Eventually, I see why. Just over the Oxford Station roundabout, little brightly-coloured tents are pitched on both sides of the pavement. They're camping in the streets? Everyone's crowding about. Loads of food stalls and a bunch of portable loos have been set up too. Despite all this, I only see a couple police officers – they'll need a lot more than that if a riot breaks out. What the hell's going on?

I switch on the radio and cycle through the chat stations. To my great annoyance, but also benefit, a certain someone's name is constantly mentioned. Several stations in, something relevant comes up: "Think I might go join them over in Regent Street, actually."

"Really?"

"Yeah. Let's do it together."

"We can't just leave the studio," the guy mutters.

"It's worth it, for a chance to see K-Rin. What do you say?"

I raise my eyebrow at the stereo player while they pause.

"Oh, what the hell?" the guy says. "Let's do it!"

I scrunch my face up at them. They're nuts. Guess everyone's come here to see her, what, because she was spotted at the BBC building one time? Well, at least I'm where the action's happening. While my car's stationary, I take several pictures through the window and capture some video.

After parking up in the closest multi-storey car park possible, I head out into the sea of fans. Tempting to get up-close footage of these campers but

I don't want to be noticed. If one person recognises me, a whole swarm could descend – don't have time for that. It's times like these I curse my height. Should've worn something different, but I've pulled my jacket's hood up at least and keep my focus on my phone's sat nav. Whenever anyone tries to talk to me, to check if I'm who they think I am, I dodge around them and disappear.

At the base of a U-shape of pale bricks and windows, sunlight funnels in to illuminate the teal glass-panelled BBC building. I'm finally here. I march across grey tiled stone. Carved into every other tile is a different place name. Some people sit about, on their phones or munching snacks. Others briskly pass me in both directions.

In front of the double set of revolving doors stand two hench security guards, arms crossed and decked out in those cliché dark sunglasses. How the hell will I get past them? Is my identity enough? Why is a place like this guarded anyway? Have people literally been storming the gates, trying to find any sign of K-Rin?

Before I approach, I press record on my phone and slide it in my back jeans pocket. My stomach should be tightening, but it doesn't. Maybe I have more confidence in myself than I thought. I stop in front of them, pull down my hood, and clear my throat.

"Hello. I'm–"

"Maddix Aitken."

I smirk. "Could you let me in, please? I'm gathering info for my latest video and I was hoping someone here could help me."

"You can go in," he says stiffly, "but don't expect any straight answers."

Huh. Interesting response – relieving, but also potentially frustrating. He steps aside, so I waste no time slipping through the revolving doors. A large, bright reception greets me. Almost a shame to step onto flooring this clean and shiny.

Behind me, I hear a commotion. A camper I noticed earlier's having a go at the security guard, his shouting muffled: "Why'd you let him in and not me?"

"'Cause you're not *him*," the guard shouts back. He jabs his finger in the direction of the main road. "Now get out of here."

Wow. Crazy to hear a security guard, or anyone, saying that about me. Before the dejected camper gets a good gander at me, I spin and walk off. For some reason, this privilege does feel briefly exhilarating.

As I head to the long, reflective reception desk on the left, I can barely hear the camper shouting, "Who is he? Who is he?"

They shout back, "Get out of here!"

Thank you, guys.

The dapper young receptionist behind the desk's Perspex screen straightens as I approach. His eyes widen. "Maddix Aitken." I smile at him and he adds, "How can I help you?"

Pity that's not awe in his voice – more like anxiety.

"I was hoping someone had info on K-Rin's whereabouts, considering she was here on Monday. I've driven a long way to meet her." I try to mimic my fake friendly tone from the interview. "I want to thank her, for everything, in person."

He glances sideways, towards the impressive spiral staircase and lifts. Looking out for a manager?

"You know," I continue, "I find it odd that no-one's reported sighting her around here. This area's so busy."

Although because of the busyness, you'd find it almost impossible to spot her. Maybe that's the point.

His cheeks flush. He goes completely rigid. Doesn't blink. "If I tell you what happened, you'll spread it around in seconds, and I'll lose my job. Being in such close proximity to where she was: it means everything to me."

Poor lost soul. At least he's not denying seeing her.

I lean forward. Stare straight into his eyes. "I promise I won't leak anything. I just want to meet K-Rin myself. No-one else will know."

Why am I saying that? If he reveals anything worthwhile, I'll want to release it, but I'd need his permission first. I go to correct myself, but nothing comes out. I feel sick.

"Everyone in this building has sworn to secrecy," he whispers.

While struggling not to get annoyed with him, I display my sweetest smile and say, "You can tell one person, especially me. K-Rin asked everyone to respect me, didn't she?"

I expect him to glance around again, but he stares at me. Perspiration starts dotting his forehead. Is he scared? Part of me wants him to be so he'll spill. I don't blink either, and will him with my gaze to co-operate.

"No-one knows how she got in," he mutters. Oh, that actually worked? "They checked the CCTV. She didn't come in through the entrance or any of the other doors. The news presenter said he just found her in the room he interviewed her in."

So not only is she a master hacker, but also a master trespasser. Intriguing.

"What about when she left?" I ask.

"We couldn't figure out how she got out, either. Once the interview was over, everyone tried talking to her, but she silently got up, walked into the nearest back room, and vanished. No other doors in there, no windows, no CCTV." He suddenly laughs. "She truly is a miracle."

How the hell did she manage that? Well, her bunny jumped out of a TV.

"Was there a TV in that room?" I ask.

His eyes glass over as if thinking. "It was a mini dressing room. We have TVs in all our dressing rooms."

I feel myself smirk triumphantly.

Of course. Normally, I wouldn't believe it, but I know her trick. Everyone else in the world has no clue what they're dealing with, and never will. It's too much to comprehend. But not for me. I know what she is, or at least how she travels around unseen. I can't track her down. I'll have to lure her out. Directly asking for us to meet hasn't worked so far. I'll need to think of another plan, or be in the right place at the right time.

"Is that news presenter here today?" I ask. "The guy who did the interview with K-Rin."

"Oh, he doesn't work here anymore." This makes me raise an eyebrow. He smiles. "He said he'd start volunteering at a local soup kitchen while trying to set up his own charity shop."

Wow. Quite a leap. Again, shame he's brainfucked, but at least he's doing good with it. There'd be no point discussing his meeting with K-Rin if it really is just a blur to him. Another great shame.

"Okay, well, thank you for the information." I lower my voice. "Could you do one more thing for me, though? Is there a back exit I can use so I don't have to navigate that crowd again? I'm trying not to get mobbed."

*

Connelly shifts his weight on the sofa, frowns ahead at the TV, then at me. "I've heard you say some crazy shit over the years, but this–"

I hold up my phone. "–You heard the guy. They're covering it up. Plus, I managed to find a policeman after I left, and he was just as brainwashed, if not worse. He said the police totally support K-Rin and don't see her sudden mass popularity as an issue, as long as everyone stays peaceful.

And I think it's working." I quickly bring up the Internet tab on my phone and show him. "Have you seen the news? A wave of criminals have been turning themselves in or admitting their crimes. I skimmed over it yesterday but there's been more today."

With that in mind, maybe Princess Preciosa's assassin will come forward at last, even if five years later. Was it an inside job and massive cover-up by the Royal Family after all?

Connelly studies the screen briefly. "You seriously think that's *her* doing?"

"She said she believes the world would benefit from more positivity. And ever since people heard that song, they've been acting high or out of character."

"That's a big stretch." His eyes widen. "Not to mention you saying she can move through TV screens." He glances me up and down. "How much have you drunk today?"

I nearly roll my eyes, but guess I can't blame him. "I'm totally sober. Look, you saw that rabbit jump out of the screen. Why can't K-Rin do it too?"

"I've been trying to forget that happened."

"But it did." I lean closer. "Conn, you can't block out the truth."

He smacks his hands down in his lap. "I don't understand the truth!"

I drop the phone on the sofa. Grasp his hands. We lock stares. What can I do or say to convince him?

"Please believe me, Conn."

His brow gradually relaxes. Eyes glaze over for a few moments. Is he reconsidering?

He sighs quietly. "I do believe you. This is all just...frightening me."

Well, that first part's a relief. Didn't he reckon I was making a 'big stretch', though?

"Me too," I say. "She has to know that I've worked out her secret by now, although what will she do about it?"

"What if she threatens us? I mean, who even is she, really? How much power does she have?"

"I'm going to find out." I release his hands to cup his soft face. "Try not to worry, okay?"

He nods slowly. I really expected him to fully fly off the handle about this, but my touch seems to soothe him. Thought *I* might freak out more too. There's a confidence in me that keeps me sane – no idea where it's coming from, but I'm immensely grateful for it.

9

The world's not ready for this. There's plenty of weird shit out there that can't be explained, but no-one wants to find out their idol isn't real, at least not in the conventional sense. Words alone aren't proof – I've already experienced that first-hand. Even if I could get hold of that music video's other version and show everyone, they'd say I edited it myself, that it's fake. They'd say the same if I caught K-Rin jumping in or out of a TV screen, just like with the rabbit. For such a critical populace, they still fall prey to her charms. What the hell is she, a siren? A witch? I've never believed in such things, but how can I refute what I've seen? You'd think my years of drinking and delving way too far into conspiracies has driven me mad. But Aki witnessed and heard the same as me, and Connelly saw the rabbit leaping out of the TV. Paranoid schizophrenics don't share hallucinations.

I won't post the gossip I caught yesterday. I, like everyone else at the BBC Broadcasting House, will swear myself to secrecy. For now, I want to keep my mind off the impending disastrous meal with Connelly's parents tonight. So I research into what K-Rin could possibly be. 'Entities that can move through TV screens' yields nothing relevant, and 'entities that brainwash through song' only brings up articles about how music can and has been used to hypnotise people. This is all pretty standard stuff, about music's effect on the body and subliminal messages. Nothing points to any beings that specifically communicate or hypnotise through music, except sirens through their voice. But they're Greek mythological half-bird-half-human beings. Not sure that's what we're up against. In any case, has she been planted by a government, or a powerful underground organisation? Google can't possibly answer that.

Shinpi's easier to tackle for now. Why would K-Rin have a rabbit? Is he literally an Easter present, as that vet jokingly suggested? Or is K-Rin using him as a kind of magic trick? Where do I even begin? What do I think of when I imagine scary rabbits? Definitely Watership Down. I type it into Google and brace myself. I remember being pretty traumatised by the film as a child. Connelly claims he wasn't fazed by it, but I don't buy that. Trying to avoid pictures as best I can, I find a page of quotes and one in particular catches my attention: "All the world will be your enemy, Prince with a Thousand Enemies, and whenever they catch you, they will kill you. [...] Be cunning and full of tricks and your people will never be destroyed." Reminds me of my current predicament, of what the world thinks of me after what I said about K-Rin. It *could* be worse – it's not like they're gunning for me yet – but the similarity is slightly uncanny. If I were to use this quote to help towards my survival, though, would I be onto something?

I shake my thinker. Need to move on. I should look at rabbit symbolism. Unsurprisingly, Google throws up all sorts: fertility, new life, sentiment, desire, prosperity. As spirit guides, they represent a time to look before you leap and are totem animals for creative problem solvers who need to switch directions fast. Apparently, dreaming of them predicts a long life. In the Chinese Zodiac, they're seen as one of the luckiest signs, bringing 'a long, peaceful life filled with beauty, love, and prosperity.' Certainly some running themes here. Most interestingly, though, rabbits are associated with moon deities, signifying rebirth or resurrection. I can't help re-reading those last words several times. I add this to the notes in my Word document and make sure to highlight it. I'll look more into this in a bit.

Further into my research, I find that Judaism and Christianity see rabbits as unclean. Fascinatingly, in Christian art, depending on context, they represent both positive and negative ideas: unbridled sexuality and lust, or the steep path to salvation. It's open to interpretation whether the rabbit's a symbol of man falling to his doom or striving for eternal salvation. That last part also gets added to my notes and highlighted. This is brilliant stuff, and I already feel closer to understanding what and why Shinpi could be – that is, if any of this abundant symbolism's true.

Moving on. Their connection to moon deities: in Chinese folklore, the rabbit's a companion of the Moon goddess Chang'e, 'constantly pounding the elixir of life for her', but in some versions it 'pounds medicine for the mortals'. An Aztec legend states that the god Quetzalcoatl walked on Earth as a human and elevated a rabbit to the Moon after it offered itself as food. The god then returned the rabbit to Earth and said, "You may be just a rabbit, but everyone will remember you; there is your image in light, for all people and for all times." There's also a Mesoamerican legend of the gods Nanahuatzin and Tecciztecatl setting themselves alight to become the Sun and Moon. Because of Tecciztecatl's hesitation and 'cowardice', another deity threw a rabbit at his face so that the Moon would not be as bright as the Sun. So in both Asian and indigenous American folklore, for different reasons, an image of a rabbit is imprinted on the Moon. I'm not sure if any of it connects, but it's interesting to read about nonetheless.

K-Rin being a moon deity doesn't entirely make sense. What does she want with Earth, and why does she communicate/brainwash through music? Have I gone too far down the proverbial rabbit hole? At this point, I feel like anything's possible. The universe is complicated. Inevitably, K-Rin is too. The idea of meeting her unnerves me, especially now I know she's not human. If she wanted to get rid of me, she would've done it by now. Her shit doesn't work on me, but it doesn't on Aki either, and now he's gone. Why would she keep me around, when I have an ever-growing audience? Maybe because my audience makes no difference; they're still enamoured with her, and I don't think I can change that.

Sipping my second Caffeine Focus this morning, I continue researching deities associated with rabbits. Might as well keep going. We have Eostre, Anglo-Saxon goddess of the spring and rebirth; Freya, Norse mother goddess, giver of fruitfulness and love, associated with Holda the Norse moon goddess; Hermes, Greek god of the spoken word who held rabbits sacred as a fleet-footed messenger; and Wenenut, rabbit-headed Egyptian goddess who is the female counterpart to the hare-headed god Weneu. There's even a Chinese deity, Tu'er Shen the rabbit god, who manages the love and sex between homosexuals. The story behind that has no relevance to my situation, but I can't help peeking.

K-Rin could well be a goddess of spring, with her flower dress and beloved bunny. In that interview, she said she wants to inspire people to make a positive impact. She wants everyone to believe in their own potential and find true happiness. It's like she's trying to inject new life into the world. Or is that just what she wants us to think? Also, where does the TV thing fit in? I'm sure I won't find concrete answers on the Internet, but I've made a good start, I reckon.

The further the day goes on, and the more I ruminate on everything I've researched, my mind goes into overdrive. Lost count how many coffees I've had, again. I genuinely believe a spring/moon goddess-like deity, posing as a singer, has brainwashed the world into adoring her, and gifted me her pet rabbit in an attempt to keep me quiet. There's never been a better time to drink. Vodka's always slowed down my thoughts, but after my recent benders, I really can't stand the idea of it.

Wait 'til Connelly hears all of this when he gets home. No. He'll dismiss me. But I feel like I need to spread the word. Show people what I've found, as well as that clip of the receptionist's voice from yesterday. It could get them using their thinkers properly again. I could even slip in what I found out about Shinpi's hair – I haven't recorded it yet, but surely it only adds to my speculation about what he really is? Others deserve to know.

With my newfound enthusiasm, I hop back on the computer and bring up a Word document. End up staring blankly at the screen for what feels like ages, though. Can't even think of how to start. I need to bring all the information together, but energy suddenly drains from me. My thinker hurts more by the second. Why did I think this was wise? People will think I'm madder than they already do, and claim I used a paid actor for that voice clip. I didn't get his permission anyway. I can't post *any* of it online – if K-Rin discovers I've even remotely sussed out her true identity and intentions, she might find a way to silence me permanently. To keep both me and Connelly safe, I have to lock this all inside. It already feels heavy and uncomfortable. I've never kept a secret like this.

I spend the day tidying up my inbox instead, and sift through the never-ending messages. Unbelievably, I have between two-and-a-half and three million subscribers. If this trend continues, I'll hit several million by the week's end. That interview I did yesterday should help boost it too. I just want to sprint down the street, screaming joyously. It's hard to focus on any fear I have from this K-Rin situation now when I'm literally living my dream.

Instead of rocking back and forth in my darkened studio, questioning life and wondering what the hell I'm going to do, I enjoy a long, hot shower. I close my eyes, and let the water soothe me. As I run my hands through my hair, down my neck, and across my chest, I feel detached. Strange to feel this while sober. I just push past it and try to go back to revelling in my success.

After stepping out and drying off, I flop backwards on the bed. A strip of sunlight from the gap in the curtains slices my naked body in half. Sighing, I melt into the soft, warm quilt. Won't let fear overcome me. I'll lie here and bask in my growing attention, in Connelly's accelerating adoration of me. My light thinker and this golden euphoric rush make me wonder if someone spiked my coffee. My arms lift above me and hands rest on the pillows. Can't help replaying the other night, how amazing I made us both feel. I want him here right now. Want to do all kinds of things.

Phone vibrates once on Connelly's computer desk. Who could that be? Sighing, I pull myself up and grab my phone. A massive message from Kya:

'Maddix! You didn't tell me BBC were interviewing you! How cool is that? I have my own interview with Vogue tomorrow. Sent them the photoshoot pictures and they paid me to feature exclusively on their site and in next month's issue! They're desperate to get anything K-Rin related, no matter how last-minute. So's the public – ever since your mum's interview, loads more people have asked me for your contact no. I haven't shared it, don't worry. Anyway, I'll split the Vogue money with you, of course =) Also, thanks for dropping my name and handle in your video! People should believe the bunny was the real deal now. Anyway, see you tonight and we can talk more!'

My eyebrows stay raised as I read the whole thing. I trust her not to give out my details, unlike a certain mother of mine. And she's right; no-one *has* questioned the rabbit's authenticity in those photos. I'm unsurprised she got a Vogue interview, although it *has* been a while. They've paid her not to publish her images anywhere else? That's a first for her, I believe. They must've been impressed. How much is she getting? My apprehension about seeing her briefly returns. How will I be around her after last time?

Sitting on the end of the bed, I start replying: 'That's brill. I'm happy for you.' I type, 'No worries about the money – it's all yours,' then stare at the words. I don't know why, but my thumb deletes them. Instead, I write, 'Really generous of you to share your pay with me. It was great collaborating with you.' I frown at the screen. That first part isn't entirely humble of me, especially as I still owe her for the Black Cow! What's wrong with me? I shouldn't accept that money. It's her job. I drove there and loaned her the rabbit, but I'd never expect anything for it. Nevertheless, my thumb hits send.

I gaze up at my reflection in the floor to ceiling mirror opposite me. For several moments, I lock eyes with myself. How did I get so proud?

Anyway, best get on. Need to tidy up those research notes I made then go through all of my latest video statistics and comments.

*

When Connelly gets home around 6, he quick-changes into a fresh shirt and swaps his work trousers for jeans. I got dressed into my smart black jeans and long-sleeved dark-green check shirt hours ago – just need to tidy up my hair a bit. Resting my thinker against the fabric headboard, I watch him from the bed as he uses the mirror to comb over his own fringe. I lower my knees to see his butt.

"They were crazy today," he says.

Half in a daze, I say, "Oh, yeah?"

"It's bad enough that instead of producing sketches for our new summer catalogue design, Roxy spent all day on an A3 portrait of K-Rin to go on her DeviantArt account, right? The boss, and everyone else then gushed over it. I went on that site and there's thousands of K-Rin drawings, digital art... even of Shinpi."

I hadn't thought to check that site, but I'm not particularly thrown. Has anyone drawn me since my popularity increase?

"But then our Events Co-ordinator got everyone into a meeting to share his ideas on K-Rin themed parties, and now everyone's working on it to make it a reality."

I frown. "People would actually ask you to organise that? How would it look? Lots of flowers and bunnies?"

"Pretty much." He chucks the comb on the chest of drawers. "No different from our Easter theme. In fact, they're basically replacing it with K-Rin. They're hoping to get more ideas from the music video she releases on Sunday."

I shake my thinker despairingly.

"Get this, though: he chose me to head the project."

Understandingly, he doesn't sound happy about it, but I'll say it anyway: "Oh, wow. Uh, congratulations."

He meets my gaze in the mirror. "Yeah, except we both know why they chose me. Everyone spent the rest of the day asking me questions about you, the rabbit, my sister, anything we know about K-Rin." He sighs. Guess that must be a kick in the balls. All I can do is give a slight sympathetic cringe. He continues, "So I'm writing up a draft advertising campaign for the new theme based on the suggestions they give me. Boss said I couldn't simply amend the Easter one – it needs to be 'totally different'." He uses air quotes there, and groans. "God, I can't wait for this craze to die already. Apparently, pet shops are filling up with white bunnies, and Facebook and Instagram are blowing up with cosplayers."

"Mm. I haven't gone on those today, but I've seen some K-Rin makeup tutorials on YouTube."

The pet shops don't shock me, either, although they didn't have any of bunnies when I went there the other day.

He tightens his belt. "And just think: out of everyone, Vogue still picked Kya."

"Yeah. Well, she did a good job. And she had a certain little prop that no-one else did."

Nodding slowly, he turns to me. "Speaking of which, is he fed and watered, et cetera?"

"Yep. All ready for a night by his lonesome, much to your parents' disappointment."

He raises an eyebrow. "Yeah. We're not lugging that hutch over there, and I don't care how well-behaved he is, if we lose him in Kya's house or garden, we may never see him again."

I really don't think that'd happen, considering how unnaturally still that thing stays, but it'll be nice not to have to keep an eye on him all night. You know, with my influence and the fact that Connelly doesn't seem as brainwashed by the song anymore, I'm curious about something... When was the last time he was around Shinpi?

"Do me a favour and come with me," I say, and thrust myself off the bed.

"What's going on?" he says with shifty eyes.

I grasp his hand and pull him out of the room. "A test."

He lets me take him into the studio.

I flick on the light and gesture towards the hutch. "What colour is he?"

"Seriously? This again? We don't have time to mess about."

"Will you just look? Please."

I'm struggling not to bounce on the spot from anticipation.

Sighing under his breath, he finally glances at the hutch. His focus lingers there, and his expression turns graver.

"What have you done?" he asks.

"Nothing. Why?"

He leans down to peer in closer. "He's fucking grey all over!"

I almost laugh. "Fascinating."

"No, it's downright disturbing." He straightens and jabs his finger towards me. "You swear you did nothing?"

I raise my hands. "I swear on both our lives."

He stares for a short while longer, at me and the creature in the hutch. He keeps trying to dispute that this thing is otherwordly, but he has to accept it now.

"It must be my influence," I say. "Those closest to me start to see the truth."

173

"Maddix," he says abruptly. "We literally do not have time to deliberate this right now."

So what if we're late? This is important!

"We need to get up early tomorrow morning as it'll be Friday," he goes on. "Have you packed your overnight bag?"

I have to stop myself from grabbing and shaking him. Why are his priorities always in the wrong places?

"Yes," is all I respond with.

"And I know you're sober at the moment, but I need you to go easy on the booze later."

"I meant what I said at The Gold Lotus. I need to treat you *and* myself better. I'm only on coffee tonight."

Plus, me getting drunk around his parents never goes well.

He raises his brow, like he doesn't believe me at first. "Okay. Well, that's good."

Eventually, he smiles, which reassures me. Maybe it was my unchanging expression that showed I was serious. Whatever the case, even though at the time I wasn't aware of where exactly the words were coming from, I do mean them now.

During the forty-five-minute drive to Epsom, I distract myself from the dread of tonight by scrolling through DeviantArt K-Rin drawings on my phone. Connelly still won't let me talk about Shinpi's colouring – guess he's overwhelmed, so we'll have to frustratingly hold off for the night. Anyway, the artwork: as usual, the talent level ranges from amazingly photorealistic to awfully misshapen. Connelly's right: Shinpi's on here. Quite the little celebribunny. I make an appearance every once in a while too. Among the artwork I've seen before – a small handful of fan drawings that were so good I incorporated them in the banner image on my YouTube page – I spot some new ones. Each picture has me holding Shinpi, though, and looking happy. It's a cheek, and a bloody lie. But I guess I *have* been projecting a humbly grateful image to the public. Seeing myself represented like this sickens me.

The best drawing of K-Rin I've seen is her in the usual attire, sitting proudly on a throne of flowers with Shinpi in her lap. Clearly not AI-generated, the artist's nailed that smug expression, enough to make me angry. It's almost like she's gloating at *me*, because she knows I can't do anything to stop whatever she's planning. It's hard to keep my research from earlier a secret from Connelly, especially during these silences. A great deal of this artwork does depict her like a goddess, floating in the sky, surrounded by light. It feels like if she isn't one already, the world will soon change that.

We park next to Connelly's parents' shiny BMW estate car then crunch across the gravel driveway to Kya's house. They always have to own the latest, fanciest model – ironic considering it usually sits outside a semi-detached town house in Croydon. Connelly and I have consistently stuck with our reliable Hyundai i20 and second-hand Vauxhall Corsa, respectively, for several years now.

Stopping under the tall porch, he mutters, "No matter what, please be civil."

"I'll try my hardest."

He sighs and rings the bell. I take a deep breath and tell my nervous stomach pangs to clear off. I'd like to see them take a dig at me now – I've accomplished way more since we last saw them.

The front door swings open, and a slice of that disturbing darkness from before sweeps through me. I don't want it, but can't seem to banish it. A grinning blonde Kya says, "Hey!"

She steps aside to let us in. As Connelly scrubs his shoes on the doormat, he says exactly what I'm thinking: "What happened to the pink?"

She lifts her ponytail above her non-thinker then lets it slip strand by strand through her fingers. "Fancied a change."

Surely we all know that's not the real reason? She's even wearing a flowing white dress and flat flowery shoes. I can't believe she's done this to herself. I try to contain my reaction, but I've no idea what my face is doing. At least she doesn't look totally like K-Rin this time, so I'm not consumed by that horrible pure hatred, but I'm still having trouble dealing with it. This is ridiculous. I'll have to pretend everything's okay, for everyone's sake.

After scrubbing my boots too, I hang up my jacket, push the door shut behind me, and follow them down the wide hallway. The place is silent compared to Saturday night; only our footsteps echo around us. A lush savoury chicken smell wafts from around the corner. I wasn't that hungry before, but I am now.

She leads us through the L-shape of hallway, dining area, and kitchen. Dressed way too formally in a dark evening dress and suit, Jade and Ed loiter by the central worktop, sipping their drinks. Looks like Jade's on the bubbly as usual and Ed's on good old-fashioned water. I expect them both to give me that awkward half-smile with expressionless eyes. I've never understood how it's possible for people much shorter than me to peer at me down their noses. Only Ed does, though; Jade lights up.

Connelly goes straight over to hug them. "Hi, Mother. Father."

"Hi, my dear." Jade kisses his cheek. "Great to see you, and Maddix."

Does she mean that? Can't say I agree after last time. I nod to them both anyway.

She checks around. "Did you not bring the bunny?"

There it is. I contain a grunt of annoyance.

"I told you, Mum," Connelly says diplomatically, "it's too much hassle to lug him over, and he won't have anywhere proper to sleep."

She waves a dismissive hand. "Oh, yes. That *is* a shame, though. Is he really as tame as he looks, Maddix?"

I rub the back of my neck. "He does seem to be a zen master."

She chuckles. Ed appears to watch me with interest, because of the subject matter, I suppose.

"What beverage can I get you, Conn?" Kya says. "Wine?"

Thank you for moving on!

"Yes, please," he says, and sighs. "I could do with a glass."

"And Maddix?" She glances me up and down. "No vodka bottle tonight?"

"I'm strictly on coffee at the moment," I say.

The parents' eyebrows rise at me. Surely they're pleased too?

"Okay." Kya also sounds shocked.

Connelly's smile is so cute I want to push him against the worktop and make out, his family be damned.

"Black," I tell Kya. "Extra strong."

She spins on her heel and sets about boiling the kettle and retrieving the wine from the fridge. Meanwhile, I catch Ed's stare again, but he quickly focuses on Connelly.

"Things sure have been exciting for you two this week," he says.

Connelly opens his mouth to speak, but I get there first, to make Ed look at me again: "It's been mental. Thanks to K-Rin, my channel's really soared. Of course, I can't give her all the credit."

Ed nods. "Quite an achievement."

Have I finally impressed him?

Jade's intense green eyes fix on me. "Is it true you don't actually know her?"

"I don't." I feel like I'll never stop clarifying that. She's asking with the same intrigue as the besotted fans in my comments section. My thinker tilts. "You guys aren't obsessed with her too, are you?"

"Well," Ed says, "we certainly recognise talent when we see it."

I smirk at him to disguise my glare. Yet another remark that I'll never know was aimed at me or not.

Kya brings Connelly his wine. "For the first time ever, my parents and I agree on music."

But she likes electronica, not pop or whatever K-Rin's trying to emulate.

Connelly hides an eye roll by sipping from his glass. Jade chuckles, in that unbearably posh way like she's from Buckinghamshire or something. If the Durands are into K-Rin, some undeniable brainwashing's behind this.

Jade sips her own wine. "Kya, honey, those photographs of you with that adorable bunny-rabbit are gorgeous."

She straightens, as if to appear taller. "Thank you. It'll be amazing to be on the front of Vogue again."

"That's our girl," Ed says, raising his glass.

Connelly stares into his wine with that awkwardness he always has when standing between his gushing parents and their pride and joy.

I know he hates me doing this, but I can't help cutting in with: "Connelly's designing a new campaign for K-Rin-themed parties."

Yep, his eyes have widened and now they're shifting between us all.

Kya gasps and gently smacks his arm. "That's such a great idea."

Ed nods slowly with apparent approval. Good.

Jade's shiny pink lips grin as she says, "Indeed. Sounds wonderful. I can imagine it's a bright and colourful feast for the eyes, beaming with positivity."

I struggle not to throw up in my mouth.

"That's the plan," Connelly says.

"You have to show me when it's done," Kya says. The kettle clicks, so she goes over to pour the water into a mug.

I follow her over and lean on the side. "What's cooking? Smells good."

"Spring chicken casserole." She glances over at the large steaming pot on the hob. "Never made it before, so I hope it's all right."

After stirring my Caffeine Sobriety, she hands me the mug. I thank her, place it on the side, and say, "Don't suppose you have any spices you can chuck on my portion?"

"Thought you hate spicy stuff?"

"Oh," Connelly says, "he's totally into it now."

I clasp my hands together as if begging and her eyebrows flick up. She moves along a little, and checks inside an overhead cupboard. "Think paprika's the strongest I've got."

"That'll do," I say. "Please."

She places the small pot near the hob. "Dinner will be ready soon, so all of you make yourselves comfortable."

We can try.

"Can we do anything to help, honey?" Jade says.

"No, thanks." She lifts the lid of the boiling pot. "I've got it all under control."

Her parents cross the room to the made-up dining table. Don't fancy being with them any longer than I have to. Ed for obvious reasons, and Jade: she's usually tolerable, but today she's way too chipper about this K-Rin thing. I take a careful sip of Caffeine Calm, clink the mug back down on the side, and tell them I'm going to the bathroom. Slight lie, as I think I'll go in there and sit on the toilet lid for a bit. Connelly watches me move away and around the corner with a wary expression. I told him I'm not drinking tonight, so he shouldn't be worrying.

As I pass the glass-panelled living room doors, I do stop, but not to go in and peruse the alcohol selection. I peek in at the darkness. That's where this all started, where I saw the alternate version of the song. What will I see on Sunday when she releases the 'real' video? How will it affect everyone else? Surely they can't be brainwashed any more than they have been? Should I try to stop it? What kind of power do I have, though? I doubt I can convince people not to watch it, but I don't want to just sit back and wait for shit to happen. If she has bad intentions for the world, and I'm the only one who's aware of it, I have to do something.

Kya's quite the cook. Everyone's tucking into their plates of chicken, onion, broccoli, petits pois, new potatoes, and pesto. Mine's got that tiny paprika kick to it. Jade and Ed keep complimenting the food. Isn't three times enough?

"So, Kya," I say, and clear my throat, "what did Jade and Ed get you for your birthday?"

Ed gives me a tiny glare. I know he hates when I shorten his name, but too bad.

Kya sips her wine. "They gave me a wine hamper last week for the party, then tonight they gave me these beauties."

In turn, she indicates to her earrings and necklace: a matching glass teardrop set with pressed flowers inside. They do look pretty. I nod with approval, but can't help wondering if a certain spring goddess inspired them.

"You really do look even more like K-Rin now," Jade says.

There it is. Kya seems to beam with pride. Connelly and I exchange a glance.

As I chew long and hard on a piece of chicken, Ed says, "Maddix, you've been making very outlandish claims recently. Do you honestly believe them, or are you doing it simply for attention?"

Kya's grin falls.

I was wondering how long it'd take for him to challenge me. He hasn't even heard the worst of it.

Jade widens her eyes at him. "Edmund. I'm sure Maddix wouldn't do that."

I appreciate her support; she does sometimes stand up for me when he's unnecessarily being a dick.

He ignores her and carries on eating. Won't even look at me. Typical. Connelly tenses up in my peripheral. His knife and fork pause on his plate, mid-cut. I don't want another argument, but Ed's an expert at instigating them. Hopefully, with no Russian Chaos in my system, *I* can control my tongue a lot better.

I swallow my food and straighten up. "Everything I've posted has been, to the best of my knowledge, true."

Ed frowns. "Even about how you got the rabbit?" He glances up at Connelly. "Son, tell me it didn't jump out of your TV."

Connelly focuses on his plate. "I don't know how it got in."

I can understand not wanting to admit that to them, but at the same time I wish he'd stand by me. Guess he's not outright denying it, though.

"However he got to them, K-Rin sent him," Kya says. "That's all that matters."

Neutral, as always. If only her parents could be like that.

"No, honey." Straightening up, Ed rests his knife and fork on his half-finished plate. "It matters more that Maddix isn't trying to fill your

179

brother's head with lies."

I start overheating. Grasp my cutlery tighter. Not only is he speaking about us like we're not here, but he's talking shit. If drunk, I would've blurted an expletive at him, but now, I'm trying to pick the right thing to say.

Connelly stares hard at him. "Father, don't do this. Please."

"What, worry about you?"

I focus on my food and continue eating. Just listen to your son, for once.

"You're very reserved tonight, Maddix," he says. Why can't he shut up?

I struggle not to huff. "I'm just trying to be respectful to our host. I'm pretty sure Kya doesn't want us arguing at what's supposed to be a peaceful birthday dinner."

He lifts a hand. "Of course. I'm sorry, Kya. I only say all of this out of concern."

Yeah, right. You should be more concerned about yourself: how you, your wife, and daughter have clearly been brainwashed.

I stay quiet as much as I can for the rest of dinner while everyone else discusses what they've been up to recently, inevitably referencing K-Rin whenever possible. Jade only used to ask me surface-level questions about my channel before – and I was grateful for even that level of interest – but now she wants to know the ins and outs of how I make my videos and what the bunny's like to work with. I suppress my annoyance and keep it brief. Connelly doesn't admit his opinion on the whole situation, or how much it's stressing him out at work. He cares so much about not causing conflict that I'm surprised he's not lying and nodding along with them. I think he's just as sick of the subject as I am. My usual compulsion to drown myself in vodka isn't there whatsoever. I've no clue why. I've never been able to tolerate his parents while sober. Maybe I'm finally growing.

Jade helps Kya load the dirty plates and cutlery into the dishwasher, while Connelly gets out dessert bowls and searches the fridge for whatever we're having for pudding. This, of course, leaves me alone with Ed. I take a deep breath, let it out silently, and stare at him until he finally meets my gaze.

Annoyingly, his eyebrow arches. "I suppose you're quite the celebrity now."

I nearly say, 'Jealous?' but rein it in.

"I'm nowhere near Kya's level of fame," I say, "but I've gained *a lot* of

180

supporters since last weekend."

Technically, I reckon I've surpassed her, but I don't want to voice that.

His eyes narrow. "It's hard to imagine all these people would support someone who is avidly against K-Rin." Trying to goad me again. If he didn't frustrate me this much, I might feel sorry for him. "There's always been something off about you. Even without the booze, you're insane."

I can't help beaming at that.

"How is that funny?" he asks.

"Because I'm one of the only sane people left in this world."

He shakes his non-thinker, as if appalled.

I cross my arms. "Don't you find it even weirder that you, of all people, are into her?"

"Well, normally, you're drunk as a skunk and hate spices. People change."

He does have a point. My changes happened pretty much overnight too. But this isn't about me.

I lean forward and rest my elbows on the table with my thinker in my hands. Stare into his eyes, daring him to do the same. But he can't.

"Would you look at me for more than a few seconds?" I mutter.

Frowning at the table, he laughs under his breath. "Why?"

Wow. It really is that hard for him.

"Show me some respect," I say.

He scoffs quietly. "You've hardly ever shown me respect, and I'm your elder."

"Oh, I have so many years on you."

I mentally shake myself. Don't know what I meant by that.

He looks at me. "Excuse me?"

At least he's maintaining eye contact, despite how awkward it is.

"I said *show me respect*, like K-Rin told you to."

Will he listen to *that*? His suspicious expression starts to glaze over.

Connelly joins us to lay down the bowls.

"What we having, Conn?" I ask.

"It's called an orange upside-down cake." Kya brings it over and places it in the centre of the table on a round gold plate. "Made it myself."

On a nicely browned cake base, a bunch of orange slices form the petals of a blossoming flower. The sharp citrus tingles my nose but otherwise smells lush. Her cakes have always tasted amazing, and once everyone's settled at the table again and I take my first bite, she proves that tonight is no exception. In fact, the sharpness has me promptly going for a second slice.

Every now and then, I catch Ed watching me. I just smirk at him again. I like making him uncomfortable. Not sure things will ever improve between us. He's never tried to get on with me, even when Connelly and I first got together. It's like I'll never be good enough for his son, his family, or my own. Now I'm actually doing well for myself, but he, Mum, and Dad still don't fully approve. I bet if I start banging on about how amazing everyone's new idol is, only then will they change their minds.

A crisp breeze relaxes me as I sit on the edge of a pool lounger, gazing into the purple-lit water. I love that the house is far enough away from the main road not to hear any cars. It's just me, relishing the dark silence. Feel like I could stay out here for hours. Relieving to take a break from all the drama, but part of me wants to dive into my phone to check out the latest comments, messages, and gossip. In general, I haven't felt this clear for years. I've spent too long cooped up in our studio, hunched over a screen filled with crazy theories. Sure, without it, I wouldn't have built my career, but I should've gone out more. Maybe then I wouldn't be considered so 'insane'.

The patio door to the living room slides open and shut behind me.

"You all right out here?" Kya says.

I glance over my shoulder to smile at her. Through the glass, I spot the others on the sofas, chatting. Can't help wondering if Ed's complaining about me – by his deep frown, I'd say he's complaining about *something* – but I also kind of don't care. A warm sense of peace flows through me, which usually happens after several drinks. Seeing Kya come towards me, though, with her ever-growing likeness to the spring goddess, that peace starts to cloud over. I hate that part of me wishes she'd go back inside. She perches on the lounger next to me and peers into the pool too. The purple lights reflect in her eyes.

"My dad's not making you uncomfortable again, is he?" she asks.

"No more than usual."

She sighs.

"Don't worry about it," I add. "I did also come out for some fresh air."

She traces the tip of her flowery shoe across the tile. "I wish you two could get along. Wish he wasn't so judgemental."

I shrug. "It's been ten years. Don't think he'll change now."

"But *you* have." She studies me. "There's something different about you."

Oh, really? She leans closer and takes a decent look. I should feel uneasy, but I just stare back. I'm not the only one who's different. That unexplainable, dark part of me may wish she'd bugger off, but while she's here, I might as well ask:

"Do you really want to be like K-Rin?"

She doesn't blink, but seems to hesitate. "Yeah."

"But you know hardly anything about her."

I doubt logic will beat brainwashing here, but it's worth a try.

"She's just...perfect. I'm not sure how I can really say that, but I just know it's true."

Her soft voice is filled with an admiration that I wish she'd show me instead. Why am I thinking this? I should be mad that one of my closest friends has been brainwashed, not jealous.

"I want to meet her," she says, and gazes at the sky. "I'm hoping I can get her attention with the photoshoot."

I find my focus on the sky too, picking out the endless patterns of stars. "It's hard to say what'll get her attention."

"I can't believe she won't even talk to you. But I'm sure she has her reasons."

I'm sure she does. She thinks she's above me, like one of these bright burning stars. Even stars stop burning eventually.

"Kya," I say, almost transfixed now, "do you ever feel this hot glow inside when people compliment you?"

"Well, compliments are always great."

"But do you get this overwhelming satisfaction when you're in the spotlight? Like a rush. And you burn so hot that you could explode."

Just thinking about it gets me riled up.

"I do," she says. "It's why I wanted to become a model."

I nod at the sky. "Don't you think it's unfair, that K-Rin bursts into the world and gains everyone's love and admiration in a matter of days?"

She hesitates. "I guess."

Was that a successful crack, or at least a chip?

"Why does she deserve the attention more than anyone else?" I say.

"...Because she's going to bring a positive change to the world. She already has."

"You have too: think of all the fans you've brought joy to, the money you've given to charities. You fought your way to where you are. You didn't have everything handed to you. *You're* an inspiration."

My eyes drift back down to her. A slight frown ruins the elated expression she had only moments ago. I hate to poison her happiness, but she does deserve recognition more than K-Rin.

"I'm proud of everything I've accomplished." Sighing, she glances down at herself. "But I'm not exactly getting any younger."

"Age means nothing."

She scoffs. "It does in this industry."

"Then show them it doesn't. You're way prettier than K-Rin." This makes her flick up her eyebrows as if in disbelief. I tilt my thinker. "Look at me." She does, so I say as clearly and seriously as possible, "She's a trickster, Kya. Don't let yourself get sucked in like everyone else. You're better than that."

The longer she stays silent with an unwavering intensity, the more I reckon it's sinking in. Can my words be enough to convince her? They should be, after all these years of knowing each other.

I lean in even closer. "Do you trust me?"

Her frown disappears. Tone falls flat: "Yes."

Good to hear. I shouldn't have doubted it.

"Do you believe me," I ask, "that K-Rin's not to be trusted?"

"Yes. I believe you."

Why am I grinning? Because I'm happy to have broken through to her? How was it that easy?

I still have her locked in a stare as I murmur, "Tomorrow, in your interview, you tell them what you believed before, that she's an inspiration to you. Don't be afraid to lie to keep the spotlight. You're going to steal it from her. You'll be a better K-Rin than she ever was. You're Kya. Beautiful. Confident. More and more people will adore you, and not her. She's a nobody. She literally spawned from nothingness." Neither of us have blinked once. Her focused eyes tell me she's taking this all in, so I finish with: "We're going to send her back to where she came from."

After a few moments, she nods slowly.

For the next hour and a half, Kya seems rather withdrawn as we all watch TV. I would've thought seeing the creation of these huge flower sculptures would impress her, but honestly I think she's a little shaken. The colourful towering rabbit is definitely the most spectacular. I keep bracing for it to come to life and leap out of the 60" TV. Eventually, Jade has to mention how much K-Rin would love this show. Kya smiles uneasily and sips her wine. She'll have to get much better at hiding her feelings.

Once it's over, Jade leaves the living room to collect her coat. Kya and Connelly follow her out. I push myself up to leave too, but Ed lingers in the doorway.

"Tell me," he mutters with a serious tone, "what did you say to Kya out there?"

Shouldn't be surprised that he picked up on her behaviour.

"What do you mean?" I say.

"She hasn't been the same since she came back in after talking to you. Did you upset her?"

I cross my arms. "If you look at me properly, I'll tell you."

With a clenched jaw, he finally meets my eyes.

"I didn't upset her," I explain. "Quite frankly, you did."

His hard frown only worsens his wrinkles. "What?"

"She wants us to get along. But that's impossible when you keep criticising and judging me. When are you going to accept me for who I am?"

I expect him to shrug me off, or least bite back a passive-aggressive retort. But strangely, he now can't tear his gaze from me. He's gone rigid. Seeing him this uncomfortable satisfies me more than he'll ever know, but why's his expression turning blank like it did at the table earlier?

"You're absolutely right," he says, and sighs. "I'm sorry I've caused so much animosity."

I feel like falling over.

"Edmund, you coming?" Jade calls.

Footsteps from the hallway draw nearer. Connelly appears behind Ed. "Everything okay?"

My arms unfold. I can barely process what just happened.

Ed seems to smile genuinely at me, for what must be the first time ever. "I'll see you again soon, Maddix. Take care, and all the best for your channel."

I can't even answer that. He slips past Connelly, who watches him saunter down the hallway towards the front door. For once, his suspicious eyebrow is very much warranted.

Not long after her parents have gone, Kya tells us she's off to bed, to get

185

plenty of sleep for the big day tomorrow. She seems shattered. Think she had a few glasses of wine, and on top of all that cooking then me breaking through to her, I reckon she'll sleep well tonight. Doubt I will, though. She says that Connelly and I can obviously stay up, so we do.

I step out into the garden again for more refreshing night air. Pacing around the edge of the purple pool, I try to wrap my thinker around Ed's one-eighty. Did I finally get through to him? Even after all these years, it seemed too sudden, considering how he was earlier. I easily changed Kya's mind too... What the actual fuck?

The patio door slides open and shut again. Connelly this time. He approaches the pool and stops at the edge with his hands in his pockets. We stand opposite each other with the water between us. The purple glow across his face almost entrances me.

"Thanks for staying calm tonight," he says. "I know my dad was pushing it."

"Mm."

"What was that as they were leaving, though? Was he being serious?"

I almost laugh. "If he was, then things have just got extra bat-shit."

He frowns. "Do you know what's wrong with Kya, too? I asked her but she dismissed me."

"I managed to convince her that K-Rin's an imposter."

His eyes widen and he murmurs, "Did you tell her about the TV screen teleportation thing?"

"No, just that she's not who she claims and Kya deserves the limelight more than her."

His frown relaxes a little. "I thought you said everyone was brainwashed. Has it worn off for her already?"

"I don't know, but I got through."

He sighs with relief. "Good. That means you can help other people too."

I screw up my face playfully in thought. "Hmm. Nah. Not yet." Naturally, this makes him frown again, so I explain, "I've realised tonight that it's best the general public don't believe the truth, for now. K-Rin thinks she can take over. I want her to think she can. Then right when she's on the verge of winning everyone's complete and utter devotion, I'll rip it all out from under her."

"How? You don't even know what you're going up against."

I smirk, and it feels strange. "I've got a better idea now. She feeds on adoration." Takes one to know one. "I'm going to convince everyone not to

186

trust K-Rin, and to worship Kya instead."

"How the hell are you going to do that?"

"Power of suggestion. It's crazy, but I seem to have it."

"Well, it hasn't worked on them yet. How will it later on down the line?"

"I'm stronger now."

He holds out his arms. "What the fuck are you talking about, Maddix?"

Normally, I'd hate him getting worked up at me, but I remain assertive. "I can influence people, make them believe whatever I want. I didn't know how before."

As much as I should be, don't feel like I have time to be overwhelmed by that fact.

He hesitates. "Say that's true. You're going to let everyone, including my parents, stay brainwashed temporarily, until the 'right' moment so you can say a big 'ha ha, fuck you' to K-Rin?"

"Yep."

Plus, I want to appreciate Ed's attitude change towards me a little longer.

He practically gawps at me. "Maddix, if you do know how to unbrainwash the world, as fucking mental as that sounds, you've got to do it sooner rather than later. You said yourself that she could have bad intentions. What if you're too late?"

I cross my arms. "I won't be. Trust me."

"Really?" He scoffs under his breath. "I'm not sure I even know who you are right now."

I shouldn't have been totally honest with him. That adoration he had for me's been cut drastically. I need it back.

He goes to turn but I stop him: "Conn. I'm sorry." He seems to study me from across the pool. I try to sound sincere as I add, "I didn't mean any of that. I'm just pissed at her for doing this, for tricking everyone. I shouldn't be petty." I place a hand on my chest. "I'll do what I can to change people's minds before Sunday."

We're locked in a stare for several seconds, then he sighs and nods. At least he appears to believe me. But his last words still bother me.

"The thing with the rabbit," he says. "It *has* been on my mind all night... I'm just struggling to accept it's possible." Wish I could ease that tense frown and help him come to terms with it. He says, "Are you still going to try to meet K-Rin?"

"I can try, but I don't think she'll let it happen. She would've responded by now."

He glances down. "Maybe you shouldn't. Who knows what she'll do? It's probably safer to stay away."

Especially if she really is a goddess, although for some reason part of me isn't even scared about that. I *am* different, but I've no clue why or how.

"I'm still me," I assure him.

After another few moments, he softly says, "I know."

So he trusts me about that. Shame I've lied to him about K-Rin, but it's a necessary evil.

10

An early morning shower in Kya's shiny guest bathroom boots me into gear for the day. Being up and about before mid-morning is alien to me – I should do it more often, but the booze has always made it virtually impossible. It's been odd being able to fall asleep without it, too. Well, I said I'd improve myself, so this is a great start.

From a stool at the central kitchen counter, I enjoy my Caffeine Kick and scroll through the messages on my phone. All more of the same, really, but since my BBC interview, several YouTubers have requested to host one of their own with me on their channel. Just for views, no doubt. Some of these are big names, and I'm almost flattered, but they're jumping on the K-Rin bandwagon, and I can't tell them anything I haven't already. I should do them the courtesy of politely declining, but every time my thumb hovers over the reply button, it swiftly swipes to something else.

From around the corner and down the hallway, I hear light steps pattering down the stairs. Must be Kya, especially since Connelly only got in the shower a few minutes ago. She whips around into the kitchen. Under the white leather jacket she wore at her party, a beige dress flows down her body: a smart but casual outfit for her Vogue interview. She leans both hands on the counter, and looks down apprehensively at me.

"What is it?" I ask.

"My agent's booked me in to appear at Cavendish Square Gardens tomorrow. He wants me to pose as K-Rin in full costume, to draw in as much attention as possible." She sounds uncharacteristically nervous. "He thinks the more pictures people take and upload, we can get K-Rin cosplay trending and more people will want to do it themselves."

I sincerely hope that doesn't happen, but it probably will.

"How will this benefit you?" I ask.

"It's 'another chance to gain more popularity and hopefully interest from other magazines.' Guess we can combine it into a meet and greet – haven't done one of those in a while. He's already throwing around the idea of an autograph and picture event in the near future." She'd normally be ecstatic about that, but instead she sighs and grimaces. "Are you free to go there with me tomorrow?"

"Uh, sure." Should be interesting to see the turnout and how people react. Maybe they'd want to meet me too. "You want me to be your camera guy? Or will Connelly be doing that?"

"I do have my usual photographer coming, and yeah, it'd be cool if Connelly could make it to get some extra shots for Instagram. But you: I'll need your *support*. That's why I was also going to ask are you free to come with me to Mayfair today, as backup?"

I glance down at my mug, take another sip, and say, "Well, I don't have any plans. Yeah."

She smiles. "Oh, thank you so much. I just feel like I need your advice, on what to say."

"You've spoken to Vogue before."

"I know, but I've never lied to them. I need to act like K-Rin's still my inspiration. Feels weird saying this, but I'm not sure I can pull it off."

At least she didn't revert to her brainwashed state overnight.

"What time's your interview?" I ask.

"Twelve."

"And how long roughly from here is Mayfair? An hour or so?"

"Yep. We'll have time to go over what exactly I should say at a coffee place."

I grin. "Brill."

"And since I need to be in the area again tomorrow, I'm going to ask my assistant to sort a hotel room for tonight. It'd probably be best if you had one too so you don't have to do loads of driving."

"Mm." Will be nice to get out of the flat for another night. But what kind of hotel will she have us stay at? "How much do you think a room will be?"

"Well, it depends what we can get at such short notice, but don't worry about that. I'll sort it for you."

Central London, short notice: it'll be treble figures for sure. I'd certainly appreciate her helping me out. Until I get my new substantial YouTube and Patreon payments this month, I can't even afford a room at a Travel Lodge.

"I'll pay you back in about a couple weeks," I insist. "I still owe you for the Black Cow too."

"Okay. We'll work something out." She pulls out her rose-gold phone from her jacket. "Let me ring my assistant a minute."

I nod, and she taps on her phone while pacing to the dining area. As I finish my mug, I watch her talk through her requirements with her assistant. I need an assistant to go through all my messages and comments. Makes me think of Aki again. His phone in my jacket still hasn't rung or buzzed. My anxiety regarding his disappearance seems to have dissipated completely. It honestly feels like he was never there. If it weren't for me playing back this video we did together, I'd reckon that were true. Why am I not worried anymore?

Kya returns to me and slips her phone away. I turn off the video and straighten up.

"Right," she says, "we're booked into the Courthouse Hotel. Best rooms they had were Double and Queen. And I normally get the Queen anyway."

"Then I assume you have rightfully taken it again?"

She shrugs. "We can swap if you want, although there's no difference other than size and it's thirty quid dearer."

"You have it." I smile. "I'm sure a Double's big enough for me." Although now I'm picturing myself splayed out on a super king bed, soaking in the peace and privilege. One day.

*

I'm actually rather excited about this, especially tomorrow's event at Cavendish Square Gardens. It's a pretty place, and the weather's meant to be dry and sunny; it should be perfect. People might want pictures of me too – the idea of that doesn't intimidate me as much as it normally would, and I'm completely sober.

On the drive home, Connelly seems pensive. Maybe he's antsy about going back to work, or jealous that I get to go with Kya to Vogue House. As tomorrow's Saturday, he can at least join us for the photography/meet-and-greet event – like Kya said, he can get some snaps straight on Instagram for her. He could come to the hotel after work today and spend the night out with me. He's always wanted to stay in a five-star hotel. Shouldn't leave the rabbit alone for two nights in a row, though. We haven't taken enough trips together. Need to see more of the country, of the world. With my recent pay rises and the forethought of a bunny-sitter, I'm sure we can make that a reality soon enough.

"Thank you for getting along with everyone last night," Connelly speaks up at last. "I know it was still touch and go in places, but overall I think it went really well."

I'm glad he thinks that, and I'm happy it did too.

"It certainly did compared to usual," I say. "How come you're so tense, then?"

He scrunches up his face a little. "I'm fine."

Okay, I don't believe that for a second, but I daren't question him.

Once we're home, I quickly check on Shinpi. Seems fine. Made the food and water disappear again, huh? I top them back up then grab my small powerbank from the desk – will need that tomorrow.

Connelly pops in to say goodbye. I go to him and kiss his cheek. Hopefully, that'll help relax him.

"All the best for work," I say. "Let me know if anything crazy happens."

He sighs. "Crazy's the new normal."

I snigger. Isn't it just?

"Good luck to you too," he says. "Be safe, stay out of trouble, and keep me updated."

I salute him. "I'll do my best."

"Okay. I'll meet you tomorrow morning at Cavendish Square Gardens, yeah?"

"Mm-hmm. And Connelly..." My hands cup his face. He stares into my eyes. I feel like I need to reassure him, and there's something I want to hear from him. "I love you."

He slowly smiles. "I love you too."

That golden glow engulfs me again. I can't get enough of it. But we're both on a tight schedule now, so I pull away from him.

To save me driving, I get a taxi to take me to Mayfair. Just as expensive as a twenty-four hour stay at any of the car parks in the area, and Connelly can drive us back tomorrow. At least Kya lent me cash for the fare, but I'll be paying her back when I can, and I mean it.

I use the thirty-five minutes in the taxi to go through the never-ending comments on my recent videos. It's exhausting seeing all these people saying the same things. Guess I've always had controversial opinions about certain topics. I mean, I don't believe in lizard people, Bigfoot, or Loch Ness Monster. But certain governments poisoning water supplies to brainwash the masses? Likely true. The 1969 Moon landing? Fake. Cloning celebrities to cover up their murders, suicides, and disappearances? Maybe true now, actually. And a spring deity who can travel through TVs, entrancing the world with her music? Absolutely true. They don't believe me yet, but they will. Now I have three million subscribers, my influence will only continue to grow.

The taxi drops me off on the busy Hanover Street, right outside the

Benugo coffee shop. I step out into the brilliant sunshine. The breeze still warrants me keeping my jacket on, and I pull up my hood again so I'm less likely to be bombarded. Looks like Kya has the same idea with those dark sunglasses. She sips from her cappuccino mug at a small table a few feet from the entrance. Another mug rests in front of the empty seat beside her.

Joining her at the table, I slot my rucksack between my feet, peer into the steaming mug of black coffee, and inhale with a smile. "For me?"

The corners of her glossy lips flick up. "I assumed you'd want one."

"Yes, yes, yes. How much do I owe you?"

"It's on me."

"Oh." I grin and cradle the lovely, hot mug. "Thank you kindly."

Although, all of a sudden, I have a craving for an espresso.

She sips her cappuccino again, and through her shades, I can make out that she's staring ahead at the road. She frowns a little and murmurs, "Ever since last night, I've felt this awful hole inside me. It's silly, really."

I feel slightly guilty for doing that to her, but it needed to be done, for her sake.

"Are you absolutely sure?" she says.

Shit. There's still doubt. Well, the only proof I have is that recording, I suppose. So I pull out my phone, connect my earphones, and bring up the file ready to be played.

"Have a listen," I say, and hand it over. "Recorded it at the BBC Broadcasting House."

Frowning, she pops in one earphone and taps the screen. I don't know what conclusion she'll draw from it, but she should at least see that something weird's going on with K-Rin. She gazes at the phone as if confused. Gently sipping my Caffeine Composure, which is honestly better and richer than anything I can make at home, I wait for her to finish. I didn't get a lot while I was there, but it's still significant.

"She broke into the BBC?" Kya removes the earphone. "And vanished into thin air?"

"Yep. And they're all covering it up."

Her gaze briefly drifts away. "You haven't released this?"

"No. Keeping it quiet for now." My tone stays low, even though the passing cars probably mask my words from anyone nearby. "Don't know what the BBC will do if I reveal this secret."

She shakes her thinker. "This is bloody strange."

193

"But definitely her style. How do you think her song aired in the first place? She hacked the stations. This should be the biggest security scandal in years, but no-one cares."

"If no-one cares about the hacking, though, why are the BBC worried about the public knowing about the break-in?"

It hasn't clicked for her yet.

"It's the nature of the break-in," I say. "They can't explain it. But I can."

"How did she get in, then?"

Usually, there's no way she'd believe me. This new skill of mine will do well here.

I clasp my hands together on the table and lean right in. I'd tell her to concentrate on my eyes, but she already is. "She moves through TV screens. Well, I guess she could through other devices too, considering she controls what information they show. But whenever she's on a screen, she brainwashes people to love her. That's why she went to the BBC. She told everyone that she wants to bring positivity to the world, but anyone, or anything, that has to brainwash people, must have different intentions."

Her expression doesn't alter for several moments.

"You're right," she says blankly. "It makes sense now. I think I knew deep-down that something was off. She's brainwashed everyone." Her eyes widen, and apprehension returns to her voice. "Even Mother and Father."

"Yes." I stifle a relieved sigh. "So we have to stop her."

She grimaces. "This is all worse than I thought. What the hell am I supposed to say at the interview?"

"Just be yourself, until they mention K-Rin. Put yourself back in that frame of mind when you admired her, think about the ways she inspired you, while keeping the truth inside."

"Shouldn't we expose her?"

"*I'm* going to expose her. You're going to pretend you were 'fooled' like everyone else. If you admit your true opinion right now, your fans will disown you." Behind her shades, her devastated eyes dart around. Smiling, I gently say, "Kya, look at me." She does, like a classic bunny in headlights. "You don't have to keep up the act long," I explain. "Before she releases her song on Sunday, I'm going to release a video of my own. By then, I should have nearly if not more than four million subscribers who'll listen to my words and believe everything I say about her. They'll share it with their friends and family. They'll lose their adoration for her, and she'll lose her

194

power."

"How do you know they'll believe you?"

Because you are.

I keep smirking. "I have my ways."

Just before midday, we walk not even a minute further down the road to Vogue House. Thankfully, it's not as packed around here as the area by the Broadcasting House. Our seven-floor building looms impressively over us, part pale and part dark-bricked, with the sun reflecting in its fifty or so windows. Kya's been muttering phrases to herself, as if preparing for a job interview. She reckons they'll see through her. They will if they hear her practising lines.

"Remember to breathe, okay?" I say.

Her shoulders relax with a sigh. "Yeah."

"You did Drama at college, right?"

"Mm-hmm."

"This is just another performance. You can do it."

She nods slowly. "Okay. I'll see you in about an hour. You can entertain yourself until then?"

"Yep. I'll have a wander. See if I can find a nice place for lunch."

"Cool." She half-smiles. "See you later."

"Good luck," I say as she heads inside the tall glass-panelled entrance.

I'm pretty confident she won't slip up, but her nerves do worry me a little.

Enjoying the sunshine, I carry on down the long stretch of road past a tiny park and various posh business establishments. I'd go on my phone to check what's around, but I fancy the surprise of finding out for myself. Every person I pass, I expect them to recognise me, but no-one shows any visible signs. I know I've got my hood up, but *someone* has to notice me. Most of them look preoccupied with their phones or like they're on their way somewhere important. The disappointment burns in my chest. Why, though? I *don't* want to be spotted!

I reach a wide crossroads and pick a random direction: left. Ah, so this is Bond Street. Black and white flags line the tops of each shop: Victoria's Secret, Fenwick, Montblanc, Boss, Dolce and Gabbana, Emporo Armani, Canali. I wouldn't dare step into any of these designer places, nor would I want to. Oh, but what's this? A bloody nice black leather zip-up jacket in the Canali window. Sure would look better and attract more attention than the tattered one I'm wearing now. But for nearly £2000, they can keep it. I go to shake my thinker in disgust, but I'm frozen with my focus fixed on that price tag. Why is it suddenly appealing? And why am I also drawn to the dark-grey suit a few mannequins along? I rarely wear them, but this one's so sleek and sharp. Again, though, it's nearly as much as the jacket. I've never understood why people with that much cash would splurge on something they could get ten times cheaper elsewhere. Does it fill them with pride to wear these big names? *Does* it get them noticed? I feel like if I had the money, I'd go in right now and buy this stuff. I'm sure I could find a smarter waistcoat for Connelly too. He'd probably flip at the cost, but he'd soon forget that when he's being admired in it at parties. With the way things are going, I could make it happen. For now, I'll have to move on.

As I wander over the Maddox Street crossroads, I smile at the similarity to my name and fantasise about what it'd be like to have a road named after me. Why stop there? How about a district? I want to make that big of an impact on a place. If I let K-Rin carry on brainwashing the world, it's only a matter of time before she gets her own district, or bigger.

It gets busier the further down I go. Another stretch of 'classy' shops lies ahead. To avoid ogling what I can't have, I focus instead on the bustling clusters of bodies. They all still seem too busy or buried in their phones to notice me. Guess three million subscribers isn't much compared to the amount of people in the world. I have the aggravating urge to shout out, to be heard, to be seen, but keep my hood up. What's so important, though? I manage to catch a glimpse of one guy's phone screen: he's enjoying the K-Rin interview, no doubt for the hundredth time. Another guy's watching my latest video. I'm right here! I shake my head.

Over the next crossroads, it's more of the same. Where are the restaurants and cafés? Might be time to consult my phone soon. On both sides, past the stream of cars, I see more shops and townhouses. I go left so that I don't stray too far from the area.

On the corner of a T-junction, I find a coffee bar. Don't know what Kya fancies today but the menu looks healthy enough for her usual tastes. The chicken livers on toast with mustard sound appealing and certainly get my gut grumbling. Not sure what she'll think of the décor, though – looks a bit mental in there with all those paintings on the walls and I know she's not much of an art lover. I make a note of the place on my phone anyway then continue ahead up Conduit Street. More clothing shops. By the time I reach the end and emerge onto a wide main road, Regent Street, my feet burn a bit. Kya must be well into the interview now. Wish I could sit in on it. Maybe I could steer the conversation if she gets off track. As it is, it'll be too late to repair any slip-ups she's made. I just have to pray for the best.

Down the right of the road, I spot the red banners and flags that mark the Hamleys toy shop. Good to see it's still standing. Is it just as magical inside as when I was young? Mum and Dad took me there on a few occasions and I must've spent a couple hours each time exploring the many levels. Puzzle games were my thing: anything that involved using my thinker. Dinosaurs, too, because I found them intriguing. It'd be pleasantly nostalgic to look around there again, and interesting to see if and how it's changed over the years, but my feet take me in the other direction.

I walk for what feels like forever down Regent Street until I reach the entrance to the underground station. I'm officially getting tired and achy now, and I can't find any more damn places to eat, not even anywhere to grab a coffee. So I bring out my phone. What's nearby? Looks like I missed a few restaurants down the side-streets. I wouldn't mind Japanese, to be honest – that'd guarantee plenty of spicy dishes. Of course, though, this is Kya's day, and she probably already has a favourite place around here.

As I make my way back towards Vogue House to wait for her, I freeze. A guy and his three young grinning girls swoop by, but the girls are in rainbow dresses, flat shoes, and flower crowns, all with flowing wavy hair. Coincidence? No way. Looks like the K-Rin cosplay might by catching on faster than Kya's agent expected. I'm surprised it's taken this long for me to see solid evidence of her influence other than more flowers than usual in shop windows. Normally, I might've found it cute, but it only makes me crave some Russian Oblivion.

*

When Kya emerges from Vogue House, she throws her arms around me, taking me aback. Did she screw up? Her musky perfume makes me light-headed, but thankfully she pulls away.

She sighs. "I'm glad that's over."

My eyebrow arches. "How did it go?"

"Long story short: it went fine, I think." She *thinks*? "I'll give you the details over lunch. So, where are we going?"

Kya's up for Japanese too, so we agree on Wagamama. The few-minutes' walk up the road and halfway down Great Marlborough Street gifts us an awkward silence. I'm desperate to hear about the interview, but as she annoyingly wants to wait 'til we're at the restaurant, I tell her about my mini exploration through the endless fashion shops. Unsurprisingly, she loves Bond Street. Guess she would if she actually has the money to spend. When I think about myself having that kind of fortune, I always imagine splashing it on upgrading to a bigger flat and better equipment for my videos. I still want all that, but now I'm obsessing over that £2000 Canali jacket.

Wagamama sits in a row of terraced townhouses. Inside, the central benches are quite packed. I remove my hood and Kya takes off her sunglasses. Each face turns to us then starts muttering to each other. What are they even saying? Good stuff, I hope! Is this what eating in public's going to be like from now on? Maybe I should start properly disguising myself.

We take our place at the stools by the large window. I drop my rucksack between it and my feet. We're probably less likely to get disturbed here, which right now is ideal considering what we need to discuss. Many people stare at us as they pass the window, but I can't tell if they recognise us or are curiously peering into the restaurant. Oh, they're taking pictures. They actually tore their attention off their phones long enough to notice us.

"Ignore them," Kya whispers. "That's what I have to do."

I repress the flattery I feel and try my best not to engage with them. As long as they don't harass us, I suppose they can take as many photos as they like.

"Did you see what happened last time I ate out?" I murmur back.

"I know, but we should be able to do what we want, too."

She's right, but I don't want *all* this fuss. To add to my building frustration, Kya says we should order food before getting stuck into the conversation. I go for chicken yakitori skewers and firecracker chicken. Easy choice. She spends an extra couple minutes deliberating, but settles on wok-fried greens and tofu harusame glass noodle salad. Apparently, she's 'treating' herself. I try to stifle my laugh.

As the waitress comes over to take our orders, she welcomes Kya personally then says to me, "Oh, and you're Maddix A., right?"

I straighten up on my stool and smile. "Hello."

"Oh my God." Her small round face lights up. "It's nice to meet you."

Nothing beats this feeling, but the pride isn't very humble, so I push it down.

Once the lady's typed our order onto her pad, she almost skips off. I hate to sour the moment, but without this K-Rin controversy, no-one would be even half as excited to see me.

I lean into Kya. "Tell me everything."

"Okay," she mutters, even though she needn't against the noise in here. "They mainly focused on the photoshoot: how and what I used to assemble the outfit, what brand of makeup, et cetera. They asked me about the bunny and how I came to meet him. Obviously, they already know you and I are step-siblings."

I nod along.

"They asked me if I've ever met K-Rin," she continues, "which, of course, I replied no to. I said, 'I'd love to, but I'm sure everyone would.' They kept nodding enthusiastically to everything I said, so they seemed to buy it."

I watch some cars go by the window. Thankfully, our tiny crowd of groupies is gone. "Sounds like you did a good job. Well done."

She smiles down at the window counter-top, but sadness glazes over her eyes. As I'm trying to think of how to reassure her, the waitress returns with my Caffeine Reflief and Kya's peach iced tea. We both thank her and she floats off with a grin. Kya gulps a quarter of her glass and gazes outside. How can you make someone feel better when they find out their hero's a liar and quite possibly not even of this Earth?

"I get how hard this must've been for you today," I tell her. "But it's for the best. I couldn't let you go on being brainwashed like that."

"I know. Thank you." She cups the glass with both hands and stares intensely into it. "I *am* grateful. It's just... I kind of want that feeling back." It must seriously be like a kind of high. She frowns deeply. "When you prove the truth to the world, imagine the depression."

"That's still better than being stuck in a false state of bliss. It'll be real. And people will heal over time." Her expression doesn't change, so I add, "She wants everyone to adore her. Who knows if she's really got worse intentions behind keeping everyone in a trance? But we can't afford to test it out." I move in closer, praying this will destroy any doubt. "We'll be saving lives."

Sighing, she looks at me again. "I know. I'm just a bit thrown, and scared."

I am too, but feel like something's pushing my fear down so it doesn't control me. Guess that can only be a good thing.

"We need to stick together, okay?" I say.

Her focus fixes on me for several moments then she says, "Yes."

The food smells out of this world. They've also given us double portions, and offer all of it for free. At this point, kind of unsurprising. Will I get every meal out on the house now? Kya seems over the moon. Says she had a bunch back in her early days, but never here, so it's likely through my influence this time. That does make part of me feel especially proud again, but leaves a bad taste in my mouth. Just like this chicken skewer; the spiciness is non-existent.

I scrunch up my face. "Disappointing."

Kya chuckles. "Can I try?"

"Go ahead."

I offer the stick towards her, cupping one hand under it to catch any sauce that may drip. She places down her chopsticks, leans in close, and carefully bites off the next chicken piece. Okay, I thought she'd take the stick from me, but that works too. She chews for a few moments then straightens up.

"So?" I say.

"I think it's bloody spicy. Maybe your standards are too high."

My eyebrow darts up at her. "Pfft."

Well, the firecracker chicken ticked my boxes at least, and there was plenty of it, so I still leave satisfied. We cross the road to the Courthouse Hotel. I can finally dump off this rucksack. It's not exactly heavy – it's just a nuisance to keep carrying around. Kya already dropped off her things with reception earlier. I should've done that too. Guess I feel better knowing my stuff can be stored safely in my room now that it's time for us to officially check in.

The hotel stands much taller than the London Palladium next to it. The pale-bricked building looks old but still pretty posh with plants in front of every arched window and the London Coat of Arms crest engraved in stone at the top. Above that, a tall white pole holds the British flag that crinkles in the breeze. From a distance, this place almost blends into the

Turner House building beside it. I wouldn't have expected a five-star hotel to be nestled snugly in a row of other establishments, but that flag pole certainly catches the eye.

Once inside, we traverse the shiny marbled flooring to the reception desk on the left made of reflective silver strips. Two large circular lights hang from the white ceiling, leading to a split staircase with a strip of purple running up it. They've modernised the hotel's interior, but the dark wood panelling still shows its age. I'm gawping around while Kya collects our key-cards from the suited guy behind the desk. A woman in a suit comes out of a side room wheeling a suitcase. Kya thanks her and refuses her offer to take it up to the room. I'm surprised she doesn't make the most out of her five-star experience. Kind of wish I had a suitcase to ask this woman to bring up for me.

As we ride the smooth, wide lift up, I contain the urge to gush over how impressive the place is. I'll do that in the privacy of my room. I get off at the first floor – Kya's the next one up – and we say bye. She says we can meet later for dinner. I dread how much the hotel's restaurant will charge, but at least the food should be fancy as fuck. Connelly would love it here.

Treading across the purple carpet, I try not to focus too long on its dizzying white circular patterns spreading down the corridor. The creamy walls help open up the space, with sunlight flooding in through the tall windows. Definitely the smartest-looking hotel I've been in. All I've ever known is Holiday Inn and the like – some have been nice for sure, but don't come close to this. Let's just see what the room's like. Where is it down here exactly? After passing several doors, I find mine and swipe the key-card to get in.

I flick on the lights to reveal more creamy walls, sandy carpet, and a standard layout: a P-shape comprised of a short passage with the door to the bathroom, and the rest of the room up ahead. I peer into the bathroom, switch on the lights, and nod approvingly at the shiny brown marbled tiling that spreads across the floor, the side of the bathtub, and halfway up the walls. A large circular mirror hangs above the black marbled sink counter. It's a decent-sized bathroom, and I can't wait to test out that shower unit – the shower head's three times bigger than mine.

I proceed into the bedroom area. Covered in pure white sheets, the pine bed stands to the right, opposite a matching cabinet and desk. The TV's a fair size, and a tray with a kettle and various amenities sits beside it. The window stretches across the back wall, the sunlight filtering in through its white blinds, with a couple of armchairs and a small, round coffee table in front. Very cosy. I'll let Kya settle in before I go check hers out. I can only dream of the King suites. This room's decorated quite blandly compared to those, from what I could see on the website. For now, I'm grateful for the chance to even set foot in a five-star hotel, let alone sleep in its cheapest room.

Once I've slung my rucksack on an armchair, I plonk myself on the edge of the bed. A few bounces show me it's pretty firm. I lie back with my legs over the edge. Feels like a perfect balance of solid and spongy, like one of those memory foam mattresses that mould to your shape. I've always wanted one like that, but whenever I have enough money saved, it goes towards something else, usually computer-related.

I should probably update Connelly and check my YouTube messages, but I could do with a quick nap after all that walking. Plus, it's an hour after his lunch break and he might not appreciate being disturbed. So I close my eyes and let myself drift away.

*

My phone vibrates in my pocket. I fumble to check who's calling. Oh, it's Connelly. Must be annoyed that I've held off telling him about everything.

I pick up the call: "Hi, Conn. I was just about to ring you."

God, my mouth's dry.

"Oh, yeah?" he bites. "Hopefully, it was to explain why these journalists have been contacting me, asking me what I think about my husband having an affair with my sister."

My vision hazes over. Everything halts. "What?"

"There were pictures of you having coffee together. Being close. Having lunch. You feeding her chicken on a skewer. Going into a hotel. All of this is bullshit, I know, but I'm being bombarded and I've had enough. Put an end to it, Maddix. Put out a statement or something. Whatever it takes."

I sigh. Oh, thank fuck he doesn't buy any of it. What the hell is wrong with these people? Can't we enjoy a day out without it being misconstrued?

"Okay. I'll do some damage control." I hold my aching thinker with my free hand. "I can't believe they'd think this."

He huffs. "So many of your *fans* have been bugging me on social media, trying to convince me that I should step aside and let you and Kya be

202

together. I can't fucking take it anymore."

That'll be mostly Mum's fault. She should've never flapped her trap about me and Connelly.

"I'm sorry they harassed you," is all I can say. "They're all being ridiculous."

He's silent for a torturous few moments then says, "I take it that interview went well?"

"Apparently. Kya's still pretending to ride the K-Rin crazy train."

"Okay. So when are you going to release your 'unbrainwashing' video?"

I stare at the bright, uncracked ceiling. "Tomorrow."

"Before or after Kya's dress-up event?"

"After, of course."

"Maddix, you said you wouldn't delay this. You're cutting it too close to the song release on Sunday, and this shit is getting too much."

He's starting to get shrill.

"I won't let her release it," I say, ignoring the pain in my ear.

"How can you possibly stop her? All you can do is change people's minds about her and hopefully they won't be affected by hearing the song."

"I *will* change their minds. But they won't even get a chance to hear what she puts out next."

"What are you going to do?" he says gravely.

If he was with me right now, I could convince him with my eyes to drop the subject. I'll have to get more persuasive with my voice.

"We're going to lure her out tomorrow. I figure she won't want to miss a large gathering honouring her. Plenty of adoration to feed on."

"Then what? You'll ask her nicely not to release the song, to stop brainwashing everyone?"

"You know I can be convincing."

"Yes, to people. But she's not an ordinary person, is she?"

I shrug. "It's worth a shot."

He hesitates for a few seconds. "This sounds dangerous, Madd."

"You'll be with me. I'm immune to her methods, and you're more resistant in my presence. So we'll be fine, okay?"

He doesn't respond. I understand his doubt. I should be just as uncertain and scared. We can't predict how this will all go tomorrow. Whatever's inside me knows we're going to win – I just can't explain how.

11

Damage control. Both Kya and I need to shoot down these rumours. I hope my new persuasive technique will work on the masses – if it does, I guess there'll be no need for *her* to convince anyone. Now how's the best way to go about this?

My phone vibrates once in my hand. I freeze my pacing and wince. A text from Kya: 'Hi. Figure we need to talk. How about you come up to my room and we can sort it out? Gives you a good opportunity to check the place out!'

I take the lift up one floor – would've used the stairs if my feet didn't ache from my excursion today. My gut aches too, as I glare at the lift door and imagine journalists or random lurkers on the other side, waiting to snap pictures of me. Thankfully, when it opens, no-one's there.

My phone rings, though, making me jerk. Mum wants me again! It's bound to be about this shit that's going on, so I cancel the call with a snarl. I severely do not want her opinion on *anything* else, especially now. And after my previous warning, she hopefully shouldn't yap about me to the press or anyone. As I reach Kya's door, a voicemail pops up on my phone. For Christ's sake. I definitely don't want to, but I suppose I should attempt listening to it later.

I knock on the door. Within seconds, Kya's grimacing face greets me. "Hiya. Are you okay?"

Wish I could shrug it all off, but I have to be honest: "No."

Being in her presence fills me with that darkness again, but for a new reason. The mere idea of us having an affair reminds me of the kind of sickness I'd get from a seven-day hangover. I'd never sleep with *anyone* else, let alone my sister-in-law who happens to look ridiculously similar to the spring goddess everyone's obsessed with.

"Come in and let's deal with this," she says.

Kya's room already smells of her musky perfume, but it's bearable. The layout's exactly the same as mine. We move down a short corridor across silver striped carpet and emerge into the usual bed, cabinets, TV, coffee table, and window setup, except everything's bigger. The décor's more interesting, too: light-grey walls, white-sheeted mattress on a beige divan base, with the headboard built into a large matching wooden panel. Two gold lamp lights hang from the panel either side of the bed, and beside it

204

stands a mirror and two pine doors that I assume lead to an internal wardrobe and storage space. Unquestionably a nicer-looking room, and my six-foot frame would fit better in that bed, but I think what attracts me most about it is the dearer price tag, for some reason.

Kya perches on a beige leather-style armchair by the window. "You have hunger in your eyes."

I laugh nervously. "Oh. Do I?"

She smiles. "This isn't their best room, but I like it."

"Yeah. I've seen pictures of the bigger suites." My focus trails off and I suddenly remember the main reason I came up here. I run a hand through my hair and scratch my thinker. "What are we gonna do about these nosy bastards?"

She sighs. "Well, I talked to my agency and they said talk to a solicitor, but I *do not* want to take this to court. For now, I think the best thing for us to do is to make a statement to the public in writing and on camera that we are *not* together. What do you think?"

Going to court over one innocent outing is fucking ludicrous, so yes, statement it is.

I let my hand smack down against my side. "Sure."

"I'm so sorry, Maddix. I didn't know people were going to react like this."

"It's not your fault." I slump on the end of the bed. Mattress feels even comfier than mine. I resist the urge to lie down.

"Apparently, there were a few reporters in reception trying to enquire about us, but they were told to leave." We're not safe anywhere, are we? Well, at least they're gone. "How can people be this supportive of an affair? I thought they'd be against it."

I frown hard at her. "What?"

"Didn't you read the comments?"

"No. Didn't even want to look."

With another grimace, she says, "Well, they all seem to say we look great together, that we'd be a fitting match considering K-Rin gave you her rabbit and I'm now modelling her."

My sickness, tension, and anger all feel ready to explode. Usually, a glass of Russian Serenity would soothe me, but I don't reckon that would even work right now! I shoot up from the bed.

"Maddix?"

Kya sounds concerned. Her voice brings me back. I don't want to worry her.

I shake my dizzy thinker. "Sorry. I just... They've made me fucking mad."

Her face turns the saddest I've ever seen it. "I know."

"Do *my* subscribers think this too?"

"I don't know. I haven't checked your videos yet, I'm afraid."

I wipe some beads of perspiration off my forehead. I'm not sure what's worse: my supporters believing I'm a cheater and wanting to disown me for it, or thinking I'm a cheater and deciding it's wonderful.

"How about we relax for a bit," she says, "then we can write our statements? We've still got time before dinner."

My eyes widen a little. "Oh. What are we gonna do about that? Surely if we're seen going to dinner together it'll just cause more issues?"

She straightens up. "I've hired the rooftop terrace out just for us for a couple hours. We should have plenty of privacy. I'm going to pay the hotel staff to keep quiet too."

"Wow. Okay." I'd like to think that'd suffice, but I have a horrible feeling. "You know, someone could pay them extra to spill the beans about us. And as cool as it sounds, wouldn't hiring the terrace out make it seem *more* like we're together?"

She shrugs. "You're right, but we can't really win here. If we eat downstairs with everyone else, we'll only get swarmed."

She's right too, and I want to *enjoy* dinner tonight.

"Have you got anything smart to wear?" she asks. "The hotel advises a smart dress code for the terrace."

"I don't have a suit and tie with me, if that's what they mean."

And why would I? Shame I couldn't have got that one from Canali.

She chuckles. "I guessed not. Well, your jeans and shoes look fine. But you didn't pack one of your long-sleeved shirts like what you wore last night, by any chance?"

"Oh. Yeah, I've got one. And I'll sort my bed hair out too. Don't worry."

She nods and stares past me. "I got someone to drop off the flower dress outfit. It's hanging in there." She must mean the door behind me. "And my makeup artist is coming here tomorrow."

"Mm." Sudden dread fills my gut with agony instead of excitement. "How the hell is tomorrow going to go in light of everything?"

"Well, let's get those statements sorted out and we'll go from there."

She's right. No point worrying about it, especially as the control is in our hands now. I can easily picture swarms of locusts with their cameras, attacking us with false accusations and their fake adoration. But we can stop that from happening.

Back in my room, I hunch in the armchair by the window. Leave it open slightly to let in the fresh air, but keep the curtains mostly shut. I hate hiding from people, but feel that's what I have to do until I can tell them the truth. I down a glass of water. Contemplate my wording carefully as I jot my speech on the tiny notepad provided by the hotel. My gaze keeps settling uneasily on the TV. Maybe we should reconsider having screens so close by. Could K-Rin travel through my phone too? Is she listening through our devices? I don't want to be paranoid, but can't help it. I form a fist around the pencil. She's distracting me. She got me in this mess in the first place. *She* made everyone crazy. I have to make things right.

I find my focus falling to my phone again. Shit. That voicemail. I know it'll make me angrier, but leaving it there will stress me out more. So I bring it up:

"Maddix, your dad and I have heard the news about you and Kya. We always thought she'd be better for you. She's not as controlling or uptight as Connelly, and she's much more successful." My hand squeezes the phone until it hurts. "Don't worry. I promise I won't be discussing your relationship with anyone again." Well, that's a relief! "But we were thinking: with your combined incomes, you could finally pay us back for that loan. A thousand pounds could really help us out." My jaw tenses again. I should've repaid them years ago, but honestly, *this* is what they're fixating on? "Discuss it with your new lovely lady and let us know. Speak to you later."

My fist bashes down on the table.

I've read through the statement countless times. Obviously, not only do the words need to be convincing, but I need to be too. With this new persuasive talent of mine, however, I reckon I can get them to accept it. I know I haven't tested it on a crowd yet, but this is my chance. Think I'm ready.

I splash my face with water in the bathroom, dry off, and sort my hair out. Let's put an end to this. I return to the bedroom, open the curtains to let in more light, and sit on the bed, facing the window. My stomach hurts. I need a drink. Come on. Push past it. I hold up my phone, turn on the video camera, and clear my throat. I've memorised everything – don't even need the notepad anymore. Just try not to come across furious. Remember you're talking to people who like you, and you want it to stay that way.

Still keeping my face serious, I press record. "Hello, everyone. It's Maddix A. I just thought I would address the rumours going around today about me and my sister-in-law Kya." I pause, half for dramatic effect and half to centre myself again already. "She and I are *not* in a relationship. We're just friends." Oh, I need to correct that. "Well, we're *family*, too... We've been in Soho together on a business trip, and we're still planning on attending the meet-and-greet event at Cavendish Square Gardens tomorrow – hopefully we'll see some of you there. I trust this helps to clarify things, because please understand that there is nothing worse than spreading false information about someone." I don't think I've blinked once. Can feel the rage simmering, like I might go on an unscripted rant. Okay, time to wrap it up. "Anyway, that's all from me. So until next time, goodbye."

I stop the recording and sigh. Think that went all right. Let's just get it uploaded and into the public eye where it belongs.

It only takes a minute for the first wave of comments to flood the screen. The words almost blur together, and I have to read them several times before they sink in. Is this real? Are these the same people who've been commenting on my videos all these years, or are they imposters?

'Maddix, I'm heartbroken. You two were the perfect couple.'

'Pls tell us its not true! U 2 r the shining beacon of hope for us all!'

'I honestly don't know what to do with myself now. Nothing makes sense anymore.'

'Devastated to hear this. I was so excited when I saw you two might be a thing. What a shame.'

'I'm literally crying as I type. Even my cat's crying out right now. She heard what you said. You're not with Kya, and yet you were feeding her like your girlfriend in Wagamama! You made us believe!! I just started to trust in love again, and you've shattered that :'('

'I nearly fainted when I found out you went into Kya's room. You can't say that meant nothing!'

Pressure mounts on my thinker. How did they even know I went into her room? Was someone up there watching me? What the actual fuck is happening? Are they really disappointed? They're absurd! Is Kya receiving the same reactions?

I call her, and she answers after a few rings. "Hi. I just posted my video and everyone so far is fucking crying about us *not* being in a relationship."

"I know." She sounds a little stressed, like it might be getting to her too. "But the truth is out there now, and it seems like they believe us, at least."

Good point; no-one's come back refuting it yet.

"For now," she says, "let's get ready for dinner and try to enjoy the rest of the evening, yeah?"

I really *should* sort myself out, but I think it'll be difficult to have fun tonight when these comments will be plaguing my mind.

As I freshen up in my room and change into my long-sleeved black check shirt as promised, Mum rings again. Naturally, I don't answer, and don't even entertain her voicemail. She'll only be going on a tirade about my video. I slump in the armchair and check in on Connelly.

Several rings go by. Doesn't want to talk to me?

"Hi," he says, sounding fairly relaxed.

"Are you in the bath?" I ask.

"Yes. I treated myself. God knows I needed it."

I smile. "How are you now?"

"Better. I saw your video. Thank you for doing that." He seems sincere but still quite pissed, as he should be. "I haven't been this swamped with journalists since Kya first started out."

That *was* annoying – glad they calmed down over the years. I'm just glad they never found out where we live.

"Hang on," I say. "Have they been coming to the house?"

"No. They've been flooding me with messages and calls. Not that I'll answer any more of them." Glad they're not bashing on our door, then. I'm surprised Mum never revealed our address, but looks like she actually listened to me this time. "It's died down a bit now. People were more interested in you *being* in an affair."

"I know. They're all sick."

He goes silent then says, "I had to convince Mother and Father that everything was blown out of proportion. Kya's been on the phone with them too."

"What?" I scowl. "Did they seriously believe it?"

"...They *wanted* you and Kya to be a thing." I've never heard such venom in his voice. "Mother was going on about what beautiful babies you two would make."

My vision starts to haze over. The sickness returns. I have no words. No thoughts.

He sighs, probably trying to recapture his relaxation. "Now I *know* this brainwashing is for real. *Something's* going on, anyway, and you need to stop it, Maddix."

I struggle to pull myself back. "I will, Conn. I promise."

*

I meet up with Kya in the corridor and we head up to the Soho Sky Terrace. If she's upset after speaking with her parents at all, she's hiding it well behind that smile. She's more stunning than me, of course, in an ankle-length silver dress, white lacy shrug, and matching stiletto heels. Hopefully, I look good enough not to get chucked out. With some planning ahead, I could've come dressed to the nines and turned everyone's thinkers. But oh well. Next time. Maybe I can wear that Canali suit or jacket.

The mild air smells cleaner up here. Down both sides of the narrow wooden terrace lie empty two-seater glass tables with chairs made of silver wicker and metal. Interspersed between these are tall potted plants and standing outdoor lights. The city stretches out beneath us under a deep orangey-pink sky.

A suited waiter guides us across the terrace to the centre: Kya's "favourite spot". We have this all to ourselves for two hours? How much does that cost? I can't deny this insane jealousy, but at least I've been given the opportunity to enjoy this privilege. We sit at one of the tables, which presses against the glass barrier, and the waiter hands us our menus. Does *he* think we're together? Will he stay quiet about this?

The lights of the passing cars below catch my attention for several moments, until the waiter asks if there's anything we'd like straight away. I ask for an espresso and Kya requests a jug of water with ice. He nods then disappears.

I glance through the menu and my eyes latch onto the spiciest thing there: teriyaki beef skewers with soya chilli vegetables. Price isn't too high, but I can't say the same about the alcohol.

"Over a hundred quid for a bottle of vodka?" I mutter.

She smirks. "I know. But you won't be ordering one anyway, will you?"

"No. And normally, I wouldn't at that price, no matter how desperate I was. But makes me wonder: if it costs that much, how decent must it be?"

"Mm." She glances at her menu then back at me. "You know, it's good that you're easing off the stuff. Every time I see you these days, you're..."

She seems to be searching for the nicest word, so I just outright say, "Off my face?"

She cringes slightly.

I sigh and watch the cars below. "I know I drink too much. I thought I'd go into withdrawal, but I haven't at all."

"That's...surprising. But I'm glad. And I bet Conn is too."

My thinker tilts, and eyes wander back to her. "Does he ever mention it?"

She doesn't blink. With my stare, I demand her to tell me.

"He's been worried about you for a while," she says. "He just hasn't known how to broach the topic with you."

I grit my teeth behind closed lips. Guess I've known that. Why does he find it easier to talk to her than me about our problems?

"What else does he say about me?"

"You spend too much time in the studio," she says a little too quickly. Well, I knew that.

I frown. "I'm earning money for us."

"But you two aren't as close as you used to be."

How can she say that so matter-of-factly? I wanted the truth, but her blasé tone is pissing me off.

I heat up in my jacket. "Okay, since I started this job, we may have been a bit distant from each other. But he still adores me. We've been doing great this week."

For the most part. I guess.

"I imagine I've screwed things up between you two with this bloody rumour," she says. The guilt makes her voice crack.

"We're fine. And it's the rest of the world's fault. Well, technically K-Rin's for brainfucking them."

Tears reflect in her eyes as she watches the street below. "My parents are driving me nuts. Mother keeps asking when my baby's due."

I go to tell her how ridiculous I think that is as well, but a voice behind me cuts in: "You're pregnant?"

I glance around at the waiter. Before I can refute him, Kya jumps in with: "I am *not*."

As long as he takes her at her word.

He bows his head. "Apologies. Are you ready to order, or would you like more time?"

He moves around to the side of us and places down our jug of water and my small espresso cup. Might as well order quickly so we can be left alone again. With a forced smile, I say, "Yes. I'll have the teriyaki beef skewers and Kya will have the grilled chicken supreme, please."

Holding his hands together in front of him, he nods. Guess he's got a good memory – not that there's much to remember.

Kya seems to shudder, as if waking from a daydream, and asks him, "Can I also have a glass of Mamaku Sauvignon Blanc, please?"

She might as well get a bottle of wine from an off-license down the road for the price of the glass she's ordering, but I get why she'd prefer this. The waiter nods again, collects our menus, and strides off.

"People honestly need to mind their own business," Kya says while pouring water from jug to glass.

"Agreed. But let's try to forget about them." Tonight's supposed to be about relaxing, but I do need to run through something with her first: "Tomorrow, at the Gardens, I'm expecting K-Rin to show."

Her eyes contract. She pauses with the jug spout hovering above my glass. "Would that be good?"

"Yes. I'm going to convince her not to release her song."

Still frowning, she tips the water into my glass. "I'm not sure she'd listen to you."

Why does everyone doubt me? I watch her pull away and set the jug back down. She takes a sip and gazes expectantly at me. I slowly smirk.

"What is it?" she says.

I want her to believe me, truly.

I lean forward. "Stare into my eyes and pay attention to what happens."

Her eyebrows twitch again, but she says, "Okay," and does as I say.

What can I make her do that she'd never do of her own volition? I don't want to humiliate her, either. I peer at the street below to make sure no-one's walking past.

"Pick up that jug," I tell her, "and chuck the water over the barrier."

Without hesitating, she takes it and empties the water into the street. We're high up enough not to hear it splatter on the pavement over the noise of cars. I smile, and feel that powerful rush I've grown to love.

Her blank face explodes into a gawp. She peers down at what she's done, and her hand carefully lowers the jug back onto the table. Does she get it now? Fear shines in her eyes. I don't want her to be afraid, but I can understand why she would be. She seems speechless.

The waiter returns and sets down her glass of wine. She stays silent, so I thank him for her and say, "Sorry, but could we please have another jug of water?"

As soon as he leaves with our previous one, Kya sips her wine and focuses on the table. I finally sip my delicious espresso and rest back.

"I'm sorry," I say. "I needed to show you what I can do."

She laughs under her breath, but her gaze remains on the table. "You never told me you're a hypnotist."

That word makes my stomach turn. I refuse to be compared to that devious bitch.

"I'm not," I say.

"What would you call yourself, then?"

An influencer? Coercer? Manipulator?

I drink more, and watch the cars again.

"How long have you been able to do that?" she asks.

Good point. I don't know where it came from. Barely even questioned it. It just feels natural.

"I don't know," I say.

The first time I noticed it was talking to that BBC receptionist, but I feel like it's been in me for a day or two longer.

"Tell me honestly, Maddix." She doesn't look at me. "Have you lied to me about any of this? About K-Rin?"

"No." I try my hardest to contain my frustration. "I'd never do that to you. You know me."

"I'd like to think I do, but..." Grimacing, she shakes herself. "That really freaked me out. You have to promise me you won't do that again. Okay?"

What would she think of me if she discovered how many times I've used it on her over the last couple days? Will she figure it out? I bloody hope not.

"I promise." Although distressingly, I might end up breaking that one. "Do you see, though, that I have a good chance of convincing K-Rin to back off?"

She sighs then nods and swigs from her glass. "What if she doesn't show tomorrow? And even if she does, how will you get a moment alone with her? Everyone will flock around her as soon as she appears."

"I just need to catch her undivided attention. That's all it should take."

Her eyebrows push together. "I hope you're right. And if she doesn't show–"

"–I'll have to rely on the video I release telling people not to watch or listen to that song. I'll record it tonight and have it ready to go. I may now be able to influence people, but I can't do it too early because I don't know how long my influence lasts."

It's clearly not permanent because even though I only just last night convinced Kya not to trust K-Rin, she's already interrogating me about it twenty-four hours later. This is why I need to ensure that song *doesn't* get out.

"What if this thing you can do doesn't work over video, though?" she says. "You know it works face-to-face, but..."

I hadn't even considered that. Normally, I would.

"Everyone seemed to accept my speech earlier. They should do next time. But I should probably do another test, just in case."

After a ridiculously tasty but admittedly awkward meal, we return to our respective rooms. That could've gone better if I hadn't used my persuasive thing on her. She doesn't hate me now, does she? I needed to show her. I don't want to manipulate her; everything I do is for her benefit and K-Rin's downfall. I want Kya to rise above her. We'll make it happen. I'll just have to do some 'coercing' along the way.

I turn on the bedside lamps and switch off the main lights. Love this warm, luxurious atmosphere. Soaking it in, I pull off my jacket and boots and flop on the bed with my phone. Haven't checked YouTube in two hours, so I bring up the app. How many subscribers now? My eyes contract at the four-point-one million. How is this happening?

Need to record the warning video, but first I want to revel in this sparkling rush. It only radiates more when I check my Patreon: eight thousand patrons. The number glows. This is brilliantly insane. The BBC interview obviously helped my publicity. When payday comes, I'm definitely splurging on that jacket, better studio equipment, and putting money aside for a deposit on a new place for me and Connelly. Might even be able to convince people to send me more... Okay, why did I think that?

I really need to get on and test my power – feels scary and wrong, but also slightly cool, referring to it like that. I video call Connelly, praying he hasn't fallen asleep in the bath. Thankfully, when he answers, he's in a loose shirt on the sofa.

He looks wiped. "Maddix?"

"Hi, Conn. I was wondering if you could do me a favour, please?"

He raises an eyebrow. "Depends, if you promise to stop doing stupid stuff."

What have I done this time?

I frown. "Like what?"

"Like booking out the whole hotel terrace and having a romantic evening dinner with my sister?"

Oh, come on. He knows that's not what it was. But hang on, if *he* knows about that, then...

"Did that fucking waiter squeal?" I say.

"There's pictures of you that people took from the street."

My eyes bulge. They must've been lurking in the shadows on the other side of the street. "What the fuck? Why can't we do *anything* without being watched?"

"Because you're celebrities and you sat right by the edge of the bloody rooftop of a hotel that those idiots know you're staying at! What did you expect?"

I huff. "I know. I shouldn't be shocked. It's just we needed to get away from everyone so we could talk about K-Rin and not be bombarded."

He gives me that unimpressed glare I sorely hate. "They saw Kya pouring water into the street and now they're questioning the quality of the food and drink at that place." That *is* unfortunate. "Please take better care with what you two do." As if he needs to tell me that – I'm already frightened of every move I make at the moment. "You may have told everyone you're not together, but now they're confused again."

I rub my forehead. "We'll handle it. Besides, I'm going to record that unbrainwashing video."

"Yes, you do that."

Talking of which: "I do need your help, though."

He sighs. "What do you need?"

Don't know how he'll feel about this, but it's another necessary evil. I stare into his eyes through the camera lens. "I need you to look at me."

"I am."

Here goes. Carefully, I say, "Tell me, with absolute conviction, that you fucking hate romantic drama films."

Without hesitation, he passionately says, "I fucking hate romantic

215

drama films."

Bloody hell. It genuinely worked!

He glances down then frowns at the screen again. "Maddix, what was that?"

His tone's a mixture of disturbed and like he's about to reprimand me.

"Proof that my persuasion skills are as good as I thought," I say.

"Maddix, I didn't even resist. How did you do that?"

I almost laugh. "I've no clue, but it means my video's going to work!"

He looks stumped. "Uh, I... I don't like this."

Seeing that fear does somewhat kill my excitement. Don't want him reacting the same way Kya did. Why didn't I consider that before?

"I'm sorry I used you as a test. I won't do it again."

"Damn right you won't." His eyes narrow. "You haven't always been able to do that, have you? This is new."

"It *is*. I can't help wondering if K-Rin has something to do with it... but it'll be her downfall. I'll make sure of it."

His gaze wanders. If I can prove to him the good I can do with this gift, he might feel less uneasy about it.

"I'm going to record that video now," I say, "but I won't release it until tomorrow. Don't know how long my influence lasts exactly, and I'm hoping Kya's event will lure K-Rin there. Then I can show everyone the truth and she can watch them all turn against her."

"Maddix, stop delaying." He seems to beg me with his wide eyes. "Please, do this now."

The call hangs up. My thumb's where the hang up icon was. Was that an accident? Well, I need to get on with the video anyway, so I can phone him back later.

I glance around the room for the best spot to record. Unfortunately, I'll have to flick the main lights back on. The bathroom probably has the brightest lighting, but I don't want to shoot what's supposed to be a serious video in there. So I push myself up, go over to the room's door, and turn on the lights. I cross to the window and sit in the soft armchair, facing into the room so that I'm not backlit. My stomach twinges for a moment then settles. I know exactly what I'm going to say.

I bring up my phone's camera, raise it in front of my face, and ready myself. Shame I couldn't do this with my professional setup, but this will have to do. I stare into the phone's tiny circular camera with intensity and tap record. I'll skip my usual introduction and dive straight to the point.

"Look into my eyes and listen to me. Do not watch or listen to K-Rin's song. She is brainwashing you. Do not trust her. She is forcing you all to love her. Make your own decisions, because if you let yourself become powerless, who knows what else she will do? For you, your family, and all those you care about, do *not* engage with her or anything she releases. Share this video on every platform you can, right now."

There. Can't make it much clearer than that. I stop recording, and lower the phone. Need to make this accessible to as many people as possible, and my words won't reach those who don't understand English. Will subtitles in different languages work? I'm not fluent in any other language, so Google Translate will be my best bet. But how can I possibly cover all the languages in the world? I won't be able to add subtitles very easily on my phone, either. Should've brought my laptop. Should've been more prepared.

Squeezing my phone hard, I screw up my face. If I can get the message out in a selection of the top spoken languages, at least the majority of the world will get it. So what are they? A quick Google search reveals English, Mandarin, Hindi, Spanish, French, Arabic, Bengali, Russian, Portuguese, Indonesian, Urdu, and German. Okay, one of those is obviously covered. The others I'll have to loosely work out, unless Kya happens to know any of them.

I move to sit at the desk opposite the bed and place my phone beside the little pad of paper. As I open Google Translate on my phone, I think about what I said in the video. I select the option for English to Chinese. Before I even type anything, the Chinese words flash into my thinker.

Frowning, I mutter, "Kàn zhe wǒ de yǎnjīng. Tīng wǒ shuō."

Since when can I fucking speak Chinese? Is that even correct? I shake my thinker. What was the next one? Hindi?

"Meri aankhon mein dekho. Meri baat suno."

What the actual hell? I've never even remotely studied these. I re-open my Google search for the most spoken languages. Let's see. Spanish:

"Mira a mis ojos."

A shiver runs through me. How can I know this? I work my way down the list:

"Regarde dans mes yeux. Anẓur fī 'ainayya. Amar chokhe dekho. Posmotri mne v glaza. Olhe nos meus olhos. Lihatlah mataku. Schau mir in die Augen." My voice sounds so alien. I gaze at the wall in pure disbelief. "What the fuck?"

I've no clue how I pronounced some of that. I'm impressed with myself, but thrown. I can't explain it, like many other things this week. I'm going to take full advantage of it, though.

I record my brief speech in the eleven languages – for brevity, I conjoin Hindi and Urdu to speak in colloquial Hindustani. Then I thread the videos together in my basic editing app and make a note of the timestamps so I can add them on YouTube while the whole thing's uploading. The video's six-and-a-half minutes, much longer than I'd prefer, but most people will only have to watch the thirty-five-odd seconds of the clip in their language. After detailing the timestamps for each language at the beginning of the video, I save it on YouTube as a draft, ready to publish when the time comes. If all goes to plan, I won't have to release it. If K-Rin backs off and never makes another appearance, the public's adoration will fade. I'm sure I can convince her, but it doesn't hurt to have a backup plan. It's taken me a bit longer than usual to put this together, as all I have is my phone, and now I'm all for collapsing in bed. Very tempting to grab myself a drink from the minibar as a reward, but my body stays put.

The longer I lie here, the more detached I feel. Is this like one of those dreams where I can speak multiple languages without actually knowing them? Does what I said actually make sense, or is it only right to me? Connelly will probably be both impressed and freaked like I am. Doubt he'll believe they just spawned in my mind. This is superb, though. With all these languages under my belt, I can reach a wider audience. I'll record in English, but I can provide embedded subtitles. Might need to hire a trusted editor to help – I won't have enough time to translate every video ten-plus times. With my massive influx of patrons, I can certainly afford it.

Loud buzzing makes me jerk. Not my phone. It's Aki's. I dart up in bed, reach across to the bedside cabinet, and grab it. Unknown number, of course, but I answer anyway. Can't believe someone's finally calling.

"Hello?" I say.

"Maddix?"

That's not seriously him, is it? "Aki?"

"Thank God. I hoped you'd found that phone."

That's what he's leading with?

"Where have you been?" I ask, heating up. "You left me passed out in Brockwell Park."

"I don't know what happened. I swear it." His voice cracks, like he's scared, and sounds a little different. "Someone found me in an alley not far

218

from the park that afternoon. I've been in a coma for four days. Only just woke up this morning. Hospital said I didn't drink enough for alcohol to be the cause."

Is this really him? His accent's changed, like it's got more of a Japanese inflection. Anyway, he wandered to an alleyway and randomly fell into a coma? Not sure I accept that.

"Are you still in hospital?" I ask.

"Yes. They have to test more... Anything else happened with you?"

Where do I even begin? But first, let's start with him.

"A lot," I say, "but what's up with your voice, man?"

"...Nothing. This is how I *should* sound."

Okay, I don't like this. He's being super suspicious.

"What was the first video of mine you ever commented on?" I ask.

He hesitates for a few seconds. "Uh, The Strange Unsolved Murder of Princess Preciosa. Why?"

Why did he hesitate? Maybe he's still groggy. At least he got it correct.

"Never mind," I say. "Anyway, K-Rin appeared on BBC to announce she's releasing the full version of her video on Sunday. I'm going to lure her out at Cavendish Square Gardens tomorrow and convince her not to. If that fails, I have a video ready commanding everyone not to watch or listen to it."

"Oh God. You think that'll work?"

I withhold a sigh at yet another person doubting me.

"Yes. I can make people do things now. And I also seem to know a shit-ton of languages." Let's test to see if I really am as good as I appear. "Are you fluent in Japanese?"

"Of course."

"Okay. Well, before today, I think I understood about three words of Japanese. But now I can tell you: K-Rin wa megami no yō da. Kanojo wa denshikiki o tsūjite idō dekiru." I laugh at the absurdity of all this. "Does that make sense?"

After a few moments, he says, "Uh, yes."

I wait for him to elaborate, but he doesn't. "And?"

"I'm a bit lost. You think K-Rin's some kind of goddess that moves through devices, but you reckon you can talk her out of releasing her song?"

"Yes."

Another few frustratingly silent moments pass. "Maddix, I thought I've

219

been crazy the last five years. I haven't been in control of my actions. I knew endless languages too. They disappeared since my coma. I was strong. Could make people do whatever I wanted. I did..." His voice chokes. "...terrible things." What's he talking about? He practically whimpers, "And now it's happening to you."

I frown hard at the dark curtains. "What are you saying?"

"Something brought me to you. Everything I've done and said recently, it wasn't me. I finally feel myself again, because it has you now."

My thumb hangs up the call. Turns off the phone. I want to hear more. Want to call him back. But I can't. I physically can't. I stare at the phone, screaming at my fingers to move. It terrifies me, but my face doesn't twitch at all.

12

My thinker lifts from the pillow then my legs swivel and push me out of bed. Didn't want to sleep in my shirt and jeans, but I had no choice. Something's forcing my every move. You. You've been here all week, lingering and influencing, but now you drive me completely. Is it because of what Aki said? What could I have done anyway? How is this possible? Have I gone mad and need help, or do you – you imposter – know what you're doing and I need to trust you? You want to take down K-Rin, right? So do I. When the deed is done, will you let me go? I can't even hear your thoughts. Talk to me!

You just silently move me forward to get ready. We're meeting Kya downstairs for breakfast. How will you treat her? And oh God, what about Connelly? How much say have you had over what I've done this week, especially with him? I might feel appalled and violated if I wasn't so bewildered. As you strip my clothes off in the hotel bathroom, those feelings start to take over. You've shared, and possibly driven, some incredibly intimate moments with me recently.

You push down my anger and switch on the shower. The water warms up instantly. My legs step into the marble bathtub and the water caresses me. I try to take comfort and relief in it, but you're stretching my lips into a grin and pissing me off again. I just want to scream, "Why me?" But the more I think about it, the clearer it becomes. I have an immunity to K-Rin, and a YouTube audience, which continues to grow. I fucking hate that without her, or you, whatever or whoever you are, I wouldn't have been nearly as successful. Please, when this is over, promise me you'll leave. I want to be solely in control. I want to be the one who's liked and admired. Promise me.

"I promise," my mouth says.

Three rows of square dining tables stretch down this tall former courtroom, lit brightly by the large high windows. I would've loved to check out the bar area last night and its renovated cells that we could've lounged and drunk in. But drinking's not your style – I did wonder how I wasn't going into withdrawal. Guess you want me to stay sharp, and that can only be good considering what'll go down today.

As Kya and I wait at a table for breakfast – another free meal, apparently – my eyes dart about. The wooden-panelled walls give the room a vintage but smart look. Again, I feel a little underdressed compared to the few other people in their suits, who thankfully appear too involved in their conversations to notice us. Maybe they're on business trips. So are we, technically. I'm glad Kya hasn't got into her K-Rin costume – don't want to draw attention yet, and don't fancy having breakfast with anyone who remotely resembles her.

She seems to be having trouble maintaining my gaze for more than a couple seconds at a time. I can't say with certainty who 'hypnotised' her last night. I know I wanted to show her what I can do, but it's not really *my* skill, is it?

"Are you okay?" you ask through me. Does she look okay?

"I'm freaking out, to be honest," she mutters. "I don't know what's going on."

I want to tell her she's not talking to me, that she should watch what she shares. Just have to pray you stay nice to her – if you want her help today, you will.

"What do you mean?" you say.

She straightens up slightly, but keeps her focus on her steaming cappuccino. "I feel like I'm losing it... The pictures from the photoshoot we did: they're different. Well, Shinpi is." Oh, really? Has the same thing happened to her as Connelly? "I thought someone had manipulated the pictures, but I went back into my phone's photo gallery and he's grey in those too." How interesting. She glances at me and whispers fearfully, "Why has he changed?"

You grin. "Because you have. You're beginning to see the truth."

She shakes her thinker. "I always wondered what you were talking about: him being black." At least she never called me a liar for it. "It's scaring me. And I'm kind of bricking myself about later."

"We can both do this." My voice sounds so soft and smooth. "Just pretend this is a normal publicity event."

"I am." She chuckles. "They always make me nervous. And now I have even more reason to be."

"You need to be confident today." My eyes stare at her, as if waiting for hers to meet them. No. Don't do this again. It may help us, but she shouldn't be manipulated like this. "Kya." This gets her attention. "Believe in yourself."

She stares at me for a few moments then nods slowly. Her shoulders relax and she sips her cappuccino. I'm glad we've alleviated her nerves, but you've already broken the promise I made to her. Having this much influence does make me feel powerful – I can't deny that – but this power's borrowed. It'll go as soon as you leave me. If I had full control of it, I'm unsure how I'd use it. I could make anyone like me. No-one should have that power, though. I need to *earn* others' respect, not steal it like a certain brainwashing deity we all know.

"I've been thinking about something," you mutter. "This may sound a little crazy, but this relationship rumour... I think we should play along with it."

I almost want those words to leave my mouth again because I swear I didn't hear that right.

Understandably, she must be in disbelief too as she blankly says, "What?"

You smile. "People all over the world were devastated when they found out we *weren't* a couple. Imagine how much happier they'll be if they heard that we are. Doesn't matter if it's true or not." She's watching with avid attention, as if taking in every syllable. You're making sense, but I seriously hope she's not buying it! "This can only be better for *both* our careers. Don't you agree?"

Don't go along with this, Kya. There has to be a part of her that realises she's being coerced into something that's going to hurt everyone involved! Maybe it's being crushed down into a deep corner of her mind and struggling for control, just like me.

"I... I'm not sure."

Come on, Kya. Fight back. She chews her lip for a short while. My body tenses – are you getting nervous that she might refute you?

She meets our intense gaze again, and eventually sighs. "You're right." I shrink even further into my corner. She keeps her voice hushed: "I don't like lying to people, but it *would* make them happy. It *would* also boost my career a bit more. If I'm honest, it *has* been dwindling for the past year or so."

This can't be real. She can't be saying this. My life can't truly be about to end.

You take a sip of your espresso at last. "Good. We'll announce it after the event. Don't want to draw attention away from what we're actually there for."

She nods, without any hesitation this time. This terrifies and angers me to the core, and I wish I could help her.

You must've been studying how I eat all week because you're taking the same size bites and chewing and swallowing the same fast way I always do. Unless you, like me, want to get on with the rest of the day. It's hard to enjoy any bit of this fancy fry-up, as all I can think about is what if I get stuck like this, forever observing my life while a foreign entity decides everything for me? My fear returns big time, but you have a knack for squashing it down and stopping me from expressing it. I'm helpless, and powerless, and I just want a drink or ten. I hate that I want to stay inside that deep part of my mind, keep my eyes closed, and not be a part of it. But I can't. If there's a way to break free, I have to keep trying.

*

While Kya returns to her room and gets into costume with her makeup stylist's assistance, I soak in the last of my room as you perch me on the bed. Can't move my eyes from my phone screen, though, and these messages are more important anyway. I'm close to five million subscribers. I'd cry out and hop around, but my body stays still and I feel a smirk. You certainly experience joy differently. My thumb deletes all interview requests from the smaller channels, and marks the ones from channels with over a million subscribers. I've always considered a few thousand to be impressive, but you obviously have other standards. I regularly watch some of these guys – it'll be amazing to meet them. I just hope I'm back in control by then.

In the ocean of messages, we spot one from Tinfoil-Canis, sent last night shortly after our phone call. My thumb deletes it without even opening it. For fuck's sake. What does Aki have to say? Is he trying to help me? I don't think he knows how to regain control if you were riding him for, what, five years? Does that mean Aki himself was never my 'biggest fan'?

My throat sniggers.

A call comes through from Connelly. I never did ring him back last night – I'm surprised he didn't try getting hold of me until now. Maybe he gave up with me. As soon as you answer, I'm going to scream out to him as hard as I can. But of course, you hang up the call and deny me the chance. You do, at least, send him a message: 'Sorry, can't talk. Heading over to the Gardens with Kya. Also, don't know what happened last night – maybe there was a bad connection, as I tried calling you back but nothing went through. Sorry about that. Anyway, see you soon. And can you get me a coffee, please? :)'

Making me lie to him already? Sick bastard.

*

As soon as Kya's ready, she texts me to meet her in the hotel lobby. You leave my rucksack with reception to pick up later. As she emerges from the lift in that flower dress and crown, with her golden hair all flowing and wavy, that dark hate I felt at the photoshoot returns. Is it mine or yours? Maybe both. You force a grin on my face either way. She drops off her suitcase at reception too then checks us out. We haven't said a word to each other. I want to thank her for temporarily footing the bill for my room, but my lips don't move. I loathe how ungrateful you are. You just watch how smitten the guy behind the desk is with Kya.

"You really do look just like her," he says with wide, unblinking eyes.

Kya manages a smile. "Thanks."

As much as I hate her uncanny resemblance, it can only aid us today.

We take a taxi to Cavendish Square Gardens – it's only an eight-minute walk, but that's plenty of time to get mobbed. The driver makes me edgy as he keeps glancing at us in the rear-view mirror. The K-Rin look-a-like next to us is obviously capturing his attention, but does he recognise me too at all?

When he pulls up alongside the Gardens, I expect you to lean forward and convince him not to charge us. Guess that'd be too suspicious to Kya, and we need her to keep trusting us, so you stay silent and she swipes her card.

Waiting for us beyond the entrance's short black gate are two suited guys in dark shades. I've seen them at several of Kya's publicity events. We'll need them more than ever today. Connelly did post an announcement on her Instagram yesterday, as well as a reminder this morning, so it's short notice, but I reckon loads of people will show for this. A few people passing by have already stopped to snap some not-so sneaky photos on their phones. I can't help hoping I'm also the subject of their interest, but have no idea if that's my thought or yours. The bodyguards lead us away from them, down the grey-bricked path into the Gardens. They're just as tall as me, but I wouldn't want to take them on with those broad shoulders and stocky arms.

I've never been here but it looks stunning. The blooming trees block sight of the buildings surrounding the Gardens, almost to the point that you can pretend they're not there. This large circular patch in the centre of Cavendish Square brings a welcome relief from the endless onslaught of bricks and windows. I do like the city, but I've been meaning to take a break; once this K-Rin business is over, and providing I regain control of my body, I'm whisking Connelly away to somewhere more rural, or even a beach. Both of us need it.

We approach the centre of the Gardens, where four paths meet to form a concrete circle around the base of a white statue that looks like something once stood atop it. Right before this, at the foot of a thick tree, stands a mini platform roped-off from the public. How many hours will Kya have to pose on that before K-Rin appears? At least she can sit if her legs get tired, but she should be used to being on her feet all day. Good job she's wearing flats instead of heels.

As we stop in front of the platform, a guy with a chunky camera around his neck approaches and greets us. It's the same photographer from the shoot the other day. He starts running through with Kya what she needs to do. Your attention wanders to the several people peering over at us from the benches around the statue base. Unsurprisingly, they pull out their phones. You give a small cringey wave, and they lap it up.

Kya slips under the red rope to step up onto the platform. A stream of sunlight shines through the trees down on her, almost making her glow. Won't take long for her to draw people in. She does look absolutely ravishing, but also so much like K-Rin that my fingers squeeze into a fist inside my jacket pocket. I think you hate K-Rin with a much more savage passion than I do. The level of hatred frightens me. It feels personal.

Any nerves Kya still has seem to slip away as she straightens and lifts her thinker high. We did tell her to believe in herself. It's always comforting and inspiring to see her confidence, no matter how it's brought about. The bodyguards stand either side of her, and I stay opposite, with the path between us. You bring out my phone to take a string of pictures, while the photographer snaps his. Before we know it, those people from the benches spawn in front of her to do the same. They're four young women and a guy, each of them asking her different questions:

"Where'd you get the dress from?"

"Have you met K-Rin?"

"Where's the rabbit?"

"Are you hyped about the song release tomorrow?"

"Can we take a selfie with you?"

Smiling, she replies, "The dress was custom-made for me by my designer. I haven't met K-Rin, sadly. The bunny couldn't come today. I *am* excited for the song release, yes. And of course you can take some photos – just make sure you stay in front of the rope, please."

So she carefully kneels on the platform and they all in turn snap their selfies with her. Just as I'm starting to feel dejected from them not noticing or talking to me, one of the women turns to me and says, "Can we please take a picture of you too, Maddix?" You grant her permission, and her friends want in as well. It still surprises me that anyone who likes K-Rin would think favourably of me, but I should bask in this attention and recognition while I can – don't mind it in small doses. I don't even have to beg you to do this; you get straight in there and pose with them. You even know how to smile like me: lips closed, one side quirking up. Once they've got what they want, the people thank us then scurry off, giggling like children. My thinker shakes slowly at them. Oh, man, they don't even know yet that I'm Kya's future fake boyfriend too.

Not many people are here yet, but we *have* arrived twenty minutes early, to be fair. Will this place get swamped? If so, we may need more than two guards. The idea of being surrounded by fans thrills me – no, it must thrill *you*, because I'd be daunted. It could get out of hand, and there might be too many bodies for us to notice K-Rin showing up. Every person who passes stops to grab a picture of Kya, and a couple of clusters stay a little longer to gawp and record videos.

A few guys approach me. "New fans," apparently. They admit they only watch my videos for the controversy about K-Rin. Interesting that they want the controversy and not any scrap of information they can get about their idol. My thinker nods along to everything they say with a smile that feels so strained that I'm glad I can't see it. I'd need several shots to be comfortable talking to this many strangers in quick succession, but you don't bat an eyelid.

As they ogle Kya again, I spot Connelly approaching in my peripheral. You turn to him with a grin. I try to scream out, 'Help! I'm being controlled. Don't listen to anything I say!' But nothing comes out. His expression's tense, and only worsens as he frowns at the gathering around

Kya. He's in his usual blue shirt, waistcoat, and jeans combo: smart and sexy as ever. Shame he's radiating anxiety right now. Does he sense that everything's about to be taken away from us?

He hands me the takeaway coffee cup he's holding. You say, "I love you so much," before planting a kiss on his cheek. Slimy arsehole. You don't deserve to share any intimacy with us, but it's much too late for that. As usual, Connelly briefly glances around with reddening cheeks from being kissed in public. Everyone's eyes are on Kya anyway. Why are you even being close with him if you're going to announce the relationship with Kya later? Keeping up the façade?

"You're still going through with this crazy plan, aren't you?"

He must be mad at me for not listening to him. Looks like you and I had the same idea, or maybe it was yours and you made me think it was mine?

You sip our Caffeine Indulgence. "Yes, but the crowd needs to get much bigger to attract you know who."

"I really don't think this'll work, Madd."

I'm not sure it will now, actually, but *you* seem so sure. You lean me into him and say, "There's no way she'll let someone else hog all the attention." Our eyes lock. "Trust me. She'll show."

"Okay," he says.

This makes me sick. Every time he's accepted what I've said this week, has it only been because you've forced him to?

Connelly backs off as soon as six more people approach, but half of them fire questions at him while the others pounce on me. There's so much noise that I can't hear what they're saying to him, only the grating enquiries for me: 'Have you met K-Rin yet?' and 'What do you think will happen tomorrow?' Neither you nor I can answer that last one, not with certainty. Where were all these fanatics yesterday when I was out and about? Too busy stuck in their phones. Guess they *would* all be drawn here today. I imagine it stings for Kya, that a bunch of these people rushed over here thinking she's K-Rin, only to then look fairly disappointed. I'm just glad none of them are asking about the relationship, but maybe that's because Connelly's right there.

The crowd grows. Being on the same level as all these bodies, a substantial portion wanting my attention, is so stressful and claustrophobic that I want my own platform to stand on. I can't even see Connelly anymore. Hope he's not being verbally assaulted by anyone, considering what he told me before. I want to check on him, or drag him away, but you're talking to as many people as possible, being so overly nice that I want to puke. The odd person does end up mentioning the rumour and how sad they are, but you thankfully tell them you don't want to discuss it. I would've thought you'd take this opportunity to use your mind control on everyone. You've been on high alert for K-Rin, I think, and so have I. How much more packed does this place have to get to lure her out? I've only ever seen her on a screen, so it's hard to picture her out here.

This really is getting too much. Where the hell is Connelly? You obviously don't care enough to look for him. I need control back. Please. I know you can hear my thoughts. Stop fucking ignoring me.

"Stop panicking," you say.

How, when I'm imprisoned and can't move anyway thanks to this insane, noisy crowd? Give me control, now, for fuck's sake!

You throw back my thinker. Shut my eyes. Grin at the sky. Bathe in the endless chatter, bustle, and excitement. It all floods inside me, like oceans of Russian Euphoria.

A deep, loud driving beat erupts around us. You glance about. That rhythmically rising and falling bassline. It's been a week since I've heard it, but I'd recognise it anywhere. Where's it coming from exactly, and how? Why today? This shouldn't be happening. Everyone else searches for the source too. As those synths join the beat, they all start to realise it's that amazing song they love. Is that a little black speaker up in that tree behind Kya? Her wide eyes stare up at it. There must be others dotted around the park. It's a setup. K-Rin knew we'd be here today, and she has us all trapped.

I want to yell at everyone to stop listening, but the music's so loud, how can they? My body pushes through the muttering crowd as K-Rin's soft voice sings, "The party's going on in here." Guess I'm hearing *their* lyrics as my defences no longer need lowering. They haven't fallen into a silent trance yet, so maybe they need K-Rin's visual aid. I'll take any small mercy I can get right now. They're still consumed enough by it that they don't seem to mind us barging through them. Where's Connelly?

What are you doing? You're making me climb onto the base of the central statue – not too difficult considering my height, but I can certainly feel my newly acquired strength in action for the first time. I could easily get arrested for being on this thing, though the one police officer I can spot seems to be as focused on the song as the others. My eyes locate more speakers hidden about the park in spots that I never would've noticed unless specifically searching for them. What are they even hooked up to? There are no leads. Are they wireless, or maybe even magic, because who knows anymore?

"Everyone, look at me," you shout.

No-one does. They all just type on their phones or hold them up as if recording. Now there'll be an infinite number of copies. Will they get deleted as soon as they try uploading them online, or will K-Rin allow it this time?

"Maddix!" Connelly shoves through the crowd towards us. At least he's not affected. Obviously, my influence on him really is strong enough to fight against that bitch's techniques. He makes it to the front of the statue and peers up at us. "What should we do?"

I can see Kya trying to fight it too, doubled over with a grimace and covering her listeners. I'd say let's run from this place, but we can't let those people get sucked in by whatever K-Rin plans to do next.

"Find as many speakers as you can," you demand. "Destroy them."

Connelly nods and heads off through the crowd. My gaze settles on the speaker above Kya's thinker. How will we reach it? Can we chuck something at it? We don't have time to stand and ponder. What will happen when the song ends? It was three-and-a-half minutes long, if I remember right, so we must have half that left.

My body jumps down from the statue base, landing in a perfect crouch. Then you spring me up and towards Kya. We don't even have to worry about getting past her guards as they stand there bobbing their non-thinkers. With this strength, though, we could probably knock them out, actually. Instead, you make me dodge around to the side of the platform then launch me onto the thick tree trunk behind them. Okay, so we *are* climbing! You scramble up using the bark's knobs and ridges. I've climbed trees before, but never this well. It scrapes and scratches my hands – they'll be sore for a while – until they grab the speaker and rip the noisy thing from the tree branch. It smashes on the grass below. Some people step back and gasp. My controlled thinker whips around to see Connelly in the crowd, raising a speaker and thrusting it into the ground. The people nearest him start shouting:

"What the hell?"

"What's wrong with you?"

I'm glad this snapped them out of it, but then they get in his face to prod and push him. I thought this music was supposed to relax them? Now we know what truly happens when someone threatens to take it away right in front of them.

You drop me to the ground. I brace to break my legs, but they land in another impossibly perfect crouch. What the fuck are you? You shove the angry bodies aside with ease, and crush my fear again. Guess I should gladly let you take control if we stand a higher chance of surviving the crowd.

"Hey," someone roars at Connelly, who's caught in a full nelson, "you're the guy who's standing between Maddix and Kya. Now you do *this*?"

You battle through to them. Please make it on time! A guy in front raises his fist at Connelly. You grasp the twat and throw him aside. Thank you! My eyes lock with the guy who's still gripping Connelly. You command him to let him go, and he does. Connelly staggers forward and glowers back at him. You can't force everyone to leave us alone at once, and we can't get to every speaker before the song ends with all these crazed people around. Our best bet is to flee.

"We need to get Kya out of here," Connelly says.

She's still on the platform, covering her listeners. The song's on its last chorus. Like a smug bitch, K-Rin sings, "Everything glistens, and it always will. You will have it all." No, they won't. *She* will. She'll have their mindless devotion and admiration, without earning it.

Snarling, you grab Connelly's hand and guide us through the terrifying, writhing crowd. People keep shouting at us, and whenever anyone tries to touch us, you either lock eyes with them and tell them to "fuck off" or simply shove them away. We reach Kya, who's hunched over. Her useless guards jam to the song's final drawn-out synth notes. They could get us out in one piece – maybe they'll return to their senses now the song's over.

My hand releases Connelly so you can hop onto the platform and help her down.

Connelly wraps his arm around her and asks, "Are you okay?"

She nods frantically and glances around. "It stopped."

It has, and doesn't seem to be playing again. The park fills with animated chatter, but several angry voices shoot our way:

"What's your deal, Maddix?"

"You think you can just ruin it for everyone?"

"You guys are fucking nuts!"

"Get the hell out of here!"

Why are they surprised I wanted to stop them listening to it? Have they not actually watched my videos?

"You're being brainwashed," you cry out, and try to lock gazes with as many people as possible.

Many of them relax their frowns as if taking it in, but others manage to shout:

"You really are crazy."

"Bring the music back."

"Just shut up already."

"Kya, tell him to leave!"

Hearing the crowd reject me like this cuts deep. They keep hurling questions at Kya:

"Did you set the music up?"

"You don't believe him, do you?"

"Why were you covering your ears?"

With a wavering voice, she replies, "I didn't know the music was going to play. I was shocked at how loud it was. I have audio sensitivity."

She hasn't answered their question about believing me, but I guess that's harder. As a few of them try moving closer, the bodyguards finally step in front of us. Kya's no longer on the platform behind the rope, but that wouldn't have provided much protection. We need to do more damage control, particularly for her.

"Kya loves K-Rin just as much as the rest of you," you shout above the racket. "But I know the truth."

"Stick to your videos," a red-faced guy calls. "What gives you the right to fuck up everyone's fun?"

Others agree with him and chuck out their own obscenities. This isn't looking good for me. You shouldn't have started destroying the speakers. Everyone's now turning against me, and K-Rin's obviously not going to show.

"We should leave," Connelly says to me. He edges back, but my hand stops him.

Ignoring the shouting, you pull out my phone and open the YouTube Studio app. Are you doing what I think you are? Yes, you are. This has to work, or I don't know what will.

As soon as the video goes live, a great deal of the crowd glance at their phones. I wouldn't be surprised if they're all subscribed to me and just received the notification. That does feel good. Some put in their earphones, but I hear the video playing from the others' phone speakers at staggered times. Whoever isn't looking at their own phone peers over another's shoulder. The whole crowd is watching. Connelly narrows his eyes and tilts his ear to them, while we wait intensely. Their expressions stay blank, until the video shifts to my speech in Chinese. Eerily, their eyes drift to me. Did it work?

They burst into incomprehensible, heated chatter. A voice in my immediate vicinity calls, "So it's really true?" I can't tell which of them said that, but others utter variations of: "I can't believe K-Rin would do this" and "We have to let everyone else know." It shocks and pleases me how quickly you've influenced them. Pride wells up inside me, and I think it belongs to both of us. Everyone's tapping away on their phones, hopefully spreading it far and wide. It's a short matter of time before the whole world changes its mind about her.

A hand touches my shoulder. This startles me, but you simply turn my thinker to see Kya unblinkingly glaring up at us.

"No more games," she says in a deep but clear tone. "Meet me at the London Stadium."

What? You don't react, only seem to wait for more.

Kya shakes her thinker and rolls out her shoulders. Frowning now, she says, "What's going on?"

My lips smirk. "Don't worry. Everything's okay."

Is it? I don't think it is! Will you let me in on what that was? Oh, you're just going to silently move my legs forward? Great.

You stop beside the guards. "Look at me." So they do, and you command, "Make sure no-one gets to me."

Once they nod, you take off past the noisy crowd, with one guard clearing a path ahead of us and the other protecting the rear. You dismiss the onslaught of interrogation. This is beyond nerve-wracking, but their bulky frames and the new strength I've been imbued with do reassure me.

Connelly's shouts for me promptly get drowned out. I need to turn back for him. Don't want to be apart. Don't even know what I'm plummeting into. This is all so overwhelming.

When we make it out of the park and head towards the road, I feel like I can breathe easier. But my anxiety still simmers. I hate being like this! As my arm hails the nearest taxi, I remember what Kya said. We're going to London Stadium? Are we finally going to meet who I think we are?

The sun glares over London Stadium. I've never been here before. So to come for the first time to confront a God-knows-what that threatens to make the world her bitch is pretty daunting. A staggering structure encages the arena, its white poles joining together to form a ring of diamonds. The taxi drops us off on the empty road beside it. Grass and trees face opposite, with skyscrapers far in the distance. It's relieving to be away from the city noise, but I would've at least expected to hear something from inside the stadium. No-one's even manning the small security booth at the perimeter fence. After we've left the taxi and convinced the driver to bugger off without his fare, you pass between the security bollards with ease. I know, like everything, taxis are overpriced, especially in London, but this is wrong. What other illegal actions am I about to unwillingly commit? I'd be shaking if it weren't for your steel nerves.

We move through the car park. No vehicle nor person in sight. Is this place deserted? On a Saturday afternoon, it should be packed. The further around the building we walk, the more the dead silence intimidates me. Did she clear the place out? What will she do to me? I just want to hold Connelly and never let go. But I may never see him again. Can't even hear his voice because my bastard pilot has turned off my phone to stop it ringing.

Through a glass-panelled entrance, we saunter over a shiny, bare black floor space. The footsteps echo. Dozens of circular lights shine down from the low ceiling, which soon stretches up to allow for a criss-cross of moving escalators. Where is she in this immense place? Will she appear to us, or does she expect us to find her? I guess our best bet's the pitch. You seem to think the same as you take us down an escalator.

On the ground floor, we find ourselves going through large glass doors into a long, wide red corridor. We pass different depictions of the West Ham crest and logo of the two crossed hammers. I've never been into football – more indifferent to it – but I'd gladly rather watch a match here than face her. Beyond a pair of open black-framed glass doors, at the end of a green stretch, a blinding light streams in. As we move further towards it, I feel like I'm not only being pulled forward by you but by something much more powerful, like fate itself. I don't usually believe in that stuff, but who knows now? My feet touch tough artificial grass. The light at the end of this dark tunnel draws distressingly closer. I'm yanking painfully hard on a locked steering wheel. There's no way you'll let me turn away from whatever awaits us out there.

A sea of red and white seats on three ascending tiers encircle the vast pitch. Lighting rigs hang from a complex structure of white poles that curve upwards to meet the edge of the open-top roof. The bright sky peers down at us, making me feel like a speck, but you carry on striding forward like you own the place.

You turn me right and head toward a domed stage setup at the far end of the pitch. A figure with blonde hair and a multi-coloured dress stands alone, front and centre on the stage. It's her all right. She never did mention any collaborators. I can't even see any equipment, save for stacks of large speakers. Is she scoping the arena out for a potential concert, or about to do something I can't comprehend? Can't believe she's actually in the same physical space as me. Hopefully, whatever happens, you can handle her.

The closer we reach the stage, I notice she's behind a delicate black microphone stand. She places her hands on her flowery hips, and lifts her thinker with a clenched jaw. She's undoubtedly pissed at us, and I'm still trying to run the other way. All this time, I've been desperate to confront her, but she might be able to vaporise me for all I know.

My feet stop a few car lengths from the stage. She stares down at us like dirt. You fold my arms. I feel my lips smirk. Don't get cocky with her – she'll only get madder.

You breathe in the fresh air deeply through my nose. "Etivni eht rof sknaht. Uoy dnif reven d'I thguoht."

What on earth just came out of my mouth?

K-Rin's voice stays at normal volume, the mic obviously turned off. "Gniod er'uoy tahw dnatsrednu t'nod I. Liaf ot siht tnaw uoy od?"

I pound against the inside of my skull. What the fuck are you guys saying?

She opens her mouth again, but you snicker, hold up my hand, and say, "Hang on. Maddix wants us to speak in proper English."

Yes, please!

She sighs. "Why are you doing this? Who's really in control?"

You smirk again. "Maddix and I want the same thing."

Not right now we don't. And you're talking as if you know each other. Who the hell's inside me?

She frowns at us like we're insane. "But the world can be a happier, more peaceful place."

Does she honestly want that?

"You can brainwash them, but it won't take away their true nature. Did you see how they were reacting to us trying to take their precious music away?" You press two of my fingers into my temple. "That can't be programmed out. It exists for a reason."

"Not everyone at that park was behaving violently. I *am* making a difference. You've seen what's already happened with the world's crime rates. If I can bring pure peace to the majority, the others will follow."

My hand drifts back down. "Everything needs balance, or *chaos* will follow."

Despite her seemingly noble intentions, that's what I would've said.

"We have no proof of that," she says matter-of-factly.

Considering she travels through electronic devices, she clearly hasn't watched many doomsday films.

You hold out my arms. "You want to risk destroying this planet you love so much?"

Could she really do that?

"Why do you turn on me now?" Her voice cracks, as if hurt. "What happened to our plan? Did you never support my dream?"

"Never," you whisper. "Can you guess why?"

She only frowns.

"You're not doing this to save the planet," you say. "You just want the fame and adoration." Her jaw clenches again. I've seen that look on Connelly many times: knowing the other person's right, and absolutely loathing it. You widen my eyes and move nearer to the stage, as if to force her to crane her neck further downwards to focus on us. "You get your own special body that can travel through those electricity waves. If I did that, I'd fry my host." Envisioning that is a new level of horror. You make me grin. "But we're made from the same stuff, remember?" What does that mean? "I'm an attention whore too... At least I admit it."

I guess I'm as guilty as both of you, in a sense. Maybe that's another reason you chose me.

That righteous, hateful expression remains, her hands still firmly on her hips. Shaking her thinker slowly, her tone deepens: "You used me."

You scoff. "And I thought I was the smart one."

"How could you do this? We made Shinpi, together, so that we could both get what we wanted faster. I had *your* interests at heart too, and still do."

My mind clouds with that darkness I've experienced so often thanks to you. "How will the world truly appreciate me if they're too busy obsessing over you?" She has no answer for that. "You've always shone the brightest. And you don't deserve to." The words scathe my tongue. Am I seriously being ridden by a jealous rival? "Just accept it: this ain't your year, sis. It's mine."

Her eyes sharpen. Brows push together. The betrayal and hatred almost burn right through me. Are you really related?

"No," she snaps. "As soon as I sing into this microphone, my music will travel to every sound transmitter across the globe, and they'll be mine again!"

She grasps the microphone stand. My hands and feet scramble painfully up the tall front of the stage before I have a chance to process what I'm doing. You grab a clump of wavy hair from the back of her thinker, yank her away from the stand, and drag her down. Her slender body smacks onto the stage floor. The sound sickens me as a crack joins it. She doesn't cry out in pain, only stares wide-eyed at us. My knees straddle her soft, flowery hips. What are you going to do? Is there really no way to stop it?

"You know," you say through my gritted teeth, "you've always had the same weakness as me." I feel the snarl slide into another grin. "You talk too much."

And my hands crush her throat. Her eyes bulge. Mouth shoots open. She tries to prise my wrists away. Those awful choked gasps send terror through my soul. I scream for the violence to end, for you to spare her. You just push down harder. I feel the conviction, and the power. I don't want to be a murderer. This can't be the answer!

She should surely be dead by now, or at least unconscious. The blood vessels in her eyes haven't even burst. My body may be blocking the sun's glow, but her face persists to shimmer. Is it even possible to kill her this way? Her gasps have fallen silent, but she's still very much alive. I'm relieved, but what will she do when we let go?

My grip on her neck gradually releases. Her mouth hangs open, and her chest heaves as if trying to make a sound, but it seems to catch in her throat. I feel a smirk on my lips. Do you not want her dead? You lift off her but keep my feet either side of her hips. Triumph flushes through me.

You're proud of your work. Have you destroyed her voice? Without that, she's nothing. I don't know how to feel about this. We may have just saved the world.

My body slowly twists and steps off her. You scuff to the edge of the stage then step off. After straightening up from our clean, crouched landing, you stride across the artificial grass. Is leaving her the best thing? I try to check on her, but my thinker fixes forward. What will she do? You seem confident enough to walk away, so is it completely over for her now? Without her voice, she can't hypnotise the masses anymore. But how permanent is it? Will she seek revenge?

As we continue across the pitch, with the sun shining gloriously down on us, I hear a calm voice echo through me: 'The world is ours now.'

13

What do you have planned for us? This and the horrible memory of choking K-Rin plague me as you take a taxi back towards Cavendish Gardens. You switch my phone on again. Multiple messages and missed calls from Connelly and Kya. Not surprised at all. They must be going out of their minds. Did they make it out of the park okay?

You ring Connelly and press the phone to my ear.

"Maddix, what the hell's going on?" He's shrill again, but for good reason. "Where are you?"

Smiling, you rest my skull back against the faux leather headrest. "I'm sorry I took off. Had no time to explain. K-Rin called me to London Stadium."

"What happened? Are you okay?"

"It's over. I convinced her not to sing anymore."

Will you tell him how? I honestly hope not.

"Oh," he says after a pause. "Are you sure?"

It *is* a stretch to believe, but it won't be as soon as we look into his eyes and say it.

My thinker rolls sideways to watch the industrial buildings crawl by. "Absolutely sure. Where are you?"

I do also want to know that, but I don't want you near him anymore. I want you out of me.

"The Courthouse Hotel," Connelly says. "We had to run out of that park and get a taxi away from that fucking crowd. Now we're holed up here and everyone's outside, waiting for us. I think someone spotted us and word spread."

His voice waivers a little, like he's scared. I would be too. We need to get them out of there.

A sigh slips from my nose. "I'll deal with them. Just stay put. I'll be there soon."

"Uh, okay."

My thumb ends the call. I hate hanging up on him without saying bye. You want to check my subscriber count, it seems. Eight million? What the actual fuck? I don't even know how to process this. It's simply unbelievable, beyond anything I could imagine. My announcement about K-Rin must've worked.

You bring up the phone's camera, hold it in front of my face, and tap

239

record.

"Hello, everyone," you say smugly. You gaze right at the camera, clearly preparing to use your mind tricks again. "So, I found K-Rin. I made her tell me what she was planning to do to you all. She would've released that song and brainwashed every person on earth to love her. You would've been her *slaves*." One side of my mouth curves up. "But I stopped her. Convinced her to back down. And now she's gone. I was right from the very beginning." You laugh, like the proud prick you are. "I'm really grateful to those of you who've supported me. It doesn't matter that hardly any of you believed me before, because I know you will now."

You record the same message in a few different languages – you'll probably do the rest when we have more time later – and string the clips together as one video. By the time we reach Soho, the video's published to YouTube for the world to absorb. Maybe it's for the best that everyone believes us. We're telling the truth. K-Rin claimed that she wanted the best for us, but we essentially *would* have been slaves. Your hypocrisy's on another level, though. You don't care about saving the planet. You just don't want her hogging the limelight.

My phone vibrates in my hand. I've never heard from Mum so much. I'm grateful she hasn't been spreading any further information about me, but I dread what she has to say. Now I can't even truly speak to her.

As soon as you answer, I try to scream out, 'Help me, Mum. I'm trapped!' But what comes out is what I usually want to say when she calls: "What do you want?"

"Maddix?" she says. "Is that you?"

No!

"Yes," you say.

"I'm very sorry. Both of us are. We should've never doubted you." She actually sounds serious. It hurts more than anything that they needed to be brainwashed to finally apologise to me. "We're so proud of you for stopping her."

"Yes. Thank you, son!" Dad? It hurts even more, knowing I can't reply.

You seem to channel my spite as you say, "Thank you. That means a lot." You smirk out of the window. "But I'd like it even more if you stop calling. You've never truly cared about me."

How much do you really know about that? Can you see my memories? It's not that I *want* them to stop calling – deep down, I appreciate that they do at all. I just wish they'd do it because they want to, not because they feel obliged to. Guess you reckon they'll never change. I don't know what I think anymore.

"Maddix, darling, you have to stop talking like that." Normally, she'd sigh with frustration, but her voice is cracking, and it stings to hear. "We love you."

"Yes, we love you, Maddix," Dad echoes.

When was the last time they told me that? Do they mean it? How can I process this?

You snigger. "I have no interest in fake love. So, Laurel, Ronnie, consider this your last conversation with your son. We're done here."

You hang up.

How could you say that? You don't get to decide this. Call them back. Tell them you weren't serious!

Of course, though, you just shake my thinker. How will Mum and Dad take it? Will they keep trying to contact me? Return to the UK after all in a desperate attempt to reach me? Or will they accept it and move on with their lives?

Well, by the time we make it back to Mayfair, neither of them have rung.

As we leave the taxi, without paying yet again, we watch the large cluster of people by the hotel entrance from across the road. I don't even want to go near them, although surely their opinion of me has only improved if they've seen my latest video? Why hasn't the hotel set the police on these people? Actually, looking closer, there *are* a couple of officers, but they're shouting with the crowd for the hotel to open its doors. Wow.

How will we get through them? We need their attention, but it's too loud. My thinker snaps to the taxi. As it goes to move off, my hand smacks against the door. It halts. What are you making me do now? You lean me down level with the window, which lowers all the way.

We lock eyes with the driver. "Hold still for a minute."

He blankly nods.

You scramble my body onto the taxi's roof, and have no problem balancing. As crazy as this is, it might just work, and I doubt we'll even get in trouble.

"Hey, everyone," you scream. "Look at me!"

You'd just love that.

With staggered reaction speeds, all non-thinkers turn to us. Every pair of eyes widens at the sight of me. The racket dies down, with only a handful of people left muttering to each other. The officers aren't even commanding me to get down.

"Step away from the hotel," you call.

Just like that, the herd separates. A powerful rush hits me. I can't deny how satisfying it feels. We didn't even need to make eye contact with every one of them. How many have seen the latest video? I'd guess most, if not all, judging by their awed expressions. They're either recording me or taking pictures. That feels good too. I think we're both revelling in it as you hop off the taxi and stride between them to the hotel entrance.

Before you go in, you turn my thinker to the two officers and say, "Do your jobs and get these people out of here."

They nod then bark orders at the two clumps of bodies to disperse. Okay, as much as this mind control thing sickens me, *that* was slightly cool.

The hotel doors open for us. We step in and the receptionist quickly shuts and locks them again.

"Don't worry," you say to him. "The police are handling it now."

"Oh." He peers through the glass and sighs. "Brilliant."

"Where is Kya?"

"Room 103. Her security guys are stopping other hotel guests from entering, though."

You smirk. "Well, they won't stop *me*."

You ride the lift up. Don't know if you feel pain like I do, but after all the walking and standing around we've done, I'm grateful. The bodyguards from earlier step aside as I approach Kya's door. She'd normally never dream of setting foot in a standard double room, but they must've had nothing else available for her to hide in.

Some people linger at the end of the corridor, seemingly pretending to act casual but keeping watch on the room.

"Get lost," you call over to them, and they scurry back through their doors. I'm impressed, again. The guards obviously couldn't get them to completely bugger off, but a couple words from me and they're gone.

We enter the room and close the door behind us. My feet take me down the short corridor into the main area. Sitting on the end of the bed, still in K-Rin attire, Kya lifts her hands away from her blotchy face and seems to sigh with relief when she spots me. My fingers wrapping around her neck flashes in my mind. It terrifies me.

From the chair in the corner by the window, Connelly darts up, hurries over, and throws himself at me. His warm arms, musky aftershave, and the knowledge that he's safe relax me for all but a few seconds as I remember it's not technically me hugging him back. Please, this K-Rin fiasco's over. Let me fucking have control again.

My nose silently inhales the caramel of his shampoo from the top of his thinker. "I missed you."

Don't you dare say that, especially if you don't mean it. He just squeezes me then pulls away.

"We saw your video just now," Kya says. "What was she like?"

"Did she do anything to you?" Connelly asks, glancing me up and down.

You gently cradle his hand with both of mine. "I'm fine. And she was...ridiculously self-righteous."

"How the hell did you convince her to back down?"

Don't tell them. I feel sick just thinking about them finding out. I know we didn't kill her but it was still horrific. Unless you do reveal the truth and force them not to think anything bad of it.

"I have power over her," you explain, almost gloating, and let go of Connelly. "That's why I've been able to resist her. She sent Shinpi to try to hypnotise me. But it didn't work."

It fucking did. It happened that day you visited me in Aki's body. It was why I hallucinated and fainted in Brockwell Park. Why can't Connelly tell it's not me speaking? He must've twigged *something* over these last few days, because seriously, how could my soulmate not even notice it's not me staring back at him?

"What should we do about that rabbit?" he says.

"He poses no harm. He's ours now. And he's done wonders for the channel."

Connelly nods. He should be questioning this more. I don't want him agreeing with everything I, or you, say!

"Did you find out what K-Rin is?" Kya asks. "I mean, she's not human, is she?"

How will you answer this one? I'm dying to know too.

My gaze shifts slowly between them. "She's something beyond our understanding. Born from the stars." I feel like you're choosing your words carefully. Of course, this description doesn't just apply to her, does it? "She's been around since the beginning of time, and was ready to finally take this rock for herself." That smirk creeps back to my lips. "But she had one weakness."

They both frown at me, as if deep in thought and struggling to comprehend.

"Why you?" Connelly says.

Good bloody question. Even before you brainwashed and possessed me, I had a resistance to her. Aki did too. Who knows how many of us there were? But I guess only one being had the power to choke the voice out of her.

My shoulders shrug. "No idea."

Come on!

I feel you grin. You're fucking loving this, keeping me in suspense. Who the fuck do you think you are?

Then that smug voice slithers through my skull: 'I'm you.'

*

Being taken over with no control whatsoever is the scariest and most maddening thing that's ever happened to me. The worst part – I thought it'd be the powerlessness, or even having what I treasure most being ripped away from me – but it's the not knowing how long I'll be stuck like this. Will you ride me 'til my body wears out? As it is, these last two weeks have felt like forever. It's been an insanely uncomfortable mixture of torture and paradise. The attention won't stop rolling in. We've done so many interviews I've lost count, and this one tonight's the biggest yet. I'd be downing shots like a nervous wreck in preparation, but you're so fucking cool about it. Shouldn't surprise me anymore.

I've never previously had the pleasure of visiting the pristine, modern White City, despite living in London my whole life. Never had much reason to. Now we're checked in at the fancy Princess Victoria Hotel, which I look forward to lounging about in later, and being made up for the camera backstage at the BBC Television Centre. I've hated this woman prodding my face with makeup brushes, although she's made my hair dead smart by combing and gelling my fringe back – that was your suggestion, and I have to admit we wear it well. We look bloody dapper in this dark-grey Canali suit you had to go back and buy. I do appreciate you getting that leather jacket too, but how can you justify dropping £3000 on clothes but expect free meals and won't pay a single taxi fare? Can you actually answer me this time?

As you check out my body in the full-length dressing room mirror, I hear your words grate against the inside of my skull: 'There's prestige that comes with telling people how much you spend on your attire.'

Prestige? Try douchebaggery. That money could've gone towards better recording equipment! Guess we can invest in that next month – with the abundance of revenue I've been getting from the channel as well as Patreon support, we'll have plenty to play with. We'll even be able to afford a deposit for a mortgage in no time. Oh, but I guess we don't have to worry about that at the moment, do we? Anyway, I'm sure the price tag doesn't make us look any better, although this suit fits perfectly and shines handsomely in these overhead backstage lights.

'You like it too. I *know* you do.'

I hate to admit it, but seeing myself like this does fill me with a slither of pride.

It's all too surreal, exciting, and frightening. In a twisted way, I'm glad you're steering the helm, because I'm unsure how I'd handle it. I've never been on TV. I'm trying to tell myself it's no different than talking on camera at home, but there's a live studio audience here. From the small backstage waiting area, I hear them cheering and clapping over the loud, explosive intro music. Inside, I'm taking endless deep breaths to calm myself, but you, of course, just slump on this faux leather sofa with my thinker reclined. When someone slips through the glass-beaded curtain, you straighten me up.

The long, flowing ruffles of an emerald-green dress catch my eyes first. They stretch up to meet a strapless, sequinned bodice, above which hangs a matching sparkly earring and necklace set that, knowing Kya, is white gold. Her hair's scraped up into an impressive ponytail – nice to see it purple instead of K-Rin blonde – and thick black makeup frames her lively eyes.

"Maddix." She beams. "You look stunning."

You smile. "I was about to say the same."

I still can't tell when you're being sarcastic, but at least it *sounds* genuine. She really is gorgeous tonight, but I'm finding it harder to look at her.

"Thank you." She clip-clops over to join us on the sofa. After lowering herself gently, probably to avoid creasing the dress too much, she takes a steadying breath. "I can't believe I'm finally on the Robert E. Carney show,

245

and with *you*."

It *is* pretty crazy. He normally invites on actors and musicians. Through the wall, I can barely hear the guy animatedly addressing the audience. We'll be on any minute now. Fortunately, you suppressing my emotions means that I'm not overwhelmed with anxiety. I don't know how much being on this particular show interests you – I just have a feeling you're grateful for the attention.

You lean me forward to rest my elbows in my lap and dangle my hands between my knees. My thinker turns to stare into her eyes. Once we have her locked, you say, "Remember what we discussed: don't talk about yourself too long, and always try to guide the conversation back to me. Okay?"

Her lovely smile has died. She nods. Why must you continue to violate her like this? She deserves more limelight than us. She's worked her whole life to get this far. Do you even realise how hypocritical you are, you selfish, manipulative dick?

You push me back down with a suffocating squeeze. I keep scratching at these walls, but every time you do this, my strength depletes.

A woman in a black polo shirt and trousers with a lanyard around her neck flies into the room to collect us. She tells us to switch on our tiny microphones, mine clipped on my suit jacket collar and Kya's over the top edge of her bodice. We wait in a short dark corridor with the woman in front of us, keeping hold of a door handle and listening closely in her earpiece.

Robert Carney's voice booms louder than ever from the stage, and even muffled through the wall I can hear him saying, "This has been a hell of a crazy time recently. I don't know about you, but I've been desperate to know more about what happened that day. So it's my pleasure to invite to the stage two very special people: UK fashion model Kya Durand, and one of YouTube's fastest rising stars, the saviour of Earth, Maddix Aitken. AKA *Your* Power Couple!"

I really detest that phrase, but being named 'saviour of Earth' has a lovely ring to it. The audience applause starts. This is it. Kya nudges us and raises her eyebrows. You lift my thinker and smirk.

"Follow the arrows on the floor," the woman instructs us again, "go to Mr. Carney, shake his hand, and sit on the sofa." Yes, we went over this earlier. As soon as the music kicks in, she flings open the door. "And go."

I don't have much chance to linger and stew in my annoyance at her stiff attitude towards us. I'd like to think she's overjoyed inside about meeting us but just can't show it.

My legs follow Kya out into the bright noise. The epic, jaunty music can't quite drown out the cheering and clapping. As my eyes adjust to the stage lights, I can make out hundreds of grinning faces. I wish I could stop and revel in it for a few moments. It's not as scary as I imagined. It helps that, thanks to you, my legs aren't wobbling. You stride closely behind Kya to centre-stage, where Robert Carney waits for us. Dressed in his signature mauve silk suit jacket with his silver hair spiked up as usual, he grins and rises from his neon desk to shake our hands. It was strange meeting him earlier, and still is. I've watched this programme for years, and never dreamed I'd be here. The camera certainly hides the wrinkles around his eyes. As much as I hate makeup, at least it covers *my* imperfections.

Kya and I move around the desk to carefully sit on the shiny purple sofa beside it. It's so soft I could sink into oblivion. Might not be a bad idea. You seem to deliberately stay on the edge and lean forward slightly so I can't enjoy it at all. Arsehole.

The sound dies down. We're quickly overheating under these lights, making me wish we'd kept the jacket off, but it's worth a bit of sweat to look this good. As you subtly glance over the dark sea of faces, I have to wonder if any part of you is self-conscious or does that side of you not exist? My eyes find Connelly and his parents smiling at us from the centre of the front row. The last thing he said to us was how proud he is – even Jade and Ed are, at last. Do Mum and Dad feel the same? Are they even watching after you blocked their numbers? The spiteful part of me hopes they are, then they can see what I've become. If only I could've achieved this without you.

Robert resumes his place at the painfully lit-up desk. He clasps his hands together in front of him on the metal surface. "Welcome, both. It's an honour to have you here."

Weird hearing him say that. Just two weeks ago, I was a nobody at Kya's party. I had five-hundred thousand subscribers, but that's insubstantial compared to what I have now. I swear I'm not ungrateful, but five-hundred thousand doesn't get you global fame.

"Thank you for having us," Kya says graciously. She hooks one leg over the other and rests her hands on her knee. Her gaze hasn't flitted once to the audience – think she's trying to keep her composure.

Aren't you going to say anything? Or are you wrapped up in your own self-importance?

"Yes," my mouth finally says. "Thank you very much."

My voice is deeper, as it always is through a mic. Guess it's *your* voice now.

"You both look amazing," Robert says, which gets a grin from Kya. He chuckles. "Maddix, you do scrub up well." He glances out at the audience. "Doesn't he?"

Is that a compliment? Everyone laughs – not *at* me, right? Thankfully, your confidence stops me from going red. You just casually pan my vision across the studio to smirk at them all. Please don't make me seem like a pompous arse. 'Pot, kettle,' you whisper. No. I've always strived to be modest, and now you're pissing all over it!

Robert clears his throat. "So, it's been a crazy couple of weeks." He doesn't know the half of it. "The world was almost completely brainwashed by the singer known as K-Rin. And it's all thanks to you, Maddix, that this didn't happen."

You nod my thinker slowly.

"Am I right in saying you haven't seen her since?" he continues.

"She's still missing, yeah."

"She'll be facing pretty heavy time when the police find her, *if* they can contain her."

"I think she'll be found if she wants to be."

That's true. She's probably hiding in the airwaves somewhere.

"Mm." Robert turns to Kya. "It must've been quite a shock for you, Kya. It's a shame, too, because you had a smashing cosplay put together of her. You really were her spitting image."

On the large screen above and to the side of his desk flashes up a photograph of Kya during her initial K-Rin photoshoot, holding Shinpi and smiling into the camera.

She twists her body briefly to look up at it. Her tone saddens, and her disappointment certainly isn't put on: "She was my idol. I was absolutely devastated when I found out the truth, as were many others."

"Yes. I remember that guy who interviewed her on the BBC: he gave up everything he had so that he could do all this charity work in her name. When he found out who she was, he was fuming. He didn't exactly come out in the best light, did he?" Yeah, he cursed her profusely for making him 'waste' his money and possessions on charity. There were certainly better

248

ways of expressing that anger. "K-Rin's true nature sent a wave of depression across the world–"

"–That depression, though," you cut in, "is likely a side effect from the brainwashing. I mean, there *are* people who are feeling it because they genuinely like her, of course. But the extent to which that many adored and idolised her in such a short space of time was impossible through organic means."

"Well, I'm sure I can speak on behalf of everyone when I say we are truly grateful you were able to resist her." Narrowing his eyes, he leans forward. "I can't believe some people thought you were in on it."

You roll my eyes with a snicker. "I know. Well, I've been *thoroughly* investigated by the police *and* MI5, and naturally, they found nothing suspicious."

Because you forced them to turn away and forget about us! I mean, I *am* relieved; we won't have to sit in those daunting interrogation rooms anymore and they'll finally leave me and Connelly alone. But I *need* them to investigate me so they can discover your unwanted presence in my body. Unsure how they'd find that out exactly, but...

"Everyone should have taken your word for it," Robert says. "We *all* see the bunny as black now. If that's not proof, what is?"

Ironic that it took another wave of brainwashing to undo the first.

"People still seem to love Shinpi," he goes on. "Is it true he has brainwashing powers too?"

"Some people think he does. Others don't... It never worked on me."

Liar. What does Robert believe?

"In that case, I'm glad it didn't." He laughs, and all my soul can do is sigh. You just make me smile – I hope it doesn't look as fake as it feels. "I remember you had to do a bit of damage control for him."

"Yes. He shouldn't be blamed for the mistakes of his previous owner. He's only a rabbit."

He nods in agreement. "Mmm."

"He's pretty much an integral part of the channel now. It's growing more and more by the day."

"How many subscribers *do* you have?"

If he's a fan, he wouldn't have to ask. Might just be for others' sake, though.

With a pride I wish belonged to me alone, you say, "Just over one-hundred million."

"Wow. Yes, that's astonishing." He shakes his non-thinker as if in disbelief. "Apparently, that puts you in third place for biggest YouTube channel."

"It does."

I don't need a mirror to see how smug my face is. At least try to sound and look unpretentious about it. It's mental how rapidly we've shot to third. I never thought I'd make it to the top one-hundred. All those sponsorship requests rolling in didn't seem real. I appreciate the extra money, of course, but I loathe that you made me stoop so low. Corporate sell-out.

"And Kya," Robert says, "I believe you've also gained several million Instagram followers over the last two weeks."

"That's right. I'm honestly humbled." Her grin stretches almost too wide. "But it's nothing compared to Maddix."

I desperately want to tell her not to sell herself short, that she shouldn't be dictated to about how to feel, how to act, what to say. But you're just too fucking strong for either of us to fight.

"You should still definitely be proud of yourself," Robert says, as if hearing my thoughts. She just glances at the shiny black stage floor with an awkward smile. For Christ's sake. Robert turns his focus to me again. "Now, Maddix, I know you haven't really spoken in much detail about your confrontation with K-Rin. Would you mind sharing a few details with us? Loads of people are dying to know."

How will you spin this? You're not about to admit on live TV that you strangled her.

My eyes drift over the waiting faces in the audience then you arch an eyebrow at him. "What exactly would *you* like to know, Rob?"

"Well, I guess what's been pressing on my mind the most is what you said to her and how she reacted. You haven't been very candid about that."

You lace my fingers together and let them rest between my knees as you lean me forward. During your explanation, you don't blink once or break eye contact with him. "When I got to London Stadium, she tried to use her tricks on me, to pacify me. I told her that wouldn't work, that she should stop what she was doing because it was wrong. I said, 'You can't just brainwash people. The world needs balance.' She didn't understand at first. She was too hell-bent on forcing everyone to love her to see what the consequences would be." At least most of this is true. Robert just listens with rapt attention. "I don't know what plans she had for us all," you add, "but we would've been slaves, with no wills of our own."

Robert shudders a little. "How did you convince her to stop?"

You straighten me and lift my thinker. "Quite simply, I overpowered her. Because of my resistance to her mind control, I was able to use sheer will to drive her away."

If you weren't skilled at mind control too, no-one would buy this bullshit.

"That truly is amazing." Robert gawps out at the audience. I'd call him foolish for falling for it, but this has nothing to do with intelligence. "Can everyone just take a few moments to show their appreciation?"

He starts clapping, and cringingly, the studio erupts in applause. Even Kya joins in. You make me gaze out at them and breathe in the hot air. A rush floods in and leaves me giddy. I do love this too. I can just imagine everyone watching at home taking part as well. This, along with Connelly's bright eyes and adoring face, almost make all these lies worth it.

"Maddix," Robert says as the applause fades away, "why do you think K-Rin told everyone to respect you if you were the only one who could bring her down?"

You shrug. "She was buttering me up, luring me into a false sense of security. 'Keep your friends close, but your enemies closer.'"

"Mm. Makes sense... Can you give us an inkling as to what's next for your channel, then? Now that K-Rin is gone, will you go back to covering conspiracies?"

"Yeah. I mean, new conspiracies crop up all the time, and I find them absolutely fascinating." Is that right, or do you find the *fame* fascinating? You haven't done any conspiracy videos so far, only stupid vlogs with that fucking rabbit. "I plan for Shinpi to continue being a main feature of the channel, since he's so mysterious. Thinking about taking him on trips to various places, maybe even hire out a nice beach somewhere for an afternoon."

You *know* I've been craving the beach for a while, and now I'll have to spend it there as a prisoner. You'll undoubtedly use it as an excuse to show off my body too, won't you?

"Ooh," Robert muses. "Exciting."

"And, you know, I'm always open for suggestions."

Thanks for that; we'll be inundated with even more dumb shit!

"Great," Robert says. "So, Kya, what will you be up to?"

She whips her ponytail back over her shoulder. "Well, since Vogue's K-Rin-focused issue never went forward, they redid my interview and asked me to model the new Louis Vuitton range to include in their next issue."

"Ooh. Very nice."

She grins, her teeth almost sparkling in the light. "I know. I'm ecstatic to be modelling for them again. And I have several more photoshoots coming up this year. I'm not allowed to discuss them yet, though."

"Oh." His eyes widen. "Why the secrecy?"

My leg starts jigging. Getting impatient, you selfish dick?

"I'd like to surprise people with a few," she says, "and others have some details to sort out before they go ahead. But I can say with certainty that you'll be seeing a lot more of me this year." She chuckles. "And Maddix."

My leg stills.

"Brilliant. I can't wait." He seems genuine enough. "It's definitely going to be a big year for you both. And I think a lot of people are excited that you two are going on this journey together."

You reach for Kya's hand and squeeze it. "There's no-one I'd rather do it with."

She smiles widely at us, but I can almost hear the screams behind her eyes. The audience goes, "Aww." I can't help cringing at them, and scoffing at your arrogance. You really think you've won, don't you?

To have this many people looking in awe at me truly is a blessing and a curse. They all gather with their cameras behind a rope barrier in the large Television Centre foyer. Kya and I pass by, but stop for photos, of course: some individual shots, some together, then more intimate. I'm just glad you don't kiss her in private too. Each flash excites me, and must be doing the same to you, but you remain upright with a cool composure. Thankfully, a couple of security guys swiftly lead us outside. The fresh air eases the headache brought on by those stage lights. I'll have to get used to them for now, I suppose.

That sleek, shiny black Mercedes waits for us in the small car park. The white lights dotted around reflect off it. I loved being chauffeured here, and can't wait to get back in. Our closely-shaven driver with the smart suit slides out to open the back passenger door. Connelly steps out in his £1000 waistcoat and grins adorably at me. God, I miss him so much. They must've picked him up from around back. I think he enjoys being driven about the city too. Guess it's the rush of importance that comes with the smell of clean, new leather, the space to stretch our legs out, and the chauffeur calling us 'sir'.

Kya and I join Connelly by the car. As she climbs in carefully, you make me grab his face and press my lips passionately against his. I still can't work out if you get anything out of this other than the satisfaction of torturing me. Can you even love anyone else besides yourself? Will I ever again get to be the one touching, kissing, and talking to him? He grips my waist, squeezes himself into me, and slips his tongue inside my mouth, even in front of the driver. I'm not sure Connelly wants me. He wants *you*, who you've made me. My heart can't take it.

He pulls away slightly to stare up at me. "You were great in there. Totally at home."

You make me smile. "Thank you for coming."

"You really do look handsome in that suit. And you two make a good couple." How the fuck can he say that last part, brainwashed or not? He does sound slightly bitter, though. He glances down, and grimaces. "Maddix, you've been gone for two weeks but it feels like two months."

My thinker tilts. "It's okay. I still love you, and you've got enough money coming in for the rent, plus extra."

"But I miss *you*."

And I miss him too!

You dare to sigh under my breath then pull him closer and whisper, "I'll come visit. It'll be our secret."

He chuckles. "Or maybe Kya will have to invite me 'round for dinner more often."

"We'll work something out. This week, though, I'll need you to come with me to the solicitors." You straighten then very matter-of-factly say, "We need to file for divorce."

It takes me a while to register the words that left my lips. Everything darkens at the edges, as if closing in on me. You snap it back into focus.

Connelly gives the tiniest frown. "What?"

He should be exploding, but I think he's experiencing the same bewilderment as me.

"It only makes logical sense," you say. "How would it look to the public if we're still married but I'm dating your sister?"

He smiles strangely, and mutters, "I know you told them we were splitting up, but I didn't think you'd go through with it. We can keep up the act and *pretend* to–"

"–We're getting divorced," you say sharply. "That's that."

No. I won't believe this... Can't.

He nods, but I can see the fight raging in his eyes.

You stroke his face with the back of my hand. "Don't fret. Remember what I said before: I still love you, and you'll be provided for. You won't lose me."

He *has* lost me, and himself. All he can do is accept your bullshit, but I can't let this go on. I won't let you destroy us.

You release Connelly, and keep smiling. "Now get in the car."

He nods again, without questioning me, but he *should*, like he always has. He just joins Kya in the car.

As we watch him, a dark figure hovers in our peripheral. Someone's lurking behind and to the side of the security barrier on the other side of the car park, peering over at us. My body tenses. You're actually nervous? Hang on. I know that studded beanie hat and small frame. What's he doing here?

You get the chauffeur's attention and gaze straight into his eyes. "Wait for me."

He nods too, shuts the door, and stays perfectly still waiting for my return. My legs set off towards the security barrier. What are you planning? Surely you can't do anything in front of witnesses? Unless you brainwash everyone to forget afterwards.

The closer we get, the clearer Aki's expression becomes. He glares, with clenched fists by his sides. He stands on the edge of the pavement, so he's not blocking the barrier – must be why the two guys in the security booth here haven't told him to bugger off. I get how pissed he is, but if he wants what's best for himself, he should stay the hell away from us.

Smirking, you stop before the barrier and cross my arms. "Don't know when to quit, do you?"

He snarls. His dark eyes burn. Is he even scared of you, or just acting his arse off?

"Get out of his body," he says, hushed but firmly. Still odd hearing his real voice.

A snigger scratches my throat. Guess it *is* slightly amusing that he thinks that'll convince you. What else can he say at this point, though?

"Aww," you say. "Aki, I didn't realise you missed me that much."

Predictably, his frown deepens. "You don't belong here. Maddix doesn't deserve this."

"What, global fame and success?"

"You know what I mean."

You shrug my shoulders. "I'm only giving him everything he wants. You jealous?"

You've also *taken* what I want. Connelly's all that matters now!

Aki scrunches up his face.

"I was you for five years and got you nothing but closer to a YouTuber you didn't even know existed," you say.

So you really were my number one fan. Aki had no choice in donating £50 a month to me. Had no choice in *anything* he did. Please, I don't want to stay powerless like him, like I am now. How many times must I beg?

You press a hand to my forehead. "He's just like you, though: always thinking and complaining and never shutting up for one fucking second."

What do you fucking expect?

Aki narrows his eyes. "I don't know who or what you are, but I'll find a way to bring you down. There'll be others out there like me and Maddix, somewhere, who can help."

You sigh. "The bunny already scouted them all out. You and I made them disappear, just like this." You click my fingers. He flinches and grimaces. He did say he'd done terrible things... But there *were* more of us? Seriously, Aki, just back off. This isn't worth your life. "That last one, in Spain, Princess Preciosa: she was a tougher one." Stop there a moment. That was *you*? All this time, I've been associating with the elusive monster I've been researching into! "But if I can take someone like her down, how easy do you think it's gonna be to get rid of you?"

Why didn't you use her instead of me? Well, you do seem to thrive on drama, and me being a conspiracy theorist fits nicely into that, doesn't it? Although there *is* plenty of drama to be had by being a princess. 'Yep, guess again,' you taunt.

Aki's frown eases a little. His eyes glance away for a fraction, enough to catch the light and reveal a glint of fear. Is killing him the only way to make him leave us alone? I guess your mind tricks don't work on him, otherwise you would've used them by now.

"Or maybe I should set the bunny on you to fuck up your brain," you say. "Your choice."

Aki, do the sensible thing here.

"Even if you brainwash me into silence," he says, "or *kill* me, your light will fade. Success only lasts so long. People will see through you."

You scoff, and seem to pause dramatically. "People see what they want to see."

He continues to glare at us, seemingly strong in his conviction, but his fists tremble.

Your confidence and bravado truly scare me. I have to believe what Aki says, that your power will wear off after a while. Because yes, you've given me pretty much everything I dreamed about, but through what means? Manipulation. Fraud. And now I'm a slave to you.

"If you'll excuse me," you say, and start to turn, "my chauffeur's waiting."

You have to flash him one more grin before striding back to the car. Well, at least you didn't hurt him. Why not? Is he not worth the effort? Suppose he's no threat. Whatever the case, I'm grateful you passed up yet another occasion to make me a murderer.

You slide into the back of the Mercedes with Connelly and Kya then the driver closes the door and takes his place at the front.

"Maddix." Kya huffs with a smile. "Thank you for finally gracing us with your presence."

You pull the seat belt across me and click it in tightly.

"Who was that?" Connelly asks.

Aki must've been in too much shadow for him to see properly. I know you won't admit who he was or why he came here, though.

"Just a fan," you say.

And they're happy to leave it at that. They're already too used to not prying further into anything you say.

The chauffeur starts the engine, which hums smoothly. He reverses in a curve then glides to the exit barrier.

You observe the glass panel separating us from the driver then direct my focus past Connelly to Kya. "Kya, my dear: Connelly and I will be filing for divorce tomorrow, so you and I can get engaged. We'll announce the engagement together on the BBC News next week."

The haze around me returns. I should've known that was your intention. The public have already been practically demanding it. But this can't happen. It's all a huge, sick disaster.

Kya seems to go vacant, and Connelly visibly tenses. As soon as you place my hand on his knee, he relaxes a little.

"You got that?" you prompt Kya.

Her eyes widen and she nods with an uncanny smile.

You rest my thinker back against the soft leather and smirk.

I can pretend none of this is happening, shut myself off from it like I normally do, but I can't live this way. I've wanted admiration for as long as I can remember, but no-one admires me. Everyone loves *you*: the thing that's destroyed my liberty, and fucked with those closest to me. I thought nothing could ever crack me. I've made a living out of searching for the truth, but something I'd never even considered snaked its way inside. Now I'm a prisoner, hoping, and praying, that if I can't figure out an escape, another truth seeker can come break me free.

Printed in Great Britain
by Amazon

31964054R10148